# More praise for HELLION

"Erotic with a capital E."
—*Atlanta Journal & Constitution*

"Magnificent . . . Lush, passionate . . . *Hellion* is Bertrice Small at her very best! Once again, [she] proves herself to be the reigning queen of romance."
—*The Literary Times*

"*Hellion* is delightfully wicked. The escapades that occur in the d' Bretagne castle will stay with you long after you've finished this thoroughly enjoyable story. Bertrice Small weaves her magic into a basketful of carnal surprises."
—*Affaire de Coeur*

# HELLION

*Bertrice Small*

FAWCETT GOLD MEDAL • NEW YORK

A Fawcett Gold Medal Book
Published by Ballantine Books
Copyright © 1996 by Bertrice Small

All rights reserved under International and Pan-American Copyright Conventions. Published in the United States by Ballantine Books, a division of Random House, Inc., New York, and simultaneously in Canada by Random House of Canada Limited, Toronto.

http://www.randomhouse.com

Library of Congress Catalog Card Number: 96-90699

ISBN 0-449-15038-6

Manufactured in the United States of America

First Trade Edition: January 1996
First Mass Market Edition: March 1997

10  9  8  7  6  5  4  3  2  1

*For my best friend on the East End,*
*Andrea Aurichio*
*What would I do without you, babe?*

# Prologue

# ENGLAND

*August 1100*

King William Rufus held his Easter court at Winchester. At Pentecost he was in Westminster. At that time, a village in Berkshire reported blood welling from the earth, and many who claimed to have seen it attested to it. When word of the phenomenon was brought to the king, he laughed.

"These English," he said. "They are such a superstitious lot."

The priests shook their heads glumly and muttered amongst themselves. The king was a most ungodly man who lacked respect for portents and all things holy. He would surely meet a bad end, *and* his wicked companions with him. But those who knew William Rufus best appreciated that while he might be a harsh man with little patience for those whose beliefs were rooted in ignorance or fear, he was fair with those who served him honestly.

The fat season for red stags began August first, and William Rufus was at his hunting lodge in the New Forest with several companions and his youngest brother, Henry. Many were surprised that Henry Beauclerc—so called because of all the Conqueror's sons, he was best educated—was so friendly with the king, for William Rufus's heir was not Henry, but rather their eldest brother, Robert, Duke of Normandy. Still, the prince seemed to hold no grudge, which was unusual in an age that lived by conquest.

On the second day of August the hunt was scheduled to begin at dawn, as was customary, but early that morning a

3

foreign monk spoke with the king's friend, Robert fitzHaimo, telling him of a warning vision he had had in the night. The king agreed not to hunt that morning, although he did not fear the monk's vision. He was dyspeptic, having eaten and drunk far too much the night before.

"I am so filled with an ill wind," he mocked himself, "that the deer would hear me coming from a great distance and hide; but we'll hunt this afternoon."

So after the midday meal William Rufus and his companions went into the deep forest to stalk deer. Finding a spot near a stream with the well-muddied tracks of beasts all about, the king dismounted, waiting silently in the bushes for a stag to come to drink. He knew that his companion, Walter Tirel, was nearby. The other hunters had scattered, as was the accepted routine in such a hunt.

Suddenly, without warning, an arrow flew through the air and buried itself in William Rufus's chest. Astounded, the king grasped at the arrow, stumbling noisily into the clearing by the stream. He had heard no one, but then his eyes met those of his assailant. A face stared from the foliage. The king smiled, recognizing the face. His look was one of admiration, almost approval. Then he fell facedown in the mud as death reached out to claim him.

The greenery didn't even rustle as William Rufus's assassin slipped away. Walter Tirel entered the clearing, looking about him. Seeing the king, he raised a mighty shout of alarm. Within moments the place was filled with the king's other companions, including Henry Beauclerc, open-mouthed and astounded by the scene that greeted them.

"*Mon Dieu*, Walter! You have killed the king!" Robert de Montfort said for all to hear.

"*Non! Non!*" Tirel replied. "*Not I, my lord!* The king was dead when I arrived. We were together, but he hurried on ahead of me. I found him so. I swear it!"

"It was an accident, I am certain," Robert fitzHaimo said.

"You are known for an honorable man, Walter, and had no cause to kill the king."

"Is this place cursed?" de Montfort wondered aloud. "The king's brother, Richard, was killed all those years ago in a similar accident, and last spring his own nephew died the same way. A hunting accident."

"It was not my arrow that killed the king," Walter Tirel said doggedly.

"Yet it must be your arrow," de Montfort said, bending down. "See, it is one of the two the king gave you himself this day. Do you not remember, Tirel? A blacksmith came with six arrows before we left this afternoon. The king praised the smithy's craftsmanship. He kept four of the arrows for himself, and gave you two. You do not have two now, do you?"

"I shot one earlier," Tirel insisted. "You yourself were there when I shot at that first stag from a-horse. I missed the beast and could not find the arrow. Do you not remember?"

"It is an accident," fitzHaimo said soothingly. "A tragic accident. There is no blame to assign. Perhaps, though, it would be best if you returned to your lands in France, my lord. Poix, isn't it? There will be some who are hotheaded enough to seek revenge for this unfortunate incident. To horse, my lord, and do not look back!"

Walter Tirel, Count of Poix, did not need to be encouraged twice. He was not so stupid that he did not realize something was amiss. However, he did not wish to take the blame for something he had not done. Mounting his horse, he galloped off, not bothering to stop at the royal lodge, but heading straight for the coast and the first boat he could find to take him to France.

*"The king is dead,"* Robert de Montfort said softly.

*"Long live the king,"* fitzHaimo replied solemnly.

William Rufus was buried the following day, a Friday. On Sunday, the fifth day of August, his brother Henry—who had not even waited to bury his sibling, but instead hurried to Winchester to secure the royal treasury—was crowned at

Westminster, despite his father's wishes that Robert succeed
Rufus. Henry, the youngest of the Conqueror's sons, based his
claim on the fact that he was the only one to have been born in
England.

"I am," he boldly told the barons, "the only legitimate heir of
the king of England, for my father was England's king when I
was born, and my own birth took place at Selby in Yorkshire.
My brother, Duke Robert, was born while my father was Normandy's duke."

King Henry promised to correct all the abuses of the previous monarch, but his eyes were on Normandy, the duchy
belonging to his eldest brother, Robert, who was on crusade.
To this end he sent out to all the landowners in England,
demanding their fealty. Henry needed to know England was
completely loyal when he went to reunite his father's original
holding with England. There could be no question of the two
territories being separate, *and* there could be no question that
Henry was the rightful king of England, and lord over both
places.

# Part I

# LANGSTON

*Winter 1101*

## ▓Chapter 1

"Y ou must have a wife, Hugh Fauconier," the king said with a smile. He reached out to take his bride's hand, giving it an affectionate squeeze. King Henry had been married just a little over a month. While the queen had been chosen for political reasons, he liked her well enough, and she him. They got on quite nicely for two people who had not known one another until the day of their marriage.

Edith, renamed Matilda to please her husband's Norman barons, was a very pretty young woman, with her mother's dark red hair and gray-blue eyes. And like her mother, she was a devout young woman. She had planned to enter a convent until Henry, seeking to secure his northern border while he sought to conquer Normandy, asked the Scots king for his sister's hand in marriage. The bride was quickly sent south, for the Scots king never knew when he might need the military strength of his English brother-in-law. The fact that Edith/Matilda was also a direct descendant of the last Anglo-Saxon rulers did not go unremarked.

Those near the king turned now to look at the object of his attention. Hugh Fauconier, knight, was a Saxon. He had known the king almost his entire life. "I should enjoy a wife if she would bring me as much joy as the queen has obviously brought you," he replied graciously, "but, alas, my liege, I have not the means to support a wife, nor lands on which to settle her."

"You do now," Henry replied with a small smile. "I am returning Langston to you, Hugh. What think you of that?"

*"Langston?"* He was astounded. All his life Langston had been but a dream. Langston was his father's ancestral home, but he had never known his father, who, with his grandfather and two uncles, had died at Hastings. Upon hearing the news of the battle, his mother had, with incredible foresight, packed up the family's valuables and fled west with her servants across England to her father's home. Hugh had been born seven and a half months later. After his mother's death, his maternal grandmother, a Norman lady distantly related to the Conqueror, had raised him. Langston had been given to a Norman knight loyal to King William.

"Circumstances have changed since my father's time," King Henry said softly. "Come and see me privately after the meal, Hugh. I will explain all to you then, my friend."

The court was at Westminster celebrating the Christmas season. While the queen's presence had brought women back into the royal circle, it was a subdued time, for the king was still in mourning for his brother, William Rufus. Then, too, there was the very distinct possibility that Duke Robert of Normandy would, come spring, attempt to overthrow his younger brother's rule in England.

Caught between his two brothers, one a duke of Normandy and the other a king of England, Henry had struggled his whole life to please them both. It had not been an easy task, and in the end his elder siblings had signed wills making the other his heir should he die without issue; and thus cutting off the younger Henry.

Then Pope Urban II had preached a call for a crusade to free Jerusalem from the Saracens. Duke Robert, tired of the factional fighting in his duchy and in the neighboring states about him, and longing desperately for a little adventure, had answered the pope's call. First, however, he'd had to mortgage Normandy to his brother, William Rufus, so he would have the silver to mount such a glorious expedition. The term of the loan was three years. At the end of that time, Duke Robert would repay King William Rufus and reclaim his lands. Robert had been on his way home from the first crusade covered slightly in glory, traveling with a new bride, Sibylle, the daughter of Geoffrey of Conversano, Lord of Brindisi, a nephew of King Roger of Sicily, when William Rufus had been killed in the New Forest, and Henry, the youngest of William the Conqueror's sons, had moved quickly to secure the treasury and have himself crowned King of England.

The barons, whatever their reasons, had not rebelled. Most believed Henry a stronger man than his eldest sibling. With Duke Robert's return, however, there was apt to be a war. The king needed all the friends he could get, for many of his lords held lands in both England and Normandy. Their loyalty would be decided based upon which of the Conqueror's sons they considered likely to win such a conflict.

Hugh Fauconier sat himself down upon a bench, still stunned by the king's words. *Langston!* He was to have Langston back. How pleased his grandparents would be. He wished his mother had lived to see this day, but she had died almost immediately after his birth.

"You lucky devil!" His friend, Rolf de Briard, poked him with a finger. "What did you do to deserve such good fortune, Hugh? It cannot be just because you raise the finest hunting birds in all of England." Rolf raised his cup to his tablemate, then drank down a healthy gulp of wine. "How big is the estate?"

Hugh shook his head. "I haven't the faintest idea, Rolf. I've never even seen it. I'm not even certain exactly where it is, except that it is in East Anglia. My grandmother, Emma, always spoke of its beauty. She saw it once, when my mother was married to my father."

"So the king could be gifting you with something totally worthless," Rolf considered. "What happened to the lord to whom it was given after Hastings? Is the land tillable? Is there a dwelling? How many serfs and freedmen? There is a great deal to know."

"And I'll know none of it until the king decides to tell me." Hugh laughed, his equilibrium returning in light of Rolf's good, practical common sense. "Will you come with me when I go to Langston?"

"Aye!" Rolf responded enthusiastically. He had come to court to make his fortune, and he was bored. Hugh's offer held the promise of adventure.

When the meal was over, and the musicians played softly, Hugh Fauconier arose from the trestle table where he had been sitting and moved to a spot below the high board, where the king might see him. He stood silently and patiently until finally the king's page came to lead him to a small, windowless room furnished by two chairs and a table.

"You are to wait here, Sir Hugh," the lad said, and then departed.

Hugh did not know whether he should sit or not, and decided to stand until the king came and invited him to seat himself. He paced the little room nervously. Then suddenly the door was opened and King Henry entered, the page coming behind him with wine and two goblets.

"Sit down, Sir Hugh," the king said jovially. "Wine for us both, my lad," he instructed the young page, who swiftly complied, then exited the room, leaving the men to their privacy. The king raised his goblet. "To Langston," he said.

"Langston," Hugh Fauconier said, echoing the king's toast.

Henry quaffed half the goblet, then spoke. "Langston was given to Robert de Manneville after my father came to England. He was barely more than a boy, but he saved my father's life on the battlefield. My father, as you know, was a man who knew how to reward both loyalty and bravery. He was impressed by de Manneville's dogged loyalty.

"De Manneville had a little estate in Normandy, unlike some who had come with my father to England. He married, had two sons, was widowed, married again, had a daughter.

Several years ago he decided to follow my brother, Duke Robert, on crusade. His eldest son went with him. The younger remained on the estate in Normandy. The daughter, who was born here in England, has always lived at Langston with her mother."

The king paused a moment to take another drink of wine, then continued. "Sir Robert and his son, Sir William, were both killed at a battle called Ascalon, some seventeen months ago. The younger son, Richard, was so informed, and married almost immediately. Sir Robert had made out a will before he departed that named William as his heir, and Richard, should William not survive. His English lands, however, he entailed upon his daughter, Isabelle. The girl is fifteen, I am informed.

"After my brother's death in the New Forest, I sent to all those given lands here in England by my father, and then my brother, asking for their fealty. Many have given it. Among those who have not is Isabelle of Langston. Twice I have sent to her demanding her allegiance, but she will not answer my summons to come to court and pledge herself to her king. She is without the guidance of a man to advise her in her behavior. Yet what if she has ignored my call because she has been so counseled by her brother, Sieur Richard in Normandy? What if she has pledged herself to my brother, Robert? I am led to distrust this maid, Hugh.

"Do you know where in East Anglia Langston is? It is just a few miles up the river Blyth from where it empties into the sea at Walberswick. There is a stone keep overlooking the river that Sir Robert built on the site of your grandfather's hall. It is virtually impregnable, and quite strategic to the safety of the area. Langston Keep must be held by a man whose loyalty to me is without question. I believe that you are that man, Hugh.

"Though you have never laid eyes on your ancestral home, I know I can trust you for many reasons, and the most important of these reasons is that you have no lands in Normandy. You have no loyalties to be divided as I once did; as so many of my most important and strongest barons do. My brother will come in the spring to attempt to wrest England from me. If I have enough men like you to rely upon, I can easily retain what is mine, and I mean to do just that. Then I shall regain Normandy.

"The late Sieur de Manneville, however, placed Langston in his daughter's hands for but one purpose. It is her dower portion. I cannot in the name of chivalry send the girl and her widowed mother packing. I therefore instruct you to take the girl as your wife. As a noble English orphan it is my right to arrange her marriage. Her family can neither complain nor forbid me. There are no legal encumbrances to prevent it. You are not pledged to anyone, and neither is this maid. I shall send one of my own priests, Father Bernard, with you to assure the two women that this is my wish, and no ruse to steal Langston or dishonor the lady Isabelle. He will perform the marriage between you and the girl, and bring me word that all is as I have ordered. Should the girl's brother complain of my actions to his liege lord, my brother Robert, you must hold Langston firmly for me."

"How soon do you wish me to leave, my liege?" Hugh Fauconier asked the king. He was not nearly as calm as he appeared to be. His heart was hammering with a mixture of excitement and anticipation; but he would show nothing but respect before his king.

"You will need a day to have your squire pack up your belongings, Hugh," the king said. "I will send a messenger to your grandfather, Lord Cedric, informing him of my wishes. I hope that now you are to become a landowner, and a husband, you will not stop raising your wonderful birds. They are the finest I have ever known."

"Once I have settled myself, sire, I shall send to my grandfather for breeding stock. Neither my uncles nor my cousins have any interest in the birds, and will not be jealous."

"I am happy to know that, Hugh, for I should not like to see the talented line of Merlin-sone disappear. Your family has always bred the best hunting birds. Did you know that my father first met your grandfather when he came to Normandy years ago to enter a competition with his birds? That was when Lord Cedric was first won over to my father's cause. His loyalty to my father after King Edward died, and his effort to quiet the Mercian countryside, were greatly appreciated." The king smiled at his companion. "I am taking up too much of your time, Hugh, and you have much to do before you leave for Langston."

"I should like your permission to take Rolf de Briard with me, my liege," the knight said.

Henry nodded. "Aye, he is a good man to have guarding one's back, Hugh. Take him with you."

Hugh stood, and then kneeling before the king, placed his folded hands in the monarch's. "I am your man. I will faithfully hold Langston for you as long as I live, sire," he promised.

The king raised Hugh Fauconier up, kissing him on both cheeks. Then he gave him a small carved wooden staff, signifying that Henry had passed Langston formally into his vassal's possession. Bowing, Hugh departed the chamber.

Behind him Henry smiled, well pleased with his day's work. He had knighted Hugh Fauconier himself many years ago. His childhood friend had pledged his loyalty to him. His fealty to William Rufus, of course, took precedence to such an oath; but when Henry had become king last summer, Hugh had renewed his vow, and now once again for Langston. There are few I can trust like this man, the king thought. There are others who consider themselves closer to me; others richer, and certainly more powerful than this knight; but none are more loyal. There is no malice in him. The king drank down the wine remaining in his cup, and went to join his wife.

"Well?" demanded Rolf de Briard as Hugh rejoined him. "What have you been given, my friend, and is it worth the trip?"

"I have no idea as to the land involved, but there is a relatively new keep of stone, Rolf, not timber and earth. And I have to marry the girl. All in all it's not a bad bargain."

*"What girl?"* Rolf exploded. "There is a girl? What's her name? Is she pretty? Better yet, is she rich?"

"She is Isabelle of Langston, the daughter of the previous tenant, and I haven't the faintest idea if she is rich or pretty, Rolf." He went on to explain the history of Langston to his friend, and the king's concerns over his bride-to-be's unwillingness to swear fealty. "The maid is probably frightened by the situation, and still mourning her father and brother. She is gently bred, and helpless in this matter. I'll set things to rights in short order, and have the little bird singing a song of love by spring."

Rolf laughed. "The little bird will be closely chaperoned by her mama, my friend, and that good lady may prove a problem. She will have an influence upon her daughter that you will not, being a stranger."

"Once she is my wife," Hugh Fauconier said seriously, "Isabelle has no choice but to answer to me first. If the mother proves difficult, I shall send her off to her stepson's in Normandy, Rolf."

Bold words, and a bolder plan of action, Rolf de Briard thought, but then Hugh Fauconier had always been a direct man. Each had been sent to court at the age of seven to be raised there. Neither had any real prospects. Hugh was an orphan, and Rolf a younger son. They had immediately become fast friends. Queen Matilda had raised and educated them with her youngest son, Henry. They had traveled regularly back and forth between England and Normandy with the court, learning first as pages, then as squires; finally being knighted just before the first King William had died. The good queen, as she had been known, had predeceased her husband by four years.

The court of the second King William was a totally different affair. William Rufus had little respect for overpious and pompous churchmen. He was a direct, forthright man who rewarded loyalty with loyalty and generosity; and disloyalty with a swift, harsh hand. His was a totally masculine court of young men in splendid costumes. There were rumors, none of them proved, that the king preferred pretty boys to pretty girls. The king smiled and neither denied nor confirmed the rumors. As no one man emerged as favorite, rumors were all the Church had. Yet the king never married, nor sired any bastards.

There were tales, Rolf thought, that he and Hugh could have told, but they never did. The king was simply a man's man. He had no time for softness. Rolf and Hugh did their duty and bided their time. It was the only life they had. Now, however, Hugh was to have land of his own. Rolf, whose heart was a good one, was delighted by his friend's luck.

The two knights departed for Langston two days later, accompanied by their squires and Father Bernard, an older man of surprising vigor. They rode for four days, crossing Essex, and then went on into Suffolk. The January weather was cold, wet, and uninviting. They saw no one along their route but an occasional farmer driving his livestock from one pasturage to another. The priest had arranged for them to stay at night in the guest houses of the religious orders scattered about the countryside. A small coin gained them a hot supper, a safe bed, and oat stirabout, bread, and cider after mass before they left in the morning. There was no breakfast without attending mass, Father Bernard warned them.

"I haven't been so well-churched in years," Rolf said with a grin as they rode along on the last morning of their journey.

The priest and the squires laughed, but Hugh only smiled, more interested in the countryside about him. The area was said to be flat, but although it lacked the hills of his childhood home, there was a gentle roll to it. There were broad meadows, and fine stands of old trees. The buildings they saw were timber-framed and plastered, the roofs thatched neatly, for there was no building stone of note in the vicinity. There was an air of comfortable prosperity to the region, as well there should have been.

There were small ports that were home to fishing fleets and

also welcomed trading vessels from the Baltic and Dutch states. The landscape was rich with cattle and sheep. The Suffolk area of East Anglia had been the most populated Saxon region in England owing to a law called Partible Inheritance, which allowed a man to divide his estate equally between all his children. This was not the custom in the rest of England.

As the road wound through the gentle terrain, Hugh realized that they were curiously isolated from the rest of the world. None of the large, important roads ran through the area. The air was cold and damp, the silence almost overwhelming. Away from the court and its distractions, he realized that winter was a colorful time. The branches of the trees were black against the gray sky. In the marshes the reeds and grasses ran the gamut of color from reddish-brown to gold, springing from the rich, dark earth or the ice-edged marshlands of the rivers and streams that seemed to crisscross the landscape.

The countryside, he could see, was good for pasturage, as well as for growing crops. He wondered exactly how much land Langston possessed, and whether it had enough serfs to work it. What did they grow? Did they have both cattle and sheep? A mill? With every step his horse took, Hugh Fauconier was more and more eager to see his ancestral lands.

"There, my lord, just ahead, and across the river," Father Bernard said. "It is Langston Keep, if I am not mistaken."

They were on a small bluff overlooking the Blyth. Hugh scanned the countryside. "There is no bridge," he noted.

"Then there has to be a ferryman somewhere," Rolf replied practically.

They directed their mounts down the incline and along the riverbank until they were almost directly opposite Langston Keep. There they saw across the river a flat, bargelike vessel, but there appeared to be no one about. Then Hugh's squire, Fulk, spotted a post hung with a bell on the shore. Nudging his horse over to it, he rang the bell vigorously, and a moment later a figure was seen running to the ferry.

"Good lad!" Hugh praised the young man. Then he looked

across the Blyth to Langston Keep. It was, the king had said, situated upon the site of his grandfather's old hall. It was indeed of stone; and he was curious as to how the stone had been obtained. The keep was rectangular in shape, two stories high. It was set upon a motte, an earthworks mound, as was customary; giving it added height from which to spy upon the countryside about. The motte was surrounded by a wide, deep, water-filled trench. The top of the motte was enclosed with a wall, and from within the enclosure rose the keep. A wooded drawbridge stretched across the water to the keep's entrance gate. It is very impressive, Hugh thought.

Then the ferryman was upon them, and there was no more time for contemplation as he waved them aboard.

"You cannot take all of us," Hugh said, noting the size of the vessel. "Fulk, Giles, you will cross after we have, for you have the pack animals in your charge." The two squires nodded.

The river was not broad, but while it looked smooth as glass, there was a strong current to it. The ferryman was obviously an expert at his task, and soon had them on the other side. The two knights and the priest made their way up the bluff, across the drawbridge, and through the barbican into the keep's bailey. Within they could see the entry to the tower itself, and a stables. A young serf boy ran to take their horses. From the dwelling an elderly man came to greet them. Upon reaching them, he stared hard at Hugh Fauconier, moving closer to peer into the knight's face.

"My lord Hugh," he said in a trembling voice. "How can it be? They said you died at Hastings, and your sons with you." Tears welled in the servant's eyes, running down the grooves age had made in his old face. With a shaking hand he reached out to touch Hugh. "Be you real, my good lord? Be you real, or some ghostie come back to haunt us?"

"What is your name, old fellow?" Hugh asked the servant.

"Why, I be Eldon, lord. Do you not remember me? But then I was but a lad when you marched out to fight the Norman invader," came the reply.

"And I, Eldon, am the grandson of your Lord Hugh. Do you remember my mother, the lady Rowena? When she fled Langston after the great battle at Hastings, I was but newly planted in her belly. I am named for my grandfather, and my father."

Understanding dawned in the servant's eyes. "You look just like your grandfather," Eldon said. "Welcome home, my lord Hugh! Welcome home to Langston!" He shook the younger man's hand vigorously.

"Will you bring me to the lady of the keep, Eldon?" Hugh said.

"Aye, lord, and right proud I am to do so," was the answer. Eldon turned and led the three men up the steps of the keep into the dwelling.

The first floor of the building was below them. Hugh knew that it would be used mostly for storage. This main level was where the lord and his family would live. They were in the Great Hall, and Hugh could see several doors that opened off of it leading to other chambers. The hall had several attractively arched windows running down one side of its length. Opposite the entrance was a raised wooden dais upon which was set a fine table covered with a snow-white linen cloth. There were two large fireplaces. Next to one of them a pretty woman sat at a loom, weaving.

"Lady," Eldon called out as he approached her, bowing. "Here be Lord Hugh come home to Langston." He gave no further explanation.

The woman arose. "Welcome, my lords," she said in a sweet voice, "although I do not understand what old Eldon's words mean. He has a tendency to wander a bit these days, but he has always served this house loyally, and so we make allowances. I am the lady Alette de Manneville. May I ask, my lords, who you are?" She turned before they might answer. "Eldon, wine for our guests," she ordered, then turning back to the three men, smiled prettily.

"We thank you for your gracious welcome, my lady Alette.

I am Father Bernard, the king's chaplain," the priest introduced himself. "I have come from King Henry with several messages for you. The young man is Lord Hugh Fauconier. His companion is Rolf de Briard. We have ridden together from Westminster."

*"King Henry?"* The lady Alette's pretty face was confused. "Does not King William Rufus yet reign in England?"

"King William died this Lammas past, lady," the priest answered her. "Did you have no word of it?"

"Nay, good father, we did not," she said. "We are very isolated here at Langston, being far from any roads of consequence."

"But did you not receive a royal messenger twice in the past few months? In early September, and then late November, I believe it was."

"Aye, my lord, we did," the lady replied. She was a lovely creature with sky-blue eyes and rich blond hair that was neatly braided and covered with a sheer white veil. "But the messenger did not say from which king he came. Perhaps he did not think it necessary, nor did we think it necessary to ask." She shrugged lightly.

"Did you not read the message, lady?" the priest continued.

"Nay, good father, for the messenger said 'twas for the lord of Langston, and my husband is away with Duke Robert on crusade. Besides, I cannot read. I gave the bearer hospitality, and put the documents away for when my husband returns."

The priest looked at Hugh, who said, "This whole matter has come about through a misunderstanding, Father. The messenger in his arrogance did not inform this lady of one king's death and the other's ascension. What shall we do?"

"The confusion changes nothing, my son," Father Bernard answered. "King Henry's orders still stand." He turned back to the lady. "Seat yourself, madame. There is much I have to tell you. My lords, pray be seated also." The priest settled himself on a bench opposite the woman. "Your words tell me, lady, that no one has come to inform you of your lord's death last

August in a battle called Ascalon. Your stepson, William, also died."

She grew pale for a moment, crossed herself, and then taking the goblet of wine offered her by Eldon, sipped it slowly. Finally she spoke. "No, good father, I was not told of Robert's death. Richard, I assume, is now Sieur de Manneville? Of course, he would be."

"He has taken a wife," the priest said. "Perhaps in the excitement of it all he forgot his duty to you, lady."

"No," she said. "He did not forget. From the moment I married their father, my stepsons were disrespectful to me. May God and His Blessed Mother assoil my lord's soul." She bowed her head a moment, but shed no tears, the priest noted. When she raised her head to look at him again, she asked, "Why has the king sent you to Langston, my lords? This manor is of no importance, nor was my late lord. Why is King Henry concerned with us? What are we to him, good father?"

"The messages sent you, lady, were for your daughter, not your husband. King Henry sought her fealty. When she did not give it to him, he became concerned, for Langston is most strategically located. Should England be threatened by invasion, keeps such as yours, on and near the coast, are its first line of defense." The priest's gray eyes probed the woman's face for any sign of deception or fear, but Alette de Manneville showed only curiosity in what he was telling her. "Sir Hugh," Father Bernard continued, "is the grandson of Langston's last Saxon lord, Hugh Strongarm. After Hastings his mother fled west to her father's house, where he was born. When he was seven, he was sent to court to be raised by Queen Matilda, for his grandmother, the lady Emma, was King William's kin." He stopped so she might absorb all this.

"Pray go on, good father," the lady Alette finally said.

"When King Henry learned of your husband's death, and that you and your daughter were bereft of guidance; when he did not receive the reassurance of your daughter's fealty as heiress to Langston, he decided that it would be best that Langston be returned to its only legitimate heir, Hugh Fauconier, his childhood friend and companion, for the king knows that Lord Hugh's allegiance to him is complete."

"Then," said Alette de Manneville, "we are to be displaced and disinherited, good father? What will become of us?"

"Nay, lady, the king is not without feeling. He would never dispossess you and the maiden. The king has determined that your daughter shall marry Lord Hugh. She is of an age, and, it was learned, has no betrothed husband. Thus," the priest concluded, "the difficulty shall be solved most amenably. Langston will, I am certain, most gladly accept the grandson of Hugh Strongarm as its lord; you shall not be deprived of your home, and your daughter shall have a most honorable knight for a husband."

*"I shall marry no man I do not choose myself!"* a determined voice said loudly from the entry to the hall. The owner of the voice strode boldly into the room. To their surprise, she was dressed in boy's clothing; only her long single braid of hair gave testimony to her sex.

*"Isabelle,"* Alette de Manneville said, her voice pleading.

"Oh, madame, do not, I pray you, look like a cornered doe. It is not a look that becomes you," Isabelle of Langston said scornfully.

Rolf de Briard rolled his eyes and restrained his amusement, but the priest looked scandalized by the girl's words.

"Do not, lady, speak with such disrespect to your mother," Hugh said quietly. If he had been hoping for a petite blue and gold creature such as Alette de Manneville, he was now doomed to disappointment. The girl was tall for a female, slender, but big-boned, and her hair was a flaming copper color. The green-gold eyes she now fastened on him were both angry and hostile.

"And who are you, sirrah, to instruct me in my behavior?" Isabelle of Langston demanded furiously.

*"Belle!"* her mother half whispered, but was patently ignored.

"I am, I fear, lady, to be your husband, which gives me the power of life and death over you. For now I choose to let you live," Hugh finished with a small attempt at humor.

*"I shall marry no man I do not choose myself,"* Belle repeated.

Father Bernard rose from his warm seat by the fire, and taking the girl by the arm, pressed her firmly into his former place. "The king has decreed, my lady Isabelle, that you shall marry this good knight, heir to the last Saxon lord of Langston. Your father and elder brother have perished on crusade. No woman can hold a keep for the king, even so small a keep as this one is."

The girl's face, hard before, now crumbled at the revelation that her father was dead. She struggled to keep her tears from overflowing her eyes. "Then I shall return to my brother Richard's house in Normandy," she said stubbornly, "but I shall not marry some Saxon scum!"

"Oh, Belle!" her mother burst out. "You know that Richard will not have us. Besides, he has married, and Manneville is smaller than Langston. You've never even been there. It's dark and gloomy. I hated it! All the years I was married to your father, I was forced to bear the insults your half brothers heaped upon me for the sake of peace. Oh, they were careful not to show their disrespect before your father, not that he would have chastised them. Rather he would have somehow found cause to blame me. The only thing I ever did that pleased Robert de Manneville was to bear you. In the beginning he was furious that you were not another son. Only when you began to show signs of being like him did you become his adored darling. As for William and Richard, they showed you favor because it pleased Robert, not because they cared for you. Neither of them ever cared for anyone save themselves. Richard will not welcome you, my child, believe me. He no longer has to satisfy your father."

"How dare you speak of my father with such insolence, madame?" Belle demanded. "He was a wonderful man, and I loved him."

"And he loved you, at least as much as he was capable of loving, my child," her mother answered, "but I only speak the truth to you. Your brother will not have you, I am certain, and why would you want to leave Langston? It is your home. You love it. Be grateful the king has provided you with a suitable husband, and you will be allowed to live your life even as you have always desired to live it, here at Langston. Do not struggle against yourself, Belle."

"You are so weak," the girl sneered. "How can it be possible that I am your daughter? I am nothing like you, madame. My father would see me dead rather than married to a Saxon!"

"An event easily arranged," Hugh Fauconier said dryly, and he fingered his sword, his blue eyes serious.

Rolf de Briard snickered, but his amusement turned to surprise as the girl pulled a short sword from beneath her cloak, standing to defend herself.

*"Belle!"* her mother shrieked, and Father Bernard crossed himself.

Hugh stepped swiftly forward and yanked the weapon from the girl's hand. Then jamming her beneath his arm, he smacked her posterior with several hard blows before forcing her back onto her feet before him, his hands gripping her shoulders hard. "Now listen to me, you hellion," he said in a hard, grim voice. "Your father, God assoil him, is dead. King Henry has restored Langston to me and decreed that you should be my wife. The king is my good friend. Had he known what a virago you are, I am certain he would not have imposed such a wife upon me, but would have had you clapped in a convent instead. I am not a harsh man, lady, and so I will give you a week or two that you may get to know me. Then Father Bernard will marry us and return to my liege lord with the news we have fulfilled his desires. Do you understand me, Belle?"

*"You hit me!"* she said in a fierce voice.

"It is not my custom to strike women," he answered, not for one moment betraying the fact that he was indeed ashamed she had driven him to such action. Not that he had been wrong to chastise her for her behavior; it was his right. Both the Church and the law gave him total jurisdiction over the girl. His grandfather, Cedric Merlin-sone, however, had always said that when a man resorted to violence with either a woman or an animal, he had lost the battle.

She glared up at him. "I should sooner end my days in a cloister than marry you, you *Saxon!*"

"Sadly, lady, the choice is neither yours nor mine to make," Hugh answered her. Then releasing her, he said to Alette, "Take your daughter to her chamber, madame, and remain with her until she is calm again. Then return to me, and we will talk."

"I hate you! I will never marry you!" Isabelle spat out as her mother tugged at her sleeve, pulling her from the Great Hall.

"Good night, hellion. God give you sweet repose," the new lord of Langston answered her.

"Whew!" Rolf de Briard said as the two women disappeared through a door. "Forgive me, Hugh, but what a termagant! Send Father Bernard back to the king to tell him. Better the girl go to the convent than you be saddled with her for all your days. Surely the king has among his wards some sweet maid who would make you a far better wife."

"While I hesitate to encumber some unsuspecting religious order with such a vixen," the priest said thoughtfully, "I am inclined to agree with Sir Rolf. I wonder if the girl is not mad."

Hugh Fauconier shook his head. "Let us give her a little time to become used to all the changes that have been set before her. I do not want to reject her out of hand if there is a chance I may win her friendship. Remember, Isabelle has sustained a great shock. Her father is dead. She has been presented with that news, along with a complete stranger to marry. She is afraid, I think, though she would deny it vehemently, believing fear a shameful thing."

"You have too kind a heart," Rolf sighed. "The girl is simply a bad-tempered shrew."

*"They call her Belle from Hell,"* came the darkly whispered comment. "The Langston folk are mortally afeared of her, lord."

The three men turned to look at old Eldon. Then Rolf burst out laughing. Even Father Bernard allowed himself a small chuckle.

"I shall call her *ma Belle douce*," Hugh said with a twinkle in his blue eyes. "When I am training a particularly difficult falcon or hawk, one that bites without provocation, I win it over with soft words, little treats, and a firm hand, until it learns to trust me. I shall manage the hellion in the same manner, until she becomes a soft-spoken angel, glad of heart and happy to do my bidding."

"I think you a madman," Rolf declared. "The Blessed Mother herself could not tame that girl. If the wench were mine, I should school her with a dog whip until she either did my bidding or I killed her." He thought a moment. "Or she killed me," he amended.

Now it was Hugh who smiled, and when he did, his whole face lit up. He was a plain man, rather than a handsome one. Tall, and big of bone, he had a long face, a long nose not unlike the beaks of the birds he was famed for training, and a long, big mouth. His eyes were among his best features, round in shape and a clear light blue. His smile was broad, showing his white, white teeth. His whole demeanor was serious, almost severe, until he smiled, and when he did, the smile extended all the way to his eyes, and his teeth flashed. Unlike many men, he did not shave the back of his head. His dark blond hair was straight and cropped moderately short.

"Let me see what I can do to tame this wild bird the king has so generously bestowed upon me. If the task proves an impossible one, my friends, then I shall cage her. She will be a challenge, but I think I can subdue the lady Isabelle."

# Chapter 2

*A*lette De Manneville shoved her daughter into her chamber with an unaccustomed force. Shutting the door behind them, she barred it and then whirled about to face her daughter. "Have you lost your wits entirely, Isabelle?"

The girl was astounded by her mother's behavior. Alette was a meek, softspoken creature who had never before shown temper, or uttered a harsh word to her. Much of her own disdain for Alette stemmed from the fact that her mother never spoke up in defense of herself or her ideas. "I cannot imagine what you could possibly mean, madame," she replied with as much hauteur as she could muster. "You cannot expect me to stand by while Langston and I are parceled off to that long-faced Saxon thief."

*"Isabelle!"* There was utter exasperation in Alette's soft voice. "Whatever men may think of women, we have intelligence. You are not stupid. You are, in fact, a very clever girl. King Henry is well within his rights to confiscate Langston. Even I can see the lay of the land. Your father worried about it constantly, which is one reason he went on crusade; to escape being torn between England's king and Normandy's duke, as all the Norman barons' families are. That is why he gave you Langston, and Richard, Manneville. Neither of you will be subjected to divided loyalties. You are English, your brother a Norman. Your choice is clear.

"Because we did not answer the king's call for fealty, he grew fearful that Langston meant to declare for Duke Robert.

We are too strategically located to be allowed to do such a thing. That is why King Henry returned the estate to the heir of its original owner. He knows he can trust in his childhood friend. He even honors your father's memory by giving you to Hugh Fauconier as a wife, thereby assuring us that we will not lose our home. It is a good arrangement all around."

Alette de Manneville pushed an errant lock of her golden hair from her forehead. "Do you know how fortunate we are, you little fool? A less thoughtful, a less Christian man than King Henry would have done nothing for Robert de Manneville's widow and innocent daughter. And do not dare to prattle to me of your half brother, Richard. He will not have us! It is time you faced some truths, my daughter. Your father married me for two reasons: to care for the two sons his first wife, the lady Sibylle, bore him, and to get other children.

"William was nine and Richard five when Robert and I wed. They were horrible little boys, always polite and obedient in your father's presence; always rude and disobedient toward me, though defended by that wretched old dragon of a creature who had been their mother's nurse. I might have won them over except that she encouraged them in their behavior. It was her way of keeping her mistress's memory alive.

"You think your brothers loved you, Belle? They did not! When you were but two months old they put you in a willow basket, carried you to the riverbank, and prepared to drop you into the water below. Had the watchman not seen them, I should not have you today, for surely you would have been killed. Their old nurse begged me on her hands and knees, tears streaming down her face when I had thought her incapable of tears, for witches do not cry, not to expose their horrendous misdeed to Robert. He would have beaten them senseless had he known. I did not expose them on the condition that they never come near you again while you were unable to defend yourself from them. The old nurse swore to keep them from you, and to give her credit, she did."

"Why did you have no more children?" Isabelle asked,

curious suddenly, for her parents had been wed twelve years before her father had departed on his crusade to the Holy Land.

"Your father became incapable shortly after your birth," Alette said bluntly. "I was glad, for though I was a virgin when he married me, I believe him to have been an unfeeling and rough lover. A woman, even one lacking in experience, instinctively knows such things."

To her great mortification, Isabelle blushed at her mother's frankness. Her elegant, noble father had been her ideal. To learn that he was less than perfection was disquieting.

"My marriage, however," her mother continued, "is not the point of this discussion, my daughter. Your marriage is."

"I will not wed with that plain-faced, great gawk of a man," Isabelle said stubbornly. "Could not the king have sent me a pretty fellow like his companion? Besides, if I am not willing, there can be no marriage, can there, madame?" She smiled smugly, and then gasped with surprise as her mother lashed out, slapping her cheek hard.

"Are you really so dense that you cannot fully understand what I have just told you, Isabelle? You no longer have choices. Langston is not yours. If you do not marry Hugh Fauconier, who will you marry? Who will have a landless, dowerless girl? Especially one with such overweening pride, and a bad temper. And what is to happen to me, my daughter? Do you care at all? Must I walk the dusty roads of England in my old age begging charity? Even you cannot be *that* heartless, Belle! *You cannot!*"

Isabelle burst out laughing. "Madame, you are hardly ancient. In fact, you are most beautiful, and yet young. Can you not obtain another husband who will house us both? Why do *you* not wed Hugh Fauconier? That would certainly be an ideal solution."

"For you, perhaps, but not for me. I would not marry again if I could. Widowed, I am free to manage my own life. I am quite content to remain that way, which is just as well for there is no one here to have me. Be sensible, Isabelle. Hugh

Fauconier seems a good man who will treat you well if you would but allow him the opportunity and say a kind word to him."

"He is a Saxon, madame. You know how my father felt about Saxons. He did not like them at all," Isabelle reminded her mother.

"This man is the king's friend, Isabelle. The priest says that he was raised with King Henry. If the king has accepted him, how can you reject him? Even your father would not deny his liege lord. *You must wed him!*"

"I will not!" Isabelle stamped her foot angrily.

"You will remain in your room on bread and water until you change your mind," Alette said, equally angry. She knew how her daughter hated being penned up. Isabelle spent her days out of doors, rain or shine.

"I will run away," was the defiant reply.

"And where would you go?" her mother demanded scornfully. "To your precious Richard? Even if he were willing to shelter you, Belle, what would become of you? You should end your days an unpaid servant in your brother's house. Without this estate, you have no dowry. For now you have your youth, and you have beauty. True, you are not the ideal woman so fashionable today. You are too big a girl. But there might be some man of your brother's acquaintance who would be willing to have you for his leman. Your hair and skin are without flaw. Still, would you choose that kind of a life over being the lady of Langston? No." Alette held up her hand as Belle opened her mouth to reply. "Say not another word to me, Isabelle. I will leave you now to think about everything we have discussed this evening. I know you will come to a sensible solution." Unbarring and opening the door, she went through it back into the Great Hall. Alette locked her daughter's chamber behind her before joining the two knights and the priest by one of the fires.

"Sit, madame," Hugh said graciously. "Is the lady Isabelle calmer now, and over her initial shock? I realize it cannot have been easy for so sensitive a female to have learned of her father's death in such a manner. It is obvious she loved her sire well."

"He spoilt her," Alette de Manneville said quietly, "and while I appreciate your kindness, my lord, let us not dissemble with one another. Isabelle is not sensitive. She is willful. I was not allowed to discipline her, for my husband found what he referred to as her magnificent spirit both admirable and amusing. In truth, however, I have discovered that strength of hers a virtue since my husband's departure. I have not the steadiness needed to hold Langston together. Belle does. She was born here, and she loves it best of anything else in her life."

"Enough to marry me without further ado?" Hugh queried.

A small smile touched Alette's lips. "She is not yet ready to concede defeat, my lord. She is filled with anger and defiance. I have told her she will remain in her room, to be fed only on bread and water, until she sees the sense of it all."

He nodded. "Perhaps a few days alone will help her to see reason, madame. Will you send the steward to me in the morning? I must inspect Langston thoroughly to see what needs to be done so that we are ready for the spring planting."

"There is no steward, my lord. He was an old man, and died three years back. I did not know whom my husband would choose to replace him, and so I did not. Isabelle has run the estate ever since. Nothing has been written down, of course, but my daughter has a good memory for facts and figures. We have managed well enough."

"Then we cannot keep your daughter locked away tomorrow. I need to learn about the estate as quickly as possible," Hugh said.

"Will you have the keys, then?" Alette asked him, holding out her iron ring which held all the keys belonging to Langston.

He shook his head. "They are yours until Isabelle becomes my wife, madame," Hugh said.

"In that case," Alette said, rising from her seat, "I will see to the meal, my lords, and you will, of course, need to know where you are to sleep. I shall need a day or two to clear my belongings from the solar. I regret there are but two guest chambers. Two of you shall have to share, but I shall leave you to decide that among yourselves." She curtsied, and hurried off.

"What a pity the king did not arrange for you to wed the widow instead of the daughter," Father Bernard said. "She is a charming and most well-behaved woman. A man would be fortunate in such a wife."

"She is lovely, I will agree," Hugh replied, "but I prefer a bit more spice, good father. The daughter suits me well enough. There would be no surprises with the lady Alette."

They were shortly invited to the high board, and the supper was served. It was a simple meal: a platter of meaty prawns that had been broiled lightly and were served upon a bed of fresh green watercress; a rabbit stew in a winy brown gravy, flavored with leek and carrot; a fat, juicy capon surrounded by roasted onions; fresh baked bread; a chunk of golden butter; a rich, runny piece of Brie cheese; and a bowl of brown russet pears. Three pitchers were placed on the table. One held cider, one ale, and the other a dark red wine. There was even a little dish of salt.

"My husband," Alette explained, "liked variety, and preferred to help himself to drink." She sat next to Hugh, with the priest to her left, while Rolf de Briard was seated on the other side of his friend.

The table was set with snow-white linen, silver goblets, and plates. While there were spoons for the stew, and each diner had a personal knife should the need arise to cut anything, they ate everything else with their fingers, picking from the platters. The hall was comfortably warm, with the light from its two fires and the candles casting a friendly golden glow over everything. Hugh noticed that there were no rushes upon the floor, and remarked upon it. Alette explained that she did not like rushes, even when herbs were sprinkled amongst them.

"They only encourage dirt, my lord. When garbage and

spittle are worked into the wood, one can never get rid of the stink. My floors are swept daily. I keep bowls of herbs and dried flowers for sweetening the air. I do not like noxious odors, and the dogs have a tendency to pee among the rushes. A clean floor intimidates them."

Hugh smiled. His grandmother Emma said the same thing, and would not allow rushes in her hall, either. "I agree," he told her.

It had been decided that Hugh and Rolf would share one chamber, and Father Bernard would take the other. Neither room was large.

Following supper the lady Alette excused herself and retired to her solar. Hugh had suggested that she remain in her apartment until his marriage to her daughter was celebrated, but Alette would not hear of it.

"You are the lord of Langston now, Sir Hugh," she said firmly. "It is only right that you have the lord's place. But I thank you for your courtesy in offering. I am glad for your coming, unexpected as it was, and I will be happy to have you for a son." She curtsied to him, and then turning to the priest, asked, "Will you say mass in the morning, good father? It has been a long time since we have been so blessed."

"I shall be saying mass every morning that I am at Langston," Father Bernard replied. "You might also tell your people that I shall be happy to hear their confessions at any time they care to come to me."

"I thank you," Alette said, and curtsied to him. Then with a small smile she bid the three men a good night and retired to the solar.

"A charming woman," the priest approved.

"A lovely woman," Rolf de Briard said slowly, his eyes following Alette as she disappeared through her door. "She is the ideal female."

"Christus!" Hugh swore, and then he grinned sheepishly. "Your pardon, Father. Rolf, I have never heard you speak in such respectful terms of any woman but your mother, and then rarely, for you are a bawdy fellow by nature. Has the widow caught your heart?"

Rolf shook himself like a wet dog, saying, "It would not matter if she had, Hugh. I have naught to offer a respectable woman. I am but a poor knight with no home of his own."

"Your home is here at Langston now, my old friend," Hugh told him. "I need your sword, and I need you. The lady Alette told me that the steward here died three years ago. Isabelle has been running the manor without keeping any records, as she neither reads nor writes. You do, Rolf. Will you be Langston's steward? It is not a lowly position I offer you, and I will treat you fairly. Father Bernard can draw up the agreement between us."

Rolf de Briard thought a long moment. It was a wonderful offer. Apart from returning to King Henry's court as one of many landless knights, he had no other prospects. To be steward of Langston would offer him a prestige he had never hoped to attain. He would now be able to take a wife. More important, he and Hugh were longtime friends and got on well together. "Aye!" he said enthusiastically. "I'll be Langston's steward, Hugh, and I thank you for the opportunity."

"Then that's settled," Hugh said, pleased. "In the morning after the meal we shall inspect the estate with Isabelle for our guide. She knows it best. We shall need to soothe her feelings, which will, I suspect, be even more ruffled by our interest and the decisions made here tonight. I think we had best to bed now."

Father Bernard held his first mass in the Great Hall at daybreak, for there was no chapel or church at Langston.

"We shall build a church," Hugh said firmly, and the priest smiled.

Isabelle stood by her mother, silent and sullen. There were two women servants with them that the men had not seen the night before. Afterward, when they made to escort the girl back to her room, Hugh spoke up.

"With your permission, my lady Alette, I would like Belle to accompany Sir Rolf and me this morning on our inspection tour of Langston. She will need her breakfast if she is to ride with us."

"As you wish, my lord," Alette murmured, lowering her head to hide the twinkle in her eyes, the tiny smile on her lips.

"I have no wish to ride with you, Saxon scum!" Belle snarled.

"Nonetheless, *ma Belle douce*, you will," he said. "Your mother has told me that you have stewarded Langston for three years. No one will know it better than you. I need your help, madame. Besides, would you not rather be outdoors than confined to your chamber?"

Belle glared at him. Damn the man, she thought irritably. He was so wretchedly smug. She wanted to deny him, but the thought of spending the entire day in her little chamber was very disagreeable. She knew her mother would insist she not be idle, and would force her to sew, or worse to weave, both of which she absolutely hated. "Very well, my lord," she said grudgingly. "I will show you Langston, but do not think you have won me over, for you have not! I consider you my mortal enemy."

"Be warned, hellion, I have never lost a battle," Hugh said.

"Nor have I, *Saxon*," she responded fiercely, and then without another word Belle stamped up to the high board and sat down.

The servants were quick to serve her, ladling oat stirabout into her trencher of warm, newly baked bread. They poured cider into her cup. Belle ate hungrily, spooning the cereal into her mouth, swallowing her cider greedily.

"In future, ma Belle," Hugh said quietly so that only she might hear him, "I would have you wait until Father Bernard has said the blessing."

"As you will, Saxon," she answered him, knowing he was right, but reluctant to admit it. Leaning across him, she reached for the cheese.

Grasping her wrist, he forced her hand back. "Allow me, *ma Belle douce*," he said, taking his knife and slicing her a piece of the hard, yellow cheese.

"Must you call me *that*?" she growled at him, taking a bite of the cheese. "I am *not* your sweet Belle, Saxon."

"But I believe that once I get through the briar hedge you have placed around yourself, I shall find a sweet Belle," Hugh answered.

Belle burst out laughing. "Blessed Mother!" she said mockingly.

He grinned at her engagingly. "Ahhh, I have made you laugh, ma Belle. You are very pretty when you laugh," he complimented her.

"I laugh because you are such a fool, Saxon," she told him. "Do ladies at court fall swooning into your eager arms when you prattle such nonsense to them? I certainly shall not!"

He chuckled, and turned his attention to his breakfast. She did not realize it, but he had already begun to breach her defenses.

When the meal had been completed, the servants brought them basins of warm water in which to wash their hands, and linen towels to dry them. Then Hugh, Belle, and Rolf moved outside into the bailey, where the horses were awaiting them. One of the female servants hurried after Belle, wrapping a cloak about the girl. A young stableboy knelt, and not even looking at him, Belle stepped upon the boy's back and mounted her palfrey. It was a dappled gray mare, and she leaned forward to pat the creature gently.

"Will you lead the way, ma Belle?" Hugh said.

She threw him an impatient look. "Since you do not know your way about yet, Saxon, of course I shall lead the way!" Then she urged her mount into a walk, moving off through the keep's barbican gate.

Below the keep's motte the small village of Langston was clustered. In times of emergency its inhabitants could easily flee into the safety of the keep's stout stone walls. There was a single street along which the villagers' houses were located. Most of Langston's citizenry were craftsmen, although some of the more important servants also had cottages for their families. The buildings were of timber, and plaster washed pale blue, ochre, or white. Beyond lay the fields and farms belonging to the manor.

"How is it," Hugh asked Belle, "that the keep and its walls are of stone? There is no stone quarried in Suffolk, Essex, or Norfolk."

"My father had the stones dragged on sledges across the fens from Northamptonshire," she told him. "The keep is only twenty-five years old. He began it the year my brother William was born. Until it was built, the old Saxon hall stood on the site. It took five years to complete. But the lady Sibylle, my father's first wife, did not choose to live in England. My father came twice a year to Langston then. His time was spent serving the king, and then the king's son. When he married my mother in Normandy, he immediately brought her to England because he wanted to make it their home. I was born here."

"I was conceived here," he told her.

*"What?"* Her tone was startled.

"My mother's family," he said, "come from near Worcester. She was married to my father in the June before Hastings. Her family, of course, supported Duke William, soon to become England's king. My father's family supported Harold Godwinson, but my mother loved my father and, I am told, held her peace. When word of the battle and King Harold's defeat was brought to her, she packed all the valuables and returned to her father's house. She was enceinte with me at the time. She died shortly after my birth. My grandmother Emma says she could not bear being separated from my father, who was killed at Hastings. She lived just long enough to birth his son and give me my father's name."

Isabelle said nothing. She might be willful and hot-tempered, but she had a soft heart, although she rarely showed it. His story was touching, even if he was a Saxon dog. Now they rode down the village street, and she pointed out the houses of the cooper, the tanner, the carpenter, the shoemaker, the smithy, the tinker, the potter, and the miller.

"You are remarkably well-supplied with craftsmen," Hugh noted.

"You may credit your family and not mine for it," Isabelle allowed grudgingly. "They were all here when my father arrived. Beyond this village, my lord, are two other small villages. We shall get to them today. Those who till our lands live in them."

The villagers had spilled out into the street as the party rode past. They pointed and whispered. Finally, when the riders came abreast of the smithy, Isabelle spoke again.

"We must pay our respects to Ancient Albert. He is the village headman, and will be offended if we do not stop."

They drew their mounts to a halt, and there beneath the canopy of the smithy an enormous white-haired old man sat sprawled in a chair. By his side was a slightly younger version, and then four even younger men. The elderly man peered at Hugh, and then commanded him to move his horse closer. Gazing up at the new lord of Langston, he finally said in a surprisingly strong voice, "He is of Strongarm's line, the exact spit of him."

"This," said Isabelle, "is Ancient Albert, the smithy."

"In truth, lord," Ancient Albert said, "I do not smith any longer. My son Elbert and his sons do the work, and good work it is, I promise you, for I have trained them all."

"You knew my grandfather?" Hugh said.

"Aye, and your father, and uncles, too. I am the oldest man in these parts, lord. I have lived eighty winters. Your grandfather was a fair man. Your father, who was called Hugh the Younger, took after him. I remember your young uncles, Harold and Edward. Such mischievous laddies, always after the girls in the village, and them happy to be caught." He chortled, then shook his head. "Too young to die, they was, but your mother did the right thing fleeing back to her family after the battle. Oh, there was some who criticized, but she saved the line of Strongarm; and made it possible for me to see the day it was restored to Langston. Is it true what Eldon has told us? Is it true you have come home, Hugh Strongarm?"

"Aye," Hugh said, greatly moved by the old man. "I have been restored as Langston's lord by our good king, Henry, God save him and grant him long life! But, Ancient Albert, I am not known by my father's name. I am called Hugh Fauconier, Hugh the Falconer, after the prize birds I raise. Soon they shall fly over Langston."

*"And the lady?"* Ancient Albert asked, looking up at Isabelle. "She is to be sent away?"

"You'd like that, wouldn't you, you old reprobate?" Belle snapped.

"The lady is, by order of the king, to become my wife," Hugh told the assembled villagers. "As you respect me, I will demand that you respect my lady Isabelle as well. She has stewarded these lands honestly the past three years, caring for you all and seeing you came to no harm."

"And squeezing every groat of rent from us," a voice in the crowd called out.

"It was her duty to collect the rent, and yours to pay it. You have not suffered that I can see," Hugh replied. "I see no signs of starvation or illness among you. As serfs and freedmen, you owe that rent to Langston. You have been too long without a master, I fear. Now you have one again. The knight who rides with me is Rolf de Briard. He is to be Langston's new steward. He is a fair man and will not mistreat you, but neither will he allow you to fall into slothful ways. There is also a priest, Father Bernard, with me. We will build a church together. Until then mass will be held in the Great Hall each daybreak. For those who need marriages and baptisms celebrated, he will tend to your needs if you will but go to him."

"God save your lordship!" Ancient Albert said approvingly.

"And God bless all here," Hugh Fauconier replied.

Then the three riders moved on, passing through the village, out into the countryside beyond. There the fields lay fallow in the weak winter sunlight. Beyond them the river ran into the sea.

"I saw boats on the riverbank," Hugh noted.

"Three or four families earn their keep by fishing," Belle said. "What we do not use they are allowed to sell."

"And what crops are grown in the fields?"

"Wheat and rye. Oats, barley, some hops for the beer. Beans, peas, and vetches. The kitchen gardens also grow lettuces, carrots, onions, and leeks. My mother has an herb garden for both cooking and medicinal purposes as well. The kitchen is on the lower level of the keep. Our gardens lie behind it. There is a good-sized apple orchard, and trees growing peaches, plums, and pears. We have wild and bird cherry, too," Belle told him.

He could see both cattle and sheep grazing in the winter meadows. There would certainly be domestic fowl. The marshes were full of water fowl. The woodlands bordering the estate would be home to deer, rabbit, and other forms of wildlife. It was a good estate, with everything needed for survival.

They visited the other villages, making themselves known to the serfs and freedmen living there. Their welcome was warm, but no one appeared surprised by their arrival, the gossip having traveled well ahead of them. Belle spoke little except to answer Hugh's questions. They returned to the keep in mid-afternoon to find that Alette had a fine, hot dinner waiting for them. And when they had eaten, she surprised them yet again.

"You have not bathed in several days, I am certain," she said. "If you will come to the bathing room, I will see to your needs."

"You have a bathing room?" Hugh was pleased.

"The keep is small as castles go," Alette replied, "but we do not lack amenities. The two latrines are directed into a single sluice that flows underground into the river," she told him proudly.

The bathing chamber was another marvel. It had a large stone tub that was oblong in shape, into which cold water could be pumped. There was a small fireplace where water could be heated just beyond the tub. The large kettle that hung over the coals had only to be tipped down the slanted incline of the tub to bring the temperature of the bathwater to a more comfortable degree. A larger fireplace on the opposite wall from the tub warmed the room. There was a table with towels, and other accoutrements for bathing. When the bath's drain was uncovered, Alette told them, it emptied into a sluice that ran into the latrine's sluice, thus keeping it clean.

Father Bernard said he would bathe when the others were done.

Alette brought Hugh and Rolf to the bathing chamber, asking, "Which of you will go first?"

"I will defer to my guest," Hugh said, bowing to Rolf.

"Nay, my lord, no longer a guest, but Langston's steward," came the polite reply. "I must defer to my lord." Then he, too, bowed.

Hugh laughed. "I'll argue no further with you, Rolf. I long for that bath." He began to strip off his garments, handing the individual articles of clothing to the pleasant-faced older woman who attended the lady Alette.

"This is Ida, my serving woman," the keep's mistress told him. "Get in now, my lord, while the water is hot."

"Does not Isabelle help with the bathing of guests, lady?" Hugh asked.

"I thought her too young for such duties," Alette answered.

"She must learn," Hugh said. "Have Ida fetch the girl so she may help you. I will send her away when Rolf bathes." He climbed into the water and sat down upon the bathing stool.

"Fetch my daughter," Alette told her serving woman quietly.

On her return, Ida reported, "She says she will not come."

Hugh looked to Rolf. "Bring my lady," was all he said.

They heard the screech of outrage even before the door to the bathing chamber was kicked open to allow the steward entry with his captive. Isabelle was thrown carelessly over Rolf's shoulder, and she was kicking wildly, beating upon his back with clenched fists. When he set her upon her feet, she furiously hit him as hard as she could.

*"How dare you lay hands on me, you oaf!"* she screamed. Grinning, he blocked her second blow.

"I asked him to bring you, *ma Belle douce*," Hugh said. "As my wife, you will be expected to bathe honored guests. Your mother tells me you have no experience in this art. It is time that you learned. There is a sea sponge on the table. Take it up, and after you have dipped it in the liquid soap, scrub my shoulders."

*"I will not!"* she spat.

"Your touch must be gentle, but firm, ma Belle," he told her calmly, ignoring her open defiance.

Isabelle crossed her arms over her chest, staring mutinously at the back of his head. "Have you no ears to hear, Saxon? *I will not bathe you.* It is a ridiculous custom, and besides, as long as she lives, my mother is the lady of this keep, not I."

"Madame, you will wash me," he said, his tone hardening.

"You cannot make me," she returned smugly.

"Belle," her mother besought her, "the lady of the keep is the lord's wife. Once you have wed Hugh Fauconier, I must retire to the background, my daughter, and you must take up these duties, not I."

"When I am my lord's wife I shall," Isabelle said, "but not a moment before then, madame. Of course, such a union is yet in doubt."

*"Ma Belle douce* is shy," Hugh said with false sweetness. "It pleases me that she be so demure and retiring. It but adds to her charm. You will watch your mother, ma Belle, and learn from her. I shall not require you to bathe me until we are man and wife."

"Go to the devil!" Isabelle snapped at him. "I will not remain here to see you pampered like some overweening infant." She whirled about, but Rolf blocked her way, smiling blandly.

"You have heard the lord's instructions, lady," he said.

*"The lord's instructions?"* The girl looked at him, outraged, and then kicked him as hard as she could in the shin.

"Owwwww!" Rolf yelped, hopping about as Isabelle pushed past him and was gone out the door.

"Ahhh, lady," Ida said, a disapproving look upon her face, "the girl should have been beaten long ago. May God have mercy upon you, my lord Hugh. The wench is possessed by demons for certain."

"Add more hot water to the tub, Ida," Hugh answered her. "It grows cold." Then he turned his head, smiling up at Alette. "Do not fear, lady, I will tame her in time," he promised.

"She has a kind heart for animals, my lord," Alette said, tears in her bright blue eyes, "but with people she is so impatient." Then without another word Alette washed Langston's lord. When she had finished, she dried him off, wrapping him in a warm towel. "The solar is yours now, my lord. I cleared my possessions from it today. I will sleep with my daughter until she is your wife, and then, with your permission, keep the chamber for myself. Ida will take you and see you comfortably settled. Go quickly lest you catch a chill."

He wanted to protest, but he did not. She had done what was correct, for the lord's chamber was now his by right. She would have been embarrassed, and not just a little offended, had he refused her, even out of kindness and consideration for the lady herself. "I thank you, madame, for your courtesy," he replied, and followed Ida from the bathing chamber to his new quarters.

Alette now turned to Rolf de Briard. "Come, my lord," she said to him, "do not dally, for the priest has yet to wash himself."

Rolf masked his shyness at disrobing before her, as he

quickly handed her his clothing and climbed into the tub just vacated by his friend. He had thought Alette the loveliest woman he had ever seen when he first laid eyes upon her. Now, he realized that he was still strongly attracted to her. He was not certain what to do. "How old are you?" he suddenly asked, surprising her.

A rosy glow suffused her, and she was relieved that his back was to her so he could not see it. "I am thirty," she told him. "I was fourteen when I was married to Robert de Manneville, and just fifteen when Isabelle was born. Why do you ask?"

"I am thirty-two," he answered, and then grew silent.

"Do you have a wife?" she asked him after a short time. She was diligently scrubbing his short white-blond hair.

"Nay. I could never afford one. I am a younger son of a third wife," he explained. "Were my eldest brother not the generous man he is, I should never have had the means to become a knight, but Ranulf, God bless him, always had a soft spot for me."

"It helps to have someone who loves you," Alette agreed. "I was orphaned at the age of four, and put into my uncle's care. He was a hard man, but eventually saw that a husband was found for me."

"Did you love Robert de Manneville?" Rolf asked boldly. He had no right to do so, he knew, but somehow he had to know.

"He was my husband," Alette said quietly. "I gave him my loyalty, my honor, and my respect. He asked no more. He sought a wife to raise his sons and give him other sons. In that I failed him." She rinsed his hair, pouring a bucket of warm water over it, and handed him a cloth to mop his face. "You are clean now, my lord," she said, and he arose to be toweled. "Have you fresh garments to wear in the morning, or shall I have the laundress wash these tonight?"

"I have other clothing," he answered her as she wrapped a warm towel tightly about his loins.

"Then seek your bed, sir, before you catch a draught," Alette ordered him, and she smiled sweetly.

"Lady, I thank you for your attention," he replied, and departed the bathing chamber.

Alette released some of the water from the tub, and then, adding more hot water, went to find the priest so he might bathe. After checking to see that the fires in the hall were banked, she found Ida and instructed her to see the bathing chamber was cleaned when Father Bernard had finished his ablutions. "Then come to bed, Ida. Belle's room will be crowded until she weds the lord, but you will have the trundle, and my daughter's serving woman will sleep upon a pallet."

"The sooner the girl weds, the better," Ida said, her look disapproving. "She needs correction, and only a husband can give it to her. God forgive Lord Robert that he would not let her be disciplined as a child. She is like some wild creature, my lady."

"Better to pray that the new lord does not grow angry and ask King Henry for another wife," Alette fretted.

"Go and rest yerself, my lady," Ida told her, patting her mistress's arm. "It will look better in the morning, I am certain. Surely lady Isabelle can be made to see reason."

"May God and His Blessed Mother hear all our prayers," Alette replied fervently.

# ▓Chapter 3

*L*angston Keep was not a large establishment. Off its Great Hall, at one end of the building, was a buttery and a pantry. The solar was located behind the Great Hall at its far end. It took up two-thirds of the space, with the bathing chamber taking up the rest. Along one wall of the Great Hall three doors opened into small rooms, one of which was Isabelle's. It was separated from the other two, which were used for guests, by the fireplace. The household servants slept in an attic above the hall. Below was a huge space for the storage of foodstuffs, weapons, and other dry goods, and the kitchens as well.

Hugh and Rolf learned that the keep had no mesne, or organized military personnel. The porter was a doddering old fellow. There were no watchmen or men-at-arms. Hugh understood how providential the arrival of two knights with their squires had been.

"How would you have protected yourselves if you had been attacked?" he asked Belle. "Langston has been a sitting duck for too long, and only your isolation has protected you." He was almost angry.

"Who would attack us?" she demanded scornfully. "Besides, the villages would rally if there was danger."

"Your serfs would run into the woods and hide," he said bluntly. "It is debatable if they would even remember to take the livestock with them. You and your mother could have been killed, or worse."

Rolf went into the villages, asking who would prefer life as a man-at-arms to tilling the soil. He returned with a respectable troupe of younger sons ready and eager to be turned into soldiers. Half a dozen slightly older men who had offered their service would be trained with the younger men, but would become watchmen for the keep. The elderly porter would be replaced by his grandsons. Daily the men marched upon the bailey green, usually under the watchful eyes of the two squires, Fulk and Giles, who also taught their fledglings how to use spear, pike, and crossbow. Sometimes Rolf or Hugh would come to watch, and make suggestions.

As Langston's steward, or seneschal, it was now Rolf's duty to administer the estate. He would handle routine legal and financial matters, and direct the serfs and freedmen. In a larger household the various domestic departments would each have had a head, answerable to the steward, but Langston was far too small for such grandeur. Rolf preferred leaving the handling of the keep's staff to Alette for the time being. To his great surprise, Isabelle proved enormously helpful as well. The household's records up to the death of the last steward were meticulous. The previous holder of the office had been both thorough and careful in his management.

As Belle could neither read nor write, she had kept all the facts of the estate's business in her head, memorizing them down to the smallest detail. Now she sat patiently with Rolf in the Great Hall for several mornings, dictating the details to him as he carefully transcribed them into the estate books.

"Her memory is absolutely faultless," Rolf told Hugh admiringly as they rode out one afternoon to Langston's farthest village to see what repairs were necessary to the cottages before spring. "I could not help but ask my lady Alette why her daughter was being so cooperative with me when she resents our presence so bitterly. My lady says that her daughter is actually relieved to have a steward to take over again because she prefers being out of doors to having the responsibility of Langston on her slender shoulders. I think the lady Alette dissembles a bit with me, for Isabelle of Langston loves her lands dearly. It must be a wrench for her to give up her authority. Still, she is no fool, and must realize she has no choice in the matter.

"Isabelle accepted the responsibility willingly when she had to," Rolf continued. "For a maid to fulfill her familial obligations so thoroughly is very commendable. If you but tame the wench, she may make you a good wife after all."

"She was a good administrator?" Hugh asked his friend, impressed by Rolf's praise of Belle.

"Aye! The serfs may complain, and claim to be glad to have a lord over them once again, but it is only because they resented having a woman rule them. She was every bit as hard as a man with them, seeing that the rents were paid on time, that the fields were tilled and harvested properly, that a fair price was obtained at market. She has not allowed the villages to fall into disrepair, or the poachers take too much game from the woodlands. Aye, the lady Isabelle did very well for Langston in the absence of its lord, Hugh."

Hugh Fauconier was pleased by Rolf's words. There could come a time, and not so far away, when they would be called upon to serve the king in a military campaign. It pleased him to know that Isabelle would be able to manage in their absence.

Everything was going smoothly but for his courtship. Belle remained fiercely hostile. There seemed to be no level upon which he could approach her in a tender manner. Rolf, he noticed, however, seemed to be girding up his courage to approach the widowed lady Alette. He had not spoken of his feelings, but Hugh had eyes in his head, and saw the direction in which his friend's interest lay. I shall have to build a house within the bailey for my steward, he thought, smiling.

The next day dawned gray and damp. It had been very cold all week. Nonetheless Belle put on her cloak and disappeared from the hall shortly after breakfast. Hugh watched her as she made her way across the bailey to the granary. She entered it, and exited a few minutes later carrying a cloth bag. Fascinated, he decided to follow her. The landscape being relatively flat made it easy to keep her in sight, and he kept far enough behind her as to not attract her attention.

Isabelle walked briskly over the frosty fields. The ground was hard beneath her feet. There was no wind, and a pearlescent sun tried hard to force its way through the milky sky, but was unsuccessful in its attempt. Ahead, Belle could see the river. A thin coating of ice had built up along its banks. The tall, deep gold reeds with their feathery heads stood like silent sentinels in the morning light. An upturned cockle was drawn on the shore. Reaching it, Belle sat down, staring out across the water. Just a few miles downstream lay the sea.

Hugh stopped, watching the girl as she sat in silent contemplation. He had never seen her so calm, so at peace.

A small flock of snow geese flew low over the river, setting down in the water near Isabelle. She did not move even as they came swimming ashore and then waddled out of the water. The geese gathered about the girl's feet. Reaching into the bag she carried, she began spreading the grain for them. The birds ate quickly, greedily, and when they had finished, they settled down about her, preening, one or two meandering up to have their necks rubbed. Hugh Fauconier was totally fascinated by the scene. Then, at some unheard signal, the geese hurried with much clacking back into the water, and swam off up the river. He wondered about it until he saw two large white swans emerging from the reeds. They are such ungainly birds on land, Hugh thought.

Isabelle stood up now, and reaching into her bag, tossed grain to the swans. When they pressed themselves around her, Hugh worried, for swans were notoriously mean and could bite cruelly. Belle, however, stood unafraid. The swans were obviously old friends. Hugh understood the patience needed to gain the trust of such feral creatures, for he had raised, tamed, and trained hawks and falcons his entire life. He had sensed from the beginning that Belle herself was such a creature. Now, seeing her with the geese and swans, he realized that if wild birds could be brought to eat from her hand, there was, for all her willfulness and temper, much good within the girl who was to be his wife. He had seen enough. Turning, he followed the almost invisible path through the fields back to the keep.

"Will it snow?" Alette wondered aloud that evening as they gathered in the Great Hall.

"By morning," Belle answered her mother. "The damp was almost visible in the air. It has been quite cold for several days now, and there has been no wind all day, madame. The beasts have been brought from the fields. I saw them being driven in as I returned home this afternoon. The serfs know the weather almost as well as I do."

"Are the snows heavy in winter here, ma Belle?" Hugh inquired.

"They are mostly light, but sometimes great," she answered him. "Why did you follow me today, my lord?"

"You saw me?" He was surprised. He had been careful.

"First I heard you. You are a big man, and move noisily. Then I saw you," she answered him, "out of the corner of my eye as I fed my flock."

"I wanted to see where you went," he answered honestly.

"Did you think I went to meet a lover?" she demanded, an edge to her voice. "I do not like being spied upon."

"I did not think you had a lover," he said quietly.

"*What?* Am I not desirable enough, then?" Her tone was sharper.

"I think your sense of honor is far greater than any passion you might feel," Hugh told her. "In our short acquaintance you have not appeared to me to be light-skirted, ma Belle."

For the first time since they had met, she smiled at him. There was no doubt his reply had pleased her. She said nothing more on the matter.

"Do you play chess?" he asked her.

"I do," she said, "and I am very good. Neither of my brothers could beat me, my lord. Can your masculine pride stand the thought of being beaten by a woman? I neither ask nor give quarter."

"Fetch the board, ma Belle," he told her with a smile.

The table was brought, and the pieces taken from a carved ivory box to be set up upon the board. They began to play, silently at first, then jibing at and mocking one another as each took an opponent's piece. Belle swiftly won the game, but Hugh only laughed, demanding an immediate rematch, which she willingly agreed to give him.

"Do you think he is making any headway with her?" Rolf quietly asked Alette as they sat together by the fire, sipping wine.

"My daughter is an enigma to me," Alette replied frankly. "I admit that I have never quite understood her. She has her father's bold spirit, not mine, I fear, and what is good in a man is not perhaps good in a girl."

"You are so fair," he said suddenly, surprised by his own boldness.

"*What?*" She was not certain she had heard him aright.

"I said you are so fair," he repeated with more assurance. "Has no one ever told you that, my lady Alette?" Rolf de Briard had brown eyes, and they warmly surveyed her. "I am of good birth," he said, "although mayhap I do not have the right to speak to you thusly."

"I do not know if you do or not," Alette replied. "No one has ever called me fair, although my aunt once told me I was pretty enough."

"Did not your husband say how lovely you were?" He was astounded. How could Robert de Manneville look at Alette and not acknowledge her beauty, her sweet face, her gentle voice? She was pure perfection in Rolf's eyes.

"Robert married me for children. He was fond of saying all cats were alike in the dark," Alette said. She thought a long moment, and then shook her head. "Nay, he never said I was pretty, my lord."

"Lady, I have not a great deal but my position, which I owe

to the kindness of my friend, Hugh, but I should like to court you," Rolf told the startled woman. "We are of an age, and not related by blood. I can see no impediment to it, can you?"

"My lord, you flatter me beyond all words, but you would but waste your time. I do not mean to wed again," Alette said softly. Her heart was beating rapidly, as if she were a young girl with her first suitor. Robert de Manneville had certainly never been so courteous in his pursuit of her. Rolf de Briard wanted to court her.

"Why will you not marry again, lady?" he questioned her.

"As a widow, my lord, I have far more personal freedom than I would as a wife. A wife, in my opinion, has little more liberty than a serf. My daughter has little respect for me. I believe her reluctance to take Sir Hugh as her husband stems from seeing my plight as her father's wife. A husband may beat his wife, mistreat her, flaunt his mistress in her face. All this she must accept without complaint. I have been happier than I have ever been in my entire life since my husband went on crusade. While I mourn his passing, for I am not an unfeeling woman, I rejoice in the fact that he will not return to hurt me ever again. He showed more kindness to his dogs than he ever did to me."

"I am not Robert de Manneville, lady," Rolf told her. "I should cherish you and love you all my days if you would one day accept me for your husband." Reaching out, he took her hand and, bringing it to his lips, kissed it. Then he turned her hand over, pressing his mouth hotly first against the inside of her wrist, and then her palm.

She shivered, and when their eyes met, Alette was almost overwhelmed by the look of deep passion in his brown eyes. She could not speak.

"Let me court you," he said, his voice low, personal, and very intense. "Let me show you that not all men are cruel and unkind, sweet lady. If when you have gotten to know me you are still of the same opinion you hold now, I shall endeavor to understand, but give me a chance to prove otherwise to you."

"You are most persuasive, sir," she replied breathlessly. She had never felt *this* way before. Robert had certainly never looked at her with such deep feeling in his eyes, and in his voice. When he had met her for the first time, he told her quite firmly that her uncle had given him permission to marry her. There had never been any talk of love. *Of courting.* He would condescend to take this orphan girl with her tiny dowry off her uncle's hands, and she would mother his children in return. It was a business arrangement, and nothing more.

"Will you let me be your knight, lady?" Rolf said softly.

"Perhaps a little while," she answered him, finally able to find her voice, "but, sir, I make you no promises."

"I understand," Rolf replied, his heart soaring. He would prove to Alette that not all men were cruel and thoughtless to their ladies. Eventually he would show her that he was worthy to be her husband. Had not that brute, Robert de Manneville, understood what a precious possession Alette was? He was a fool, then!

She rose from her seat. "It is late, sir," she said.

"I will escort you to your chamber, my lady," he replied, standing.

The hall emptied, but for Hugh and Isabelle, bent in serious concentration over their chessboard. While she had won the first game, it had been mainly because he had underestimated her skill. Her respect for him began to grow grudgingly when she realized that, and saw that he did not intend to allow her a second victory over him if he could possibly help it.

He was not like any man she had ever known. While she had loved her father, who was indulgent of her, she had hid her fear of him, for she was never certain if the swift violence he often exhibited toward her mother might not be turned upon her one day. In her secret heart Belle wondered if she would have been brave, or if she would have given way to fear, as Alette so often had before her husband. Robert de Manneville had been kind to his only daughter, but she had still been a child when he went away. Now she was almost relieved that he would never return.

Her brothers had been another matter. William, the elder, was ten years her senior. Though she would have never admitted it to her mother, Alette had been correct when she said he tolerated her only for their father's goodwill. On the rare occasions they had been alone, William enjoyed taunting his half sister with the fact that his mother was of far, far more noble birth than her mother. Yet Belle knew her mother's kin were of the nobility, and more than just respectable. He also mocked her for being bigger than other girls her age when petite was the ideal for women of breeding. "You are a carrot-topped calf who will one day grow into a carrot-topped cow," William liked to tell her. Fortunately, he spent most of his time in Normandy as he grew older, so she was spared his nastiness. She was quite delighted he would not return from his crusade, and even more so that he had left no wife or legitimate issue.

Richard de Manneville, the younger of her father's two sons, had been less hostile to his little sister. Six years her senior, he had spent more time than his elder sibling in the lady Alette's care. He had a mercurial temperament, unlike the stolid and snobbish William. Usually he was kind to Isabelle, but sometimes when there was no one about to see, he would lash out at her angrily, overwhelmed by jealousy that she would have Langston, and William, Manneville. There was not enough money to put him with the Church and assure him a position of importance. Richard de Manneville would have to make his way as a knight. He would have to earn his own prestige and fortune.

Such a fate did not appeal at all to Richard. Sometimes in his anger he would pinch his little sister where it would not show. His thin fingers were adept at rendering her black and blue. Belle quickly learned to defend herself from her brother, sometimes using her fists, sometimes kicking out at him. Such behavior never failed to amuse him. It would set him to laughing so hard that his rage swiftly dissolved. Isabelle could imagine Richard being absolutely delighted when his brother was killed in battle, leaving Manneville all to him.

And these were the only men of her own class that she had ever known, Belle thought. Oh, occasionally a noble visitor would pass through, requesting a night's lodging, but they would ride in late and depart early, leaving no visible impression upon her. For over four years she and her mother had lived alone at Langston except for the servants. For three of those years, since she was twelve, she had managed the estate without any help from anyone. She had been very frightened when the old steward died, but unless she wanted them to starve, or to have her serfs rebel or run away, she knew that she had to take charge and be strong. Any sign of weakness would have led to their ruin. Until the male peasants, serf and freed, understood she was *lady* of the estate in deed as well as fact, they would try to bully her.

Each day she would ride out, no matter the weather. She delegated authority where she could, but oversaw all with a very sharp eye. What she did not know about planting, threshing, and harvesting, she quickly learned from the women on the estate, who in defiance of their men wanted the lady to succeed. Belle even learned to prune the fruit trees herself. She was not afraid to alight from her horse to chase poultry into the barn in a sudden storm. She administered justice, turning a blind eye to the tenant who poached an occasional rabbit from her fields to feed his family; hanging the bully who had been previously warned, yet stepped boldly from her woods carrying the carcass of a dressed deer, which he then proceeded to try to sell for profit to her villagers. The family of the illegal hunter was fiercely driven from her estate, for Isabelle knew to allow them to remain would be but to court trouble. The people of Langston respected the lady, even if they did not all like her. If I had been a man, Isabelle thought bitterly, my actions would have never been considered unusual.

Now she was faced with Hugh Fauconier, knight. Heir to the last Saxon lord of Langston. Sent by a king she didn't even know, to take over not just her lands, but her person. Why, Isabelle wondered as she pondered her next move upon the chessboard, why had she never considered the possibility of a husband? Her father had never discussed the matter, although she realized that if he had not gone away, a betrothal would have been made and a marriage settled by now. Somehow in those years without him, she had become used to being her own mistress, *and she liked it*. She did not want to give over her authority to a husband. *Langston was hers!* She moved her knight piece, realizing even as she did it that it was a very bad move.

"Check," Hugh said quietly, taking her knight. Then, "Why did you make such a foolish move?"

"I had lost my concentration," she answered him honestly. "I was thinking of something else, my lord. You have won this game fairly, I think." She even gave him the tiny vestige of a smile.

"What were you thinking of?" he asked her.

"You," she said, surprising him.

*"Me?"* The sandy brows over his blue eyes rose questioningly.

"I know that you are not to blame, my lord, but I do not think it fair the king take Langston from me," Isabelle said. "I know I am only a woman, but I have kept my lands peaceful and prosperous."

"What would you do if there were a war?" he asked her quietly. "How would you defend Langston from attack? How would you meet your obligations to your liege lord to send soldiers in his defense? You cannot go into battle for the king, or train others in warfare. And who is your liege lord, Belle? Will you pledge your fealty to King Henry, or to Duke Robert? What if your brother claimed these lands for himself? What would you do?"

"Is there to be a war?" she queried him.

"Probably in the coming spring, or summer," he said. "King Henry will prevail, of course, but Langston is too close to the sea. Should your brother, who is the duke's man, come here to find you and the lady Alette alone, he would certainly take these lands for the duke's good. The king will not have it, ma Belle. You are not some silly little girl who does not understand what I am telling you. You have courage, and intelligence. These are words I never thought to use in reference to a woman, but they fit you.

"Langston must have a lord to defend it, and you must have a husband, unless, of course, you have a calling for the religious life. If that be so, I should not stand in your way. I would dower you fairly into the convent of your choice. Your mother could then return to Manneville in Normandy. Perhaps your brother would not like it, but he would have no right to refuse his father's widow shelter and sustenance."

Isabelle arose from her seat, and walking over to an arched window, looked out into the darkness. "It is snowing," she said, seeing a buildup of white flakes upon the stone sill outside. She heard the scrape of his chair. She heard his footsteps stopping behind her, and then his arm slipped about her slender waist. She stiffened.

"Why are you afraid to marry me?" he said quietly.

"It is not you, my lord," she told him. She could feel his warm breath on the back of her neck. "I am afraid of no man. I have no calling for a religious life. I simply wish to be free. No woman who is a wife is free. You may beat me without justification, or cast me aside without cause, and I have no recourse. English law and Church law are both on your side. My father was not unkind to me, but he was never good to my mother. I should rather remain unwed than live that kind of life. Oh, you may promise me not to be that way. Perhaps you might even mean it as you said the words, but in the end it would be the same for me as it was for my mother," Belle concluded.

"My mother died shortly after my birth, and my father at Hastings, as you know," he began. "I was raised by my grandparents. Never in all my life did Cedric Merlin-sone raise his hand to his wife, the lady Emma. My grandmother has a fierce

Norman temper even as you do, ma Belle, but even her out-
bursts could not make grandfather angry enough to beat her.
Many men would have, I know that, but not my grandfather.

"My grandparents have lived their lives together as equal
partners, even as King William and good Queen Matilda did,
may God assoil their souls. That is the kind of marriage I offer
you, Isabelle of Langston. You will not be my servant. You
will be my companion. You will be the mother of my children.
If I must go to war in the king's name, you will be my regent
here at Langston. I do not know how else to reassure you than
to tell you these things. Neither of us has a choice in the matter.
The king has said we must marry. I have pledged my loyalty to
Henry Beauclerc, and will obey his commands. I know you are
an honorable woman. Can you do any less?"

"Will you put your words in writing?" Belle demanded.

"Would you sue me then, *ma douce*?" He was amused.
"Besides, you cannot read, and would not know if the words
were true."

"I trust you to make them true, my lord," she answered.

He was amazed. "You would trust me, Belle? Why?"

"Because you are not like my father, or my brothers," she
said simply.

It was the most astounding avowal of faith that had ever
been given to him. To refuse her confidence would be
unchivalrous. "I will have Father Bernard write whatever
words you dictate, ma Belle, and I will sign it in your presence.
In return you must do something for me. I want you to learn
how to read, and to write. You will be a much better chatelaine
for it. Will you promise me that?" He turned her about so that
she was facing him.

"Who will teach me, my lord?" she wondered.

"Father Bernard will teach you," he told her. "Will you
learn?"

"Aye, my lord, I will learn, and gladly, but will he also teach
me numbers, too?" She looked eagerly up at him. "If you and

Rolf de Briard go away and leave me in charge, I must be certain the books are properly kept; that we are not cheated."

He nodded, thinking as he did that she had the most beautiful eyes. Not the soft blue of her mother's, but a mysterious green-gold, like a sun-dappled pond in the deep forest. Unable to help himself, he brushed her lips with his.

She drew back, her eyes darkening, half angry, half puzzled. "Why did you do that, my lord?" she demanded.

"I but sealed our bargain with a kiss, ma Belle," he said seriously.

"Is such a thing always done?"

"Have you never been kissed before?" he answered her question with a question, knowing the answer before she spoke it.

"Who is there to kiss me, sir, and why would they want to?" Isabelle said irritably. "I am not some giggling serf girl, eager for a tumble in the woods. I saw my father kiss my mother only once, when he went off upon his crusade with Duke Robert."

"Kissing is a fine, old sport," Hugh told her with a quick smile. "My grandfather loved catching my grandmother unawares and giving her a loving kiss. We shall learn to know one another better if we practice kissing on a regular basis, ma Belle."

"You are making fun of me," she said. "I do not like to be mocked, my lord. There is absolutely no practical use for mashing one's lips together that I can see."

Hugh chuckled. "You are young, and you are innocent, ma Belle," he told her gently. "In time I will show you how the skilled application of kissing can bring about a useful conclusion. Besides, it is permitted that a married couple kiss whenever and as often as they like."

"We are not married," she said, her tone dark. Then she somehow lost her breath as he pulled her hard against him.

"We are going to be married, and very soon, ma Belle," he replied. His free hand cupped the back of her head firmly. "Close your eyes," he said. "It is better when you close your eyes, *chérie*."

Why am I complying with such a silly request? Isabelle wondered, even as her dark lashes brushed her pale cheeks. His mouth closed warmly over hers, pressing firmly, and then a frisson of enjoyment raced down her spine. She was astounded, and pulled away from him, puzzled.

"What is it?" he asked.

"I felt . . ." She thought a moment. "Pleasure," she finally decided. "Aye. Your kiss gave me pleasure, my lord."

"Then I have succeeded in my purpose, ma Belle. A kiss should be pleasurable," he explained.

"What follows kissing?" she demanded of him.

"There is more to kissing than you have just experienced," he said softly, gently running his forefinger down her elegant, long nose. "In time we will explore everything together, but for now I think you should find your bed, ma Belle. Your mother will wonder where you have gotten to, and I would not fret her." He released his hold on her.

For a moment Isabelle wasn't certain her legs would function as they should, but then she curtsied politely to him, and turning about, walked across the hall, through the door into her chamber.

The room was dark. Carefully, she wended her way around the pallet and the trundle where her servant, Agneatha, and her mother's, Ida, were snoring in deep sleep. Since her mother had moved from the solar, Isabelle had been forced to share her bed with her. She had had absolutely no privacy. It might be almost worth marrying Hugh Fauconier to obtain her portion of the lord's chamber, which was certainly much larger, and far less crowded than this room was now. Reaching the unoccupied side of the bed, she sat down a moment to draw off the soft shoes she wore in the house. Standing again, she undid her belt, laying it aside on a stool by the bed. Next she removed her tunic and her skirt, placing them atop the belt, then climbed into bed next to her parent.

"I will marry him," she said low to her mother, whom she sensed was not yet asleep.

"Why?" Alette asked, curious. "Did he beat you in chess, and thereby win your respect, Isabelle?"

"I won the first game, he the second. We talked. He will not be like Father, madame. He has agreed to sign a paper. He wants me to learn to read and to write. The priest will see to it," the girl told her. "There is, after all, as you have said, no choice. The king has commanded, and Hugh Fauconier is the king's man. Can I show less loyalty?"

Alette could feel the tension draining from her body. "When?" she asked her daughter. "Did he say when we will celebrate the marriage?"

Isabelle shrugged in the darkness. "Let him decide, madame. It makes no difference to me." She rolled onto her side, indicating to her mother that their conversation was over.

Relief poured over the older woman. She wondered exactly what it was that had caused Isabelle to cease her opposition to the king's command. *He has agreed to sign a paper.* What on earth had Isabelle meant by that? Alette wondered. What could a paper have to do with convincing her unruly daughter to cooperate? Blessed Mother! She was going to have to speak to Isabelle about . . . about . . . *it.* Could she let the girl go to her marriage without some knowledge of what was to come? Of what was expected of her?

Alette thought back to her own wedding night, and she shuddered. Robert de Manneville had been a virtual stranger; a neighbor of her uncle. She had seen him perhaps half a dozen times in her life. He was old enough to be her father, and he had a beautiful, proud wife who was the envy of every man of rank for twenty miles around. Then her aunt mentioned one day that poor Sieur Robert had suddenly been widowed. Several months afterward her uncle came to her and told her that their neighbor needed a new wife. He was willing to accept Alette despite her small dower.

"But why me, Uncle Hubert?" she had innocently asked. "Surely Sieur Robert can find a greater name to wed with than Alette d'Aumont."

"Indeed," her uncle had agreed, "but he wants a wife now. Those two unruly sons of his need a mother. Sieur Robert will want other children as well, for the lady Sibylle was in delicate health for many years. You're a good strong girl, Alette. You'll suit him well."

There had been nothing more left to say. She was certainly given no choice. What she did not know was that no other family would have Robert de Manneville marry one of their daughters. He had a fierce temper. He had also adored his late wife. No woman following in Sibylle de Manneville's footsteps would suit him, be she the most beautiful girl, the wealthiest heiress. Hubert d'Aumont, however, saw a chance to ally his family with a better family. He would have given de Manneville his own unmarried daughter, but she was only ten, not old enough yet to be mounted or produce children. His niece was all he had. He gladly sacrificed her to his ambition.

In the hour before she was brought before the priest to wed Robert de Manneville, her aunt Elise came to her. "I wanted to tell you all that you would need to know to please your lord in your bed sport," she began, "but Sieur Robert has forbidden me, saying he will school you himself. Your uncle cravenly agreed with him, but I think them wrong. Still, if I speak to you of what you must know, Sieur Robert might sense it and be displeased. Then your uncle will beat me, Alette. I will tell you this only. Yield to your husband in *all* things, my child. Do not defy him in any manner. He is a hard man, and had the choice been mine, *ma petite*, I should not have given you to him."

With these rather frightening words ringing in her ears, Alette d'Aumont was wed to Robert de Manneville. Her uncle, she knew, had gone into debt to pay for the feast that followed. When it was over, she was mounted before her husband on his huge warhorse so that they might ride across the fields to his home. It was during that ride she was given a taste of what was to come. Guiding his mount with his sinewy thighs, Robert de Manneville fondled his trembling bride's round little breasts as they rode. He had had a great deal of wine to drink, but he was not drunk. One hand crept up her leg beneath her skirts.

"Have you ever had your *petite bijou* tweaked, Alette?" he asked her, turning her face to place a wet kiss upon her lips.

She looked at him dumbly, not having any idea of what he meant. *"Mon seigneur?"* Then she gasped as the tip of his finger began to rub at a particularly sensitive spot of flesh she hadn't been aware she possessed. She squirmed, but he snarled an order for her to remain still. It was virtually impossible, although she struggled to obey him. Then, to her further shock, he pushed a single, thick finger into her body. Terrified, she began to sob as the finger moved deeper inside of her, stopping suddenly.

"Good!" he said as if to himself. "You are intact. Your uncle did not lie to me. I haven't had a woman since my Sibylle died, Alette. My juices have been pent up these last months, and I'll not wait another moment to satisfy myself." He drew his big horse to a stop in a stand of trees. "Now do exactly what I tell you, Alette," he said as he lifted her from his lap. "Pull up your skirts, and straddle the horse as I set you before me," and when she had obeyed him, he continued, "Now lean forward, my petite, as far as you can."

She complied, but said as she did, "I cannot keep my backside from lifting up, monseigneur. If anyone should come along, I would be shamed."

"Be patient, *ma petite*," he said in an almost soothing voice, and he ran his hands over the milky flesh so sweetly displayed. Drawing his own ornate tunic up, he fumbled for his manhood, pulling it from his drawers. It was hard, and rampant. Raising himself slightly in his stirrups, he drew the girl back toward him, a hand upon her belly to steady her, his other hand seeking the proper passage in which to insert his raging weapon.

*She felt it.* She felt it pushing into the passage his finger had but lately occupied, but whatever it was, it was bigger. Alette whimpered, half afraid, and with the beginnings of pain. "You are hurting me," she sobbed to him. "Please do not hurt me!"

His fingers now dug into the tender flesh of her slender hips. Forcing her forward again, he thrust hard once. She screamed. Twice. She pleaded. And finally a third time while she shrieked with pain. "Be silent, you little bitch," he snarled. "The pain will ease, and your cries are spoiling my pleasure." He pumped her hard, finally shuddering, and sighing gustily. "Ahhhhh! Aye, that will do until we get home, *ma petite*. I intend to have you several times tonight." Pulling her skirts back, he lifted her into her former position, kicking his mount forward to continue their journey.

Silent tears poured down Alette's face. Why had her aunt not warned her of this horror? The passage in her body he had so cruelly invaded ached terribly. She struggled to regain her composure, for they would soon be at her new home. She didn't want to embarrass either her husband or herself. When they arrived, he dismounted first, lifting her down, introducing her to his sons, his servants. Alette greeted them all politely, kissing her stepsons, who glared in unfriendly fashion at her. She could barely stand. She was in dreadful pain, but she walked proudly into the Great Hall and stood accepting the toasts of de Manneville's staff. Then she was escorted to her chamber, where Ida was already waiting.

"I will attend to myself, Ida," she said quietly, dismissing her serving woman lest she discover her shame. Alette quickly undressed, and was mortified to find her chemise stained with bright red blood. Was her flow upon her? The blood had run down her thighs. She felt so raw where he had used her. Before she might wash, however, the door to the chamber opened and Robert de Manneville entered.

Seeing the bloody garment, the stains upon her legs, he grinned, pleased. "I did a good job of deflowering you, *ma petite*," he said, and began pulling off his clothing.

The hours that followed were a horror in her memory. Her husband seemed insatiable in his lust for her. By morning she thought herself half dead, and her fair body was covered with scratches and bruises. Each night that came after was a repeat of the first, until finally she was able to tell him that she was with child.

Isabelle was born eleven months after their marriage. They were living at Langston then, and when she had healed from the birth, her husband, try as he might, was unable to function with her as he once had. It was, Alette recalled, the answer to her prayers. After that, however, he became more abusive toward her, but she knew she should rather suffer his beatings than be at the mercy of his lust ever again. It was all she knew of the physical relationship between men and women.

How could she explain to her daughter the pain, the degradation, the horror of the marital act? Isabelle was rebellious enough. If she knew what was in store for her, she would change her mind. What would happen to them then? No. Every woman must suffer a man's lust. Isabelle would be no different. She would tell Isabelle nothing. *Nothing!*

# ❧ *Chapter 4*

*I*t was yet dark in the Great Hall of Langston as Father Bernard prepared for the mass. Several young female serfs worked at reviving the fires in the fireplaces. Quietly the priest set out the small jeweled crucifix he always carried with him on such journeys, drawing it forth from its velvet bag, setting it reverently upon the high board which would serve as the altar. The young boy delegated to serve him placed two silver candlesticks on either side of the crucifix, affixing pure beeswax tapers into each, grinning delightedly at the priest's smiling nod of approval.

There is so much to be done here, Father Bernard thought as he looked about the hall. He had already performed several marriages, and baptized any number of babies. He had even seen off two old souls, easing their passage from this world into the next with the last rites of the Church, and had blessed the graves of those who had died over the last few years without benefit of clergy.

Hugh had promised to build a church, and the priest knew the young man would keep his word. Langston needed a church. The keep needed a chapel. *And they all needed a priest.* He had wanted to stay here from the moment he had seen the place. The king did not need him. He was but one of many royal chaplains, but the people of Langston needed him. It would not be a rich living, he knew, but they really needed him here. He would speak to Hugh.

"You look almost grim, good father," the subject of his thoughts said, startling him. "Is everything aright?"

Father Bernard turned to face Hugh Fauconier. "You need me here!" he told the younger man, voicing aloud his thoughts.

"You would remain on this small holding? I would be right glad of it, Father Bernard, but I am no great lord, nor likely to be one," Hugh said. "And will the king allow it?"

"King Henry has a dozen nameless priests just like me in his service," Father Bernard said, "and two dozen more clamoring to be given a place at his court. If you ask him, my lord, I know he will release me from his service that I may stay at Langston, where I may assuredly serve God better. I am of no importance to the king."

"Certainly we must ask him," Hugh replied with a slow smile. Then he was all business. "I have promised Langston a church. We will build it together, good father. You may live here in the keep, or have your own house. You will have the church's portion of rents and goods for yourself. For now I cannot promise to give you anything but food and shelter until I have better learned the condition of this manor."

The priest nodded. "It is fair, my lord," he said.

The Langston folk were now coming into the hall for the mass. Rolf appeared, and Alette, Isabelle, and their women came into the Great Hall from their chamber. The lad assisting the priest lit the candles upon the makeshift altar, and the service began. When it was concluded, and the priest had blessed the congregation, Hugh spoke before they might all depart for their day's tasks.

"Good father, a moment, I pray you. Last night the lady Isabelle agreed to become my wife. I would have you perform the ceremony now."

*"My lord!"* Alette was taken aback. This was no way for such a momentous occasion to be celebrated. She looked to her daughter, as did everyone else in the hall.

Isabelle of Langston, however, had locked her gaze onto that of Hugh Fauconier. She was surprised by his action, yet the challenge in those smoky silver-blue eyes was irresistible. And the faint, almost imperceptible smile touching the corners of his mouth made it very clear that he knew it. It was just a trifle irritating that he taunt her so smugly, and silently. She ought to fly into a rage, terrifying them all, but she did not.

With a vanity she had not suspected that she had, she gazed at her attire. She was wearing a bright green tunic with gold thread embroidery over an indigo-blue skirt. The tunic was belted at the waistline, with a silk belt worked with gold threads. Her thick hair was plaited into a single long braid, as she always wore it. It only took her a moment or so to assess her appearance. Looking back at Hugh, she said, "I think it an excellent idea we marry now, my lord, at the beginning of the day. Then we may get about our work without interruption."

With a grin he was unable to restrain, he held out his hand to her, drawing her to him as she took it. "You have heard my lady, good father. Let us get on with it, and the congregation here may witness the event, in honor of which I shall suspend the afternoon's labor."

"Where is my paper?" Isabelle demanded suddenly of him.

"I shall have the priest write it after we have received the sacrament of marriage, ma Belle. Do you trust me to honor my word?"

"I do, my lord," she answered him.

Then before her stunned parent and the others, Isabelle of Langston was joined in marriage to Hugh Fauconier, as ordered by King Henry and agreed to by both parties involved.

"You may kiss the bride, my lord," Father Bernard said.

She expected him to brush her lips lightly, as he had the night before. Instead, however, Hugh pulled Belle into his embrace, kissing her hard upon her mouth to the lusty cheers of the onlookers. When he set her back upon her feet, her surprise was evident.

"Now, my lady wife," he said calmly, "shall we break our fast?"

"Aye, my lord husband," she replied, matching his poise.

"Your wedding day should have been something special," Alette chided her daughter as they sat eating. "Married after the mass without any warning! Do you call this meal a feast? Bread and cheese and wine? Oh, Isabelle! Why did you not refuse him so that it might have been done properly? No one would have faulted you in such a matter."

"It did not matter to me," Isabelle replied. "The king ordered the marriage. You said I had no other choice but to obey. If my lord sought to formalize our match this morning, I saw no cause to object."

Alette was astounded by her daughter's attitude, but then she had to admit to herself that Belle had always shown a lack of propriety. She should not have been surprised by such outrageous behavior.

"For whom would you have arranged this proper wedding, madame?" her daughter said scornfully. "Our only relations are in Normandy. We do not know our neighbors, for the land all around us is in the possession of a great lord who is rarely here. The marriage was well-celebrated, and witnessed in the presence of our own Langston folk. I feel no lack."

"A bride cake," Alette said weakly. "There should have been a sugar cake, and a minstrel to make music. You will have no beautiful memories. A woman should have beautiful memories of her wedding day."

"Do you?" Isabelle asked her mother.

Alette grew pale, but then she said, "I was surrounded by my family, such as they were. There was wine and cake. Then your father took me up on his horse, riding across the fields to Manneville. That was my wedding day. What will you have to remember? A hurried, sudden ceremony after the morning mass! *And cheese!*" She began to cry.

"*Chère* madame," Hugh interrupted, for he had heard it all, "I know that you must be disappointed, but we shall make up for our lack of display this day when our first child is born. Then will be a grand celebration, and I shall entrust it all to you." He took her hand in his and kissed it. "Do not weep now."

Alette looked at Hugh through wet, spiky dark blond lashes, thinking after all that her daughter was fortunate in her plain-faced kindly bridegroom. She managed a tiny smile to reassure him, retrieving her hand as she said, *"Tu es bien gentil, monseigneur."*

"It is not a bad feast, madame," Isabelle said in an attempt to emulate her husband's kindness, even if she thought her mother silly and weak as water. "The bread is still warm from the ovens, and it is a new wheel of cheese this morning."

*"Oh, Belle!"* her mother said in that tone she seemed to reserve for her daughter alone.

Hugh stood up, saying to his new wife, "I would that you rode with us this morning, ma Belle. We need to know which fields are to lie fallow come the spring. And Lent is almost upon us. Who supplies the fish we will need? Our own people cannot fish enough, can they?"

"First, Father Bernard must write my paper," Isabelle said, "and then you must sign it, my lord husband."

"Agreed!" he answered her, and called for parchment, pen, and ink to be brought to the priest.

As it took several minutes to find the required items, the servants cleared the high board of all evidence of the meal, putting the leftover bread and cheese into a basket to be distributed to the poor, as was the custom at Langston. Finally the priest was settled, a clean parchment before him, his newly sharpened quill tip inked.

"Tell him what you would have him write, my lady wife," the lord of Langston said to her.

Isabelle pondered it a moment, and then she said, *"I, Hugh Fauconier, lord of Langston Keep . . ."*

Father Bernard scribbled swiftly.

*". . . swear upon the name of our lord, Jesus, and his holy, Blessed Mother Mary that I shall treat my spouse, Isabelle of Langston, with respect and dignity."*

The priest's hand slowed, but then hearing no order to cease from Hugh, continued to take Isabelle's dictation.

*"I shall not beat my wife, nor abuse her with harsh words."*

Alette de Manneville gasped, shocked by her daughter's daring. She fully expected her new son-in-law to stop the girl, but he did not.

*"In my absence, my wife shall take on my authority over Langston, and its people, for I consider her my equal."*

Alette cried out softly, falling into a chair, her hand over her heart. *"Mon Dieu!"* she whispered, her heart beating in terror as she awaited Hugh Fauconier's justifiable wrath.

"That is all, my lord husband," Belle said calmly.

"Rolf, you and Father Bernard will witness this document," Hugh said quietly, bending to sign it. When they had, Hugh rolled up the parchment and handed it to Isabelle. "The first gift in your dower," he said with a small smile. "I do indeed keep my word, *chérie.*"

"When do I have my lessons?" she asked him.

"In the afternoons," he told her. "With your permission, we will leave the running of the household in your mother's capable hands for the time being, my lady wife. In the mornings you will ride out with us so that you are kept fully familiar with the estate. I expect that both Rolf and I will be called upon to join the king's armies come summer. You will have to oversee Langston while we are gone."

Belle nodded. "I will go and fetch my cloak," she said, hurrying off.

"While we are out," Hugh said to his mother-in-law, "you will see that my wife's possessions are moved into the solar, lady. I would know how much she understands of the intimacies that transpire between a man and his wife. What have you told her?"

"I have told her nothing, my lord," Alette answered him. "There was no need until now, but before tonight I shall advise her to yield to you in all you desire, my lord."

He saw the distaste in her eyes. She had obviously not been

happy in her bed sport with her late husband. It was good she had not told Isabelle anything, passing on her fears and aversions. "Say nothing to Belle, lady," he said gently. "I am a kind man, and will not hurt her."

Her relief was almost palpable. She curtsied to him and hurried away, her blue skirts swirling about her ankles as she went.

"You will have to woo her tenderly, Rolf," Hugh said to his friend.

The denial sprang quickly to his lips, but then Rolf de Briard sighed. "She is the most beautiful woman I have ever seen," he said. "I want to marry her, Hugh. Does it surprise you? Will you permit it? She is, after all, in your charge now."

"You could have a younger woman," Hugh said. "She is past thirty and may not be able to have children for you."

"It matters not to me," Rolf told his friend.

"Then if you can gain her favor, Rolf, I have no objections. You are her equal in rank. A knight. The steward of Langston. Your addresses will, however, have to be gentle in nature. The lady Alette, I suspect, was not happy with Robert de Manneville. He may have hurt her, making her fearful of the sweetness between a man and his wife."

Rolf de Briard nodded. "She has hinted, more by what she has not said than by anything she has, that she did not love him."

"Spring is coming," Hugh said with a small smile. "A woman's heart is more easily breached in the spring, I think, than at any other time of the year. I will leave you to your own devices for I have my work cut out for me with ma Belle." He chuckled.

"You two appear to have come to some sort of understanding," Rolf noted, a twinkle in his warm brown eyes. "My poor heart almost jumped from my chest when you asked the priest to marry you, but she did not shriek with outrage. And that document you let her dictate. No court would recognize such a thing. Both God's law and English law give man complete control over his wife. You know it, Hugh."

"I do," the lord of Langston agreed, "but Isabelle needed the reassurance that the paper gives her. She will never know the law because she will have no need of it, Rolf. I am not a brute who will be cruel to his family as her father obviously was."

"You have too soft a heart," Rolf muttered.

"Only for ma Belle," Hugh said with a small smile. "She bewitches me, Rolf. I like her spirit. I have far better ways to spend the time with her than in argument. I want my children to come from love as I came from my parents, may God assoil their young souls."

*"My lord!"* Isabelle stood at the head of the hall impatiently tapping her foot. "Are you coming? Or do you mean to spend the day in idle chatter with your steward?"

The two men laughed, and taking their cloaks from the waiting servants, joined her. Outside, the ground was newly snowy, but Isabelle informed them that the real storm would come later in the afternoon. They rode out across the estate, Isabelle telling them which fields would lie fallow in the coming planting seasons and which would be planted with barley, rye, corn, and wheat.

"We require three days' labor each week from the serfs and freedmen alike," Isabelle explained. "It is rare, once the fields are planted, that we need all their time. My father always made them give it, but I found they worked better for me if I let them go when their work was done, provided it was done well. During harvest we all work together to get the crop in, going from one field to the next, starting, of course, with the demesne holdings. I allow gleaning in both the fields and the orchards once the harvest is in safely."

"You were a good chatelaine, ma Belle," Hugh told his bride.

"The serfs resented me because I was the daughter of the Norman lord, and because I am a female; but I was hard with them for it," she said grimly. "I would not let Langston fail!"

It is strange, Hugh thought as they rode along. For all he was the rightful Saxon heir to Langston, Isabelle was more of Langston than he was, having been born and raised here. Her sense of honor and of loyalty pleased him. He hoped his grand-parents one day would make the trip from their home in the west to meet her. He somehow knew they would approve of this hellion he had been given as a wife.

The snow was beginning to fall in earnest as they returned to the keep. Smoke rose from the smoke holes of the cottages as they passed through the village. Not even a dog was left to wander the street in the lowering weather. It was almost midday, and Alette had the main meal ready and waiting for them. There was duck, a minced venison pie, a thick pottage of winter vegetables, hard-cooked eggs, bread, butter, and cheese. Those at the high board ate from silver plates and drank their wine from silver goblets. The others in the hall ate and drank from wooden pieces. Afterward a bowl of apples and pears was placed upon the high board. The fruit both looked and tasted amazingly fresh. Hugh remarked upon it.

"When we harvest them in October," Alette explained, "I dip some of them in wax to preserve them better, then store them in a dry, cool place. Now in February, the fruit tastes as if it has been just plucked from the tree."

" 'Tis very clever of you, my lady," Rolf said quickly.

" 'Twas a trick my aunt taught me," she returned.

That afternoon Father Bernard began teaching Isabelle her letters. She was an intelligent girl, and quickly mastered the alphabet. Alette occupied her time at her loom, weaving a tapestry she had been working on now for over a year. Hugh and Rolf busied themselves going over estate matters while their two squires gathered up the new men-at-arms not on duty, and taking them to the armory, taught them the proper care of their weapons. The evening came, and outside the keep the wind howled as it rose with the storm. The hall became a trifle smoky, for one of the fireplaces did not draw well. The evening meal of bread, cheese, cold meats, and stewed fruits was set out. Gradually the hall began to clear of those who did not belong there, for at Langston the hall was only used for sleeping in an emergency. The servants slept in the attics above the hall, as did the two squires.

Alette came to her daughter's side. "I have had Ida and Agneatha prepare a bath for you in the bathing chamber. Come, and I will help you, Isabelle. It is your wedding night. While you were out today we moved all your possessions into the solar, which you will now share with your husband. Agneatha may continue to share my chamber with Ida, unless you wish her with you—but not tonight."

Isabelle rose, silent. She had forgotten about this other part of marriage. How foolish of her to have overlooked the fact that she would be sharing a chamber with Hugh Fauconier. Following her mother into the bathing chamber, she allowed the three women to bathe her, pinning her own braid as she stepped into the stone tub, saying, "What is that smell? Since when do I wallow in perfumed water?"

Agneatha giggled, ducking a blow from the older Ida. " 'Tis lavender, lady. A new bride should smell her sweetest for her husband."

"Men like this stink?" Isabelle looked dubious.

"The fragrance will not be so strong once you have dried off," Alette said quietly, "but a man does enjoy a fragrant woman."

Without the aid of the servants, Belle scrubbed herself vigorously, then rinsing, stepped from the tub, clean and rosy. Ida and Agneatha carefully dried her off, and Alette handed her daughter a clean chemise. Isabelle slipped it on, reaching up afterward to loosen her braid. She sniffed critically at herself.

"I can still smell that damned lavender, madame," she grumbled.

"It is a fresh and pleasing fragrance," Alette replied. Then she pointed to a small door in the wall that Belle had never before really noticed. "It opens into the solar, my daughter. You will not have to go out into the hall." Alette kissed Isabelle on her forehead. "Good night, my child. God give you a peaceful rest." Then opening the door, she practically pushed the girl through into the adjoining chamber, and closed the door behind her.

The solar was the lord of the keep's private chamber. Belle had spent little time here, for when her father had been in residence, he had allowed none but Alette the freedom of his privy chamber. When her father had been away from Langston, Alette preferred the hall, except at night, when she slept here. There was a fireplace; the narrow windows in the room were tight, the chamber comfortably warm. In fact Isabelle could never before remember having been so toasty within the keep, whose gray stone walls seemed to husband the damp and cold. In summer it was an advantage, but in the winter it was not.

"Come, Belle, and sit with me," Hugh called to her.

She started, unaware that he had been in the room, but then she saw him in the straight-backed chair by the fire. "There is no place for me to sit, my lord," she answered him.

She saw him hold out his hand in the light of the fire. "We will share the seat," he replied. "Come."

He was a big man, and she no petite maiden. She did not see how they could share the narrow wooden chair, but she moved to his side. Reaching up, he drew her down into his lap. She stiffened with shock, then attempted to arise, but he held her firmly.

"Is this not nice?" he said to her. "Put your head upon my shoulder, ma Belle. You will be more comfortable that way."

She sat rigidly, hardly breathing. "What are you doing, my lord?" she demanded nervously of him. Why on earth was he holding her like this?

"I am attempting to have a cuddle with my pretty wife," Hugh said.

She didn't know what to answer him, and so she remained silent.

"Are you afraid, ma Belle?" he asked her gently.

*"Afraid?"* Her young voice was tremulous, yet she attempted to sound scornful. "Afraid of what, my lord?"

"Of the intimacy between a man and his wife, perhaps?" His voice was kind, even understanding. It irritated her. He was treating her like a child, and she was not a child.

"I know nothing of such intimacy, my lord!" she snapped at him.

"As a wellborn virgin, you should not," he told her. "That is why I am attempting to educate you in such matters as tenderly as I can. What transpires between a husband and wife regarding bed sport can be most pleasurable for them both. I know that I will gain great pleasure from your sweet body, ma Belle; but I would that you receive equal pleasure from me as well."

"I have seen the animals mating," she mumbled low to him.

"We are not animals," he replied, drawing her head down to his shoulder. "You are a brave girl, ma Belle, but all maidens are a little fearful of the unknown. Trust me, *chérie*." His hand smoothed her head. "Let me lead you. I will be gentle, I promise."

She didn't know how she should respond to him. She felt a trifle foolish, which angered her, but then he began skillfully to unlace her chemise. She caught at his hands, struggling with herself not to cry out.

*"Non, non, chérie,"* he softly chided her, brushing her hands away as if they were two moths. Successfully completing his task, he pushed the soft linen fabric from her shoulders, baring her to the waist.

Unable to help herself, Isabelle cried out low, but his response was to press his lips against hers, stifling the outburst. Pulling away, she pressed her palms into his chest. *"Oh, please don't!"* she half whispered. To her intense mortification, her eyes filled, a single tear escaping to rush headlong down her pale cheek.

Leaning over, he caught the tear with the tip of his tongue. His eyes never left hers.

Isabelle shivered violently, almost overwhelmed by the intensity of the emotions his act aroused in her.

Hugh saw the fear in her eyes. He drew her back into the comfort of his embrace. "Do not be afraid of me, *chérie*," he pleaded with her. "You are my bride, and you are so fair. I cannot help but desire you."

"Until you kissed me last night," she answered him, "I had never been approached by any man. I thought kissing foolish, but then you showed me it could be pleasurable. What is it you wish to do to me now, my lord? And is it pleasurable as well?"

He sighed deeply. "I would teach you, ma Belle," he told her. "I would join my body with yours in sweet communion." Mother of God! Had he ever even had a virgin before? He did not think so. It was more complicated than he thought it would be. Should he force the girl, she would be terrified, and never forgive him. He would have to be very patient. He did not think he had ever been called upon to contain his lust before. Tentatively he reached out, cupping one of her breasts in his hand. "Ahhh, *chérie*," he sighed.

She trembled, but said nothing.

It was a sweet breast. Very much like a ripe, round little apple. He fondled it, brushing his thumb across the silken nipple, which hardened almost immediately beneath his touch. He caressed her other breast in a similar fashion, then said to her, "Your little tits are by far the prettiest I have ever seen, ma Belle. I would kiss them."

*"Not yet!"* she managed to gasp, squirming just slightly in his lap as his hand slipped down her torso, pushing her chemise ahead of it. His fingers smoothed around her flat belly, then slipped lower to entangle themselves in her silken bush. Isabelle could not draw a breath. Then he was sitting her up again. His eyes seemed glazed, but his voice was commanding when he spoke to her.

"Now, *chérie*, I want you to undo my chemise as I have undone yours. I want to feel your hands on me, ma Belle." His look was intense.

She was curious, however, and very aware that the only garment he was wearing was his chemise. Unlike her garment, which extended to her ankles, his went only to his knees, and was slit up on either side of his leg and hip. She unlaced him with clumsy fingers, finally pushing the garment from him. It fell to his waist. His chest was very broad and very smooth, his flat nipples prominent and rosy. Timidly, she touched him, surprised to find his skin as soft as her own.

"That is nice," he said, encouraging her with a little smile.

Isabelle blushed shyly, embarrassed at being unable to control her hands. They didn't want to stop caressing his broad chest. Her fingers made small circles across his skin, stroking, smoothing his flesh. She could feel the warmth of him through her very fingertips. He took one of those hands now. Raising it to his lips, he slowly kissed first the inside of her wrist, and then her palm. His silvery-blue eyes never left her green-gold ones. Her breath was caught somewhere in mid-throat, and yet she was breathing. He held her hand against his cheek for a long moment before letting it go. Belle buried her head in his shoulder diffidently. It was all so new, and not just a little frightening, although she would have rather died than admitted such a thing to him.

He cradled her gently, caressing her hair, undoing the ribbon that held her braid so neatly, his digits skillfully unplaiting her red-gold tresses, fluffing it out so that it was spread about her white shoulders. He sniffed audibly, appreciatively. "What is that fragrance, *chérie*? It is absolutely delicious!" He nuzzled her hair near her neck.

"Lavender." She practically whispered the word.

He took her chin between his thumb and his forefinger, turning her toward him, forcing her head up with a firm but smooth motion. He had never really looked closely at her until this moment. She had an oval-shaped face with a faintly squared chin that housed a little dimple. Her eyes were oval-shaped, too. A quick, startled look at him and they lowered, dark, thick lashes brushing her pale cheeks. The nose was long, narrow, and typically arrogant Norman; but it was her mouth that mesmerized him. It was full and lush, and simply made for kissing. He had been unable to resist it last night. He was unable to resist it now.

Wrapping her in his embrace, he bent his head to match her lips with his. The sweet, subtle fragrance enfolding her body surrounded them, engulfing his senses. For a moment he wasn't even certain of who was seducing whom, so strong was his desire.

Isabelle shivered, but it was neither from cold nor from fear. His bare chest had suddenly become crushed against her naked breasts. She could have never imagined such a sensation in her wildest dreams. The effect of skin upon skin was enthralling. With a deep sigh she stretched her body just slightly, now concentrating upon his kiss, which seemed equally wonderful. It didn't seem to matter that he was not the handsome Norman knight of her dreams. Although she had never been kissed before Hugh had come into her life, she knew with some primitive instinct that he was very good at what he was doing. Somehow she managed to slip her arms up and about his neck, drawing them into even closer proximity.

With a groan he surprised her, drawing away. "Ahhh, ma Belle, you could tempt a saint from the path of heavenly virtue with that divine mouth of yours." Tipping her back in his arms, he ran a finger across her lips. "I have so much to teach you, *ma douce*," he murmured, his smoky silvery-blue eyes causing her to flush with the heat of his ardor. Then he gently stood her on her feet.

Isabelle blushed to the roots of her golden-red hair as her soft linen chemise fell to her ankles, exposing all of her charms to his eager eyes. When he stood and his garment fell away, too, she colored even more. Unable to restrain herself, she stared at him. While seeming a trifle awkward in his clothing, he seemed very well made without them. His limbs were long, big-boned, and nicely fleshed. He had extremely shapely legs for a man. They were covered with a light golden down, far lighter than his dark blond hair. His bush was the same, almost iridescent color. It glowed like golden threads, tightly curled, drawing attention to his maleness. Her eyes widened at the sight, and then with a small cry she turned her head away.

"I have never seen a naked man," she explained, although it was hardly necessary that she do so.

"Are you shocked?" he asked her.

She shook her head in the negative. "I think your body . . . beautiful," she finished. "Oh, 'tis not the word I want, but I know no other way to say it. Handsome is wrong, for you are not handsome, my lord. Besides, faces are handsome, not bodies."

He laughed softly. "I think all of you beautiful, ma Belle," he told her. Then he took her face between his hands and began kissing her again. How had he become so fortunate as to gain this marvelous girl as a wife? Isabelle was a form of the name Elizabeth. He would name the church he had promised to build St. Elizabeth in thanksgiving for his lovely bride.

His fervent kisses made her head spin. Feeling her legs beginning to weaken, she cried out softly. Hugh caught her in his arms, his tawny head seeking out the curve of her throat which she had innocently presented to him as her head fell back. His hot, wet mouth plotted a slow, deliberate course across and down her straining throat. He buried his lips in the hollow of her neck, murmuring low, then moved on to kiss the tops of her breasts. His hands slipped to her waist, and lifting her up slightly so that she was suspended above his mouth, he began to tongue her hard, little nipples.

*"Ohhh, Holy Mother, I can bear no more!"* Isabelle cried out involuntarily, hating herself as she did. He would surely think her a coward and despise her for it.

Hugh, however, cradled her in his arms, and walking across the chamber, laid her gently upon their bed, climbing in next to her. "Do not be ashamed," he said quietly to her. "You are so new to passion, ma Belle. It is a strong thing. Soon you will not fear it, but welcome it. My desire for you is already great, but I want you to know pleasure, too." He began to gently stroke her body with his big hand.

When her heart had finally stopped pounding so violently and she could find her voice again, she asked him, "Will we couple, you and I, my lord? I have not told you the whole truth. Once, before my brother Richard returned to Normandy, I saw him couple with one of the serf girls. He did not know I saw him. It was in the stables. I had gone to fetch my mare. While I was saddling her, Richard came into the stable with the girl. They did not see me. He forced her against a wall, pushed up her skirts, loosened his clothes, and had at her. The noises she made frightened me, but when he had finished with her, he gave her a quick kiss, and laughing they went off together. I could not really see what they did. Did he hurt her? Her cries were terrible. Yet she seemed content enough when Richard had finished with her."

"Your brother coupled with the girl," Hugh agreed, "but he did not hurt her. Her cries were of satisfaction, not pain or fear."

"Will I cry out like that?" Belle wondered aloud.

"If I please you, aye, ma Belle," he whispered, the tip of his tongue finding the whorled shell of her ear. He then blew softly, sending a shiver down her spine.

"I think you are possibly a wicked man, my lord," Belle said softly, and then, "Will you make me a wicked woman?"

"Very wicked," he murmured back at her. Rolling onto his side, he bent his head and began to kiss her breasts.

*"Ahhhhhh,"* Belle sighed nervously.

His mouth closed over a nipple and he began to suckle upon her.

*"Ohhhhhh!"* she cried as lightning seemed to scorch her very soul. His lips were so insistent as they drew upon her flesh, demanding the unknown from her. She reached out to pull him away, but instead her hand tangled itself in his tawny hair, pressing his head deeper into her bosom. Her breasts were

beginning to ache. A strange throbbing had begun somewhere in the place between her thighs. Isabelle moaned, and suddenly his other hand was caressing her belly, his fingers seeking knowingly toward the pulsation, finding it, touching it, sending a shock through her body such as she had never known. She arched herself upward to meet him, almost weeping with relief, although she could have not told anyone why. She did not know herself.

"Do not be afraid, *chérie*," he told her gently. "I must prepare you to take my manhood within your sweet virgin's body. This," he stroked the palpitating little nub of flesh with his finger, "is your pleasure pearl. If I touch it so . . ." and she cried out sharply, "you will feel delicious sensations, *n'est-ce pas, ma douce?*"

"Yessss," she hissed through clenched teeth. "Ohh, my lord, it is sweet! Do not cease, I beg you!"

With a smile she could not see in the darkness of their chamber, he tenderly began to play with her. His efforts were rewarded with little mewlings that told him he was succeeding in his endeavors.

"I want to pleasure you," Isabelle said suddenly, attempting to sit up, but he pushed her back onto the pillows.

"Not just now, *chérie*," he told her thickly. Silencing her protest with a kiss, he slipped a finger into her female channel until it touched her virgin shield, and she cried out, her head pulling away from his. Her passage was narrow, but it would widen to take him, he knew. Catching her hand, he drew it down to his manhood.

Her slender fingers ran along its length, her sharp intake of breath audible in the half darkness. "This is your desire?" she asked him tremulously. "It seems very big, my lord." The heat of his flesh was exciting. Her heart had begun to beat a fierce tattoo. Afraid, she would never admit to it. He had promised her pleasure, and she did not think him a liar. Besides, the aching and throbbing of her own body was growing by the minute. Intuitively she knew that only the joining of their bodies would give them both the release they seemed to crave. "You may have me, my lord," she said. "I am ready, but you must tell me what you desire of me, for you understand my ignorance."

She is so brave, he thought proudly. He could feel her terrified heart thumping beneath his head, which lay upon her breasts. Best to end the mystery so that their time might be better spent in pleasuring each other. That she had not become hysterical to his advances, that she was not coldly indifferent to him, portended a warm heart. "Spread your legs open for me, my *douce*," he ordered her, slipping himself between her rounded thighs when she obeyed him. Carefully he positioned himself, moving forward, pushing himself gently into her body, now both eager and fearful. The walls of her passage began to envelop and close about him. Her heat burned his flesh.

Isabelle tensed at his entry. She could feel her body opening like a flower, seemingly anxious to accommodate him. She was frightened, and at the same time very excited. She had never felt more aware in her entire life. Yet the sensuous rhythm he was initiating between them was beginning to send her senses reeling. Her fingers dug into his big shoulders, both clinging to him and encouraging him onward. *Onward to what?* "Please!" she begged him. *"Please!"*

In answer to her pleas he drew back and thrust hard, burying his manhood to its hilt within her sheath. A quick burst of pain radiated into her belly and thighs, paralyzing her for a brief moment, causing her to gasp with shock. Then it was gone. To her great surprise she began to weep wildly, and he comforted her as best as he could, caressing her, kissing the tears away. Hugh began to move on her once he was certain the pain had dissipated, thrusting and withdrawing, thrusting and withdrawing until Isabelle was gasping with obvious, open pleasure.

The pain had been sudden, and sharply hurtful, but it disappeared as quickly as it came, leaving her wondering if it had really happened at all. Then he had begun that incredible motion, and her own body was responding in kind. She was floating. She was flying. It was wonderful! Her body seemed to swell, burst, melt all in a moment's time, and when it was over she begged him, *"More, my lord!"*

With a contented laugh he pulled her into his arms, kissing the top of her very tousled head. *"Oui, chérie,* there will be more for us both, but first a little rest that we may regain our strength."

"I am now truly your wife, Hugh Fauconier," Isabelle said.

"You are truly my wife," he agreed. "When the storm is over, I shall send my squire to the king to tell him so. Father Bernard wishes to remain at Langston. We will need the king's permission. Will it please you to have a priest here?"

"Aye, my lord. What good is a church without a priest?" She snuggled against him, content for the first time in her life. "He will teach me to read and write so I may be a better chatelaine. He will be here to baptize the children when they come."

"Do you like children?" he asked her.

"I do not know, my lord," Belle admitted with a chuckle. "I have never had any. If they are like my brothers, however, I do not think I will like them at all."

"They will be like us, ma Belle," he said softly. "One day we shall go to the West Country, and you will meet my grandparents. They will tell you what I was like as a lad. But first I will go myself and bring back my birds. Langston is a good place to raise my hawks. Can you hawk?"

"We never had any birds," she admitted. "Will you give me my own merlin, my lord? And teach me how to hunt with her?"

"I promise, *chérie.* You shall have your hawk," Hugh told her.

"I trust you, my lord," Belle answered him. "So far you have kept your promises to me. I believe I am even beginning to like you."

With a laugh Hugh pulled his bride into his arms, and began to kiss her quite passionately once again. "And I am beginning to like you, too, hellion," he rejoined.

# ❧Chapter 5

$T$he snow continued through the night and into the following day. Hugh and Isabelle did not emerge from the
solar until the midday meal. The bride looked arch, the bridegroom sated and quite pleased with himself, Rolf noted with a
chuckle. They ate heartily, speaking little. Then, after the meal,
they disappeared hand in hand back into the solar. The hall
emptied as everyone went about their afternoon tasks. Alette
sat at her loom while Rolf was settled, his sword across his
knees, honing the blade to his satisfaction.

Suddenly, Alette began to weep noisily, her face in her
hands as she sobbed. "Ohh, my poor child," she said. *"My
poor child!"*

Rolf set his sword aside and hurried to her side. "Lady, what
is it that troubles you? Do not weep, I beg you!" He knelt next
to her, trying to brush her tears away with his large hand.

Alette cried all the harder.

Not knowing what else to do, Rolf put his arms about the
woman, comforting her with soft words, stroking her fair hair
gently. "Do not weep, sweetheart," he begged her. "I cannot
bear to see you unhappy. Just tell me what has distressed
you. I will do my best to make it better, Alette." He held her
tenderly.

"They did not come from their chamber until it was time to
eat," Alette sobbed. "Then he dragged her back into the solar
after they ate. My poor daughter! He must be using her cruelly.
I would not have thought Hugh Fauconier that base. I can do

89

nothing to help my child. Oh, Isabelle! I should have warned you! *I should have warned you.*" Alette looked up at Rolf, and his heart almost broke when she said, "She will never forgive me! How could she?"

Rolf had known that Alette's late husband had not been a particularly kind man; but now he was certain that Robert de Manneville had been a brutal lover who had terrified his wife. Hugh was not that sort of man. "Lady," Rolf said in kindly tones, "your daughter is a happy woman, I swear it! Did you not look at her when she came with her lord to the meal? She glowed with happiness. Hugh is a kind man. He should never misuse a woman. You are mistaken in your assumptions."

"Am I?" Alette's blue eyes were grave as they looked at him. "Why were they not up with the dawn and about their usual business? Why did he take her back into the privacy of the solar if not to use her over and over again?" She shivered with distaste, realizing as she did that Rolf's arms were about her.

"The lady Isabelle did not look either abused or unhappy," Rolf said softly, seeing her confusion and removing his arms from her person. "I have known Hugh since we were children. We shared our first woman, and have had many adventures together. He is a gentle lover. Women have always enjoyed his attentions. So I believe it to be with your daughter, my lady Alette." Rolf remained kneeling by her side where he might make eye contact with her.

Her blue eyes looked at him disbelievingly. *"Enjoy that?"*she whispered. "How could any decent woman enjoy a man's lust?"

"I think she could if it were co-joined with her own," Rolf replied. "Have you never felt lust for a man, my lady Alette? Not even once?"

"I was fourteen," Alette explained candidly, "when I was married to Robert de Manneville. Because I was orphaned young, I lived with my aunt and uncle until I was ten. Then my cousins and I were incarcerated within a local convent where we were to remain until suitable marriages were arranged for us. We saw no man there but the ancient priest who heard our confessions and administered the sacraments to us. I knew Robert de Manneville only by sight as a child for he was one of my family's neighbors. There was no courtship. He was a virtual stranger when I married him. I have known no man but Robert de Manneville. I am ashamed to say I never felt anything for him except perhaps fear, and loathing."

"He was cruel to you," Rolf said. It was a statement, not a question.

Alette gazed at him through bleak eyes. Then to his surprise she began to speak further, telling him of the horrors she had endured on her wedding night and the nights that followed, until she was mercifully relieved of her spousal duties by her pregnancy. And of afterward, when Robert de Manneville could not function with her in a normal manner, and held her responsible for his failure. She spoke of his cruelties, of the beatings she endured at his hands. Finally drained, Alette grew silent once more.

After a long moment Rolf said to her, "If you were my wife, Alette, I should treat you with respect and use you gently. I would teach you to sing with joy at my touch. You should never be afraid again, *if you were mine*." He was shocked by what she had confessed to him. Many men of his generation had a tendency to be over-rough with their women, but neither he nor Hugh had ever been deliberately cruel to the fairer sex. To take a maiden's virginity while forcing her over the neck of a horse was horrific. He wanted a chance to prove to Alette that not all men were brutal; that passion could be sweet.

"I will never marry again even if the king commands me to do so," Alette said with grim determination. "I should die before I placed myself into the keeping of another man."

"But Hugh Fauconier is now lord of Langston," Rolf reminded her. "You are already in his charge, my lady Alette."

"He will not distress me if I keep his house well, Rolf de Briard, nor will I be forced to serve his baser desires. That, alas, my poor Isabelle must do." Suddenly she was very aware again of his close proximity to her. Alette flushed nervously, and seeing it, Rolf arose from her side where he had been kneeling.

"Hugh will never send you away, lady," Rolf told her, "but you will have no real place in this household once your daughter takes up her rightful duties. What will you do then? You are yet young, and you are far fairer than your daughter."

"You should not say such things to me, Rolf de Briard," Alette chided him. "You are, I think, too bold a man."

"Nay," he said with a slow smile. "I have certainly never been called *too* bold, madame, rather the opposite; but I now give you fair warning that I mean to court you. My lord Hugh has absolutely no objections, for I have already expressed my admiration of you to him. I shall prove to you, *ma petite* Alette, that not all men are uncaring and cruel. I shall teach you to crave my touch, to enjoy it when we make love. You shall be my wife, and only my loyalty to Hugh Fauconier and King Henry will take precedence over my love for you. What say you to this?" His look was warm, his voice firm with his resolve.

"I think you quite mad, Rolf de Briard," Alette answered him. "I have already told you I shall take no man to my bed again. I will not be at your mercy as I was at the mercy of Robert de Manneville!"

"I think my lady Isabelle gets some of her spirit from her mother, not just her father," Rolf teased Alette wickedly. "You have the most tempting mouth, *ma petite*."

Startled, Alette blushed, then standing abruptly, she fled the hall for the relative safety of her chamber. Rolf de Briard *was* too bold, whatever he might say of himself. Yet his words touched her in ways she did not understand. No man had ever spoken to her as he did. Certainly not her husband. Was this what her cousins had called *wooing*? Her conversations with Robert had been mostly one-sided. He would tell her what he desired. She would obey. He would criticize her for some fault, real or imagined. She would abjectly apologize for whatever it was that displeased him.

Not once in all the years that she had been married to him had Robert de Manneville said he loved her, that he cared for her, that she satisfied him in any manner. When Isabelle had been born, he raged at her for her failure to produce him another son. He had not thanked God, or His Blessed Mother, for her safe delivery from the perils of childbirth, or for the healthy baby daughter he now had.

His two sons were little better than their father. William, the elder, seemed to hold her responsible somehow for his mother's death, although she had known neither of the de Mannevilles prior to her marriage. William had been eight years old when his mother had died from the complications of a stillbirth—a third son who was buried with her, Robert was forever reminding his second wife. Sibylle had been a woman who knew her duty. William had been his mother's particular pet, and while Alette knew she could not replace Sibylle in her son's heart, she hoped at least to be a good mother to him. He, however, would not allow it, and the horrific old woman who was his nurse, who had been his mother's nurse as well, encouraged the boy in his rudeness, in his misbehavior, in his open hostility to his young, uncertain stepmother.

Richard, her younger stepson, had been only a littler easier. The second son, he had been no one's child really. Richard enjoyed the attention Alette gave him, for at five years of age he was yet in need of mothering. Still, the poor child was torn between his kindly stepmother and his elder brother, whom he very much sought to please. In the end his behavior was scarcely better than William's, until William at age fourteen had returned to Normandy to oversee the estate that would eventually belong to him. Richard, of course, had assumed that Langston would one day be his. His displeasure in learning several years later that it would not, but would rather go to his half sister, was not pleasant.

"Could you not have spoken up for me?" he raged at his

stepmother. "A large dowry would be good enough for Isabelle, would it not? A wench with a fat purse is a respectable match for a landed man. You have worked your wiles upon our father, and allowed him to leave me landless! William warned me! He said that you loved that red-haired changeling you birthed far better than you loved me. I have been cheated. I will never forgive you." Then he had returned to Normandy, joining his brother at Manneville. Alette had not seen him since, which had actually been a great relief. Such had been her experience with men.

Now, here was Rolf de Briard, murmuring soft, coaxing words into her ear, setting her heart to beating as it had never before beat, confusing her totally! Men were absolutely not to be trusted. Had life not taught her that, even if it had taught her nothing else? Still, she had to admit that Isabelle had not appeared to be in any distress. If anything, she had had a look about her that reminded Alette of a large ginger cat that had gotten into the cream. Alette had experienced few surprises in her life, but she had to admit that this was one of them. What on earth could have turned her fierce-tempered daughter into a smiling, well-tempered young woman? Had her son-in-law threatened his bride? She had not heard any cries, although she sat up half the night in the hall listening, until Ida had come and made her seek her bed.

In the days that followed, Alette watched carefully, but she saw absolutely no indication that Isabelle was unhappy. Her daughter, in fact, was beginning to take a strong interest in the household duties of a chatelaine. She asked questions constantly about preserving food, making soap, and all manner of things relating to the running of the house. She also seemed to be the instigator in leaving the table with her husband immediately after the evening meal. Some nights they would not even stay at the high board, but rather take bread, meat, cheese, and wine into the solar, closing the door firmly behind them. Once she heard Isabelle laugh in so seductive a tone that Alette was positively shocked. The sound was positively lustful. Rolf's eyes met hers and he chuckled.

"You need not be so smug!" Alette snapped. "He has bewitched her. Like all men, he will eventually show his true colors."

"You are being very foolish, *ma petite*," Rolf told her.

Several days later Hugh and Isabelle fell into a raging argument. Isabelle ran to their chamber, angrily slamming the door shut behind her.

Hugh dashed after her, furiously pounding upon the door to the solar as he shouted, "Open this door at once, Belle! I will not be denied my own bed because of your idiocy!"

"The door is not locked, you lumbering oaf," Belle shouted back for all to hear.

Alette watched in terror as her son-in-law burst through into the solar, banging the door so hard behind him that it shook upon its hinges. Those remaining in the hall could hear the tempestuous uproar going on behind the closed door. There was much shouting. There was the sound of crashing crockery. Then suddenly all was very silent. Alette ran to the door of the solar, frantic, but she could hear nothing.

Trembling, she whispered to no one in particular, "*He has killed her!* He has every right. Ahh, Isabelle!"

"More than likely," Rolf said soothingly, "he is kissing her. It was, after all, just a lover's quarrel, *ma petite*."

"How do you know that?" Alette demanded as he gently drew her away from the solar door and brought her to sit in a chair by the fire.

"My lady Isabelle saw Hugh speaking with a *very* pretty serf this morning. The girl was shamelessly flirtatious, flaunting herself at her master. Hugh was amused. He quite enjoyed her behavior, though he did nothing to encourage her. I observed the lady Isabelle watching the wench with her husband. Have you not noticed that she has been sniping at Hugh all day? The lady Isabelle is jealous. I believe she is becoming quite fond of her husband. They are, I suspect, at this very minute resolving their differences in that age-old negotiation known to lovers the world over. Besides, Hugh is not a violent man, *ma petite*. It is more likely the lady Isabelle would strike him than he her. Your fears are, as usual, groundless."

Alette said nothing, and Rolf believed the matter solved, particularly when Ida came to take her mistress off to bed. Rolf bade her sweet dreams and continued sitting by the fire, watching the flames leap and dance amid the great logs. Then he dozed, waking suddenly at a sound he could not quite identify. Reaching for his sword, he carefully looked about the hall. All was exactly as it should be. He stood up, and when he did, he saw Alette, in her white chemise, crouching by the solar door. With a sigh he went to her, speaking gently in soft tones.

"Alette, my petite, what are you doing?" Her hair was loose, and her eyes had a wild look to them.

"I cannot hear anything," she half sobbed.

"Because Hugh and my lady are either sleeping or involved in each other, *ma petite*," he told her. Bending, he raised her up.

Alette looked straight at him. The expression in her blue eyes almost broke his heart. "I am so afraid," she said low.

He caught her up in his arms as she crumbled into a swoon. For a moment he just held her, uncertain as to what he should do. How could he return her to her chamber without arousing the two serving women who slept with her? They would raise a fine hue and cry. Then Alette's fears would be known to everyone. There was no one, Rolf knew in his heart, who could cure her of those terrible fears but a tender lover. He walked swiftly to his own chamber, opening the door without dropping her, and laid her upon his bed. Then shutting the door behind him, he disrobed but for his linen chemise, and climbed into the bed next to her.

Alette stirred. "Where am I?" she murmured.

"You are with me, in my chamber," Rolf said quietly.

She trembled. "Let me go, my lord," she begged him.

"The door is not barred, Alette," he told her, "but if you stay, *ma petite*, I will show you that you need not fear a man's desire."

"You would coerce me?" Her voice was ragged as she forced the words out. Then she shuddered again.

*"Never!"* he declared vehemently. "I would take nothing from you, Alette, that you would not freely give me. I am not a barbarian, I have told you that before. Because Robert de Manneville was a brute, you believe all men to be brutes, but it is not so. You fear for your daughter, but the lady Isabelle revels, it is clear, in the passion she shares with her husband. If you choose to leave me now, I will, of course, regret your going, but I will understand, and I will be patient. You may not believe it now, but I have loved you from the moment I first saw you. You know I want you for my wife. I will have no other woman if I cannot have you, *ma petite*."

Alette was very silent, very still. It had been many years since she had shared a bed with a man. It had been even longer since she had shared her body with a man. She shivered. She was so cold. She knew she should get up and leave him, yet somewhere, deep within her, a tiny flame of curiosity stirred. She might be frightened, but she was not stupid. Rolf de Briard was nothing at all like Robert de Manneville, and, she suspected, he never had been. Isabelle's obvious contentment with Hugh Fauconier had made Alette wonder. So had Rolf de Briard's warmhearted blandishments.

"I am no light-skirted serf," she said halfheartedly.

"You are going to be my wife," he replied firmly.

"I will never marry again," Alette declared.

"You would prefer to be my leman to being my wife?" he teased.

"That is not at all what I mean!" Alette cried, confused.

"I want to make love to you," Rolf de Briard told her, running a single finger down her nose.

"Ohhh, I do not know! I am so afraid, Rolf, and yet . . ."

He gathered her into his arms and kissed her tenderly. Softly his lips pressed upon hers, subtly beginning his arousal of her.

With expert fingers he unlaced her chemise, pushed it from her shoulders, and caressed her full breasts.

"Ahhh," Alette cried out, half fearful. She remembered how Robert used to crush and bruise her tender breasts with his cruel, greedy hands; how he had bitten down on her nipples until she screamed with pain. Rolf, however, did none of these things. His hands were gentle, almost teasing as they fondled her. When he bent to kiss the warm flesh, when he took a nipple in his mouth, she tensed in terror, but he merely suckled upon her, sending chilly little ripples down her spine.

"Ah, my darling," he told her, his voice fervent with passion, "you have the most perfect, the most beautiful breasts I have ever known!" He rained a firestorm of kisses over her palpitating bosom.

She was growing quite light-headed with his attentions. This was so lovely. Why had her husband never touched her like this? Was this what Isabelle was experiencing at the hands of Hugh Fauconier? No wonder she was happy.

"Does my touch give you pleasure, Alette?" Rolf murmured into her ear, kissing it with a tender little kiss.

*"Yes!"* she said. *Pleasure.* It was pleasure she was feeling. She had never before felt pleasure at a man's touch.

Rolf grew bolder. Slowly, carefully, he pulled the chemise down and off her beautiful little form. She neither resisted nor begged him to cease, but he could feel her tensing as if for a blow. Patiently stroking her, Rolf sensed Alette finally begin to relax within his gentle embrace. He drew her lengthwise across the bed, then bending his blond head, he began to kiss her body with tiny, warm kisses. She vibrated beneath him.

"Ahhh, dear God!" Alette sighed fervently.

Rolf smiled in the dim light of the room, which was lit by just one candle and a faint waning moon outdoors. Nuzzling up her torso, he slid his hot, wet tongue between the valley separating her full breasts. Then he drew his tongue back down her belly, burrowing into her navel with it.

"Ohhhhh! Ahhhhh! *Ahhhhhh!*" moaned Alette, whose head

was spinning with a variety of sensations, all of them utterly and absolutely wonderful. She was afire with a longing she had never before felt, had never even known existed.

He gathered her back against him. Her head fell back, blond hair cascading over his arms. Once again his kisses burned into the flesh of her straining throat, found her wildly beating heart, brushed across her breasts, which were now swollen hard and aching. His mouth closed over first one nipple; sucking, teasing it with his tongue; and then the other. Laying her back, he began a more intimate exploration, first touching the insides of her thighs, then touching her Venus mont. His fingers sought out her cleft, pushing through, finding her little pearl, beginning her awakening, kindling a heat such as she had never experienced.

Why am I letting him do this to me? Alette wondered hazily. She knew she must stop him before it was too late, before he finally threw off the mask of the lamb and became the fierce lion he really must be. She had to stop him. Her legs fell open as he stirred her to her first peak. *She had to stop him!* He was atop her. Her hands reached out to push him away, but instead they slipped about his neck to draw him closer. *What was the matter with her?* Oh, God, she could feel his weapon at the mouth of her channel. *He was pushing into her! He was filling her full! He was moving with tender passion upon her, and she wanted him! She wanted him!* She sobbed hungrily, her nails digging into the thick muscles of his broad shoulders. He was moving faster and faster upon her. Her body was responding wildly, pushing up to match his fierce downward thrusts. *And it was wonderful!*

His mouth came down upon hers, cutting off her cries of joy. Never, Rolf thought hazily, never before have I felt such sensation. Her fingers kneading at his back, her nails raking him. The tension was building within him until finally he could bear no more, and his passion exploded within her sweet body, his love juices overflowing her womb. They lay gasping in the fiery afterglow of their spent energies. Then together, clasped in each other's arms, they wept softly.

"Marry me," he begged her. "Can you doubt that I love you, will cherish you, will never abuse you? *Marry me!*"

"No," Alette said low.

Rolf swore, frustrated. *"Why not?"*

"I have told you," Alette said quietly, "that I shall never again allow any man to have control over me. But I will be your leman, for you have shown me how sweet passion can be between men and women."

"I will end by killing you," Rolf groaned.

Alette laughed. "Nay," she told him, rising from his bed. "You can only kill me with pure delight, my dear Rolf de Briard."

"Where are you going?" he demanded of her as she put on her chemise and walked toward the door.

"To my own chamber," she answered him. "If one of the servants should awaken and see I am not in my bed, they will raise a great hue and cry. It would hardly do for them to find me in your bed, would it? No one would ever expect such a thing of me."

"You are enjoying this," he accused her, and she laughed again.

"Good night, my lord," Alette said, feeling happier than she had ever felt in her entire life, except when Belle was born.

"Stay," he begged her. "Your Ida will not waken, my love. Her snores can be heard throughout the hall. She sleeps heavily."

"But Agneatha does not," Alette told him. Opening the door, she slipped through it and was gone.

"Damn, Agneatha," Rolf muttered softly. Why the hell was Isabelle's maid still in Alette's chamber? If her own mistress was not ready to have her sleep in the solar, then let her sleep in the attic with the other servants. Then Rolf had a wicked thought. Agneatha was a fine, strapping girl, and he had noticed she had an eye for his squire, Giles. Giles slept in the attic. If Giles encouraged the girl, she would be willing to take her place with the other servants above the hall, thinking to seduce Giles, or be seduced by him. Then he could take his own pleasure with Alette, whose servant, Ida, slept so hard once her head touched the pillow that not even the archangel Gabriel's trumpet would awaken her.

He needed to be alone more with his ladylove that he might rid her of this foolish notion she had about marriage. Rolf tossed restlessly, trying to find a comfortable position. "Damn Robert de Manneville and all his kind to hell!" he said grimly. Had the man been even half decent to his wife, Alette would have been eager to remarry. What kind of man needed to hurt a woman before he could gain his pleasure? Certainly the man had been a coward! Rolf finally slept.

"Do you notice a change in my mother?" Isabelle asked her husband a few days later as they rode out to assess the damage from the latest storm. She was relieved to find there was none. Actually, the snow was helping to heal the land. Sixteen months ago at Martinmas there had been a sea flood of the land such as no man could remember happening before. The tides had swept inland almost two miles, and the Blyth had risen to flood some of Langston's fields with unusually salty water. Luckily, the salinity there, several miles up from the sea, had been far less than downriver, where it would take years for the fields to be fertile again. They had gotten a crop from the flooded Langston land last year. Now, with all the rains and snows of winter it would return to normal.

"What kind of change?" Hugh responded.

"She is smiling a great deal more than I have ever known her to smile, and she sings constantly while she weaves. It is most annoying, my lord," Isabelle told him tartly.

He debated whether he should tell her the truth, deciding he really should. "Your mother has taken Rolf de Briard as her lover, ma Belle," he said. "Rolf loves her, and she is happy. It is quite simple."

"How dare you spew such a filthy lie about my mother?" Isabelle cried angrily, and, kicking her horse into a gallop, she rode off.

Hugh followed, chasing her across the fields and along the riverbank, where the geese, grazing, flew up in a panic, and finally into a stand of woods. They burst forth from the trees, galloping across a meadow. She was an amazing rider. He wondered when she would tire of their chase. Why was she so distressed that her mother had found happiness again? Perhaps she did not understand that Rolf wanted to wed Alette. Certainly when he explained it all to her she would calm herself. Then Isabelle's horse stumbled and she was pitched over the mare's head into a snowbank. To his amazement, and relief, she immediately leapt up, swearing colorfully, brushing the snow from her cloak.

Hugh jumped from his mount. "Are you all right, ma Belle?" he demanded anxiously, rushing up to her.

Isabelle looked up, and then she hit him as hard as she could with her fists. *"Liar!"* she shrieked at him, pummeling him with both of her fists. A big girl, the impact was not soft.

Hugh grabbed for his wife's hands, but she successfully eluded him, raining blows upon his body wherever she could. "Stop it, you hellion!" he shouted at her. *"Stop it!* I have not lied to you. Ask your mother if she has not taken Rolf for her lover."

"How dare you even suggest I ask my mother such a thing?" Isabelle yelled at him. "I should never offend her delicacy in such a manner, nor my father's memory, which I know she honors!"

"Your father was brutal to your mother," Hugh shouted back. "Rolf de Briard is gentle and kind to Alette. She never knew a man to be so with her. Are you aware that she believed I was abusing you because we spend so much time alone together? She would crouch outside our chamber door at night listening to see if I beat you. Twice she was found there, once by Ida and once by Rolf. Now she knows a man can be amiable and mild of disposition. She no longer fears for you. Ask her yourself, you damned hellion! I am not in the habit of lying."

Isabelle's hands fell to her sides. She seemed drained. "I will ask her," was all she said. Then remounting her mare, which was standing nearby, she rode back toward the keep.

Hugh Fauconier sighed deeply. What in the name of heaven had made him believe he had tamed her so easily? Then he laughed at himself for his naiveté. Isabelle was a wonderful bed partner. She was passionate, and quick to learn. *That*, at least, they had in common, he thought wryly; but there was far more to his wife, he was discovering, than just her amorous talents. She was intelligent, clever, and loyal. She also had a fearsome temper that had obviously not waned a whit simply because she enjoyed making love with him. Oh yes. He was a fool. *A fool who was falling in love with his wife.* Mounting his horse, he turned the beast's head toward home, wondering just what he would find there when he arrived.

When he reached the keep, Isabelle was nowhere in sight, but he saw a stable lad leading her mare into its shelter. Calling the boy to take his stallion, too, he dismounted and hurried up the steps of the porch into the hall. Alette was seated at her loom, weaving at her tapestry. Rolf was on a stool by her side, strumming his lute. Belle stood in the shadows watching them. When Rolf took Alette's hand in his, kissing it, their eyes met tenderly.

Isabelle then strode into the hall, unaware that her husband was just behind her. "So, madame," she said in haughty tones to her mother, "this is how you honor my father's memory! I am told you have become this man's whore. *Shame! Shame!*"

Alette paled, but she jumped to her feet, facing her daughter bravely. "How dare you presume to criticize me, Isabelle," she said angrily. "The father you loved was a bad husband to me, though I never complained of it. He was a bad father to you as well, though you know it not. Had he been a better father, he would have allowed me to punish you when you were unruly. That he did not is to both our detriments."

"You were too much of a mouse to dare complain to Robert de Manneville of your alleged mistreatment," Isabelle snapped.

"No one, but a man and his wife," Alette quickly responded, "knows what goes on behind the closed doors of their solar."

"How brave you have suddenly become, madame," was the sneering reply.

"Love, my daughter, has made me both brave and strong," Alette said quietly, standing proudly by Rolf's side.

"And does he love you, madame?" Isabelle said. "And if he does, why does he not make you his wife? This man wants only what is between your legs. He shows you no honor. At least my father did."

"I have asked your mother to marry me, my lady Isabelle," Rolf spoke up, "but she will not. I will, however, pursue her until she does, for I love her with all my heart. I do, indeed, honor her."

"Is this so, madame?" Isabelle demanded of her mother.

"I will never marry again," Alette said quietly. "I will not allow myself to be in any man's keeping. I will be my own mistress."

Father Bernard, who had been sitting by the fire all this time, now arose and joined the warring factions. "My daughter," he said to Alette, "such conduct does not set a good example to others. I know this is not your customary behavior. Sir Rolf has tendered you an honorable proposal of marriage. If you do not choose to accept it, then you are permitted that freedom by virtue of your status as Sieur de Manneville's widow. However, as your spiritual adviser, I must forbid you to behave in such an unchaste fashion any longer." He turned so that his stern gaze took in Rolf de Briard as well. "You are forbidden, my lord, from further carnal knowledge of this woman, Alette de Manneville, unless she takes you as her husband. If either of you disobey me, the sacraments will be denied you both. Do you understand what I am saying to you?" he concluded severely.

Alette glared at her daughter, and without a word went to her chamber, slamming the door behind her with as much force as she could muster.

"You will give me your knight's oath, my lord," the priest said. "Women are weak, but men weaker when a woman pleads prettily. Your oath, Sir Rolf."

"You have it, good father," Rolf said, though reluctantly, and he glowered at Isabelle, but she looked smugly back at him, triumphant.

Hugh saw the look. "Go to your chamber, Belle," he said quietly, but in a tone that brooked no nonsense and dared her to disobey.

She opened her mouth to protest, but his look was suddenly so fierce it quelled her defiance. "Yes, my lord," she meekly replied.

"And remain there awaiting your punishment until I come," he added.

Belle bit back the reply on her tongue, doing as she was told.

When she was gone, Hugh turned to his friend. "It is my fault. I told her the truth because she saw the change in Alette's behavior these past few days. I am sorry, Rolf."

Rolf shrugged fatalistically.

"Why will she not wed with you, my son?" the priest queried.

Rolf explained.

"Ahh," the priest said, shaking his head. "While a man does indeed have the power of life and death over his wife, and St. Paul instructs wives to obey their husbands in all things, too many men abuse this power that God has given them. Women are the weaker and gentler sex. They should be treated well, revered for their ability to bring new life into the world, and respected. You have my permission to continue wooing your lady, Sir Rolf, but there must be no further carnality until she speaks her vows with you before me. Now, go and comfort her, for she is heartbroken, I am certain. Your gentle persuasion will win her over in the end. I will pray for it."

Rolf hurried off, and the priest turned to Hugh. "My lord, I believe you have a wife badly in need of correction. It is not a task that I envy you, but you must see to it."

Nodding, Hugh moved grimly away and into the solar, where Isabelle was waiting. She glared at him angrily, inwardly frightened, as he closed the door behind him and made a great show of turning the key in the lock. Then he faced her. "Well, Belle, what have you to say about your outrageous conduct toward your mother and Sir Rolf?" he demanded of her.

"Even the priest said I was right," she defended herself. "My mother was wrong to behave like some common slut, ready to spread herself for the first man who came along and whispered pretty words in her ear."

"Your mother did not behave like a slut," Hugh said quietly. "You are new to passion, ma Belle. Tell me how you like it?"

"It is wonderful!" she burst out.

"Your mother is new to passion also. She thinks it wonderful, too, else she would not have pursued it with Rolf these past few weeks," Hugh said. "Rolf is desperately attempting to overcome your mother's understandable reluctance to remarry. I think he will in time, but you had no right to expose them publicly in the hall. Thank God no servants were about. Rolf is our steward. You could have diminished his authority with your outburst. You have also hurt your mother, and forced Father Bernard, who might have otherwise turned a blind eye, into forbidding them their passion at the cost of their immortal souls. You have behaved like a willful, spoilt child, ma Belle. As your husband, it is my duty to chastise you. I have, it seems, no other choice in the matter. Remove your gown."

*"What?"* She looked at him, astounded.

"Remove your gown, madame. You are to be spanked," Hugh replied. "You have acted like a child. You will be punished like one."

"You would not dare!" she gasped.

"What, madame, further defiance?" He raised an eyebrow menacingly.

"Did you yourself not say you are not in the habit of beating women?" she demanded of him.

"You give me no choice in the matter, Isabelle," he told her. "Now, obey me, madame. *At once!*"

Belle was dumbfounded. He actually meant it. He was going to physically punish her. A tiny thread of fear curled itself tightly in her belly, but outwardly she showed no signs of nervousness. Looking him straight in the eye, she carefully removed her gown, laying it neatly aside. Then she looked questioningly at Hugh, who was now seated on the bed.

"Come here," he said, beckoning her, and when she stood in front of him, he told her, "Raise your chemise and lay yourself across my knees, facedown, Isabelle." His look was very stern.

"I shall kill you one day," she said low.

"But not today," Hugh responded, reaching up and pulling her down across his knees. "This, Belle, is for your mother," and his hand descended hard upon her bottom. She shrieked, more from outrage than any serious hurt. "And this is for Rolf." The hand once again made contact with her flesh. "And this is for me!" He smacked her a third time. "Now, you impossible hellion, keep yelling," he ordered her. "I want everyone in the hall to believe that you are getting the punishment you truly deserve."

She heard his hand slam down upon something, and she shrieked, terrified, until she realized he was walloping their mattress and not her person. Tears of relief slid down her face and she struggled to wipe them away, all the while sobbing and crying at the top of her lungs for the benefit of those who were surely listening.

*"There,"* she heard Hugh declare in a loud voice. "That will teach you to misbehave, Isabelle. I hope you have learned your lesson and will behave with more dignity in the future. After all, you are the chatelaine of Langston Keep." Then turning her over, he pulled her into his arms, saying softly, "You were very bad, madame."

"So were you," Belle replied. "Why did you not really beat me, my lord? I did deserve it," she admitted.

"A bitch beaten does not grow to love her master, ma Belle," came the surprising answer.

"I am not an animal!" she exclaimed, struggling to sit up.

"No, you are not," he said, "and because you are not you should have more sense than to behave as you did earlier in the hall. Your mother does not owe your father further loyalty. She is young yet, and beautiful. She can have a happy life with Rolf. Are you so jealous of her that you would deny her that happiness?"

"No, no!" Belle cried. "I know my father was not a kind man to my mother, but he was always good to me. Her memories and mine come into conflict in this matter."

"Try then," he said, "to understand hers better, *chérie*," He slowly kissed her ripe mouth. "Did I hurt you?"

"You have a hard hand, my lord," she admitted, rubbing her injured posterior. "It stung."

"Good!" Hugh told his outraged wife. "Then the next time you are tempted to act rashly, you will remember my hard hand and act more prudently, ma Belle. *N'est-ce pas?*" His eyes were twinkling as he spoke.

"I really am going to kill you one day," Belle said darkly, and he laughed.

# Part II

# ENGLAND

*Spring 1101–Summer 1103*

# ❧ Chapter 6

The ewes had lambed in midwinter. The inhabitants of Langston manor considered it a good sign for the coming growing season that not one of the new lambs had been lost. Several cows had calved in very early spring, and three mares had dropped foals. Again, the new offspring were healthy, lively animals, chasing their mothers, and chasing each other through the meadows filled with asphodels. Everything was beginning to show signs of new life by the time the ploughing began. The art of fertilization was not well-developed in England, but a three-field system of crop rotation had been followed for centuries at Langston. Every third field would lie fallow, while the fields on either side of it would grow green with their crops, one planted in the winter for late spring harvest, the other planted in the early spring for a summer harvest.

The common fields were carefully divided into neat strips, and the serfs given strips in each field on which to grow crops. The serf could also pasture any animals he owned in the common pasturage, or allow his pigs to eat acorns in the lord's woodland, where he might gather firewood for himself. Serfs, like the trees growing in the forest, belonged to the land. They could not leave without their lord's permission. Obedient, loyal serfs could be fairly certain of their small cottages and strips of field; but in return for these tenuous possessions, they rendered whatever services their lord required of them.

They worked his fields in the demesne before they worked their own. They gave special favors at certain seasons to their lord, which had been predetermined. And they gave their lord payments in kind. Their flour had to be ground in the lord's mill, and woe if the miller, usually a freedman, was dishonest and took more for his payment than he should. Their bread was baked in the lord's bakehouse ovens. The serf could not marry without his lord's permission, nor could his children, although a good master rarely withheld permission if both parties were willing.

But at Langston, as on all small manor estates, the lord, his serfs, and the freedmen who made their home there, were bound together by their dependence on each other.

For his part, Hugh Fauconier owed his allegiance first to King Henry, from whom he had received his lands. The king required certain things of his vassals. They must ransom him should he be taken captive in any battle. They paid the expenses of making his eldest son a knight, and provided a dowry for his eldest daughter. Each vassal gave forty days military service yearly in exchange for his fief; attended court when required; entertained the king when necessary; and accompanied his lord on expeditions and wars when requested.

All this done, Hugh's next duty was to his lands and his people. Slowly, Hugh and Rolf were building a defense force which they would lead should it ever become necessary to protect Langston from outside marauders. Though he had gotten his manor from the king, if someone stronger desired it and Hugh could not protect it, he would lose it. As long as the new lord swore fealty to King Henry, it would be unlikely the king would object. A weak vassal was of no advantage to him. So the inhabitants of Langston were all bound together by their necessity to survive and to prosper.

The arable fields were finally all planted, and began to sprout green almost immediately. In the meadows the cattle and sheep thrived on the new grass. The orchards bloomed, giving promise of a bumper crop of fruit to come. In the kitchen gardens Isabelle and Alette, barely speaking but allied by the keep's needs, planted cabbages, carrots, onions, leeks, peas, and beans. The herb garden, also within the keep's walls, was Alette's special province. It was here she grew the flowers needed for medicinal purposes and for flavoring the food. When they had first come from Normandy, she carried some of the original plants with her.

"How long have you tried to teach me what I must know about these herbs?" Isabelle said pleasantly, trying to slip back into her mother's good graces again. In the weeks since she had exposed Alette's love affair to Father Bernard, her mother had hardly even glanced at her. Isabelle had finally realized the cost of her heedless actions. Her mother was the only woman of her class on the manor. Alette, she was discovering, had been her only friend. She was anxious to heal the breach. Alette, however, did not seem so eager to let bygones be bygones.

"You have never been interested before," she replied coldly. "Why are you suddenly so interested now?" She knelt and gently drew away some of the winter cover with which she had protected her plants.

"Because I am chatelaine of Langston now," Isabelle said quietly, "and if I am to be a good mistress over my people, I must learn whatever I can to help them. One day I will pass the knowledge you share with me along to my daughters and granddaughters."

"You have a great deal to learn," Alette responded as her daughter knelt down beside her. "This is southernwood. You will know it by its hairlike leaves. It will soothe fevers and wounds. Here is wormwood, its cousin. We use it for constipation and the stomachache. It is also used for worming, man or animal, and is a good flea repellent. It causes headaches and nervousness if inhaled excessively. You must be careful." Alette pinched a slender leaf of southernwood, and rubbing it between her fingers, held out her hand. "Smell," she said.

Isabelle sniffed. "It's sweet to the nose," she said.

"But bitter to the tongue," her mother replied.

"What is this?" Isabelle fingered some purplish, red-ridged stems. The plant had an aromatic fragrance.

"Mugwort. We flavor the beer and wine with it."

"What else is here?" Belle queried her parent.

"Tansy, mostly for cooking, but also useful for getting rid of wind. Mary's gold, an antidote for pestilence and stings, but also good for flavoring stews and pottage; for rubbing into cheese to preserve its color; and when sugared, it makes a delicious conserve. Liverwort, which when made into a warm drink eases liver troubles; milfoil to stop bleeding; and foxglove, used externally for scrofula. Pasque flowers yield green dye, and asphodels a yellow dye. The roots of the iris give the scribes their ink. Dried, we call the roots by another name, orris, and it makes a fine deodorant and room freshener. Lavender will give sleep to the sleepless, and horehound stops coughs. Borage, as well as thyme, will give courage. Balm is a memory enhancer, and sage, if eaten in the month of May, will give long life," Alette concluded. "There is a great deal more, of course, but I think if you have absorbed anything I said, Isabelle, then you have made a good start." She began to dig vigorously, aerating her plant roots. "Go on now," she told Belle.

"But I want to help you, madame," Isabelle replied.

"You have already done more than enough," Alette answered sarcastically. "I need no more of *your* help, my daughter."

"I am sorry!" Isabelle burst out. "I thought you wanton. I did not know you loved him. I would not harm you, Mother."

"*Love him?* Why on earth would you say a thing like that?" Alette demanded angrily. "What makes you think I love him? Do you believe because a woman lies with a man that she must come to love him? Do you love your husband, Isabelle? Do you even know what love is? Rolf de Briard showed me that passion need not be bestial and cruel. He proved to me that a man can be tender with a woman. He is everything that your father was not!"

*"And you love him!"* Isabelle concluded triumphantly.

Alette's face was thoughtful a long moment, and then she said, "Perhaps I do, Isabelle, but you will say nothing of it to him." She pulled herself to her feet and brushed the loose dirt from her gown. *"Nothing."*

"Why not, madame? He loves you and would make you his wife." Belle drew herself up to face her mother, shaking her skirts out.

"I will be no man's chattel ever again," Alette responded with her familiar litany. "A wife can be abused, but a man never abuses his mistress lest he lose her. I, however, am neither a wife nor a leman, for my virtuous daughter would not have it so within her house," Alette finished bitterly.

"Hugh is lord here," Isabelle heard herself saying, "and if he orders you to marry Rolf de Briard, Mother, then you must!"

"I would throw myself from the walls of this keep, or drown myself in the river first," Alette answered her daughter grimly. "Think not to force me to the altar, Isabelle, lest my death be on your conscience." She turned and walked away.

As Isabelle and her husband lay abed that night, she asked him, "Why is my mother so stubborn in this matter?"

"Because your father mistreated her," he explained patiently again, stroking her soft white breasts with his long fingers. "If it is God's will that Rolf win her over, then he will."

"And if he does not?" Isabelle demanded.

"Then they will both be very unhappy, I suspect," Hugh replied. Bending his head, he kissed her mouth in a leisurely fashion, smiling at the sound of her breath, which drew itself in sharply. "I have heard it said that you gained your temperament from your father, ma Belle, but I think there is much of your mother in you, too. She is a very stubborn, a most determined woman." He drew his wife into the circle of his arm, his other hand caressing her, slipping down the curve of her hip to fondle her bottom. "It has been some weeks since I have had to spank this sweet flesh," he murmured. "You have been a very good little wife of late, ma Belle." He kissed her hard, forcing her lips apart, plunging his tongue into her mouth to fence with her tongue.

Isabelle's head spun slightly. While she was getting used to his passion, she suspected she had not yet tasted it to the fullest. He had never before done what he was now doing, but she liked it. With a sigh she shifted her body so that she might wrap her arms about him, drawing him against her aching breasts. "Mmmmmmmmm," she purred, her sharp little nails raking him ever so lightly.

He shivered as he felt a tingle of pleasure race down his spine. "Hellion," he said softly, taking his mouth from hers, "you are still too innocent to know your own powers, and for that I thank God."

Belle responded to this by nipping at his earlobe. Then her little tongue pushed into his ear, wiggling about the whorl suggestively. She blew softly into the spiral. Her hand reached down to fondle him and she whispered boldly to him, "Your rod is already as hard as iron, my lord. Your eagerness to fuck me is apparent, Hugh of Langston. Come, and put yourself inside me, husband." She kissed his ear warmly.

"You are shameless," he teased her, his fingers exploring her nether regions, finding her more than ready to receive him.

"Aye," she admitted blandly. "I am totally shameless when it comes to your passion. *Hurry!* I want to feel you hot and throbbing within my secret chamber, my lord husband. I cannot do without you!"

"Tell me that you want to be fucked," he taunted her.

"I want to be fucked!" she quickly responded. "Ohh, Hugh, yes, please! *Now! I want to be fucked!*"

It almost killed him, but he slowly, slowly pushed himself into her eager sheath, when actually he wanted to use her roughly. He could not, he was finding out to his dismay, get enough of his young wife. Sometimes he thought that if he could, he would spend every day and every night in their bed with her. A day had not gone by since their marriage, except for the few days of her flow each month, that he had not used her several times daily. And she was as eager for him as well. Ahhh, God! *She was eager!*

"I shall have to put you in a chastity belt," he growled at her, "when I go to give my service to the king this summer." His buttocks contracted and expanded as he rode her heaving body. "Your passion is far too hot, ma Belle." He pushed her legs up so he might plunge deeper into her, for he could not, it seemed, go far enough today.

"I will always be hot for you, my lord," Belle told him, wrapping her legs about his waist. Ahh, God! He was wonderful, and she was dying of the sweetness between them. "There is no man who could possibly please me as you do!" Then Belle felt herself soaring into infinity, and her cries mingled with his as they found their pleasure.

Afterward, as they lay sated in each other's arms, Hugh said, "I must leave you in a few days' time to go to my grandfather's house near Worcester. Langston is a fine place to raise my birds, and I have promised you a merlin, ma Belle. I want a young bird, that I may train it myself."

"Can I not go with you?" she asked him. "I have never been anywhere in my whole life but here. I think I should like to travel."

"Not this time, my love," Hugh answered. "It is not a good time to visit, for there is a great deal to be done here. Even though Rolf will remain to oversee his duties, I do not want your mother taking charge of the household again. Langston is yours now. It is too soon for you to go away. It would only confuse the servants and diminish your authority. That authority must be strong, for certainly this summer sometime I shall be called upon, and Rolf, too, to serve the king against his brother, who will try to take England. Whether the battle be joined here or in Normandy, Rolf and I must go. You, ma Belle, will be left with the entire responsibility of Langston. Though you have stewarded the estate in your father's absence, your mother was always considered Langston's chatelaine. That is no longer the case. In the absence of its lord, Langston belongs to its lady entirely. Everyone will depend upon you."

"Will you ever take me to meet your family?" she asked. Though disappointed, Isabelle understood fully what her husband was saying to her. She did have responsibilities, and if they did not seem so heavy a burden when he was with her, she knew their weight well, having borne them in the past.

"If this war is not an arduous one, we shall go in the autumn after the harvest is in," he promised her with a kiss.

Hugh departed several days later, traveling in company with his squire, Fulk, and six men-at-arms, young Langston men, wide-eyed at this chance to see more of the world. Isabelle waved her husband off, disappointed, but with a smiling face. He would be gone a full month, and she was already aching with loneliness. How had Hugh managed to creep into her affections so easily? Then she laughed at herself for being a little fool. Hugh Fauconier was strong and kind. He knew how to laugh, and would not allow anyone, his wife included, to take serious advantage of him. She respected him, and perhaps she even harbored a small tender of fondness for him as well.

Hugh had been gone several weeks, and it was almost May when one day the watch on the tower called out a warning. On the other side of the river, opposite the ferry crossing, a small armed party of men had appeared. Isabelle stood atop the walls of Langston and counted.

"Ten, no more," she said. Then she turned and asked her mother, "Where is Rolf de Briard?"

"He rode out this morning to the far village," Alette answered. "Does not the leader of that troupe look familiar, Isabelle?"

"We had best send a rider for Rolf," Belle said, paying little heed to her mother's words. "We should be safe unless they attempt to swim the river. I do not think they will, for any fool can see it is a tidal river and the currents are strong."

*"It is Richard,"* Alette said suddenly. "It is your brother,

Richard de Manneville. Look closely, Isabelle. Is it not Richard?"

Giving instructions that the steward be sent for, Belle turned her gaze back across the river, straining her eyes. "It might be Richard," she said. "I cannot really tell from this distance. Besides, he was not full-grown the last time I saw him."

"What can he want?" Alette wondered nervously. "Why has he returned to England? He should be in Normandy."

"You are frightened," Isabelle said, surprised. "Why are you frightened, madame? The de Mannevilles cannot harm you."

"Richard should not be here," Alette said. "He has no reason to come to Langston. That he has is bad luck."

"He is in for several surprises," Isabelle said. "No one sent word to him of my marriage, did they?"

Alette shook her head. "No," she said. "I felt there was no need for courtesy, as he had not the decency to send to us that your father had died and that he himself had married. We do not even know who his wife is, or if there is a child."

"I no longer care," Isabelle replied. "When Richard stormed back to Manneville simply because Father had made Langston my dower, I realized that it was not us, but Langston he loved."

"Yet you never said anything," Alette cried. "You defended him at every turn! How could you?"

"He is my half brother, madame," Belle answered simply.

*"Halloo, the keep."* The cry came across the river clearly.

"Impatient as ever," Belle noted, and then she called back, "Identify yourself, my lord."

"I am Richard de Manneville, lord of Langston," was the reply.

Isabelle burst out laughing, the mocking sound carrying in the still air. "You are not lord of Langston, Richard, and well you know it! I will send the ferry across for you, and two of your men, when our steward returns to the keep this afternoon. Until then you must bide your time, brother."

*"Belle?* Is that you? God's blood, wench, you are taller than

ever. Let me cross now. We have not eaten since early morning."

"That is your misfortune, Richard," she answered him. "When the steward returns, and not a moment before. Of course you could try to swim your horses across, but the tide is soon to turn. You might drown, and be less trouble to me then. Come ahead if you wish."

Now it was Richard de Manneville's turn to laugh. "Belle from Hell, you have not changed, I can see. We'll wait, *petite soeur*."

Isabelle and her mother descended the walls and returned to the hall. Alette was fretting again.

"How dare he call himself lord of Langston! He knows better."

"He may call himself whatever he wishes, madame, it changes nothing. Langston was my dower. The king had me wed to Hugh Fauconier, and now he is lord of Langston. What can Richard possibly do in the face of that?" Isabelle demanded.

"He is like his father," Alette said grimly. "He does nothing without purpose." She took a cup of wine from the servant at her elbow and drank nervously. "What can he want?"

"Obviously he has some scheme in mind to relieve me of Langston," Isabelle responded. "He has secured Manneville, and married. I will wager he already has an heir, else he would not leave his wife. Now he thinks to take my portion." She laughed. "What a surprise my dear greedy brother is in for when he learns that Langston is no longer undefended, or his sister defenseless."

Rolf de Briard returned from the far village, brought by the servant who was sent for him. "I've already seen," he said as he came into the hall. He bowed to Isabelle, but his eyes were on Alette.

"It is my half brother, Richard de Manneville, calling himself lord of Langston," Isabelle said, and explained the rest.

"We have enough men to defend the keep against such a small party, do we not?"

"We have enough men-at-arms now to secure Langston against a far larger troupe, lady," Rolf replied.

"I believe a strong show of force is in order, Rolf. I do not want my brother to believe for one moment that there is any chance of his taking Langston from us. Richard is charming, but he is ruthless."

Rolf de Briard nodded. "Give me an hour, lady, and then I will send the ferry for him and all of his men. It is better we not leave the others to wander about the countryside. There might be others planning to join them who are not yet here. If we contain your brother and his companions within the keep, there will be little danger from the outside then. Hugh should be back within a few days."

"I will leave our defense in your capable hands, Rolf," Isabelle told him, and then she smiled, to his surprise.

A trifle nonplussed, he bowed again, and left the two women.

"Shall we see to our toilette, madame, so we may greet our guests with honor?" Isabelle suggested to her mother.

When Richard de Manneville entered the hall at Langston over an hour later, he was astounded by the sister who greeted him. Isabelle was indeed tall for a woman. Her carriage was quite imperious. She wore a light wool tunic, pale yellow in color, over a long, full skirt of green linen that fell in trailing folds. The neckline was embroidered in indigo blue and gold threads, and matched the identical embroidery on the wrists of her sleeves. A girdle of green silk cord belted the garment. Her red-gold hair was neatly contained in a gold net crispine. This was certainly not the child he had left behind when he returned to Normandy.

"Isabelle, *ma petite soeur*," he greeted her, enfolding her in an embrace. Jesu! The wench had fine full breasts. He pressed her a trifle too tightly against his chest, holding her a bit longer than he should.

Isabelle shook herself free. "Welcome to Langston, brother," she addressed him in English, and then more bluntly, "What brings you to England? Does not Manneville need your attentions?"

"Father is dead, and William, too," he announced dramatically.

"Did you think we would not know that?" Isabelle demanded, an edge to her voice. "And you have married, we are told."

"I did not think that word would have reached such an isolated place as Langston," he said, a bit surprised.

"King Henry was concerned that in the absence of our menfolk, Mother and I would be left unprotected." She turned and motioned the steward. "This is Sir Rolf de Briard, our steward. Sir Rolf, my brother Richard, Sieur de Manneville."

The two men nodded warily to each other.

Richard de Manneville then acknowledged his stepmother with a bow. "Madame, it is good to see you again." He had forgotten how young she was. And how beautiful. She wore her favorite blue, and her face was serene as he had never seen it.

"You look well, Richard," Alette replied coolly.

Langston's well-trained servants were already offering refreshments to the Sieur de Manneville and his nine companions.

"The meal will be served shortly," Isabelle said, "but first, tell me why you have come to Langston, Richard."

"Duke Robert has returned Langston to me," Richard began.

"*I beg your pardon, brother?*" Belle's tone was icy. "Langston is not Duke Robert's to dispose of, for it was an outright gift to Father and his descendants from King William. Father settled Langston upon me, not you, Richard. How dare you attempt to use your sex to usurp my lands!"

"Isabelle, you do not understand, being just a young girl, but there is to be a war soon. Langston must be secured for Duke Robert when he regains his father's inheritance from Henry Beauclerc," Richard explained. "A woman cannot hold lands.

It is unnatural. Father should have never given you Langston, but Duke Robert has corrected the situation."

"Langston is my dower, Richard," Isabelle said.

"Do you think I should leave my sweet little sister homeless and without a husband, Belle?" Richard chuckled benignly. "Not at all. I have brought you a husband, *chérie*. We have both sworn our allegiance to Duke Robert, and Luc de Sai has sworn his fealty to me. In return he will have you to wife, Isabelle, and hold Langston for us. And you, my lady Alette, will remain in your home under our protection as well. I have seen to it all," he finished, pleased. Then he called, "Luc de Sai, to me!"

A heavyset young man detached himself from the others and came to join them. He had black eyes and curly black hair.

"Luc, this is my sister, who is to be your bride," Richard said. "Is she not a fine big girl as I said?"

Luc de Sai boldly eyed Isabelle, his look lingering upon her breasts a moment too long, and he licked his lips. "Lady," he said, bowing.

"Oh dear, Richard," Isabelle said, her voice honeyed, "I cannot possibly wed with this gentleman, I fear."

"Why, Belle, maiden-shy? I should not have expected it of you." Her brother chuckled indulgently.

"Nay, Richard, I am hardly the type of woman to be maiden-shy," she answered him, "but you have been so busy telling me of all you have done for us, that you have not asked what has happened over the last long years when my mother and I were alone. What has happened is that I have already wed. I was married several months ago."

"I am the head of the de Manneville family, and you are a de Manneville, Isabelle," her brother said sharply. "You cannot marry without my permission, and I did not give permission for any such marriage. It shall be annulled."

"I like a woman well broken in," Luc de Sai spoke out. "I do not mind, my lord."

"Where is your husband?" Richard de Manneville demanded. He glared at Rolf de Briard. "Is it you, steward?"

Isabelle laughed. "Nay, it is not Rolf. My husband is Hugh Fauconier, who is heir to the last Saxon lord of Langston, brother dear. My husband, however, is not here. He has gone to Worcester on business. As for your authority over me, Richard, you have none. I was married to Hugh at the king's command, for King Henry, like his brother, also believed that Langston could not be held safely by a woman. Stay the night, if you wish, but then you would be advised to return to Normandy and to your master. Look around you, brother, we are well-defended at Langston. Your puny force cannot take it from me."

"What, Belle, do you remember me so little that you think I shall turn tail and run? Langston should be mine," Richard snapped angrily at her. "And you have become too bold for a woman."

"My husband likes me that way," Belle responded. "Langston was never yours, brother, and it never will be. How dare you come here to try to steal it away from me? You are a Norman, Richard, and I an Englishwoman. Langston Keep is held in King Henry's name, not Duke Robert's. This is England, not Normandy."

"Beware, sister, I am not as helpless as you would believe. I have powerful relations now. If I choose to take you back to Normandy and hold you captive in a convent until this matter of your marriage can be settled, what could you do to prevent me? Duke Robert stands high in the pope's favor for his crusade into the Holy Land, for retaking Jerusalem back for the Church, and I am Duke Robert's man. Then, too, you and your husband could meet with an accident, sweet Isabelle. That would leave my stepmother alone, helpless." Richard de Manneville looked to Luc de Sai. "What say you, Luc? Would the lady Alette suit you as well for a wife?" Reaching out, he pulled Alette forward. "She is really quite beautiful, isn't she? Far lovelier than the daughter."

*"Much lovelier,"* Luc de Sai agreed, licking his lips again. His eyes roved insolently over Alette's shrinking form.

"Brother, you are still a bully," Belle mocked him. "I am sorry to tell you that my mother is also unavailable for any marriage proposal, having only recently remarried herself. *She is also with child.*"

*"Belle!"* her mother shrieked. "How could you know?"

"Later, madame," Belle said, her gaze locked onto that of her half brother in a fierce battle of wills.

"To whom is my stepmother now wife?" Richard said furiously.

"To Sir Rolf de Briard, our steward," Isabelle answered. "He is my husband's best friend, and like Hugh, was raised at court by Queen Matilda, may God assoil her good soul." Isabelle crossed herself piously and then looked to Father Bernard, who had been silently observing the turmoil between Richard de Manneville and his half sister, Isabelle of Langston. "The priest can vouch for the truth of this all," she said. "He was one of the king's own chaplains until he was sent with my husband and Rolf to minister to Langston. He performed both weddings, did you not, Father Bernard?" She smiled sweetly.

"I did," the priest replied without hesitation, coming to her side. "My lady Isabelle's marriage was celebrated in late January, and the lady Alette's in March, my lord de Manneville. The king would have it no other way, for unlike his brother, William Rufus, he is a pious and devout son of the Church."

"Unhand my wife," Rolf de Briard said quietly to Richard de Manneville. He drew Alette into the protective curve of his arm, quite gratified to feel her sag with relief against him.

"I have been cheated," the Norman said grimly, "but beware, sister, for when Duke Robert takes England, Langston will be mine. And when it is, I shall send you and your mother packing with your worthless knights! You think you have bested me, but you have not!"

"Get out of my hall!" Isabelle said angrily to her half brother.

*"What?"* He looked astounded.

*"Get out of my hall,"* she repeated, gesturing forward several of Langston's men-at-arms. "I do not want you here, Richard de Manneville. My hospitality is not for those who would come into my house and abuse it. Our father and brother were killed almost two years ago, yet you could not find the time to send to us. Nor did you send word of your marriage. Even now I do not know who you have wed, not that I really care. I pity the poor girl, brother. Now you dare to come to England at *your* convenience, pretending that you care what happens to my mother and me, suggesting that one of us marry your man in order to hold Langston for Duke Robert. You are a fool, Richard! Now, get you gone out of my hall, and take your lustful, ruttish friend with you!"

"It is almost nightfall," Richard protested.

"Alfred will ferry you and your men back across the river," Belle said stonily. "If you choose to camp upon the other side, I cannot stop you, but be gone by morning, *brother.*"

"My lady, please," the priest interceded, but Isabelle stopped his speech with a raised hand.

"Do not prattle to me about hospitality or familial duties, Father Bernard," she told him. "My brother is bound by neither except if it be to his advantage. He would murder us all in our beds this night to get his way. Is that not so, Richard?"

"You were an unpleasant little girl, Isabelle," her brother replied bitterly, "and you have not changed. I always said Father should have beaten you, but then you were his only daughter. He was wont to dote upon you, more's the pity. I shall return to Langston when Duke Robert has settled the matter of England with Henry Beauclerc, *sister.*"

Isabelle laughed. "I will not expect to see you again, then, brother mine," she told him. "Now, leave my hall."

Richard de Manneville turned upon his heel, Luc de Sai by his side, and with their men they departed the keep. Isabelle climbed to the walls to watch as they were taken back across the river Blyth. Smiling grimly, she watched as they set up their small encampment. Then, satisfied, she descended back into the hall, where her mother, Rolf, and the priest awaited her coming.

"You give no quarter, my lady," Rolf de Briard said, admiration in his voice. "Hugh would have been proud of you, and so I shall tell him."

Isabelle nodded, a faint smile touching her lips. "If there must be war, Rolf, then I will be left to care for Langston. I will do my duty, I promise you all. My brother is a greedy fool."

"We have another matter to discuss," Father Bernard said quietly, and he looked seriously at Alette. "You are with child, my daughter?"

"It is no one's business but my own," Alette said defiantly.

"It is my business, too," Rolf said, "for if you be with child, *ma petite*, it is my child. I am not a man to desert his responsibilities."

"*Your responsibilities?*" Alette was outraged. "I am not your responsibility, nor is my child ... if I am indeed with child."

"My serving woman, Agneatha, says my mother has had no female flow in many weeks," Isabelle told the two men calmly.

"I have committed a grave sin in your behalf, my daughter," Father Bernard said. "I spoke a great lie when I told the Sieur de Manneville that you were married to Sir Rolf and that I had myself performed the ceremony. Now I must right the wrong else it imperil my immortal soul."

"Surely God would understand why you said what you did, holy father," Alette said nervously. Why was Rolf grinning like an idiot? "My stepson will not come again to Langston. There is little chance of Duke Robert overcoming King Henry. Why can you not all leave me be?"

"God works His will in ways we cannot understand, my daughter," the priest said. "While I do not believe that King Henry will be overcome by his brother, I cannot be certain. Only God would know the answer to the questions you pose, my lady. What I do know, however, is that you must wed with this good knight who loves you so deeply. You cannot allow his child to be born a bastard. Such an act would not be worthy of you, Alette de Manneville. Will you punish the innocent soul now nesting beneath your heart for your fears, for the wrongs done by your late husband, for the sin of your own pride?"

Alette's will began to falter, particularly when Rolf's arms tightened about her and he murmured softly into her ear, "I love you, *ma petite*. I will be good to you, I swear it on the Blessed Virgin's name. Please, trust in me."

"Come," Father Bernard said. "My chamber is private, and as spare as I could make it. It will serve as our chapel." He shepherded the two women and Rolf into the privacy of the small room, calling to Ida and Agneatha, who had come into the hall, to join them. "Now," the priest said, "with the lady Isabelle, and these two good servants serving as witness to the proceedings, we will begin."

Alette felt totally helpless. Betrayed a second time by her own child! Where had she gone wrong with Belle? And yet . . . she looked up at Rolf, and tears sprang into her eyes. His gaze was so filled with devotion and love for her, she wondered why she hadn't seen it before. He really *does* love me, she thought, amazed by the realization, and suddenly relieved. Rolf was not Robert de Manneville. Rolf loved her! They would be happy together. It was as if the ice in which she had encased her heart cracked and fell away. Catching up his hand, she kissed it, wanting to laugh aloud at the quick joy that sprang into his face. When asked, she consented gladly to become his wife.

Afterward the priest advised them, "Tell your household servants the truth of this matter, my children. If, God forbid, Sieur Richard should ever return, they will then swear your marriage was celebrated in March, and not upon the next to last day of April." His eyes twinkled. "God bless you, my children. Now leave me that I may make my peace with God for all the lies I have told this very day in your behalf." He crossed himself.

"Tomorrow," Isabelle said to Father Bernard, "we shall choose a site for the church we wish to build. And you shall have your own house, too, good father. It shall be next to our church so you may always have easy access. And you will have the church's portion of the harvest this year, and two serfs, a man and his wife, to care for you."

"I thank you, lady," the priest said, "and I know that my lord, Hugh, will approve all you have promised me."

They left him, returning to the hall where the meal was even now being put upon the table. Alette and Rolf could scarcely take their eyes from one another, and Belle could not resist teasing them.

"For a woman who did not wish to remarry, madame, you seem content enough with your lot now," she said mischievously. "Did you know, Rolf, that my mother threatened to fling herself from the keep's walls if I forced her into marriage? I somehow do not think you will have to worry about such tragedy now, however."

*"Ma petite!"* The bridegroom looked genuinely stricken.

"Belle is correct, *mon amour*," Alette replied. "You need have no fears. I am helpless in my love for you—something I certainly never thought to be." She looked at her daughter. "How is it, Isabelle, that you were wiser than I was in this matter? Is it possible that you have come to love your husband? And knowing now what love is, saw mine for Rolf even before I could admit it to myself?"

*"Love Hugh?"* Voicing the words aloud seemed to lend a legitimacy to the thought. She had not considered it before, but now it would seem she no longer had a choice. Did she indeed love Hugh? She certainly missed him, and not simply because she enjoyed their bed sport. She missed lying with him, and talking of all the wonderful plans they had for Langston one day. She missed riding by his side across the land. She missed waking in the night and snuggling next to his bulk. She missed fighting with him, damnit! "Mayhap I do love Hugh," she said thoughtfully, "if indeed what I feel for him is

love." Then she grew fierce. "But say nothing of this to him! If I do love him, then I shall tell him when I think the time is right, and not a moment before! I will wreak havoc upon anyone who divulges my secret to him!"

"Your secret is safe with us, *stepdaughter*," Rolf teased her.

"I think the steward must have his own house," Belle decided aloud. "I shall speak to my lord husband about that when he returns home." She picked up her goblet and raised it to them. "A toast to my mother, and to *my stepfather*," she said with a smile. "Long life, and many children!"

They drank, and then Alette said, "Is it not time that you had children of your own, Isabelle?"

"I am too young to be a mother yet," her daughter replied airily.

"I was younger than you are now, fifteen, when you were born," her mother replied. "You have already passed your sixteenth birthday."

Isabelle laughed. "I was just sixteen on the first of this month, madame. Besides, you sought motherhood to escape my father's unwelcome attentions. I, on the other hand, welcome my husband's attentions very much. In fact I am most shamelessly eager for his return." She took up a joint of broiled rabbit from the platter passed her by a servant and bit lustily into it.

Alette didn't know whether to chide her daughter for such lack of delicacy or not, but Rolf chuckled.

"I know just how she feels, *ma petite*," he murmured in her ear. "I am most shamelessly eager for your return to my bed. When is this child of ours due to be born?"

"Not until year's end," Alette said, trying not to smile.

"And would it harm the babe if we were to play for a bit, *chérie*?" He nibbled upon her earlobe. "Ummmmm, delicious! 'Tis far more tender than the rabbit, I think."

Isabelle burst out laughing. "Take some food and wine, *Father* Rolf. I can see you and my mother are hard put to behave with propriety at my table. Go to your chamber, and satisfy your other appetites first. Only then will you enjoy your meal, I think."

Rolf stood up and pulled Alette with him. "Madame, I thank you for your delicacy of feelings in this sensitive matter." Taking a bowl, he filled it with rabbit, bread, and cheese. He handed a small decanter of wine to Alette, then led her off to their chamber.

Belle sat alone at the high board. She was suddenly filled with a feeling of great peace, as if all was right with her world. There was only one thing lacking. *Hugh.* Surely he would be home shortly, and they could share their passion once again. Did she love him? She knew now that she did, but unless he would admit the same to her, she would not leave herself vulnerable.

# ▓Chapter 7

While Hugh was gone, a mews was built for the birds he would bring from his grandfather's home. Stones, stored in the keep's lower level, were brought up into the bailey and set with mortar to make the base of the structure. The building itself was fashioned of well-dried timbers, the cracks between the boards filled with clay from the river's edge so the wind might not get through. The roof was thatched. A stone floor laid. The whole structure was then whitewashed. Two windows were set high. The heavy oak door, banded in iron with a sturdy iron lock and round pull, was just large enough to allow a falconer to pass through it.

Inside, the single room was semidark, its two windows allowing just enough light to accustom the birds to daylight. The stone floor was covered with coarse sand, which was raked daily and would be changed on a regular basis. The mews were high and wide enough to allow limited flight. Perches of various sizes were set to suit the different birds who would live there. Some were placed high and stood well out from the whitewashed walls. Others were just high enough to keep the birds' tails off the ground. Bunches of dried herbs that would not be poisonous, should the birds eat them, were hung to sweeten the air.

Outside the mews, carefully carved low stone blocks, their bottoms cone-shaped, were driven with iron spikes, point side down, into the ground. Here the birds would be brought to *weather*, which meant to become used to the world outside their protective inside environment. Their training would require great care, and even greater patience upon the part of the falconer.

Only the nobility were permitted the privilege of owning hunting birds. Usually the birds were caught wild. Nestlings taken from their nests were called eyases. Slightly older birds, already flying, were caught with nets. These were called branchers. Hugh Fauconier's grandfather, Cedric Merlin-sone, however, was unique in his breeding of the hunting birds. Used to human contact from birth, these creatures made better and more obedient hunters. Only the female birds, larger and more aggressive, were called falcons. The smaller males were tiercels. They were considered inferior, and rarely used in the hunt. Their ability to mate and to produce healthy female offspring were their strong points.

"We have rarely spoken of the birds," Isabelle said to Rolf. "What kind will Hugh bring?" It was two days after her brother's very brief visit and hasty departure. A messenger had brought word that Hugh Fauconier would be returning this day.

"There are only two kinds," Rolf answered her. "The long-winged hawks and the short-winged hawks; but there are several varieties. His grandfather raises them all."

"What difference does the wing size make?" Belle inquired, anxious to learn what she could so she would not seem too ignorant in her husband's eyes. The ladies of the court among whom Hugh was raised certainly must know more than she.

"The long-winged birds hunt in the open, in the fields, over the marshes and the water. The short-winged birds are better suited to the woodlands, where the long-winged hawks are at a distinct disadvantage amid the trees, where they cannot swoop and soar," Rolf explained. He smiled at his stepdaughter. "Do not be afraid to ask Hugh about his birds. He will be delighted in your interest."

"He has promised me a merlin," she said.

"I would have thought a sparrow hawk more suitable for a

lady," Rolf considered aloud. "Perhaps if your mother desires a bird, I shall choose one of them for her. It might take her mind off her roiling belly."

Isabelle flushed and turned away from Rolf de Briard. The thought of her mother quickening with child was embarrassing, and an indictment to her own barrenness. How could Alette have gotten herself in such a state, and so quickly, when she, younger and surely more fertile, had not been able to prove her worth to her husband? What was the matter with her?

"Will Hugh teach me to hunt with my bird, do you think?" Isabelle asked him. "I have never had a hunting bird."

"Of course," Rolf assured her. "He will want you to be a good huntress, Belle, for you will surely help him show off his falcons to those noblemen who come to him for hunting birds."

Isabelle suddenly laughed. "Poor Rolf," she teased him. "You shall have to spend the summertime overseeing Langston while Hugh and I idle away our days hunting with his birds. Perhaps we shall ask you to join us now and again if everything is in order here."

Rolf chuckled. "I should appreciate that, my lady daughter," he replied. Hugh was right, he thought to himself. Isabelle of Langston was a little hellion, but he suspected she had never in her entire life been so free of responsibility as she was now. It did his heart good to see her happy, for he knew if that was so, then his friend, Hugh, would be happy also.

The lord of Langston returned toward midafternoon; a lad who lived at the far end of the estate in the direction from which Hugh came ran ahead, announcing the master's return. It was a slow traverse to the keep, as he traveled with a small caravan of carts, each covered by an arch of canvas and drawn by small, shaggy ponies. Hugh rode at the head of the procession, mounted upon his great horse, a large white bird upon his arm. The creature was hooded.

Isabelle stared. "What is it?" she asked Rolf.

"It is a gyrfalcon," he told her.

"She is magnificent," Isabelle said admiringly.

Hugh drew his stallion to a halt beside Belle. Immediately, a young man dashed from the group of travelers to take the gyrfalcon from him. Hugh swung a leg over his saddle and slipped easily to the ground.

"Welcome home, my lord," Belle said, her voice suddenly breathy.

A slow smile that began in his eyes lit his plain face. "Madame," he responded. Nothing more. There was no need for words between them. Bending, he kissed her in a leisurely fashion until, blushing, Belle broke from his embrace, scolding him, but gently.

"My lord! It is unseemly that you kiss me so before all!" Her cheeks were flushed, her eyes unnaturally bright.

Hugh grinned at the halfhearted rebuke. "I am ravenous after my travels, my lady wife," he said, and his blue eyes twinkled.

"The meal is ready when you are, my lord," she replied primly.

"My hunger is for other than food," he murmured low, so that only she might hear. Then, turning away, he began giving orders to the three falconers who had accompanied him. "Take them to the mews, my lads. See them fed, watered, and unhooded. I want them familiar with their surroundings as quickly as possible. Rolf, was the mews constructed to your satisfaction?"

"Yes, my lord, although eventually I should like to see it all of stone. Built of wood, the mews are vulnerable," the steward responded.

Hugh nodded. "Once the king is firmly settled, we shall send to Northamptonshire for stone, as did Belle's father when he built this keep. I see construction has begun on the church."

"And the priest's house as well, my lord," Rolf said.

"I told Father Bernard he might live in the keep," Hugh answered.

"The lady Isabelle will explain everything that has happened in your absence, but for one thing which I must tell you. Alette became my wife two days ago. She is quickening with my child."

A broad, sweet smile lit Hugh's face, and he grasped his friend by the hand, shaking it heartily. "Wonderful! How did this all come about, Rolf? Are you happy? Of course you're happy!" Hugh laughed.

Rolf grinned back. "My *stepdaughter* will tell you all."

"We shall need a great deal of stone," Hugh considered. "You must have your own dwelling within the keep."

"So my lady Isabelle has promised," Rolf explained.

Hugh shook his head. "By the Blessed Mother, Rolf, do you realize that but six months ago we were both poor knights with little hope of little more than we had? Now look at us! Husbands, and you to be a father."

"And you the lord of Langston, in full possession of the lands that once belonged to your father's family," Rolf concluded. "Aye, I am amazed by it all myself, my lord. Were it not for your generosity, I should yet be a poor knight in the service of the king instead of the steward upon these rich lands."

"Come," Hugh said, embarrassed by his friend's gratefulness, "you have not yet met my falconers. They are young lads, but saw the chance for opportunity here with me as opposed to remaining with Grandfather's household where they were but three of over twenty falconers, and the others about them all in seniority. Alain, Faer, Lind, to me!" he called the trio, who were carefully unloading the covered cages.

Placing their burdens in the mews, the three young men came to stand respectfully before their master. They were freedmen, not serfs. As long as the Merlin-sone family had bred and trained hunting hawks, their families had been falconers. The three were of medium height and build. All were brown-haired, but each had different-colored eyes.

"Come, lads," Hugh said, "and meet Rolf de Briard, my oldest friend, who is the steward here at Langston. Rolf, this is

Alain, Faer, and Lind, the best young falconers in my grand-father's house."

The three flushed and shuffled their feet as they nodded their heads in acknowledgment of their steward. "We will see just how good we are, my lord, when we have trained this new bunch we've brought with us," Alain, the spokesman for the trio, said.

"Come to the hall when you've settled the birds," Hugh told them, and then he and Rolf hurried up the steps into the keep.

"Welcome home, my lord!" he was greeted half a dozen times over by his smiling servants, and Hugh felt a great warmth suffuse his soul. *Home.* Aye, Langston really was his home. He could have sworn he actually felt the stones in the building greeting him with gladness.

"God be praised for your safe journey and return, my lord," the priest said, saluting him.

"You have been busy, good father, I am told, since my departure," Hugh answered, tossing his cloak to a servant and taking up a goblet of wine from another. "Rolf tells me you have performed a marriage."

The priest beamed. "Indeed, I did, my lord."

"And just how did it all come about, good father?"

"That," the priest told him with another smile, "must be the lady Isabelle's tale. She is very clever, your lady wife."

"Most clever," Hugh agreed, "for she greeted me at the bar-bican, and has now disappeared." He looked about the hall, but there was no sight or sign of Belle.

"Welcome home, my lord," his mother-in-law addressed him. "We are relieved to have you back."

Hugh took up both of Alette's small hands in his. "I thank you, madame, and I tender my congratulations to you upon your marriage."

Alette laughed softly, a becoming rose color staining her cheeks. "My lord, I thank you," she responded, her adoring look going to her husband.

"I am happy for you," Hugh continued, "although you were

at times more recalcitrant in the matter than I have ever seen your daughter. Where is my lady wife? I have not seen her since my arrival."

"She is preparing your bath for you, my lord, for she realized you will be dirty and dusty from the road," Alette said.

"Belle has finally learned the art of the bath?" He was surprised.

"She has tried," Alette said, laughing.

Hugh turned about and hurried to the bathing chamber, eager for the delights that awaited him. Since that time several months ago when Alette had attempted to teach her daughter how to bathe a guest, Isabelle had refused to have anything to do with such labor. He was curious to learn what had changed her mind in the matter.

"Do not dally, my lord," she told him sharply as he entered the bathing room. "The water is nicely hot, and it will soon be time for the meal. Quickly, remove your garments!"

They were alone in the bath.

"What, madame? Is it not your duty to help me off with my clothing?" he demanded, seating himself upon a stool. "Come, assist me with my boots, Belle." He looked to her, eyes dancing with amusement.

"Are you such a child, then," Belle grumbled, but she came and pulled his boots off his big feet.

Reaching out, Hugh tumbled her into his lap, kissing her soundly. A hand slid swiftly up her skirts, stroking the soft inside of her thigh.

Belle sighed, the sound one of pleasure. Then struggling up, she smacked him playfully. "My lord!" She was a picture of perfect outrage. "This is not the time for such folderol. Stand up!" She yanked his tunic over his head, laying it aside. Beneath he wore only a linen sherte, for the weather was warm. Unlacing it, she drew it off of him, too. "Take your own braies off," she ordered him. "I must see to the bathwater. It is probably cold at this point." Her cheeks were flushed. Was it the heat or the state of his sex, very visible and obviously eager, beneath his drawers?

Hugh slipped out of the remainder of his garments while Belle made a great show of testing the bathwater, adding a bit of scented oil, choosing the correct soap pot, gathering her washing cloths and brush.

"Get in! Get in!" She gestured at him with an impatient hand.

Hugh mounted the stone steps and climbed into the big tub. "Ahhhh," he moaned as the hot water immediately began to ease his aching muscles, for he had been riding for several days. He slid deeper into the water. "Ahh, ma Belle, this is heaven. You must come and join me, *chérie*. I have missed you."

"Do not be ridiculous," Isabelle said primly. "Now, behave yourself, my lord, and let me do my duty." She picked up a cloth.

"But can you not do it better in here with me?" he teased her.

She glared at him, muttering about the foolishness of men; shrieking with complete surprise as he reached out, dragging her down into the tub with him. "*Hugh!* You have gone mad!" She struggled to arise, but his arms wrapped themselves about her. "Let me go, you great oaf! The water will shrink my gown! Let me go!"

"Take your clothing off, *ma Belle douce*," he crooned at her. Then his fingers began loosening her skirts, sliding them off her, tossing them in a sodden heap upon the floor. "Your tunic, madame," he ordered her, helping her to get the soaking garment off to join the skirts. Unlacing her chemise, he flung it across the room. Fortunately, she wore no shoes in the bathing chamber, and her braid was pinned up. "Now, madame," he growled at her, "I would have the warm welcome from you that you earlier denied me." His mouth descended bruisingly upon hers.

Belle's head spun with delight. Ohh, how she missed him! Cradled in his lap in the tub, she could feel his manhood, stone hard, eager for her. One arm cradled her while his other hand played with her own burgeoning little sex, his fingers pushing into her creaminess while she moaned against his lips.

"Have you missed me, ma Belle?" he murmured against her mouth. The fingers pushed deep and rhythmically inside her.

"I . . . hardly noticed your . . . absence, my lord. There . . . was much to . . . do," Belle fibbed, and then she shuddered with her first release.

Hugh lifted her slightly, turning her to face him, and lowered her onto his own raging weapon, groaning as she sheathed him. "You lie," he said through gritted teeth, his big hands cupping her taut buttocks.

She slipped her arm about his neck, riding him smoothly while his lips moved slowly, deliberately, over her straining throat, across her swelling breasts with their aching nipples. "You're a wicked man, Hugh Fauconier," she purred at him. *"Ahhh! Ohhhhh!"* she moaned, her eyes closing as he released his passion into her, filling her full. Belle fell forward onto his shoulder as Hugh's arms embraced her. They lay that way, sated and contented, for some minutes, and then Belle opened her eyes with a start.

"Oh, Holy Mother!" she gasped. "They won't sit down to the meal in the hall until we come. How long have we been like this?" She scrambled from the tub, the water sluicing down her lush body, causing his lust to renew itself. "Wash yourself quickly, my lord," she said, flinging a cloth at him. "I must hurry to dress, and I shall bring your fresh clothes to you. Oh, hurry!"

In the hall they heard him laughing, and when the lord and lady of the manor appeared after some minutes, no one dared to mention that Isabelle was wearing different garments. The servants began trouping in from the kitchens below, carrying dishes from which arose delicious odors. At the high board they were offered broiled river perch caught that same afternoon, roasted duck, venison pie, broiled rabbit, a thick vegetable pottage, peas, bread, butter, and cheese. Both wine and ale were offered to those at the high board. Below the salt, however, the menu was less lavish. There was salted fish, broiled rabbit, a pottage, bread, and cheese. There was plenty of food, for Isabelle would not stint their retainers, and the ale flowed freely.

Hugh ate with gusto, as did Belle, but both were anxious to retire to the solar to feed the lust they had just barely stoked in the bathing chamber. Each cast surreptitious glances at the other, their eyes moving guiltily away when they met. Their hands touched and they started, laughing nervously. Patiently, they waited for the servants to clear the dishes away. Two young serfs came into the hall, one with a drum, the other with a reed instrument. They began to play softly by the fire. When Rolf drolly suggested to Hugh that they play a board game, Langston's lord arose, stretching and yawning with much show.

"I've ridden long and hard these past days," he said. "I think I shall find my bed now. Isabelle, will you come, too, or remain in the hall entertaining your mother and stepfather?"

"Ohh, I'm very tired, too," Belle said, jumping up and hurrying after her husband.

Rolf chuckled wickedly. "Hugh will ride a good deal more before the dawn, I think; and Belle be twice as tired before the sun rises."

"You are very naughty, my lord," Alette chided him, laughing.

"I must hang my garments up to dry," Belle said as they entered the solar. "I have not so many gowns that I can be wasteful."

"Hurry!" he commanded her, and when she joined him, said, "You have kept me waiting, ma Belle. You must be punished," and turning her over his knee, he spanked her bare bottom twice before turning her back again to kiss her.

Belle only laughed at him. "You will have to toughen your hand in brine, my lord, if you truly mean to chastise me," she teased him. "Those were but love taps you just gave me."

She wiggled her bottom provocatively in his lap, feeling his instant response.

Standing up, he tossed her onto their bed and flung himself atop her, pinioning her beneath him. "Hellion," he growled in her ear. "Shall I never tame you?"

"No," she laughed again, "you shall not! A tame little wife would quickly bore you, Hugh Fauconier. I am not one of your little birds, to be wheedled into obedience, nor would you want me that way."

"I am not so certain it is a wise thing that you know me so well, *ma Belle douce*," he told her.

She slipped her arms about his neck and drew his mouth down to hers. "A wife should know her lord," she murmured low against his mouth. Then she nibbled gently upon his lower lip. "How can she please him if she knows him not?" Her hand ruffled through his tawny gold hair.

"Do you want to please me, ma Belle?" he half groaned. She was driving him wild with desire. The luxurious feeling of her firm young breasts against his bare chest was wonderful. The nipples stabbing him were like sharp little stones. Shifting himself, he fastened his mouth over one and began to suckle strongly upon it.

Lightning forked through her body at the insistent tug of his lips. She almost purred with the pleasure he was giving her.

He lifted his head a moment, his eyes meeting hers. Then he repeated his question. "Do you want to please me, ma Belle?" His mouth found her other breast and he bit gently down on it.

"Ahhh," she cried low. The slightly painful sensation was really quite delicious. "Sometimes I want to please you," she admitted.

Hugh raised his head again. *"Now?"* he said.

"A-Aye," Belle responded softly. Her hand touched his face, her fingers following the line of his jaw, brushing softly over his lips, which kissed the slender digits before he separated one from the others, drawing it into his mouth to slowly suck upon. Belle could feel a tightening in her nether regions, an ache starting to build in her lower belly. *"Hugh,"* was all she could say.

Releasing her hand, he drew her over into the curve of his arm. "I am very passionate, Belle," he began, "and I have missed my wife. I am not a man to diddle a pretty serf in a hay pile or beneath a hedge. Since the morning I left you, I have had no woman beneath me. I have been gentle with you so far, but tonight I do not know if I can be gentle. I desire you greatly, *chérie*." His big hand smoothed her tangled red-gold hair, sliding down its length, slipping over the curve of her hip, down her thigh. "All those nights we were parted, Belle, I thought of you. Of your milk-white skin, and your fiery hair; of your mysterious green-gold eyes, and your luscious body. But I thought as much of your youthful wisdom, your loyalty, your deep love of Langston and its people." His hand moved up again now, catching her chin between his fingers, lifting her gaze to his. "I thought of how you will fight for what you believe in, and of your temper, which sometimes outruns your good sense. As much as I love my family; as happy as I was to see my grandparents; I realized that all I wanted to do was gather my birds and come home to you, Belle. Do you know what I am saying to you, *chérie*?"

Isabelle's eyes were filled with tears, but her voice was strong when she answered him. "You are saying that you love me, Hugh, and I am right glad of it, for I love you, too!"

Their lips met, gently at first, and then fiercely as their passion built. Her lush mouth softened beneath his hard one, yielding, giving, until the kiss seemed without either beginning or end. His lips traveled over her straining throat, across her chest, her breasts. Isabelle sighed deeply, her hands brushing over his skin with little feathery touches. Her breasts felt swollen, enormous, near to bursting from their skin. When he tongued her nipples, she whimpered, for it actually hurt her. His teeth grazed over the tender flesh, and Belle moaned.

Now his head was moving lower down her torso. For a moment she stiffened, but then her body relaxed. This was her husband. *Her love. Her Hugh.* And he had never before been this bold with her. His mouth pressed a warm kiss in her navel and moved on across the taut flesh. She almost stopped breathing when he kissed the insides of both of her thighs, but then he moved on, trailing a ribbon of little kisses down her legs, finishing with each foot. Belle giggled nervously.

Hugh startled her, however, with his next action. Slowly, slowly, his tongue began to retrace the path his lips had but recently taken, moving from the tip of her toes, up her legs to the shadowed insides of her thighs. Pushing her limbs apart, he buried his head in the nest of blazing red curls, inhaling her special fragrance. Isabelle gasped, shocked, her head spinning wildly, but there was more to come. She felt him opening her, his tongue seeking, seeking. *Seeking what?*

"Ahh, Holy Mother!" she cried as he obviously found what he had sought and his tongue moved relentlessly back and forth over her little pleasure pearl, releasing myriad frenzied sensations that rendered her faint, but yet conscious to enjoy the delicious madness that was now permeating her body and soul. She thrashed beneath his sweet mouth, aching, flying, struggling to reach the crest of the mountain; and then her passion culminated in a violent crescendo that for a moment seemed to break her entire being open, rendering her helpless as the sweetness poured over her, and she wept.

At that moment he entered her, his manhood sweeping up her channel, filling her with throbbing warmth and life. He licked the tears from her cheeks, kissing her tenderly. He took her fiercely, driving himself and her hard, feeling the hot tightening of her. Then it seemed as if she were drawing him into her body so deeply that he thought she would swallow him entirely. He could feel her fingers digging, digging, into the flesh of his buttocks, her slender legs wrapping themselves about his torso.

*"Belle! Belle!"* he groaned. "You are killing me." Then he felt himself swelling, ripening within her, followed by blessed

relief as his passion burst itself, flooding her with his love. To his great surprise, he too wept.

She wrapped her arms about him, kissing his face frantically. "What else are you keeping from me, my lord?" she managed to gasp.

Hugh laughed weakly, rolling off her. "You are wonderful, *ma Belle douce*, my sweet wife. I adore you!"

She said nothing, instead drawing him to her to rest his head upon her breasts. He felt her kiss upon his hair, and then, arms about him, she grew still, her rhythmic breathing lulling him into sleep.

When he awoke just before dawn he found himself still in her arms. He had never, he realized, in all his life felt so safe, and so at home. "I love you, Belle," he said low.

Surprising him, for he had thought her still asleep, she replied, "And I love you, Hugh."

"How long have you been awake?" he asked her.

"A moment or two," she said, "no more."

Raising his head, he gazed into her eyes. "What would you like to do today, ma Belle? Would you like to see the bird I have chosen to be yours? She is a fine little merlin."

Belle smiled, rolling onto her side, and nodded. "What other birds did you bring, my lord?" she asked. "Rolf has explained to me that you have both long-winged and short-winged hawks, but he said you would tell me the varieties you have."

"I have brought two breeding pair each of gyrfalcons, peregrines, and merlins. These are the long-wings. The first two are quite large birds. They hunt small to medium-sized game, and all manner of waterfowl. The merlins are littler birds, and hunt small creatures, both winged and four-footed." Now he rolled over and, pushing the pillows behind him, sat up. "I have two varieties of short-winged birds, goshawks and sparrow hawks. I have also brought a number of young birds, yet to be trained."

"I want to see my merlin," Belle said, climbing naked from their bed. "What is she like? Is she a good huntress?"

He laughed at her enthusiasm. "I shall tell you nothing,

madame. You must see for yourself. You must first think of a name for her, for each bird has its own name to which it answers."

They hurried to bathe the excesses of their passion away, and then dressed, stopping briefly in the hall to snatch pieces of bread with toasted cheese, which they quickly ate. Hugh's three falconers were already about their business as they approached the mews. Several birds were set out upon the stone blocks, weathering. The falconers nodded politely to their master and mistress.

"I have brought my lady to see her merlin," Hugh announced.

"Her be a fine little bird," Alain said approvingly.

Hugh led Belle into the mews and over to a low perch where two small birds sat unhooded. Reaching out, Hugh took the larger of the two upon his hand. "Here she is, ma Belle."

"She has few feathers," Belle noted, her disappointment evident.

He laughed softly, so as not to startle the creature he held. "She was just born this spring, *chérie*. Her parents are magnificent, and she gives promise of being even better."

"Why can I not have a fully grown bird?" Belle wondered.

"Because I want you to help with the training of your merlin," Hugh said. "That means you must devise a whistle signal to which she, and no other bird, will answer. She must bond with you, and be yours alone. To do this with a bird, you must be a part of her training. Now, what will you name her? No one else may name her but you, ma Belle."

Suddenly, the little falcon stretched her neck out and delicately nipped at Isabelle's sleeve.

Startled, she drew back, but then laughed. "She has named herself, my lord. 'Couper' is her name. I think it appropriate."

Hugh set the bird back on its perch. Couper, the French for *nip*. He chuckled. "Aye, 'tis a good name for her."

"How am I to train her?" Belle asked. "I know nothing about

hawks. My father once had a peregrine, but I was not allowed to touch it."

"Couper," he said, "has already been prepared for her training. Her talons have been trimmed. Some people seal a young bird's eyes by temporarily sewing them shut. I do not. I prefer to use a hood." He held up a small leather cap that he now fit over the merlin's head. "She is quite used to it," he said. "You can see the strips of leather with their brass ringed ends fastened about her legs. They are called jesses. The tiny bells attached to her feet allow the falconer to ascertain her movements." He gently stroked the young bird. "Couper has already been taught to stand on a hand. Now, Belle, I want you to whistle a phrase of song. Then put your hand against the merlin's chest, encouraging her to step on it. You must always whistle the same few notes, *chérie*. It is a signal between you. That way no one can steal your bird away from you, for it is not just the music itself that Couper will obey, it is your tone which cannot be imitated."

Belle thought a moment, and then whistled four short, sweet notes while at the same time pressing her hand gently against the bird's chest. The falcon hesitated, but Belle whistled her notes again, her hand insistent. Couper stepped upon the young woman's hand, and Belle caught her breath in wonder, her hand reaching out to caress the merlin. The bird was dusky brown with a darker banded tail. She chittered softly at Belle's touch, shifting herself nervously.

"Walk about with her," Hugh commanded his wife, "and talk to her. She needs the reassurance of your gentle voice."

"Oh, Couper," Belle said softly, "you are such a beautiful little maiden, or at least you will be when you are fully feathered. I love you already. We are going to be great friends, are we not, *ma petite*? We will learn together, for I have never had a falcon, nor have you ever had a mistress, but Hugh says your parents are fine birds, so you must be a fine bird, too. It would not do to disgrace your family now, would it?"

Hugh watched the girl moving about murmuring to the

young falcon. Now and again he could make out a word or two, but Belle's conversation was for her merlin alone. Occasionally she would stroke the creature, who quickly became used to her light, gentle touch. Finally, after a few minutes had passed, Hugh said, "Bring Couper here, ma Belle. I want you to feed her. Lind," he called to the young falconer, "bring the bucket."

Isabelle turned, surprised, for she had not noticed anyone else in the mews before, but now she could see that both Lind and Faer were there. She blushed, thankful she had not been intimate with Hugh before strangers. "What is in the bucket?" she asked her husband, attempting to cover her confusion and shyness before Lind and Faer.

"Chicken," Hugh told her. "Take a piece, and feed it to Couper."

Lind held up the bucket, and Belle drew out a section of raw poultry, offering it to Couper, who greedily snatched it from her mistress's hand using her beak and a single claw. She began to tear apart her breakfast while standing upon her other foot.

Isabelle laughed softly. "You are very greedy, *ma petite*," she said. "You have, I can see, a great zest for life." She allowed the bird to continue to perch upon her hand while it ate. When the falcon had finished her meal, Isabelle carefully placed her back upon her perch, crooning to her, telling her how good she was.

Hugh nodded his approval, his eyes meeting those of the two falconers, who nodded back at their lord, smiling. "There is a leash attached to the perch, *chérie*," Hugh said to Belle. "Tie it to one of the rings and make it fast. That way Couper is unable to leave the mews, but the leash is long enough that she may fly, yet always return to her correct perch."

Isabelle did as he bid her, and then together they left the mews to return to the hall. "Couper is wonderful!" she enthused. "I love her already, my lord. Thank you."

"You have done very well for a first lesson, ma Belle, but

the lessons will get harder, I warn you. Still, I think it important for you to train Couper yourself. It will teach you the value of the birds and the care that must be taken with them. Many," he explained, "take the birds from their nests in the wild. That is far too simple, and depletes their population. It is harder to breed them and train them. The birds bred and trained by the Merlin-sone family are prized in both England and in Normandy because they are taught well. They are healthy. Each day from now on you will work with Lind to train Couper."

"More lessons?" she teased him.

He smiled as they entered the hall. "Father Bernard tells me you write a fine hand now, *chérie*, and your reading skills grow with each passing day. I am proud of you."

"I can both read and write in English and in French, my lord," she said, "and soon I shall begin Latin. Father Bernard says I have a head for learning, unnatural as that may be in a woman. He grumbles greatly at me about it, but then he says he must continue to teach me else he might not be prepared when we give him children to teach. I am learning my numbers, too. It is far easier than when I had to keep everything in my head," Isabelle admitted.

"You will be a fine chatelaine for Langston when I go to serve the king, and Rolf with me," Hugh told her.

Belle stepped around in front of her husband, looking anxiously into his face. "Will it be soon?" she asked him.

He nodded. "I expect a summons any day now, ma Belle. As I came back across the countryside from Worcester, I heard much gossip. Many of the great Norman lords have already shown their disloyalty to King Henry. The king sent ships out in an effort to stop Duke Robert from his folly, but some of the captains have gone over to the enemy. For the moment, the brothers but spar with one another. Soon, however, there will be war; a war for England. I had hoped that this war would be fought in Normandy, but it would seem that King Henry will make his brother come to him, that he fight this battle on his own ground."

"Then that is why Richard dared to come here," Belle said, and then she clapped her hand over her mouth. "Ohhh! I did not tell you!"

"Tell me what, *chérie*?" he asked her.

"I meant to tell you last night, but I was distracted in the bath, and then *afterward*." Her eyes met his, and she could not help the giggle that escaped her. Then she grew serious. "While you were gone away, my lord, my brother, the Sieur de Manneville, came to Langston claiming to be its rightful lord. I sent him packing." Then she explained.

"You did not even allow him the courtesy of remaining the night under our roof?" he said, astounded, and then he laughed. "You were wise, Belle. You did well."

"That is what Rolf said," she replied.

"How in all of this did you manage to get your mother to wed with my steward?" he inquired, more curious now than he had been before.

"When Richard saw he could not force his man upon me, he suggested the fellow marry my mother. I told my brother that Mother was already married to Rolf, and Father Bernard backed me up. Of course, after Richard had departed, my mother had no choice but to wed Rolf. Father Bernard swore it would be a blot on his immortal soul if she did not," Belle finished, laughing.

"You trapped your quarry quite neatly," Hugh approved. "I am glad you love me, ma Belle, and are not my enemy."

"Oh, for all her protests to the contrary," Belle said, "my mother is quite content to be Rolf's wife. He is nothing like my father. The lady Alette will, I am quite certain, rule her roost without any interference from her besotted husband. We must soon send to Northamptonshire for stone to build them a house of their own, my lord."

"I would attach it to the keep," he said, "thereby making a second tower within the bailey. Its entry will be only through our hall, for safety's sake."

"That will take several years' time to build, my lord," Belle noted. "Can we not build them a house of wood until their tower is completed? With my mother's child due between Christmas and Twelfth Night, we will soon be crowded out, particularly if I should have a child."

"Are you with child?" he asked eagerly.

Belle shook her head regretfully. "Not yet," she said sadly.

"You are young," he told her. "There is time."

"But what if you are killed in this war?" Belle suddenly cried.

"I will not be," he said with such certainty that she believed him. "I have too much to live for, ma Belle, *n'est-ce pas*?"

Impulsively, she flung herself against his chest, silently imploring his reassurance and his comfort. "I will kill you, Hugh Fauconier, if anything should happen to you," she told him with perfect illogic.

Three days later the king's messenger arrived, summoning Sir Hugh Fauconier, lord of Langston Keep, and his steward, Sir Rolf de Briard, to the defense of England in King Henry's name. They were to bring with them twenty men, trained and armed at Hugh's expense. Their term of service would be until England was secured in King Henry's name.

# ▓Chapter 8

They were alone again, Isabelle and her mother, but it was different this time. Different from this same time last year. Different from only five months ago. Now she and Alette were both married. Her father dead. Her mother expecting another child. One thing had not changed, however. Langston was still hers. Once again it had been left in her keeping, but now she knew how to husband it better. Now she had the support of Father Bernard. Hugh was gone, and Rolf as well. The two young squires she had not even gotten to know yet were gone, and twenty of Langston's best young men with them. The knights and their squires had left upon horseback; the Langston men, archers all, on foot, their crossbows slung across their broad backs.

She watched them all go, looking into each familiar face as they stood in the bailey waiting to leave. How many of those familiar faces would not come home, she wondered mournfully, suddenly aware for the first time of how truly serious this all was. She had clutched her husband's hand then, silently pleading with him to have a care, to come home to her. Isabelle could not ask him to remain. She knew it was impossible. She would not shame Hugh Fauconier publicly before Rolf and his men.

"Work every day with Couper. Lind will instruct you in exactly what you must do. I want to see great improvement in the merlin when I return home, ma Belle. We will hunt together, you and I."

"Will this be a long war, my lord?" Belle wondered.

He shook his head. "I do not think so, *chérie*. While I am gone, however, I expect you to take good care of Langston, even as you have in the past. I will come back to you by autumn." He brushed her lips lightly and then left her.

Midsummer's eve came, and Belle gave the serfs a holiday from their labors that they might celebrate. The fields and gardens were lush with growth, and all signs pointed to an excellent harvest. At Langston there was no word at all as to what was happening. They were so far off the beaten track that unless a message was specifically bound for Langston, they were not likely to hear anything. In one sense Isabelle thought it was a relief; but in another it was torture.

That night the lady of Langston stood upon the walls of the keep, silently watching the midsummer fires. She could see the shadowy figures of the dancers nearest the keep. It was a primitive celebration, and Belle, knowing what all the passionate dancing would lead to, longed for her husband. Alette, however, through the early weeks of her confinement and beginning to show just the faintest of bellies, was placid and content as Isabelle had never seen her.

"How can you be so calm not knowing what is happening?" she demanded irritably of her parent. "There could have been some horrendous battle. Hugh and Rolf might be horribly wounded!"

"Then they would be brought home so we might nurse them," Alette responded reasonably. "If you are not going to eat that dish of cherries, Isabelle, I would be obliged if you would give them to me. They are absolutely delicious. Why, you haven't even tasted them."

"I don't want them, madame," Belle replied shortly. She hated not knowing what was happening. When her father had gone with Duke Robert on his crusade, she had not cared, for she was but a heedless child, but now it was her husband who had gone off, and she loved him. She couldn't understand how

Alette, if she really loved Rolf, could be so composed and so tranquil. It was absolutely aggravating! Still, the entire countryside seemed wrapped in summer, and very placid.

And it was peaceful. The king's position was a relatively strong one. He had made alliances with both King Philip of France and the Count of Flanders, a relation. Neither France nor Flanders wanted to see England and Normandy united again. It was best that the warring brothers be kept separate, and each in his own domain. Henry's other ally was the Archbishop of Canterbury, Anselm, who had been exiled during most of William Rufus's reign. One of Henry's first acts had been to recall the archbishop, who preached in favor of Henry's claim to England's throne. The king's enemies, however, were some of the most powerful of the Anglo-Norman lords. They hoped that with Henry deposed and gone, and Duke Robert, a fine soldier, but an incompetent ruler who would more than likely remain in Normandy, in his place, they would be free to rule England. The most dangerous of these lords was Robert de Belleme, who held the Welsh marches. He was both ruthless and cruel, and cared only for his family's advantage.

In July word came via a passing peddler that the Norman fleet had been sighted. Their current course would bring them to England in the vicinity of Pevensey. Duke Robert, instead, landed to the south at Portsmouth on July 19. He and his army headed for London, but Henry, a fierce fighter and far better tactician than his eldest brother, quickly moved his forces to check Duke Robert. William the Conqueror's two surviving sons met on the London road. Archbishop Anselm stood between them, negotiating the treaty that would spare England another fruitless war.

King Henry would concede his Norman holdings to Duke Robert, and pay his brother two thousand marks of silver each year. Those who had turned traitor against Henry would be pardoned, and their lands restored. Whichever of the brothers died first, and without legitimate male issue, the survivor would inherit his sibling's holdings. Since Queen Matilda was with child, this last was thought irrelevant, especially as Robert's duchess was also young and would surely bear sons.

The king, his face long and sad, waited with bated breath for the duke to accept the terms as dictated by Archbishop Anselm. *Take the terms, my dull-witted elder brother,* Henry silently prayed. He sighed gustily, and was hard put to keep from shouting his triumph when Duke Robert, grinning, certain he had bested his little brother, said, "Done, by God!"

"God bless you both, my sons," the archbishop said piously. "You have saved us all much suffering. Both Normandy and England will praise your names. My clerks will draw up the compact between you, and you will sign it in the morning. For now, let us eat together."

An enormous tent had been set up in the center of the English camp for the nobles to feast together. A rough high board had been fashioned, and three chairs were set behind it. Archbishop Anselm sat in the center, the king to one side of him, the duke on his left hand. Below, tables and benches were placed, and with much merriment the celebration began. Servants ran back and forth bringing trenchers of bread and pitchers of wine. Outside, whole sheep, sides of beef, and whole pigs roasted over open fires. Musicians moved about this temporary hall, playing and singing. For all the supposed goodwill, the king's adherents stayed on one side of the tent and the duke's men on the other.

Henry was feeling quite mellowed now. He had avoided a very nasty conflict by virtue of his own cleverness. Two thousand marks of silver was little enough to pay for England's throne. Not that he couldn't have beaten Robert in a contest of arms. His foolish brother's withdrawal, Henry thought, would give him time to consolidate his position further. The northern border with Scotland was secured by his marriage to the sister of Scotland's king. And England would be further secured by the removal of those traitors who now sat eating his meat and drinking his wine, comforted by the belief that he had pardoned them. Well, he would not destroy them for this particular fault. But he would find others, and he would rid England of men like Robert de Belleme, who held the Welsh marches in his tight grip. Shortly he would not. *And I will have Normandy, too,* Henry thought coldly. *Not today, and perhaps not tomorrow, but I will have it all the same within five years.* He smiled to himself, his eyes sweeping about the room, mentally noting the disloyal, and those loyal to him as well. He saw his childhood friend, Hugh Fauconier, with Rolf de Briard. They had answered his call, and come with twenty men who were well provisioned and, from the look of them, well-trained.

The king whispered to his page, "Go to Sir Hugh Fauconier and tell him that I would see him and Sir Rolf de Briard in my tent when this evening is over."

"Yes, my lord," the boy replied, and hurried off to do his master's bidding.

Henry saw Hugh nod curtly in answer to the page's summons. He smiled. *Faithful Hugh.* He remembered his mother telling him as a child that Hugh, treated with courtesy and respect, would be the best friend he would ever have. He could almost hear his mother's sweet voice even now, over the din in the tent. He could see her pretty face. Her youngest child, he had been her favorite, the one to whom she had left all of her English holdings.

"Hugh Fauconier may not be a great lord, or the son of a great lord, Henry," his mother had told him, "but he has good breeding. The line of Merlin-sone descends from a younger son of the kings of Mercia. His father's people were cousins of the lady Godiva, the Earl of Wessex's wife, which is why they followed Harold Godwinson into battle at Hastings. Once they pledge their loyalty, they are true to it. Hugh's maternal grandfather pledged his faith to your father as King Edward's heir long before the battle which won your father England. They are not a powerful family, nor have they great riches. Their strength is in their loyalty, and their honesty. Gain Hugh Fauconier's true friendship, Henry, and this Saxon lordling will always serve you well. You will find as you grow older, my son, that good and faithful friends are as rare as hen's teeth."

Henry Beauclerc had accepted his mother's word. She had never lied to him or played him false. He trusted her as he trusted no other. Besides, he had liked the young Saxon boy come to court to be his companion. Unlike so many of the little Norman boys he knew, Hugh Fauconier was friendly and fair. He did not cheat, and when others did, Hugh would shake his head and invariably say, " 'Tis no victory if it is not won honestly." At first the others would mock him, but gradually they ceased their cheating because Hugh's simple words shamed them. There was something about this tall, plain-faced Saxon boy that made them want to please him, become his friend. Hugh, however, while courteous to all, chose his own friends. Prince Henry was one, and Rolf de Briard the other. And as his mother had promised him, Hugh Fauconier served the sons of William of Normandy faithfully.

After the feasting was done, Hugh came to the king's tent with Rolf. The three men greeted each other affectionately. A page brought goblets of good wine, and the trio sat together for the first time in many months as old and cherished friends.

"Tell me how Langston pleases you, Hugh," the king said. "Your missive told me little more than the plain facts."

"I found the estate in good condition, my lord. Belle had managed it well in her father's absence, for Robert de Manneville had scarcely left England when the old steward died. Everything was as it should be. The most amazing thing was that because she could neither read nor write then, she kept the records of everything done, and the figures, in her pretty head."

"Then you need have no fears for Langston in your absence," the king noted. "Is it a pretty place?"

"Great stretches of fields, and softly rolling low hills, my lord. Some forest. Aye, a very sweet land. I thank you for returning it to me. There are still some serfs alive on it who remember my family."

"And the lady, Hugh?" The king's eyes twinkled. "Is she as fine as the land? She sounds a most competent and perhaps even a frightening lady for one as young as she."

Hugh laughed. "The serfs used to call her Belle from Hell, my liege," he said. "She has a fierce temper, and would not allow them any quarter. She is strict in her judgments, but none ever called her unfair. I think they resented her most because she was a female. I find her a good wife, however. I am content with Belle."

"Father Bernard is happy?" the king asked politely.

"We are building him a church, and his own house," Hugh said. "I think he enjoys ministering to Langston's folk far more than he enjoyed being one of your many chaplains, my liege. He is filled with energy at all he must do and the many duties that claim him."

"And you, Rolf." King Henry turned to his other companion. "Are you pleased with your position as Langston's steward? You will be looking for a wife soon, I have no doubt, now that you can afford one." The king chuckled.

"I have already remedied that lack in my life, my liege," Rolf told Henry. "When we first came to Langston, I fell in love at first sight with Robert de Manneville's widow, the lady Alette. She became my wife, and we are expecting our first child around the feast of the Nativity. Hugh is building us a house within the bailey of the keep."

The king laughed heartily. "You are a sly fellow, Rolf de Briard, and a fortunate one, too, I think. Is the widow pretty, then?"

"My mother-in-law is a beauty," Hugh told Henry. "Prettier than my Belle, though she be lovely, too."

"I am pleased that it has all gone so well for you, my lords," the king said to them. "I need a strong England, and loyal knights. I know I can count upon you both now that this matter with my brother has been settled *for the time being*."

Hugh and Rolf immediately understood the king's emphasis, and nodded silently. "We are always here for you, my liege," Hugh told him. Then, lowering his voice, he asked, "What will you do with the disloyal? You have after all promised to pardon them."

The king smiled wolfishly. "Indeed I have, but there are other ways of containing the rebellious, and their rebellions, my friends."

"We are with you, my liege," Hugh replied firmly.

They spoke on until finally the king admitted to being tired, and his companions left him. In the morning the king's men and the duke's men came together to witness the signing of the peace accord between the two brothers. Afterward the king called to Hugh Fauconier.

"Come and pay your respects to Duke Robert, Hugh. He wishes to speak with you about your hawks."

Hugh came forward and bowed before the duke, a handsome man with strong features and mild blue eyes. "How may I serve you, my lord duke?" he inquired politely.

"Henry tells me you are now raising those fine birds that your grandfather once raised. Is this so, my lord?"

"My mews is but newly built, my lord duke," Hugh said. "My grandfather still raises his hawks in Worcester. I have several breeding pairs, and some young birds this year, but little else."

"I want a gyrfalcon," Duke Robert said. "It must be snowy white and trained to hunt cranes. Can you supply me with one?"

"Not until next spring, my lord duke," Hugh answered honestly. "I have a fine young bird, born two months ago, of snow-white parents. Her mother is the best gyrfalcon I have ever owned. Her offspring should be even better once she is trained, but the training will take time."

Duke Robert nodded. "I am willing to wait for a bird trained by the line of Merlin-sone, Hugh Fauconier. When she is ready, bring her to me yourself so that you may personally instruct my falconer in this bird's care and feeding. Such a creature is true royalty."

Hugh looked to the king. "With my liege's permission, my lord duke," he said.

"You have my permission, Hugh, to take the bird to Normandy. Let it be a gift from me to you, Robert," Henry said graciously.

The duke inclined his head toward his younger brother. "My thanks, Henry. It will be an expensive gift, I think." Then he smiled.

The king laughed. "What will you take for the bird, Hugh? Will a quarter knight's fee do you?" He then turned to his brother. "Hugh's estates at Langston are worth two knights' fees to me each year, plus the service he renders me. He is a faithful man."

*"Langston?"* The duke thought a moment, and then he said, "Henry, I must speak to you about Langston. The son of the previous lord is disputing its ownership. He has asked me to speak to you about it."

"Is he here?" King Henry asked.

"Aye, he is," Duke Robert said.

"Call him forward, and we shall settle the matter now," the king said. Then he winked at Hugh, for he had heard the previous evening about Richard de Manneville's visit to Langston.

Richard de Manneville came from among the ranks of the duke's men, bowing first to his liege lord and then to the king.

Henry noted the younger man's error, or was it sly discourtesy? "What is your claim to Langston manor?" he asked Richard de Manneville in a stern voice.

"Langston was given to my father outright by your father, sire. I am my father's sole surviving, legitimate heir. The manor is mine by right of inheritance," the Sieur de Manneville told the king.

"Your father made a will, my lord, leaving Langston to your sister Isabelle to be her dower, and an inheritance from him. A copy of that will was among the papers of my brother, William Rufus, then the King of England, for it was written here at court and approved by him. I learned of your father's death before you even thought to inform your sister. As king it was my right to claim the wardship of such a young, innocent, undefended maiden. So I did. In my capacity as your sister's guardian, I gave her in marriage to my own man, Sir Hugh Fauconier. Your sister is content with the arrangement, as am I," the king finished. His tone was final.

"That being the case," Duke Robert said, "the Sieur de Manneville can surely offer me no further objection, or make any claim upon this manor." Duke Robert was a fair man.

Richard de Manneville's dark eyes were angry, but he knew he had no other choice than to accept the decision rendered by England's king, and his own duke. He bowed to the two men with ill-disguised bad humor, but the king was not yet finished with him.

"Come, my lord," he said in jovial tones. "You have not yet met your sister's husband." He drew Hugh forward. "My lords, greet one another, and give each other the kiss of peace."

Hugh, amused by the situation, did his king's bidding. His brother-in-law was stiff with anger, but Hugh pretended not to notice. "Come, Richard de Manneville," he said, "and let us share a cup of wine together. I am sorry I was not at Langston when you called. My good lady wife, of course, informed me of your visit."

"And did the bad-tempered wench tell you that she would not even offer me a night's hospitality beneath your roof, my lord?" Richard de Manneville said irritably. "I had hoped marriage would mature my sister, but I see you are as lax with her as was our father."

"My wife is a unique creature, Brother Richard," Hugh said, pressing a goblet of the king's wine into the Sieur de Manneville's hand. "She did not trust you, I fear, but I am certain 'twas just foolishness upon her part, eh? Women are such skittish creatures."

"That is true enough," Richard de Manneville agreed grudgingly, raising the goblet to his lips and drinking deeply.

"Then it is resolved between us, and we are friends?" Hugh said with a smile.

Richard de Manneville shrugged. "Very well," he said. "Besides, it is unlikely we shall ever meet again, Hugh Fauconier. There is little need for me to leave my estates but for my service to Duke Robert each year. I have a son now, and the promise from my wife of other children. I wish you the same good fortune. I hope my sister will prove a better breeder than my stepmother, the lady Alette. She could only give my father Isabelle in all the years that they were married. Perhaps it was for the best, however."

Hugh raised his own goblet to Richard. "I wish you a safe journey home to Normandy," he said quietly.

When the two men had emptied their goblets, they parted.

"So that is the end of it, then," Luc de Sai murmured, coming to Richard de Manneville's side.

"How little you know me, Luc," was the reply. "It may take a bit of time, but Langston will be mine one day. Let my sister and her husband believe that they have won. Let them be lulled into a sense of false security. In the end I shall triumph. Be patient."

"And your sister will be mine?" his companion asked.

"If you want her, aye," Richard de Manneville answered.

"I want her," Luc de Sai said. "I suspect her passion is as fiery as her red-gold hair. I will enjoy making her howl with pleasure."

"How basic your needs are," the sieur replied coldly.

"The simpler a man's needs are, the better, my lord. That way he is rarely disappointed," Luc de Sai responded, surprising his master with his sagacity.

Duke Robert remained in his brother's kingdom of England until Michaelmas, and everywhere the duke visited, his men caused difficulty and damage. Angered by being denied a war with its spoils, they had become difficult to control. Warned by their thoughtful monarch, England's citizens buried their valuables, sent their daughters to safety, and bore the abuse. King Henry allowed the Normans a certain latitude, not wanting to damage the fragile peace. He was as relieved as his subjects, however, to see Duke Robert and his forces embark for their brief voyage across the channel that separated their two realms. Then the king dismissed his armies, sending most of them home.

Hugh Fauconier and the Langston men returned on a rainy October morning. Hugh was happy to see his keep, and happier yet that there had been no war, that he could return with all the men who had ridden out with him in early July. Rolf beamed with delight to find Alette, her rounded belly very visible now beneath her skirts, eager to receive him. Leaping eagerly from his horse, he clasped her to him, kissing her soundly.

"Gracious, my lord!" Alette emerged from the embrace rosy with blushes and her great happiness to have him safely home.

Hugh dismounted his stallion, his eyes never leaving those of Belle's. She stood quietly awaiting him. Her elegance and her dignity both impressed and delighted him. She was every inch the chatelaine.

"Welcome home, my dear lord," she greeted him. Her look was a passionate one, although her calm demeanor would have fooled anyone not acquainted with Isabelle of Langston.

"I am glad to be home, madame," he said, stripping off his riding gloves. "Shall we go indoors? I have had enough of the damp this day, and long for the fire."

"Some wine, too, I have no doubt," Belle responded. "And the meal is almost ready, my lord. You and the men will be hungry after your many hours in the saddle." She turned, and with him following, walked into the hall. "Afterward you will want a bath, and my stepfather, too," Isabelle said. "We are ready for you, my lord."

"We will eat first, and then I will let Rolf bathe. I want to visit the mews. That young gyrfalcon hatched by my Neige this spring has been promised to Duke Robert. I am to go to

Normandy next spring and bring her to him. She is to be trained to hunt cranes."

"Then the war is over?" Belle asked, taking a goblet of rich, sweet red wine from a servant and handing it to her husband.

"It was settled without any blood being spilt," Hugh said, and explained the terms of the agreement to his wife.

"I think the king foolish to pardon those lords who rebelled against him," Belle noted. "They should be punished."

Hugh chuckled. "Do not fear, ma Belle," he said, and took a gulp of his wine. "King Henry is no fool. While he has pardoned Robert de Belleme and the others for their treason, they are fools if they think him content with the matter. The king is his father's son. He does not forget a fault done him. He will find other ways to punish them. The agreement so carefully crafted by the archbishop will not hold forever. The king means to have Normandy, and in the end he will have it. The duke is a fine soldier, but so is King Henry, who has an advantage over his brother because he is far more clever than Duke Robert. Be patient and you will see, *chérie*." He swallowed down the rest of his wine and kissed her cheek. "I hope you are well rested, madame." His look was smoldering.

The meal was served, and the hall rang with boisterous voices, as it had not in several months. Isabelle smiled to see the healthy appetites of her husband and his men. It was good to have them home again. After they had eaten, Alette took her husband to the bathing chamber, but Hugh, true to his word, hurried out to the mews, Isabelle by his side.

"Wait until you see how Couper has grown and how far her training has progressed," Isabelle said proudly. "Ah, there she is. Lind is weathering her. Good day, my darling little beauty," Belle cooed. Reaching out, she gently encouraged the merlin onto her fist, murmuring affectionate little words to the young falcon, stroking her tenderly.

Hugh nodded, pleased with his wife's ability. "Have you taken her on horseback yet, ma Belle?" he asked her.

"Twice, just this week," Belle replied, caressing the

excitable bird, who, hearing an unfamiliar voice, had grown skittish. "Easy, my beauty," she purred. "This is your master, and you must be used to his voice as well as mine and Lind's."

The merlin looked directly at Belle, her gaze arrogant, and then she began to preen her feathers vigorously as if to indicate her lack of interest in them both.

Isabelle laughed as she set the young falcon back upon her stone perch. "Lind says that next week we are going to teach her to hunt by means of the lure, my lord." She scratched the bird on the back of its neck before turning away.

"The first serious step," Hugh replied. Then looking about, he spotted the young gyrfalcon that had been promised to Duke Robert. Seeing her, he called to the falconer, Alain, who was responsible for the large hawks. "We have a royal master for Blanca," he told Alain. "She must be taught to hunt cranes before we bring her to Normandy next spring. The king has given her as a gift to Duke Robert."

"She is worthy of royalty," Alain said. "I'll begin her training in the marshes myself, my lord. She'll be ready."

"How can you teach her to hunt cranes specifically?" Belle asked him as they walked toward the keep.

"Her lure will be made from a pair of crane's wings," he said. "Would you like to see some of her training, ma Belle?"

Belle nodded vigorously. "Aye!"

He pulled her hard against him in the shadow of the porch. One arm was tight about her waist. His other hand sought and found a breast, which he fondled vigorously. His lips murmured hotly against her ear. "I want to fuck you, wife. Until I saw you as we rode into the bailey, I did not realize how much I missed you, Isabelle." Finding her nipple, he pinched it gently several times.

Her heart leapt madly in her chest. Her legs were suddenly weak. She feared they would not hold her. "My lord! What if someone should come and find us thus?" She could feel his hardness against her.

"They will say the lord of Langston Keep lusts after his

fair young wife," he answered her, his lips tickling her neck just beneath her ear. "Do not demur, madame, or I shall take you here right where we stand, and the devil take the consequences."

"You would not dare," she gasped, partly shocked, partly fascinated to see if he really would carry out his outrageous threat.

Hugh laughed wickedly, pushing his wife back against the stone wall of the porch, his mouth finding hers in a scorching kiss. Despite the ardent nature of his lips, Belle was aware that he was fumbling with his clothing. Suddenly, and without even breaking off their kiss, he slid his hand swiftly up beneath her skirts to cup her buttocks and lift her up. She tore her face from his, gasping with surprise as he entered her, iron-hard and eager.

*"Ohhhhh! Ahhhhhh! Huuugh!"* She wrapped her legs about him, panting with pleasure. "Yes! Yes! Yessss! Oh, Holy Mother, I've missed you, my love!" She kissed his face frantically, her own lust well-engaged. She didn't give a tinker's damn if someone saw them. She wanted him!

At first he pushed into her with slow, deliberate strokes of his manhood, half his early pleasure gained from the little moans issuing forth from her. Then, as his passion mounted, he moved with harder, faster strokes, making her sob as he pleasured her, making her shudder as they reached their heaven together in a sizzling burst of longing satisfied. Only then did he lower her down, slowly, holding her close against him. "Hellion," he groaned low, "you try my patience."

Isabelle laughed weakly. "My lord, I should not have believed such a thing possible. I will not tempt you again to such rashness . . . but it was wonderful!" Beyond the porch she could see the rain pouring down in silvery-gray sheets, and she realized why they had not been discovered by anyone. She nestled against his chest.

Hugh smoothed the red-gold head that lay against his tunic. He hadn't realized until just a few moments ago that she had the power to drive him to utter rashness. He was well and truly caught by the bonds of love; but it was not, he decided, such a bad thing. He kissed the top of her head. "No woman has ever excited me so, ma Belle. No one but you. I do not think I like being parted from you, *chérie*."

"I am glad of it, my lord," she told him, "for I missed you as well." Then she looked up at him with a smile. "Should we not go in now, my lord? I am certain that my mother has thoroughly bathed my stepfather by now. They will be engaged in far sweeter pursuits at this moment, I am certain."

"Not with your mother so far gone with child," he said. "Rolf knows he must contain his desire for now. We have spoken on it."

Isabelle laughed. "How little you men know of women," she said. "My mother says there are ways for a husband and wife to gain their pleasure even when a woman is full with her babe."

"There are?" He was surprised, intrigued.

She nodded. "So my mother says. Soon she will have to transmit her information to me, my lord, I think."

He set her back from him, eyes wide with delight. *"You are with child, ma Belle?"*

"I believe so, my lord," she said calmly. "My mother concurs, and she should certainly know better than I."

"How can you be certain?" His face was alight with happiness.

"I have had no woman's flow since before you went away to war, my lord. And you will notice a change already in my breasts when we are together later. If it is a son, I would be happy if he was your image, but oh, I hope our daughters will not have your face! We have not the means to dower plain girls!"

*"When?"* His voice was strangled.

"In early spring, I think," she replied.

"You cannot ride," he declared, and opening the door to the keep, drew her inside into the warmth of the hall.

"Hugh," she said, exasperated, "if I thought you were going to be such a fool about this, I should not have told you yet. How am I to train Couper if I cannot go out with her? She is mine, not yours, or Lind's. Ask my mother. I am in no danger for another month or two."

"I will not have my son endangered on a whim," Hugh said in pompous tones such as she had never before heard him use.

"*Your son,* my lord? And what of your wife, or do you suddenly just consider me in terms of my ability to breed for you?" Belle demanded scathingly. "A creature to be as easily replaced as any breeding stock?"

"I did not mean that, and you well know it, madame," he said. "Do not try to twist the matter about as you are wont to do when you cannot obtain your own way." He glared at her.

Belle glared back, not in the least intimidated. "This is my child, too," she said angrily. "I would not endanger it, my lord, I am not that selfish; but ride I will for at least another month so I may train my merlin. Couper will be confused should we suddenly cease her training. There can be no harm in it if I do not gallop. I shall but walk my mare, and stand while waiting for the falcon to return with the lure, Hugh. I will not really hunt. You may even come with me when I take Couper out so you may be reassured that I take no chances."

"I do not know," he said. "I must speak with your mother."

Belle smiled sweetly. "Thank you, my lord," she answered him, knowing that she had won her point. "Come," she said, holding out her hand to him. "You will want your bath now, Hugh."

Hugh Fauconier shook his head at her. "If I had known you were with child, Belle, I should not have been so rough with you earlier."

She laughed, and the sound was decidedly seductive. "I am not some delicate little flower, Hugh," was her response. "I rather liked that bit of naughtiness. I am only glad the rain prevented anyone from catching us at our passion." Then she laughed again, and this time the sound was most assuredly wicked.

The next · day, they rode together with Lind to begin Couper's first serious training session. Lind had fastened a thin length of line, called the creance, to the end of the bird's leash. When they reached the open field where they were to work with the falcon, Hugh helped his wife from her mount, and Lind transferred Couper to her mistress's gloved fist. Belle removed the bird's hood, all the while whistling the familiar notes to which she had accustomed the falcon over these last few months. A piece of meat, tied to the lure, was handed to her, and repeating the snatch of song Belle fed a bit of the meat to Couper, her slim fingers wrapped tightly about the creature's jesses.

Lind now took the meat and began to move away from the bird, yet keeping the lure with its meat bait clearly in her vision. Finally he stopped and placed it on the ground. Isabelle released Couper, the creance unwinding in her hand as the bird flew the short distance between her mistress and the meat. Lind reached out to take the meat, whistling the falcon's call notes to encourage her onward. Finally he stopped and set the meat before Couper. When she fell upon it, he took her up, lure and all, pulling the jesses tight, and returned her to Isabelle. The game was repeated several times, until finally Hugh called a stop to it.

"She is going to be an excellent hunter, ma Belle," he said, in praise of the merlin. "She never once hesitated in going after the lure today, and it's only her first time."

"What will happen next?" Isabelle asked her husband as she drew the dark leather hood back over Couper's bright, sharp eyes, before handing her off to Lind to transport.

They walked together across the field, their horses following behind with the falconer.

"We will play this game with the meated lure for several more days," Hugh said. "If she continues to respond as well as she did today, then we shall begin to whirl the lure in the air as you give her her call notes. If she is as intelligent as I believe her to be, Couper will quickly learn to leap from your fist and go after the lure in the air. Once she does that, the creance can be removed. Your merlin will then be able to fly free and hunt.

"We will use a rabbit skin, stuffed with meat, as bait. Lind will drag it about in front of the bird. We will teach her to swoop and pounce upon her victim by jerking her up tightly before she can gain her objective. The next part of her training will involve the dogs. They will drive a live rabbit or small game bird from its cover for Couper to hunt. Once she has killed her quarry, its heart will be removed and fed to her as a reward for her good behavior."

"Should I not be the one to drag the bait about the field?" Belle asked him.

"Aye," he answered her honestly, "but as Lind will increase his speed on horseback to give your merlin a good workout, and you have said you will not ride at breakneck speed, it is Lind who must complete this part of Couper's training. He will use your call notes, Belle, and if you wish, you may feed the heart to your bird to reinforce the bond between you both."

"I do indeed," she told him. "I am not squeamish like some."

Over the next few weeks the three of them worked together to train the merlin. Hugh also worked with the young gyrfalcon promised to Duke Robert. Her training was very much like the merlin's, up to a point. Once the gyrfalcon had become adept at hunting rabbits and smaller birds, she was acquainted with her real quarry. A live crane was staked out in a meadow, eyes sealed, beak tied so it could not fight back, its sharp claws filed blunt. Meat was tied to the hapless crane's back. Then the gyr-falcon was shown her prey. Blanca, intelligent, immediately knew her duty, and killed the crane the first time. Its heart was fed to her, and both Hugh and Alain knew the big bird would become a magnificent huntress.

Blanca was taught to recognize the call of the crane. Alain removed the larynx from her first kill, slit it, and blew into it, thereby producing the proper sound. He did this each time she was successful in her hunt. The gyrfalcon was now fed along with the greyhounds who would hunt with her, in order to foster comradeship between the creatures. The dogs were trained to help the gyrfalcon capture her prey.

Finally, the harvest in the field and the orchards was gathered, the granaries filled, and the weather grew cold. The days grew shorter and shorter. Hugh announced an end to Belle's sessions with Couper, but she did not complain, for in truth the little merlin was now well trained to hunt. Martinmas was celebrated with roast goose. The feast of the Nativity came, and on that very day, Alette de Briard gave birth to her first son, baptized Christian by Father Bernard on the feast of St. Stephen.

It was an easy birth, much to Alette's surprise, for she had suffered greatly when Isabelle had been born; but her son slid quickly from her body with barely a few hours' labor. Cradling him in the crook of her arm the proud mother declared, "I can already see he is like his father."

Rolf beamed with pride, fascinated by this tiny human with his halo of golden hair. *His son.* He had a son. He felt the tears welling up in his eyes, and when Hugh put his arm about his friend, Rolf looked up unashamed, saying, "May you be as fortunate, my lord."

"God willing," Hugh Fauconier said, looking to his wife, who smiled and nodded in agreement with them both.

# ⬛Chapter 9

"*L*ook at me," Isabelle of Langston wailed. "I look like a fat old sow! My gowns do not fit any longer, and I can hardly walk. My hair is positively lank! When will this child be born? *When?*"

Hugh pulled his wife back into their bed, his hand caressing her very distended belly. "The babe will be born when it is time for him to be born, *chérie*. Do not distress yourself."

Belle glared at him. "*Do not distress myself?* How kind of you, my lord. How noble! I am full to overflowing with your son, and you tell me not to distress myself? I can barely waddle about the hall to complete my duties. I cannot sleep for the child's constant kicking. He is a horrid little beast! If men bore this burden, Hugh Fauconier, you would not speak so lightly of *not distressing myself*! How would you like to be swollen up like some overripe fruit ready to burst?" She pulled angrily away from him, close to weeping.

He was hard put not to laugh at her anger, and yet he truly believed he understood how frustrating it must all be for her. His wife was used to being active. She hated the fact she could not hurry about as she was used to doing. And carrying a child had not improved Belle's temper. In recent weeks it had become shorter and shorter, to the point where the least word, or even a mere look, could set her to raving.

"It cannot be much longer, *chérie*," he told her. "I can only imagine how difficult it has been these last weeks, but just a little more time. Your mother says it won't be long, and she

172

should surely know." Hugh took his wife's hand in his and kissed it.

Isabelle burst into tears. "Tomorrow is my birthday," she said. "I will be seventeen. I am growing old, Hugh. *Old!*"

Again he was tempted to laugh, but he did not. "You are the most beautiful old woman I know," he told her.

"Oh, Hugh," she sniffled, suddenly, inexplicably, mollified by his kindness.

The following morning as her family gathered to wish her a happy birthday, a strange look came over Belle's face, and Alette instantly knew.

"You are in labor," she said in matter-of-fact tones to her daughter.

"I think so," Isabelle said, and then she winced. "I can feel something, Mother, and I want to push it out!" she cried.

"Good heavens!" Alette said, astounded. "Surely you are not going to deliver your child like some serf in the fields?" But the look on her daughter's face convinced her that perhaps Isabelle indeed was going to have her baby much sooner than later. "There is no time," she told the others. "Ida, Agneatha, help me get my daughter upon the high board! We have no other choice, I fear."

Before they might even move, Hugh lifted his wife up and laid her gently upon the cleared table. "Easy, ma Belle," he said in gentle tones. "Breathe deeply, *chérie*." He smoothed her brow.

"Rolf, bring a screen to shield the lady of Langston from prying eyes," Alette directed her husband. She began to remove her daughter's tunic and skirts, leaving her only in her chemise. Taking a knife, she slit the soft linen fabric on either side.

Hugh stood at the end of the table, bracing Isabelle, who was now in a seated position, her legs raised against her chest.

"Jesu! Marie!" Alette swore. "This grandchild of mine will not wait! Hurry, Rolf!"

The screen was set before the front of the high board to give

Isabelle some measure of privacy. Ida and Agneatha had
already gone for and returned with hot water, wine, clean
cloths, swaddling clothes, and the cradle for the soon-to-be-
born infant. Isabelle shrieked and, unable to help herself, bore
down. She could actually feel her body stretching, something
being expelled from her innermost regions. She cried out
again, and yet again. Hugh, his arms about her chest, whispered soft words of encouragement to her, pressing soft kisses
upon her head. Belle grunted hard, and then to her amazement
she felt free again. She heard a cry. *The cry of an infant.*

" 'Tis a fine boy," her mother said, holding up the howling,
bloodied little creature. "You have a son, Isabelle, Hugh."

"Give him to me! Give him to me!" Belle cried.

"Let us clean him off first," her mother counseled.

"No! Give him to me now!" Belle demanded, almost crying
as Alette set the child in her arms.

"Let me at least cut his cord," she said, but Isabelle did not
hear her. She was too fascinated, too enthralled by her son.

"Look, Hugh," she said. "See how tiny his hands and feet
are. I think he has your features. He'll be plain of face, as
his sire, my lord," but her voice was soft with her love for
them both.

"Shall we name him after your father?" Hugh asked.

"Nay," Belle told him. "I will name our son after *his* father.
He will be Hugh the Younger," and she relinquished hold of
the baby to her maidservant, Agneatha, so that he might be
cleaned up and set safely in his cradle.

Several weeks after the birth of Hugh the Younger, a summons
came from the king. Robert de Belleme, the Earl of Shrews-
bury, and his brothers—Arnulf, Earl of Pembroke, and Roger
of Poitou, Lord of Lancaster—had rebelled against the king.
The king's armies were assembling to be deployed along the
Marches of Wales, where the rebels had taken a stand. The
marches were an area along the English-Welsh border, and

along the southern coast of Wales. Hugh and Rolf marshaled their men, the troop having grown to fifty bowmen now.

"This time," Hugh told Isabelle, "not all will come back, I fear. This time there will be fighting."

"See that you come back," she told him. "And what of Blanca? If you answer the king's summons, you cannot possibly take her to Duke Robert. Will you offend him?"

"Send to the duke a missive telling him that I cannot come but will try to come in the autumn, or the following spring," Hugh told his wife.

Isabelle nodded, and then, kissing her husband, bravely bid him Godspeed.

Robert de Belleme and his two brothers, of the Montgomerie family, were each all-powerful men in their own right. United, they were a forceful trio. Unfortunately, they were disliked by the majority of the baronage, most of whom were far less powerful. The Montgomeries had no support in their rebellion against the king from either their own kind, from the clergy, or the people, who hated them. Why they had dared to face off against King Henry was a mystery to most. Others, wiser, believed the Montgomeries had foolishly succumbed to their overweening ambition.

Driven back into their own castles, they were forced to surrender after only three months. Each of the three lost their lands as forfeit for their stupidity; and they were exiled with their families back to Normandy, where they immediately began to plan another rebellion. Duke Robert, while he had not actively encouraged the disobedience against his younger sibling, had also not actively discouraged it. He had, in fact, very pointedly looked the other way. His wife was shortly to deliver their first child. He was not happy to see the return to Normandy of the Montgomeries, who had always been ambitious troublemakers wherever they settled.

Hugh Fauconier and Rolf de Briard returned home to Langston in late July. Six of their archers had fallen in the fray, a relatively small number, and they felt fortunate. King Henry had been very pleased by their loyalty and their support. Let great lords rebel against his legal authority; it was the small lords like Hugh who would hold England against all rebels and foreigners. He made his childhood friend a baron to reward him, and when Hugh asked if he should go to Normandy, the king said, "By all means, Baron Langston, go, and take the gyr-falcon to my brother. It will reassure him better than anything else I can do that I do not hold him responsible for the bad behavior of the Montgomeries. They are his problem now, may God help him. Poor old Robert. They will cause him more trouble, to be sure, sooner or later. Aye, go, and remain in Normandy until the Duchess Sibylle has delivered her child. Then return, and bring me all the news, both public and private, that you have managed to learn at my brother's court."

"I wish you could come with me, ma Belle," Hugh said to his wife. "If only our son were a trifle older and did not need you, *chérie.*"

"But he does need me," Isabelle replied. "I do not want to give him to a wet nurse yet, my lord." She looked down upon the bed where their little son lay naked upon a sheepskin, kicking and cooing. He was almost four months old now, and each day, Isabelle thought, he seemed to change before her very eyes.

"I have already missed much of Hugh the Younger," her husband said sadly. "It is the way of our world that I must be away so much right now. Once the king has reigned for a while, England will be quiet. Then I shall have but my knight's service each year. I shall be home to teach our son to ride and to hunt." He smiled down at the baby, who grinned up at his sire, a great, toothless grin. Hugh offered him a finger, and the infant grasped it strongly, surprising his father. "By the rood, ma Belle, he has a tenacious grip, our wee lad!" Then he bent down and kissed the child upon his forehead. "Take care of your mother, Hugh the Younger. I'll be home as quickly as I can."

"How long?" Belle asked.

"The king wants me to remain long enough to bring him the news of the duchess's delivery and learn the sex of her child. She is due to have her babe in mid-autumn. I should be home by Martinmas, if the seas are not too stormy."

"The weather is usually best either just before a storm or immediately after one," Belle told him. "Go, my lord, and do what you must. Rolf will be here, and we are well-defended now."

Hugh Fauconier departed his home once again on Lammas, in the company of Alain the falconer and six Langston men-at-arms. He took with him Blanca, the gyrfalcon, who would be given to Duke Robert; and a charming little sparrow hawk he intended as a gift for the duchess. The swallow-sized hawk had a rufous back and tail, unlike any other hawk. The sparrow hawk was definitely a lady's bird. It would find its prey and then hover over it, its elegant little wings beating rapidly, until finally it would swoop to kill.

Isabelle stood upon the walls of the keep, her son in her arms, watching as her husband rode off toward the nearby coast and the waiting vessel that would sail him across to Normandy.

Once again it was time to harvest the crops grown in the fields and orchards at Langston. Grain was threshed, and stored in the granaries. Flour was ground in the lord's mill, some distributed to the serfs and other tenants, the rest stored. Cider, ale, and wine were made to be stored in the cellars of the keep. The fields to be used for the autumn planting of spring wheat were ploughed, and the seeds sown. The animals were gathered from their summer pastures and brought closer to home, where they might be quickly herded into shelters when the weather turned inclement. Michaelmas was celebrated. The weaving of linen began.

Christian de Briard was in his tenth month of life, his nephew, Hugh the Younger, a robust six and a half months old.

Alette confided to her daughter that she believed she was quickening with another child.

"So soon?" Isabelle said, surprised.

"I am not young like you, my daughter," Alette responded. "I want to give my Rolf at least two sons before I am unable to conceive."

"What if it is a sister for Christian and me?" Belle teased.

"A daughter would suit me as well," Rolf told the women, overhearing their conversation as they sat together in the hall watching their babies crawl about. He bent, kissing his wife, then turned to Belle. "The manor is ready for winter, whatever it brings," he told her. "Everyone has worked very hard, my lady daughter. I should like to reward the serfs by allowing them a day's hunting in your fields and woods. No more than one deer per village, and two rabbits per family. Will you approve?"

"Aye," Belle answered. "They are deserving. Give them their day. Are the houses all in good repair for winter, Rolf?"

"Two roofs, one in Langston village and one in the outermost village, will need patching before the cold sets in, but I have already arranged for it, my lady. Tomorrow I have said the women and children may glean in the fields and orchards for whatever they can find. Well-fed peasants cannot be urged to any kind of sedition. The winters are hard enough."

Martinmas came, and with it a letter from Hugh Fauconier telling his wife that the duke and duchess had been delivered of a son. The duke, however, wanted him to remain on so they might hunt crane and test Blanca's prowess. The duchess had been pleased with her sparrow hawk. He would be home as soon as he could. Spring, at the very latest. Isabelle sighed, but there was nothing she could do. She was forced to accept her husband's decision. He could have hardly refused the duke's request without giving grievous insult to the king's brother.

The Nativity was celebrated in Langston's new church, which was, as Hugh had desired, called St. Elizabeth's. The church building was of a timber-frame construction, plastered and whitewashed. The roof was thatched. Hugh had wanted a stone church, but they would have had to wait much longer for the stones to be cut and then dragged over the marshes and the hills from Northamptonshire. Later, perhaps, they would have a stone church.

Langston's lord had wanted his church erected as quickly as possible. His serfs had worked diligently all summer and autumn, felling tress, cutting boards, mixing plaster, weaving thatch, in order that they might celebrate the Nativity within their own church. And next to the church was a small cottage especially built for Father Bernard, and a brand new churchyard.

On the eve of the Nativity the interior of the church was decorated with branches of yew and holly. Alette and Isabelle had been busy for days making candles of the purest beeswax for the candlesticks on the altar. The tapestry that Alette had been weaving since the departure of her first husband on his crusade hung behind the altar. It was a scene depicting Christ feeding the multitudes; a lesson, Father Bernard said, as to how a master should treat the less fortunate; a lesson that was practiced nicely here at Langston.

To celebrate the Nativity, every serf and freedman on the manor of Langston was given two measures of beer, a rasher of ham, and a loaf of bread. Each child was allocated a handful of raisins as well. As many as could crowded into the hall, singing joyously of the Christ child's birth. A health was drunk to the absent lord and to his good lady, who had seen to this happy occasion. Then the family was left alone to celebrate quietly. Isabelle, however, was pensive. There had been no further word from Hugh. She had resigned herself to not seeing him until spring. She looked over to her baby brother, Christian de Briard, now toddling with great determination everywhere his fat little legs could take him; his nephew, Hugh the Younger, crawled behind him. It was good that they would have each other as they grew up. She looked to her mother and stepfather, content and happy as they awaited the birth of their second child. Belle sighed.

The winter was a hard one, bitterly cold and wet. There were severe ice storms that damaged many of the trees in the orchards. Candlemas came, and with it the lambing, but it was a poor season. Not as many ewes gave birth as had the year before, and many of the newborns were lost in a wicked snowstorm that struck toward the end of the month. Only sheep, Belle thought, could be so utterly capricious as to have their young at the worst possible time of the year.

The spring was late, the frost refusing to leave the ground. When the planting was finally done, it was washed away by severe rainstorms and had to be done again, which was accomplished with some difficulty, the earth being sodden and difficult to plough. The winter wheat had suffered with the cold and wet. When they were finally able to harvest it, the yield was scant. None of the usual signs seemed to bode well for a good growing season.

"Pray God," Isabelle said to Father Bernard after the mass one morning, "that the summer crops are bountiful."

"Without the lord, lady, little good will happen for Langston," Ancient Albert, the old smithy, said in a quavery voice. "Where be Lord Hugh? We need him."

Isabelle took the rheumy-eyed old man's hand and said to him, "The lord is at Duke Robert's court on king's business, Ancient Albert. He will return soon. I know it."

"There will be no luck at Langston until the lord is safely home," Ancient Albert pronounced. "You does your best, lady, and loves the land, you surely does, but Langston must have its lord. Its luck is in its lord."

Easter came and went. Alette de Briard gave birth to her second son on the fifth day of May. The boy was baptized Henry, after the king. And still there was no word of Hugh Fauconier. Isabelle was becoming frantic. Where was her husband?

"We will send to the king for word of Hugh," Rolf said one evening as he sat with his stepdaughter in the hall. "Surely he will have had some word of him and know when he is to return."

"Nay, I will *go* to the king," Isabelle said quietly. They were alone, the servants having sought their beds, and Alette in her chamber nursing her newborn son. "A message would be as likely to get lost with all the correspondence the king must receive. He cannot, however, ignore me if I am standing before him, can he?"

"Belle, listen to me," her stepfather said. "You know that Hugh and I were raised with the king. There are things about our liege lord that we have not discussed before you because frankly they were of no import to you. But if you go to court, you must know that Henry Beauclerc is a very lusty man. He has always enjoyed women more than he should. Although it is said of him that his couplings are more for political advantage than passion, I know that not to be true."

"The king is a married man, Rolf," Isabelle said naively, "and I a married woman. He will have no interest in me at all. Besides, I am not going to court for pleasure. I am going to find out where my husband has gotten to, and nothing more."

"The king will look at you, Belle, and see a beautiful woman," her stepfather told her. "You cannot refuse him if you engage his lust."

"Then come with me, Rolf, and protect me." Belle laughed. "I will be a most proper lady. King Henry will not be in the least taken with me. I shall wear a wimple and veil at all times, and pretend to be shy. Besides, he will surely maintain a loyalty to Hugh that will make it impossible for him to seduce me. Shall we take Agneatha with us?"

"Hugh would not want you to do this thing, Isabelle," Rolf said. "He would forbid you, and as your stepfather so must I."

"You are indeed my stepfather, Rolf," Belle said quietly, and there was danger in her tone, a danger Rolf recognized. "You are also, however, the steward of Langston, and I,

Langston's lady. You must obey *me* in the absence of my husband. I do not have to obey you."

Rolf de Briard sighed and bowed his head. There was no place he could imprison her that she could not escape. He tried a final ploy. "Let me go to the king for you," he said. "He will speak with me for our friendship's sake."

Isabelle shook her head. "Nay, Rolf. The king would greet you fondly and invite you to join his hunting party. He would keep you with him when we very much need you here at Langston. Nay, I must go with you. We will learn what we must and return quickly to Langston. Ancient Albert is already muttering of Langston's luck being its lord. The serfs will become discouraged if such talk spreads. We must get Hugh home!"

"Very well, Isabelle," Rolf said, defeated. She was probably right, he thought. If he went alone, Henry would involve him in the activities of the court while Langston languished without him. Perhaps she could play the worried little spouse and engage the king's sympathy, not his lust. Still, Alette was going to be furious. "Your mother will not like this at all," he said to Isabelle.

"My mother is fearful of anything she considers out of the ordinary. She has never been to court, you know." Isabelle chuckled. "She will think me quite disobedient, and you a madman for aiding me."

But Alette surprised them both when she was told of their plans.

"I think it an excellent idea that you go to court and speak with the king," she said to her daughter. "We really must have Hugh home again as soon as possible. And I am pleased, my lord," she smiled at her husband, "that you will escort Isabelle, and keep her from danger. It would be unwise of her to go alone with only her servants about her. Besides, you know the king, and can help her to get an audience with him. It is a good time for you to go. The planting is finally done, and there is really nothing to oversee until the haying." She turned to her daughter. "I will look after my grandson."

Here was something Belle had not considered, and for a moment she faltered. "He is not weaned," she said slowly.

"But he is eating solid foods, for he enjoys imitating his uncle Christian," Alette said. "I have plenty of milk, daughter. I will nurse him, too, when he needs it. He is, after all, past his first birthday. Go and find your husband. You need another babe to care for, and you are past eighteen now." She laughed mischievously.

"As are you, madame, and yet you continue to have children," Belle teased her mother. Then she grew wistful. "I should like a daughter to keep her brother company," she said.

"I should like one as well," Alette said, her blue eyes twinkling as she looked at her husband.

"Madame, you have a daughter," he responded, returning her look of affection and love.

"I would like another," Alette told him stubbornly.

"In time," he promised her, "but first let us find Hugh."

Several days later they departed for Winchester, for Rolf believed, since the king had spent Easter there, he would yet be there, preferring to avoid London in the warmer weather. They took with them Belle's servant, Agneatha, and twelve men-at-arms for protection. Langston was left well-defended. Hugh's squire would serve as captain of the guard, and Rolf's squire would oversee the estate in his master's absence. Father Bernard blessed the little party as it left the keep. As they rode down the hill into Langston village, Ancient Albert blocked their way.

"Lady," he said to her, his lined face worried, "where goest thou? Will you leave us, too?"

"I am going to the king, Ancient Albert," Belle said. "He will know where Lord Hugh is. My mother is in the keep with my son, Hugh the Younger. Until his father returns, it is he who is Langston's lord, and Langston's luck. We will quickly return, I promise you."

"God go with ye, lady," Ancient Albert said, satisfied. "The little lord is in the keep with his grandma. 'Tis good. 'Tis good." He stepped aside to let them pass on through the village to where the ferryman awaited them to take them across the river Blyth so they might be on the road to Winchester.

Isabelle was very excited. In her entire life she had never been off Langston lands. She had never even crossed the river. There had been no need to do so. Everything she had wanted or needed could be found at Langston. Even if her father had lived and made a marriage for her, she would have probably remained in her home, as it was her dowry. Now, as the ferry took her across the river, Isabelle felt as if she were embarking upon a great adventure.

"I have planned our journey to Winchester, Belle, so that we will be able to shelter each night in the guest houses of convents, and abbeys," Rolf explained. "Because you have never traveled before, you may find the first few days a bit tiring."

"What if the court is not at Winchester, Rolf?" she asked him.

"If the king has moved on to another place, there are those in the government who will have remained behind. They will know where we must go. But Henry will be at Winchester, I am certain. He doesn't like London at this time of year, and it is too early for good hunting in the New Forest."

"How long will it take us to get to Winchester?" she inquired.

"Seven to nine days, providing we can make good time and have decent weather," he told her. "You will get to see London, Belle, but first we must pass through Colchester. It's a small town, and very old, but then, you have never seen a town before. It will be a good start, for London is a large, noisy place such as you could never imagine. We'll not stay there long."

They rode across the countryside until they came to a

narrow road. Turning onto it, they moved steadily south. The first night, they sheltered at a small convent, St. Mary's. Agneatha and her mistress were given beds within the convent itself. Rolf and the men slept in the guest house belonging to St. Mary's, just outside its walls. Their supper was spare: a small trencher of bread, a piece of broiled fish, a cup of cider.

"They don't treat themselves too good, do they?" Agneatha whispered to Isabelle as they sat together, separated from the nuns, at their own little table. She pulled a bit of bread off the trencher, remarking, " 'Tis stale, and the fish don't smell that good, I fear, lady." Agneatha was twenty, and very outspoken when it was warranted. "We'll starve before we gets where we're going if this is the kind of hospitality we're going to receive." Her nut-brown braids trembled with her irritation, for Agneatha enjoyed her food, as her plump form attested.

"Shhh, Agneatha, St. Mary's is obviously a poor convent. Look, the good sisters are having only pottage and bread. They've obviously given us their best. We are lucky to have a safe lodging. Rolf tells me that travel is very dangerous, and only our men-at-arms prevent robbers from attacking us. We'll feast grandly when we reach the court."

The next day they halted within five miles of Colchester. They would pass through the town the following morning. All of the Langston people were amazed by the number of people they found on the road as they moved toward the town. There were lords and ladies, with men-at-arms such as those in the Langston troupe. There were farmers driving cattle and geese into the town's market. An abbot on a beautifully caparisoned mule passed them, followed by a double line of brown-robed monks, singing plainsong as they went. And then they saw it, an enormous keep towering over the town. Awed, Isabelle gazed up, mouth open. It was the biggest building she had ever seen in all of her life; far, far bigger than Langston Keep.

Rolf smiled. "This town," he said, "has been here longer than anyone can remember. When there were Celtic tribes in England, this town was here. The people who conquered this land before the Saxons, built temples to their heathen gods when they lived here. The castle is built upon the ruins of one of those temples. Some of the bricks in the castle come from it. The cattle market for the district is here, and always has been. And the finest oysters in the world are found here," he finished.

"I could not have imagined such a place as this," Belle said.

"Do you like it?" he asked her.

She shook her head. "It is too noisy, Rolf."

He laughed. "Wait until you see London," he warned her.

They had been on the road several days, and the weather held for them. The early spring had been too wet, and now it seemed as if it were too dry. Belle could see that most of the fields they rode by were as behind in their growth as were the fields at Langston. It did not bode well for a good year, and she worried that they would not be able to get through the next winter without some starvation. She was becoming angry at Hugh. He should be home, she thought, and not running about Normandy. Langston needed him. His son needed him. *She needed him.*

Finally, as the roads began to grow even more crowded, she realized that they were nearing the great city of London. She could see the city ahead of them, surrounded by a dingy haze.

"It's from the coal and wood fires used for heating and cooking," Rolf said in answer to her unspoken question.

They passed through Ealdgate, the portal believed to be the oldest of the city's gates. The city surrounded them, and for the first time in her life Isabelle felt afraid. There were too many people. Too many buildings were all crowded together on either side of the narrow streets. She grew very quiet, looking straight ahead as if seeking an exit from this terrible place. The gray day made the city seem all the darker.

"We must cross the river," Rolf said, "to reach the road to Winchester. There is a fine bridge we'll use, not a ferry this time."

They came to an open-air market on the river's edge. Belle

breathed a bit easier being out of the grim city streets. She looked about her, astounded. There were stalls selling every kind of merchandise. One displayed bolts of cloth such as she had never seen. It glistened, and there were colors she had never imagined. A poulterer's stall was hung with chickens, ducks, geese, and game birds. A horse merchant had staked his animals out for prospective buyers to see. One booth offered glazed pottery, fine-turned wooden bowls, and spoons. Rolf stopped at the wine merchant's booth to buy them a cup of wine. He called to a pie merchant with a tray of buns upon his head to stop, and selected three buns filled with raisins, paying the man a ha'penny for his wares.

"There's the bridge." Rolf pointed as they continued along.

"I do not like this London," Isabelle said. "I will be glad to be quit of it. It's even dirtier and noisier than Colchester. Will Winchester be as bad, do you think?" She stuffed the last of the bun into her mouth, chewing the sweet raisins until they were pulp.

Rolf laughed. "Winchester will be no worse than Colchester, Belle, and you'll not have to stay long, I promise you. I will get the king to see us. Then we shall be able to return home."

They clattered across the bridge, leaving the city behind. The road they now traveled was called Stane Street. It had been built by the Romans. The weather had held for them, and Rolf thought if it continued, they would reach Winchester in another two days. He was not happy bringing Isabelle of Langston to court. What if Henry took a fancy to her? No matter what she believed, the fact that she was Hugh Fauconier's wife would not deter his lust. Fortunately, Belle, being a countrywoman, had not the elegant clothing the Norman ladies of the court would be wearing. Her glorious hair was relatively well hidden beneath a modest linen veil, her gown simple. She would appear like a sparrow next to the peacocks. With luck, the king would not be intrigued. With luck, he would tell them what they needed to know, and they would depart back to Langston.

The sun shone for the remainder of their trip, and a warm spring wind blew at their backs as if pushing them onward. At last they reached Winchester, which was, Belle immediately decided, not at all like either Colchester or London. It was a far quieter town, its Romanesque cathedral and castle dominating it. No sooner had they entered it than Rolf knew the court was still here. He recognized many faces, and there was an air of gentle bustle about the town. With a deep sigh of resignation, he led his little party to the castle.

"Ohh, isn't it exciting?" Agneatha bubbled. "Do you think we'll get to see the king, my lady? Ohh, they'll not believe the half of it when I tell it back at Langston."

"No," said Belle thoughtfully, noting the elegance of the women's clothing, "they will not." She glanced down at her practical but plain garments. Why hadn't Rolf told her? She'd disgrace Hugh for certain! She would have to make the best of it for she had no other choice, and after all, it had been her idea to come to court and petition the king. She could only hope her appearance would not go against her.

It was the dinner hour, and the king was in the Great Hall. Rolf made Isabelle and the Langston party wait outside the hall. He didn't want their presence announced so dramatically, for he was not certain how much of Hugh's visit to Normandy was public knowledge. There were always spies about, ready to report the most insignificant little bit of tittle-tattle to Duke Robert *and* to Robert de Belleme, who had sworn vengeance on King Henry for driving him out of England. Seeing a young page he knew, Rolf called him over.

"Go to the king, my lad, and say that Sir Rolf de Briard has just arrived at court and would speak privately with him if he would be so kind as to give him a few moments. Wait until you can address the king discreetly. Do you understand, my lad?"

"Aye, m'lord," the boy said, and he hurried off.

Rolf stood quietly against a wall, waiting, watching for the page to gain the king's ear. A juggler with a small, amusing dog began to entertain before the high board, the dog tossing balls to his master, then snatching them away, to much laughter. The attention of the diners was well-engaged. Rolf saw the king cock his head to one side, and in the shadow of the king's chair he could see the page. The king nodded to the lad, and Rolf could see his lips moving gently. Then he looked back to the juggler, laughing uproariously at the antics of the little dog.

The page hurried back to Rolf. "The king says he will see you in his private chamber. You are to go there now and wait for him. He will come when he can."

Rolf thanked the page and left the Great Hall. "Go into the hall," he told the Langston men. "Say you are with Sir Rolf de Briard, high steward of Langston Keep. You will be fed. Remain there until I come to fetch you, and speak little." Then he turned to Isabelle and Agneatha. "The king will see me, Belle. Come, and I will take you to the chamber where we will speak. I do not know how long it will be before he comes, so we must wait. At least you will have your privacy."

They went to the little room where Hugh had first spoken to the king regarding Langston, and where later he and Rolf had bid the king farewell. They had no sooner entered it when a page arrived with wine and goblets. He deposited the items upon the table and left. Rolf poured Belle a goblet of the liquid. The poor girls were probably starving at this point, but they had no choice but to wait. Belle thoughtfully shared her wine with Agneatha, whose belly was rumbling with a mixture of hunger and excitement.

Isabelle considered her attire. It was painfully plain, though it was one of her best gowns. Her skirts were of an indigo-blue linen. Her grass-green linen tunic was belted with a girdle made from small squares of blue and green enameled copper, each square studded with a single small pearl. The embroidery at the neck and sleeves of the gown was of real gold thread, in a foliage design. Her hair, braided neatly in its single braid, was covered by a fine white linen veil, its hem also embroi-dered in the gold thread. Isabelle discreetly brushed the dust of the road from her garments. If only she had had the time to change into better garments. If only I had better garments, she thought.

"You look fine," Rolf reassured her.

"I look like what I am," Belle responded, a bit tartly, "a country bumpkin. Why did you not tell me of the beautiful clothing the court ladies wear? I hope I shall not embarrass Hugh with my less-than-fashionable appearance, Rolf. I saw those wonderful materials in London in that market by the bridge. Can I buy some when we return home? Certainly my lady mother would enjoy having something so fine."

"I never thought much about clothing before we left Langston," Rolf admitted. "Besides, you have not come to the court to join it. We have come to find out where Hugh has gotten to, Isabelle."

"It could not hurt my case if I were to look pretty," Belle replied, annoyed. Why did men not understand these things?

"Belle," Rolf said to her low, urgently. "Remember what I have told you about the king. He has a weakness for pretty women, and you are a very pretty woman. I must warn you again that being his friend's wife would not deter him if he desired you. As I waited in the hall I learned that the queen is due to deliver a child in August sometime. She bore her first little prince too early, and the babe died. This child is therefore twice as important. The king will have eschewed his wife's bed for many weeks now. I know him well. His eye will be roving. Let me do the speaking, and for sweet Jesu's sake, keep your lovely eyes lowered and your head down. Let Henry Beauclerc's lust look elsewhere."

"Very well, Rolf, I shall play the meek and modest little wife of Hugh Fauconier lest I send you into a fit and my mother be widowed again; but I think it ridiculous. I will not leave here, however, until I learn where my husband is. Understand that, and do not fail me." Belle brushed her skirts again vigorously, shaking them free of wrinkles.

They waited. Agneatha fell asleep, exhaustion finally setting in and the too-rich wine, unwatered, going to her head.

"Poor lass," Rolf said. "It is all too much for her, I think."

Belle nodded, and then she smiled. "The wine was very potent, and I fear I let Agneatha have more of it than I should have. She is not used to such a fine brew, and if truth be known, neither am I, but I erred on the side of caution."

Finally, they heard footsteps in the corridor outside the small chamber. The door was flung open by a page, and the king entered the room. Rolf bowed low as Belle spread her skirts in a deep curtsey, head well down and eyes modestly lowered as her stepfather had suggested. Still, she could not help sneaking a look at the king, and found him a fine figure of a man, with his black hair and his bright blue eyes.

"Rolf, it is good to see you, and who is this lady?" he asked.

"My liege, may I present Isabelle of Langston, my lord Hugh's wife and my stepdaughter. We have ridden from Langston to beg you to give us news of Hugh. We have not heard from him since Martinmas."

"He has not returned to England?" The king sounded puzzled. His attention engaged by the news, he looked away from Belle. "I asked him to remain for a while with my brother's court to pick up what small bits of information he could, but I assumed he had returned home in early spring. There was no need for him to remain longer, as he could not tell me anything that I did not already know; for example, that Robert de Belleme agitates against me in Normandy and attacks my few holdings there that my brother has returned to me. There are few secrets at my brother's court, it seems, that are not public knowledge. This is most strange, Rolf."

"Then what could have happened to my husband?" Belle asked.

The king turned to look at her closely for the first time. "Madame, I fear I do not know," he said honestly, noting that Isabelle of Langston was a most pretty young woman.

"But you must find out!" Belle cried. " 'Twas you, my lord,

who sent my husband to Normandy! A falconer could have easily delivered the gyrfalcon. 'Twas you who asked Hugh to remain with Duke Robert. I want my husband back! We need him at Langston. My son is fatherless without Hugh Fauconier. Who will defend him?" Her cheeks were flushed and her eyes sparkled with her indignation.

*"Belle!"* Rolf de Briard's voice was uneasy. "My lord, I must apologize for my stepdaughter. She is an outspoken country girl, unused to the ways of your court and its protocol."

"Nay, my lord, do not apologize, for the lady is correct when she says Hugh is my responsibility." The king smiled slowly at Belle. Then reaching out, he tipped her face to his gaze, intrigued by the fact she did not shyly lower her eyes as many would have, but rather stared straight into his own blue ones. "I shall send to Normandy to my brother, my lady Isabelle, for news of Hugh Fauconier. You will be reunited with your husband as quickly as I can arrange it. Until then you must remain here at court as our guest. I like new faces, and we shall soon hunt in the New Forest. Did you perhaps travel with one of Hugh's fine birds?"

Belle moved just enough to loosen his light grip on her chin. "Nay, my lord. 'Tis no pleasure trip for me, you will understand. I but came for word of my husband. I am honored by your invitation, of course, but we cannot remain. There is my infant to consider, and it is almost time for haying. The serfs cannot be left alone for too long, with only my mother to guide them. She has not the authority to command them, being of gentle nature and mild disposition."

"Indeed," the king said, amused, and further fascinated by this girl who spoke to him in such serious and practical tones, as if he were her equal, and not her king.

Rolf swallowed hard. He would have to back Isabelle up. He knew she could not possibly see the danger she was in, but he certainly did. "My liege, I fear I must agree with *my step-daughter.*" He stressed the connection hard, hoping that that, combined with the fact that she was Hugh's wife, would deter the king from any lustful intentions. "I know Hugh has told you that it was the lady Isabelle who kept Langston whole and prosperous during her late father's absence from England. My sweet wife, Alette, is just not strong enough to maintain firm control and see to all that must be done upon the manor. We must return as quickly as possible. I know that you will send to us when you have word of Hugh Fauconier."

The king smiled. It was a flinty smile. "Send one of your men back to Langston for some birds," he said to Isabelle. "It is foolish that you return all that way only to have to wait for word from Normandy. If you remain here, that word will be delivered you all the quicker. I will send tomorrow to my brother. I am certain that Langston can survive your absence for a short time, madame, but if you are overly concerned, then Sir Rolf is free to return to his duties and his wife."

"I have not the garments to join the court," Isabelle countered. "Look at me, my lord, I am but a simple countrywoman. You would shame me and my lord husband if I were forced to appear in such clothing."

"The proper gowns can be supplied you, madame," the king replied.

"I have not the wherewithal to pay for such garments," Isabelle told him honestly. *"I must return home, my liege."*

*"Nay, madame, you must remain here.* I am your king, Isabelle of Langston, and you will obey me. Now, I must go and look in on the queen. She is great with child, and most uncomfortable. It soothes her that I visit her when she is so fretful. Remain here until a page comes for you. He will show you to your quarters. Will you stay, Rolf, or do your heavy duties call you back to Langston?" Henry Beauclerc's blue eyes twinkled with mischief and his delight at having gotten his own way. He was indeed a dangerous opponent to have.

"I will remain, my liege, for to do otherwise would be to shirk my duties to my lord, Hugh Fauconier," Rolf said quietly.

"Remember, Rolf," the king reminded him. "Your oath to

me comes before the oath you swore to Hugh." Then the king turned abruptly and departed the little chamber.

"Damn!" Rolf swore, white about the lips.

"Oh, Rolf," Belle tried to console him, "it is not that bad. I would prefer to return home, but if the king would have us stay, then stay we must. We have no choice in the matter."

"Do you not understand, Isabelle?" he cried. "The king lusts after you! I should not have brought you to court."

"He may lust all he likes, Rolf," Belle responded. "He will not have his way with me. After all, he is only a man. I may have little experience where men are concerned, but I know enough to avoid a suitor's unwelcome attentions."

"If he wants you, he will have you, Belle," Rolf said grimly. "He is the king. A woman does not put off a king."

"Why not?" she demanded. "Is a royal cock any more special than an ordinary lord's cock? How ridiculous!"

"Nay, Belle, a cock is a cock, but a king is no ordinary lord. When a king commands, his loyal subject must obey. If the king seeks to put his royal member between your milk-white thighs, you will open them willingly, for to do otherwise would be to commit treason, my headstrong girl. Oh, you would not be accused openly of such perfidy, but you would nonetheless have offended Henry Beauclerc, and he would find ways of punishing you. Perhaps he would send Hugh off to fight Robert de Belleme, who harasses his Norman possessions. Hugh could be killed, and you widowed. Then he would take over the wardship of not only your person, but that of Hugh the Younger. He might keep you openly as his mistress, or marry you off to some compliant lordling who would look the other way while the king pursued his passion for you. When you lost his favor, you would be shackled to some stranger who might not be as loving and as tolerant as Hugh has been of your impetuous behavior. I warned you not to come to court, Belle, but you would not listen. Now you must accept whatever happens with as good a grace as possible."

"I did not know," Isabelle whispered, horrified by what Rolf had told her. "Oh, Holy Mother! I can hold him off but a short time. If Hugh does not come quickly, I shall be ruined!"

"If it comes to that," Rolf said, putting a comforting arm about his stepdaughter, "Hugh need not know, Isabelle. I will not tell him, and neither must you, for his sake as well as your own."

A tear slipped down Belle's pale cheek. "Oh, Rolf, what have I done?" she cried softly. Then she grew paler. "Agneatha!" she said. "She will surely know if the king attempts to seduce me. Two might keep such a secret, but three surely cannot!"

"You must be hard, Isabelle, and I know you can be. Warn your serving woman that should she betray you, you will dispossess her. A serf without a master cannot survive, and Agneatha knows that. She will keep any secrets she must for that reason alone."

Isabelle nodded. "I grew frightened for a moment," she said. "I must keep my wits about me if I am to survive, Rolf."

"Aye, you must," he agreed, giving her a little squeeze of encouragement. Then he said, "I think we can manage a new gown or two in the court style for you, Belle. I have the funds with me. It should allow you a few days' respite from the king's attentions while they are being made. Then, when you are introduced to the court, you will be able to hold your head up and do Langston proud."

The door to the little chamber opened and a page entered. "My lord, my lady. The king has sent me to escort you to your apartment. If you will but follow me, please."

Isabelle went over to the chair in the corner where Agneatha sat, head nodding, her soft little snores barely audible. She poked the servant. "Wake up, Agneatha," she said. "Wake up!"

Agneatha started. Her head snapped up and she stared wildly about the room. "Is the king come, then?" she said, stumbling to her feet.

"Come and gone," Isabelle told her.

"He's come and I've not seen him? Ohhh, my lady!" the young woman wailed. "All this way, and I never seen him!"

"There will be plenty of time to see the king, Agneatha," Isabelle told her serving woman. "We have been asked to remain at court for a short time while the king seeks word of Lord Hugh. Come along now, for the page is here to take us to our sleeping quarters."

Agneatha beamed with delight. "Oh," she exclaimed, "I am so excited, my lady. To stay here at the court, and to see the king! What a fine treat for us. Old Ida will be pea-green with jealousy, she will."

Isabelle looked to her stepfather, unable to repress the giggle that bubbled up from her throat. What a coil they were in, and innocent little Agneatha knew but the half of it!

# ☒Chapter 10

$T$hey followed the young page through the castle, finally entering through a heavy, ironbound oak door into a medium-sized room. The stone walls were whitewashed. There was a small fireplace and a single window with stout wooden shutters. The furnishings were utilitarian, for most people coming to court brought their own amenities. There was a table, two chairs, and a bed with a trundle that could be pulled out from beneath it. While the bed had a mattress, there were no other coverings upon it, and no hangings of any sort.

"Where are you going to sleep, Rolf?" Isabelle was puzzled. The room was more than large enough for Agneatha and herself, but certainly not for the three of them. She looked for a connecting door, but there was no connecting door. "Where is my stepfather to rest?" she asked the lad.

"The king says that Sir Rolf may take his rest with the castle knights, and that he knows how to find his way, my lady," the page said.

Isabelle nodded, dismissing the boy. When she had closed the door behind him, she turned to Rolf. "You are right, my lord. The king is most determined to have his own way in the matter. He has quite effectively isolated me. Dare you remain nonetheless?"

Rolf shook his head. "You must fight this battle yourself, Isabelle," he told her. "You are clever, I know, but I fear the king is far more clever. He is a skilled hunter, and you are the prey he stalks."

Agneatha looked between Rolf and her mistress, completely puzzled. They spoke in riddles. Seeing her confusion, Isabelle explained the predicament. The young serving woman was shocked. " 'Tis wrong!" she said. "I don't think I want to see this king after all, my lady."

"A king is never wrong, Agneatha," Rolf told her gently, "and whatever happens, you must never reveal any of it to a living soul."

"Keeping this secret will be the hardest thing you have ever done," Isabelle said to her serving woman, "but if you reveal the truth to anyone at Langston, and I will know it is *you* should rumors arise, I will have you whipped and driven from my lands. You know the fate of serfs who do not belong to their lands, Agneatha. Among your family you have climbed the highest, coming in from the drudgery of the fields to serve in the keep. You are a good and faithful servant to me, and I love you well. You have served me honestly with all diligence, but if the worst should befall me, I would not bring shame to my husband, my mother, and my child. Do you understand me?"

Agneatha nodded. "I know you do not seek this, my lady," she said. "I will tell no one, and I will pray the king loses potency. Ohh, if only we were back home! My old granny has a potion that takes the vitality right out of a randy cock."

"Holy Mother!" Rolf exclaimed. "May I never displease your old granny, Agneatha." Then he turned the subject neatly. "We must go into the marketplace in the town and find bedding, else you both be most uncomfortable tonight. The trundle has no mattress upon it. And perhaps we can find some material for a new gown, eh, Belle?" He gave her an encouraging smile.

"But I am not skilled enough to make one of those beautiful court gowns," Isabelle replied, "and alas, neither is Agneatha."

"I can find you a seamstress," Rolf promised her. "Agneatha, open the window so the chamber may air while we go to market."

"How can you find me a seamstress?" Belle asked him.

Her stepfather grinned at her. "I know a number of ladies with the court," he said with a chuckle. "They will be able to tell me."

*"Indeed?"* Then she grinned back at him, and they hurried off.

In the town was a well-stocked, good-sized open-air market that did a brisk business when the court was visiting. Isabelle quickly obtained newly made feather beds for herself and Agneatha; fine linen sheets lifted from a lavender-scented bin; feather pillows; down coverlets; a brass ewer for washing, and a pitcher for water. She found bed hangings of fustian, neutrally colored with a deep blue design; an earthenware chamber pot; some candlesticks and candles.

" 'Tis expensive, this coming to court," she noted tartly.

"We'll sell the bedding and curtains back to the secondhand merchant when we leave," Rolf told her. "We'll not get much, but we'll recoup some of what we laid out." He patted his stepdaughter's hand comfortingly. Isabelle had a tendency toward frugality, which was certainly not a bad trait in a woman, particularly a woman responsible in part for the well-being of an estate. "Come along now, my lass," he said, "and let us find the merchant who sells pretty cloth for pretty gowns." He led his two charges through the market until they found a booth hung with fabric such as the two women had never seen.

Isabelle stood in rapt awe for several minutes, her head moving this way and that. Finally, she said with a great, gusty sigh, "Rolf, I cannot decide! They are all so beautiful, and," she lowered her voice, "I expect frightfully expensive. Can we afford such fabric?"

"Choose what you like, Belle," he said. "Remember, you are the lady of Langston come to court."

She turned again to the fabrics. The lavender damask would make a marvelous tunic worn over violet silk skirts. No. The mauve silk for her skirts, and she could then have a second tunic made from the violet damask. And that marvelous tawny orange brocade would make another tunic to be worn over yellow silk skirts, which would also match with a creamy white brocade that could also be worn with the mauve skirts, whose violet tunic could go with the yellow skirts as well. Before she could speak, however, they were interrupted by a voice trilling out to them.

"*Rolf? Rolf de Briard!* Oh, it is you!"

"Mavis, how delightful to see you once again," Rolf responded, kissing the woman's hand. "May I present my stepdaughter, the lady Isabelle of Langston. Belle, this is the lady Mavis of Farnley."

The two women nodded, sizing one another up as they did so. Mavis of Farnley was a very pretty woman with dark hair, bright blue eyes, and fair skin made fairer by the pink blush of her cheeks. She was dressed, to Belle's embarrassment, in the most fashionable garments: a tunic of sky-blue brocatelle which had been woven with pure gold threads, and gracefully draped deep blue skirts. She made Isabelle feel like a bumpkin.

"*Your stepdaughter?*" Mavis eyed Belle. "When did you gain a stepdaughter, Rolf de Briard? She looks far too grown-up to be your stepdaughter, I fear, and much, much too pretty."

Rolf laughed. "I married her mother over two years ago, Mavis, and not only do I have this fine grown-up girl for a stepchild, my lady wife has in that time given me two sons."

"Gracious, my lord, you have been busy!" Mavis said with a chuckle. "Where did you find your lady wife, and why have you been so long from court, Rolf de Briard? We have missed you." Putting a plump little hand upon his arm, she smiled up at him.

"I live in Suffolk now, Mavis. I am steward to Hugh Fauconier, who is the lord of Langston. The lady Isabelle is his wife."

"Is Hugh at court, then? And will I get to meet your wife, Rolf?" Mavis inquired. She turned to include Isabelle in their conversation. "I hope you know what a rogue this Rolf de Briard is, my lady. There will be many broken hearts amongst the ladies when they learn of his marriage. One day he and Hugh Fauconier were here; the next they were gone away, and none of us knew where."

"We need a seamstress, Mavis," Rolf said with a grin. "You are certainly one of the most outrageously fashionable women here at court, and I know you will know the best seamstress in Winchester. Poor Belle will not appear before the court until she has what she deems fashionable court clothing. That is why you find us here this day."

Mavis turned a critical eye to Isabelle. Then she patted the girl with her little hand. "You are absolutely right, Belle. I may call you Belle, mayn't I? We're going to be friends, I know! Your garments are perfectly fine for Suffolk. I'm a country girl myself, a mixture of Norman and Saxon blood, y'know. For court, however, a woman should be a bit more dashing. What fabrics have you chosen? Show me."

Isabelle presented her selections for inspection.

"Very nice," Mavis complimented her, "but let me suggest you choose the violet damask with the gold thread woven through it instead of the plain violet. And you will need some *passemente* braid in both gold and silver for trim. Now, for a seamstress. Master John, your most 'umble cloth merchant," Mavis mimicked the booth's owner teasingly, "just happens to be wed to the best seamstress in all of Winchester—is that not a fact, Master John?"

"Your ladyship is too kind," the merchant said, but then he turned to Isabelle. "If yer ladyship wishes, my wife can indeed make the gowns you will need for your visit to court."

Isabelle nodded. "Yes," she said.

"Have Mistress Mary come up to the castle tomorrow," Mavis instructed the cloth merchant. "She is to ask for Isabelle of Langston's quarters. She will be directed." She looked to Rolf and Belle. "Well, come along now, and we'll stroll back together. Is this your serving girl? What is her name?"

"Agneatha, my lady," Belle replied.

"Well, Agneatha, you must make friends with my Jane.

She'll tell you everything you're going to need to know about life at court. I honestly don't know what I should do without Jane. You remember Jane, don't you, Rolf? She is such a dear, loyal creature. We were raised together, you know. I suspect my father was her father as well, but no one ever dared to voice it aloud, if indeed it is true." She rattled on, gossiping merrily as they walked together back to the castle.

When they had once again reached the royal residence, however, Isabelle bid Mavis of Farnley a good night. "Our journey has been long," she said simply, by way of explanation.

"But there will be music and entertainment in the Great Hall this night," Mavis protested.

"I am not comfortable dressed as I am, my lady Mavis. When I have my first garment made, then I shall gladly join you," Isabelle responded. Then she curtsied to the other woman politely, and with Agneatha following in her wake, hurried off to her chamber. She knew the bedding would have already been delivered from the market by the lad Rolf had paid to do so. She was hungry, tired, and beginning to be a little frightened.

"Isabelle did not expect to be invited to stay at court, and she is a little bit overwhelmed by all of it," Rolf explained to Mavis.

"She is Hugh Fauconier's wife," Mavis said, "and everyone knows that you and Hugh were the king's favorite boyhood companions. By the way, where is Hugh? And why did he not see his wife had the proper clothing to bring to court? Honestly, men!"

"Hugh is not with us, Mavis," Rolf said, "and neither is my lady wife. Lest you obtain the wrong impression, let me explain that Hugh is overdue on the king's business. Isabelle became worried, and nothing would do, for she is most headstrong, but that we come to court and inquire ourselves as to his whereabouts. I must beg you, however, not to be party to any gossip concerning this matter. We thought but to come, inquire, be reassured, and depart, all in the same day."

"But Henry Beauclerc took one look at Isabelle of Langston and decided otherwise," Mavis said astutely. "Poor little innocent. Really, Rolf, you should have had more sense than to bring such a pretty creature to court. You, of all people, know what he's like when he sees a woman he fancies."

"I could not prevent Belle from coming," Rolf said. "She loves Hugh dearly, and he has been gone several months. He should have been home ere now, Mavis. You see Isabelle as a little country girl lacking experience. Perhaps that is true in one way, but let me tell you that my stepdaughter is a determined, strong-minded woman. She was still a child when her father, Robert de Manneville, departed England to join Duke Robert's crusade. Shortly thereafter the estate steward died, and she, alone, held Langston. She could neither read nor write then, and so she kept the estate records within her head. Everything was in perfect order when Hugh Fauconier and I came to Langston after her father's death at Ascalon. Langston had been in Hugh's family before Duke William's time. King Henry returned it to him, and gave him Isabelle for his wife. Now Hugh is missing, and Belle would have him back. And she will, too."

"Why, Rolf, I do believe you admire your stepdaughter," Mavis said.

He smiled thoughtfully, surprised by her observation, but he realized that it was true. "I do," he agreed.

"Is she like her mother?" Mavis wondered.

"Nay, Alette is a gentle, biddable woman who suits me quite well; but Hugh, from the moment he saw Belle, was intrigued by her. They quarrel with the same intensity as they make love." He chuckled. "I prefer my sweet-spoken Alette to her daughter, who has a tongue as sharp as the well-honed edge of a broadsword. She is quiet now only because she is overwhelmed by all she has seen in the last week."

"And, undoubtedly, by Henry Beauclerc, our sovereign, who probably made no bones about his attraction to your stepdaughter. He's been like a randy old billygoat of late, with the queen so big with child and inaccessible to his passions. He has, I am told, already impregnated two ladies of rank in his lust. The legion of his bastards certainly grows with each passing day. I hope that your poor Isabelle does not become enceinte by him. With her husband away, there would be no pretending that the child was his. What a scandal would erupt!"

"Holy Mother!" Rolf exclaimed. "I had not considered it."

Mavis of Farnley rolled her blue eyes back in her head. "Men," she said scathingly, "seldom do. You never, ever contemplate the result of your lusts." Then she laughed. "Oh, come along, Rolf de Briard, and let us join the others in the Great Hall. You have many friends here who will be happy to welcome you back to court and congratulate you on your good fortune." She slipped her hand through his arm and led him off.

Belle and Agneatha had meanwhile returned to their assigned chamber. They had hung the fustian curtains about the bed, and made both it and the trundle up. Isabelle's trunk had been brought to the chamber by the Langston men. Agneatha started a fire in the fireplace, and closed the shutters over the window so that they might be snug. It had begun to rain outside, the first rain they had seen since leaving Langston. But the room was warm and dry, and almost friendly.

"I am starving," Isabelle said. "We have not eaten since we left the monastery guest house this morning. Find the Great Hall. Rolf will be there, or some of the Langston men. Tell them you want food for us, and then bring it back."

"Let me get us some water first," Agneatha said. "Then I will find us food. I'm hungry myself." She took up the pitcher, exiting the room, to return just a short while later carrying not just the pitcher, but a full bucket of water. "The nicest young man-at-arms helped me, and he let me take the extra bucket, too," she said.

While Agneatha disappeared off again to find them some supper, Belle nestled the pitcher in hot ashes in a corner of the fireplace to warm its contents so they might wash before retiring. She longed for a real bath, and wondered if such a thing was possible in this place.

It seemed a very long while before Agneatha returned, but she brought with her bread, cheese, a joint of mutton, and a carafe of wine with two goblets. These last were being carried by one of the Langston men.

"I found Lord Rolf in the hall, mistress," Agneatha said. "He showed me how to get food, and he sent Bert back to stand guard outside the chamber. He says to tell you he'll have one of our men there at all times, and he'll see you himself in the morning."

"Have you eaten, Bert?" Isabelle asked the man-at-arms.

"Aye, my lady. The food ain't as fresh as back home, though. I'll be glad when we goes back. How long must we stay?" Bert shifted his weight from one foot to the other nervously. He'd been asked by the others to see if he could ascertain this information.

"The king has sent a messenger to his brother's court in Normandy," Isabelle explained. "We must wait for his return. Until then my stepfather and I have been invited to hunt with the king." Then she smiled at the soldier. "I'd rather be home, too," she admitted.

"Well, now you've heard it from her ladyship herself, Bert," Agneatha said sharply. "Get on outside and do your duty so we can eat at last." She punctuated her order with a swift poke in his ribs.

Bert bowed and departed.

Agneatha set a rough table for her mistress and herself. They sat down and began to eat. The bread was fresh and the cheese tasty, but the mutton was tough, and Agneatha said so as she vigorously chewed the greasy meat and swallowed it down. Isabelle was hard-pressed not to laugh, and as it was, she could not restrain a giggle.

"You're right," she told her serving woman. "It's awful. You would think the king would eat better."

"I should have brought a piece of fish," Agneatha said, "but frankly I didn't like the smell of it. Maybe it was that fancy sauce."

"When we can eat in the hall it will be better," Isabelle said. "There will be more variety—at least I hope there will be."

They had finished their meal, and Agneatha had cleared the remnants away, when there was a knock upon the door. It opened to reveal a small boy, no more than six years of age. He was very elegantly attired, and stepped smartly past Bert, who held the door open for him with great aplomb. In his hands he carried a small willow basket. The lad bowed.

"Good evening, my lady Isabelle. I am Henry Beauchamp, a page in the king's service." He handed her the basket. "My lord the king thought you might enjoy these new strawberries, my lady."

"Please thank the king for me, Henry Beauchamp," Isabelle said politely. Then, unable to resist, she asked him, "How old are you?"

"I am six, my lady, and have been in the king's service a year," he piped. "When my mother died, I was sent to court. The king is my father, you see. It was felt my chances of advancement would be better if I were with him, rather than a simple memory." He bowed again. "I shall tell the king you are pleased, my lady, and I bid you good night. God give you a good rest and pleasant dreams."

"Holy Mother," Agneatha said as the boy departed. "What a fine young sir, and so tender in years, my lady."

"Yes," Isabelle said thoughtfully, picking at the pretty little strawberries that had been set upon a bed of green leaves. The boy was the king's bastard. What if she could not hold the king off and must submit to his desires? Would she, too, be the mother of a bastard? Hugh would never forgive her. She would never forgive herself! "Did your old granny have a potion for preventing a man's seed from taking root in the womb?" she demanded of Agneatha.

The girl flushed. "Why, my lady, what a wicked thought! Such a thing is forbidden," Agneatha protested.

"Tell me the truth," Isabelle said. "That child is the king's bastard. What if I must lie with the king? How can we keep such a secret if I return home to Langston with a big belly, and my husband gone all these months? I must be able to protect myself."

"There's certain herbs, mixed together, that can help you," Agneatha said slowly. "Perhaps I could obtain them in that market we was in this afternoon. I can go look tomorrow."

"Do so," Belle commanded her.

They washed in the warm water from the pitcher, undressed, and climbed into their beds, blowing out the candles beforehand. The fire died slowly, finally crumbling into a glow of orange coals that slowly faded away into a gray nothingness. At first Isabelle could hear the faint sounds of merriment somewhere within the castle, and then at last it died away and there was naught but silence, broken only by Agneatha's soft, gentle snoring.

Isabelle lay in her strange bed in her strange room in this strange place. What a day it had been, she thought. She had seen and learned more in this single day than in all the days of their journey up till now. She wondered what her new gowns would look like. She had never seen or felt such exquisite materials as those Rolf had purchased for her this afternoon. Though the king made her nervous, particularly the way his eyes had locked onto hers, if she had not come to court, she would not have ever known such beautiful clothing existed. Before they returned home she would purchase other material from Master John for her mother, so she might copy and sew her own fashionable gowns.

Agneatha awoke before her mistress, and rising, dressed, hurrying off to the Great Hall to find them some breakfast. She gathered up newly baked bread, butter, honey, and a couple of hard-boiled eggs she wheedled from a cook's helper with a jest and a smile. A Langston man joined her, explaining he would be relieving Bert, and so Agneatha sent him off to get them a

pitcher of cider. Returning back to their chamber, she refilled
the pitcher with fresh water and laid a new fire, tucking the
pitcher back into its corner.

Hearing the activity about her, Isabelle awoke, amazed that
she had slept through the sunrise. Stretching, she greeted
Agneatha, "Good morning. How could I have slept so long? Is
that fresh bread I smell?" She threw back the coverlet and
stepped from the bed.

"Fresh bread, still warm from the ovens," Agneatha said
with a smile. "Come, mistress, and eat your breakfast. The
seamstress is certain to come this morning, and you'll want to
be ready for her."

Belle sat down and tore off a piece from the loaf, smearing
it with butter and dipping it in the honey. She popped it into her
mouth, her pointed little tongue snaking out to catch a drizzle
of honey. "That's sooo good," she said. "*Eggs!* You found
eggs!" Reaching out, she began to peel one, and swiftly ate
it down.

With a smile, her serving woman joined her, pouring
Isabelle a goblet of foaming cider. The two women ate quickly,
finishing everything that Agneatha had managed to bring back.
There were some of the little strawberries left over, too, and
they finished them off as well.

"I want a bath," Isabelle announced when they had finished
and the table was cleared away. "I am filthy, and have not
bathed since we left Langston over a week ago. My hair is
filled with dust. Go and find my stepfather, Agneatha. Our
man-at-arms should know where Rolf is. Tell him that I must
have a bath! Surely they bathe at this court." Sitting back down
upon the bed, she unbraided her hair, took up her brush, and
vigorously began to brush the red-gold locks.

Agneatha disappeared from the chamber. When her hair
was untangled, Isabelle arose, and, unbarring the shutters,
flung them open to look out the window. Below her was the
town of Winchester, the stones of its Romanesque cathedral
gray in the rainy morning light. The sky was beginning to

lighten considerably, and it appeared as if the day would be a pleasant one after all; but it was all so very different from home. Oh, Hugh, where are you? she thought. Come home to me. Please come home to me, my dearest lord. Then turning away from the window, she sighed.

There was a knock upon the door, and it opened to reveal Rolf de Briard. Entering, he kissed Belle upon her cheek. "Good morrow, Isabelle," he said. "Did you sleep well?"

She nodded. "I did, but I miss home, my lord."

"And you miss our fine bathing chamber," he said with a smile.

"I do! How do people wash themselves here, my lord?"

"I have arranged for you to have a wooden tub, and when you wish to bathe, you have but to set our men-at-arms to hauling the water," he told her. "They will bring it from the kitchens, where it is heated."

"How primitive," Belle said, wrinkling her nose. "Does even the king bathe like this, my lord?"

"I'm afraid so. He has an enormous oaken tub, bound with straps of iron. It is carried with his luggage when he travels from castle to castle," Rolf explained to her.

Isabelle shook her head. "A proper bathing chamber is better," she said. "The king sent me a basket of strawberries last night. I must admit that they were very welcome."

"He has not come here himself, has he?" Rolf asked her.

"Of course not," Isabelle said, and then asked, "Do you think he would dare? Ahhh, that is why you stationed our men-at-arms outside my door, Rolf. Thank you. I do not think I am ready yet to cope with King Henry. Damn! Where is Hugh?"

"I will do what I can to protect you, Belle, but you understand I cannot offend the king or directly oppose him," Rolf said.

"I know," Belle replied. "*I* will oppose him, however. I will not willingly give myself to such a lecher. He should be ashamed of himself, using his power and position to coerce a woman into his bed!"

Rolf said nothing further about the matter. Henry would seduce his stepdaughter with charm, and would indeed use his position and power to compel her to yield herself to him. Arguing with Belle would serve absolutely no useful purpose. She would soon learn that a king such as Henry Beauclerc could not be gainsaid. If he decided that he wanted Isabelle of Langston for his latest plaything, he would have her.

Agneatha arrived with the wooden tub, followed by a line of men-at-arms delivering the promised hot water. Rolf bid his stepdaughter farewell and departed. When the men had all gone, Agneatha locked the chamber door from the inside and helped Belle to disrobe. Belle sank down gratefully into the water, a slow smile lighting her features.

"Ohhh, that feels so good, Agneatha. Do we have any soap?"

The serving woman nodded. "Aye!" Then she produced a little cake scented with lavender. "Remember your wedding night, my lady, when your mother perfumed the bathwater, and you made such a fuss?"

Isabelle laughed as she lathered the soap between her hands and began to wash herself. "Aye, I remember! I've changed since then, haven't I? Besides," she excused herself, "my husband likes the scent."

"Ohh, my lady, do you think we'll ever see Lord Hugh again?"

"He's coming home, Agneatha, I am certain of it. *He must!*" Isabelle said in a strong voice. "Isn't it just like a man to run off and forget the time? They never grow up, do they?"

"No, my lady," Agneatha agreed, "they surely don't."

When Belle had finished her bath and washed her hair, she was dried and put into a fresh chemise. She wrung the excess water from her long hair, toweling it vigorously. It was foolish to dress, as the seamstress would be here this day, and besides, she didn't intend to leave this chamber until she could be seen in decent clothing. The men-at-arms removed the tub, first dumping the bathwater out the window onto the earth below.

They had no sooner done so when Mistress Mary, the seam-stress, arrived to take Isabelle's measurements. She was an apple-cheeked woman with a merry smile and an easy manner.

"How do you do, madame," she said, curtseying. "I have come from Master John, the draper. I understand you will need a small wardrobe for your stay at court. I have been told the lady Mavis of Farnley recommended me. A lady of great taste and style, she is."

"*Merci bien,* Mistress Mary," said Mavis as she breezed into the chamber. "Good morrow, Isabelle of Langston. I hope you don't mind, but I thought you would like my help."

"Oh, yes!" Belle said, delighted to see her new friend. "I so admired the garments you were wearing yesterday."

"Well, let's get started, Mistress Mary," Mavis said. "You brought the fabrics? Of course you did!"

Mistress Mary smiled at Mavis's enthusiasm, and nodded to her little assistant. "The mauve silk first." She turned to Belle. "This is to be for a skirt?"

"Aye," Belle said.

Mistress Mary set to work. She measured, she cut, she stitched. First a mauve-colored skirt, and then the buttercup-yellow skirt. Next came the tunic dresses that would be worn over the skirts: the gorgeous rich violet damask that was woven through with gold threads, and the delicate lavender with its intricately woven pattern. Mavis suggested that the lavender tunic be trimmed in silver *passemente*, and the seam-stress nodded her approval. Copper *passemente* was used to trim the tawny orange brocade tunic.

"That color is so good with your wonderful hair," Mavis said. "I didn't realize what glorious hair you had yesterday, as it was hidden under that modest little veil you were wearing. Mistress Mary, does Master John have a sheer material shot through with copper, and perhaps one with gold, and one with silver, that might make pretty veils for the lady Isabelle?" She turned to Belle. "Did you bring a chaplet with you, or perhaps a circlet or two?"

Belle shook her head in the negative.

Mavis looked again to Mistress Mary. "Who would you recommend?" she asked the seamstress. "It can't cost a fortune, either."

"Jacob the Goldsmith," Mistress Mary said without hesitation. "He's the most scrupulously honest man I've ever known. You can always be completely honest with him, and not have to worry that he'll gossip about your business to any other member of the court. Indeed I suspect he is the keeper of some great secrets. The king has been known to give Jacob his trade." She smiled up at Isabelle from her position on her knees, where she was pinning the orange tunic. "He'll find you a pretty piece for your veils that you need not be ashamed to wear before the high and mighty, but you'll not be forced to mortgage your estate to pay for it." She chuckled. "There, that one is done. Now, let us cut the last."

"I suppose Rolf would purchase me a chaplet if I asked him," Isabelle said thoughtfully. "I have a pretty one at home, but I never thought I should need it on this trip. Indeed, I thought I should be on my way home by this time. Ohh, that is not the material I chose for the last tunic, Mistress Mary, but my, it is beautiful."

"I switched it," Mavis said. "I went back early this morning because I kept thinking how dull that plain cream-colored brocade was, Belle. This fabric is far more striking, don't you think so?"

Isabelle looked at the creamy brocatelle, a brocadelike fabric with a slightly raised pattern. It had tiny gold-thread stars woven in it. "It is lovely," she admitted, but her practical soul was bewailing the cost of such fine fabrics that would only be worn during her short stay at court. Still, when they returned to Langston, perhaps she could have some of her new garments altered to fit her mother. Then they would both have beautiful gowns to wear on special occasions.

"Gold *passemente* on this one?" she asked Mavis.

"Excellent!" Mavis enthused. "The gold stars are charming,

but not quite enough for such a pristine color. The trim is just right!"

"Everything will be lined in matching sarcenet," Mistress Mary said.

The fitting done, the garments cut, Mistress Mary gathered up everything, folding it neatly, and placed it in a basket which she then handed to her assistant.

"How soon will you have something for the lady Isabelle?" Mavis demanded. "She will not show herself, and is confined to her chamber, until she has proper clothing. There are so many people I want to introduce her to, and her time at court is limited. It should not be spent in here."

"I can have one gown for you tomorrow," the seamstress said, "the rest, the day after." Then she curtsied to Isabelle and Mavis, saying to Belle, "Thank you for your custom, my lady."

"How is she to be paid?" Isabelle wondered when Mistress Mary had finally departed. "I have no money."

"Rolf will pay her," Mavis said. "You don't need to carry coins with you, Isabelle. That is a man's task." Then she changed the subject. "Do you play chess?" she asked.

"Yes," Belle laughed, "but not in my chemise. Let me dress."

Mavis nodded, and then said, "It's the dinner hour. I must go, but I shall return this evening and bring a board with me."

In the Great Hall, Mavis sought out Rolf and told him, "Belle and I have spent most of the day with Mistress Mary. I think you will be pleased by her transformation. She is to have a gown by tomorrow. Jacob the Goldsmith will come to show her chaplets, so be certain to pay him, too, my lord."

Rolf chuckled. "You are teaching my stepdaughter bad habits, Mavis, my sweet. She has always been a simple country girl."

"And so I think she would prefer to stay," Mavis responded. "I could see her thoughtfully assessing every coin she suspected was being expended on her finery; which she thought might be better spent elsewhere. She must certainly be an excellent chatelaine for Langston. When I have eaten, I will take the pieces and board, and go to play chess with her. I see you have stationed your own men outside of her chamber. 'Tis very wise, although they could certainly not prevent our friend from entering a room in his own house. Still, it is good."

"Isabelle understands her position, although she is certainly not happy about it," Rolf replied.

"Perhaps out of sight will be out of mind," Mavis answered him. "There are many pretty women here at court to take his fancy."

In their chamber, Isabelle and Agneatha dined on capon, beef, braised lettuces, fresh bread, butter, and cheese. The king's page appeared with a carafe of the king's own wine. It was rich and fruity, with a ruby color. Isabelle thanked young Henry Beauchamp.

"The king wonders if he might visit you in your chamber, madame," the boy said to her.

"Gracious!" Belle pretended to be astounded. "I do not think it would be proper, young sir, and besides, my new court gowns have yet to be made. I could not receive the king in *these* old garments. Please tell the king that tomorrow I shall have a gown, and shall tender my thanks for his kindnesses then. And you might ask him if his messenger to Duke Robert has yet departed for Normandy to ask for word of my husband."

The boy bowed and left her.

When Mavis returned with the chess pieces and the board, Isabelle told her of Henry Beauchamp's message from the king.

"He's certainly determined, isn't he?" Mavis said. "Well, Rolf has told me you know you cannot refuse him."

*"Why not?"* Belle asked, her eyes flashing green fire. "Why can I not refuse the king's lecherous attentions? Why must I

acquiesce meekly with a 'Yes, my liege,' and spread my legs for the royal member?"

Mavis of Farnley was astounded. "I . . . I don't know," she said. "Because he is the king, I suppose. Women just don't refuse a king."

*"Why don't they?"* Belle demanded. "A king is just a man. A powerful man, I will grant you, but a man nonetheless. Why should such a man be allowed to compromise the chastity of a respectable woman? You would think a good Christian king would want to protect such a woman, not menace her with his masculinity and his jurisdiction over her as her liege lord. It is wrong, and I shall not allow myself to be bullied!"

Mavis did not think that all of Isabelle of Langston's determination would protect her from the king, if the king's lust gained the upper hand. Still, she could see that Isabelle was not a woman to be argued with. It would do her no good to appeal to poor Rolf de Briard. If he learned of his stepdaughter's attitude when he thought her resigned to whatever happened, it would likely send him into a fit. He already felt guilty for having brought the girl to court.

"You will do what you think is best, of course," Mavis said, "keeping in mind Hugh's position, the well-being of your son, and of course, the fate of Langston." Then she laughed. "I think, perhaps, that Henry Beauclerc will meet his match in you, Belle. I do not believe that any woman has ever meekly said, 'No, my liege, and go away!' It should be quite a surprise to him, but beware your adamant refusal does not intrigue him even more than your fresh country charms," Mavis warned.

# PART III

# BRITTANY

*Summer 1103–Midsummer 1104*

# Chapter 11

*I*sabelle stared nervously into the polished silver mirror that Mavis had brought her. She could scarcely believe the elegant young woman staring back at her was Isabelle of Langston. She was wearing her yellow skirt with the tawny orange tunic. The tunic was girdled with linked copper disks enameled in yellow. A matching brooch was fastened upon her left shoulder. Her hair was neatly contained by a gold caul which was studded with tiny freshwater pearls. Over her head was a sheer gauze veil shot through with copper and held in place by a yellow enameled circlet. Belle wiggled her toes in the new soft shoes which had been dyed yellow to match her skirts. "I am really beautiful," she said softly. All her life she had been compared to Alette and found wanting; but now she realized it was just that the two were different in appearance, and Alette conformed to the fashionable ideal of beauty.

"Mary, Mother of God!" Mavis swore. "Are you just now realizing *that*, Belle? Of course you're beautiful." Then she laughed. "Looking at one's self in the waters of a pond never tells you all, does it?"

Isabelle shook her head. "No," she admitted. "My mother has a small copper mirror, but it isn't as large or as clear as your silver one, Mavis. Thank you for bringing it so I might see myself."

"And do you *now* understand the dangers you face from the king?" Mavis demanded in serious tones. "Oh, there are women at court, most of them better garbed and from more powerful families, but Henry Beauclerc will see only you, Belle. Do be careful, and do not displease him."

"I will not shame my husband willingly, Mavis," Isabelle said in a quiet voice. "Not even with a king. And the king should not allow his lust to erase a friendship of such long standing."

Mavis shook her dark head. "God help you," she said, "for surely now only He can, Belle."

The hall was a wonder, and Isabelle tried very hard to maintain her composure, but it was difficult. She could not help staring. Enormous fireplaces, six in all, lined the hall, three to a side. Above them were soaring, arched windows. From the carved and gilded beams of the hall hung banners of multi-colored silk such as she had never before beheld, and the noise was incredible. Over a hundred people inhabited the king's hall, seated at the trestle tables upon benches, their places secured by not simply their rank, but by their importance to the king personally. A man above the salt today could be well below it a month hence. The two young women found places toward the rear of the hall, settling themselves with a group of other ladies.

"This is Isabelle of Langston, Hugh Fauconier's wife," Mavis said, introducing her to the other women. "She is newly come to court with her stepfather, Rolf de Briard."

The others extended their welcome to Belle, examining her closely, nodding their approval at her garments, which, while suitable, were not above her station. "A well-brought-up young woman" was the silent consensus of Isabelle's table companions.

"I have not seen Hugh Fauconier yet, my lady," one of the women noted, "but I have seen that charming scamp, Rolf de Briard."

"My husband is overdue on king's business," Belle answered carefully. "I could not bear to wait at home a moment longer, and so my stepfather brought me to Winchester that we might seek the latest word of Hugh."

"Have you children yet?" another woman inquired.

"A son," Belle replied. "I left him in my mother's keeping."

"Ah, very wise," an older lady approved. "If not a mother's love, a grandmother's is next best. It will have been many years, however, since your mother had the keeping of an infant, I'll wager."

"Oh, no, my lady!" Belle said, laughing. "Sir Rolf has already given my mother two children, and she tells him she longs for more."

"Gracious!" the older lady declared, and then she chuckled. "Your stepfather is certainly a lusty fellow, but then, he was raised with the king, and we all know what sort of fellow he is!" This remark was followed by much worldly merriment.

Isabelle blushed. "So I have been told," she said. Then she turned away, undoing the little knife that hung from her girdle so she might spear any food offered her. Before her lay a fresh trencher of newly baked bread. While the king and his high nobles might eat off gold and silver plates, those at the back of the hall made do with hollowed-out loaves of bread to contain their food. She leaned over to Mavis and whispered, "Where is Rolf?"

"Up near the high board, I'll wager," Mavis returned. "He'll be with all of his old friends, the king's personal companions. They're a bawdy group. It's no place for an innocent like you."

Those at the rear of the hall were first offered fat prawns steamed in seaweed, and then venison stew was ladled into their trenchers. The sauce was of red wine and dill, but Belle was not certain how fresh the meat was and ate sparingly. Her cup, however, was filled with a respectable red wine. Afterward there were sugar wafers. I was better off eating in my chamber, Isabelle decided wryly.

Rolf arrived when she was barely finished with her meal. Kneeling by her side, he said softly, "I would formally present you to the king and queen, Belle." Then he smiled at her as he rose. "How pretty you look, daughter."

Belle stood, brushing crumbs and imaginary wrinkles from

her skirts. Politely, she excused herself and followed her stepfather to a place before the high board. They stood quietly,
waiting to be recognized. Belle saw the king surreptitiously
glance their way, but he made no move to acknowledge them.
They waited, and she could feel her temper rising. She dared
not, however, show any irritation. Finally the queen turned her
head, and seeing them, leaned over to whisper to her husband.
The king turned his head, and feigning surprise at seeing them
there, smiled broadly.

"Sir Rolf de Briard," he said, "and who is this with you?"
Although the king knew very well who Isabelle was, their first
introduction had been in secret, and must remain so. No one
else could know that they had already met, lest the rigid court
protocol be discommoded.

"My liege," Rolf said formally, "may I present to you, and
to our most noble and good queen Maude, my stepdaughter,
the lady Isabelle of Langston, wife to Sir Hugh Fauconier." He
bowed, and Belle curtsied.

"We welcome you most heartily," King Henry said jovially.
"I have but recently sent to my brother for word of Sir Hugh.
You will both stay with us until I have received an answer, will
you not?" He smiled toothily.

"Gladly, my liege, and you have our thanks for your gracious hospitality," Rolf answered, bowing again deeply.

Isabelle remained upright in a silent show of defiance. The
king grinned, a flick of his eye acknowledging her challenge.
Then the queen spoke. Her soft voice was tinged with the
sound of her Scots homeland. Her gentle blue eyes were guile-
less, her expression sweet. She was quite large with child.

"Have you children, my lady Isabelle?" she asked, her hand
going instinctively to her rounded belly.

Belle's anger melted. "Aye, madame, a son, known as Hugh
the Younger," she said with a smile. "He is in my mother's
care."

The queen nodded. "It is difficult, I know," she told Belle,
"to be torn between one's children and one's duty. You are

welcome to my chambers." She smiled her sweet smile at Isabelle.

"I thank you, madame, for your kindness," Belle replied, and then she curtsied to the queen, understanding that they were now dismissed.

"Nicely done," Rolf told her as they moved away.

The meal was over and the tables were cleared away. There was entertainment: a minstrel from Ireland who sang poignantly of death and noble battles; a juggler who, to Isabelle's amazement, could keep four gilded balls in the air at once; and a man and a woman with a pack of little dogs who danced on their hind legs, pirouetting across the stone floor of the hall to much clapping from the onlookers. Isabelle had never seen anything like it. She laughed, and clapped enthusiastically, a becoming flush staining her cheeks.

"Have you told anyone that you have a room to yourself?" Rolf suddenly asked her, concerned.

Isabelle shook her head. "No," she said. "Why would such a matter even come up? My sleeping arrangements can hardly be of interest to anyone else."

"If no one knows that you have been given the luxury of your own little chamber, no one will suspect that you are involved with the king," Rolf explained to her. "If anyone should discover it, play the innocent and say you thought it was due to the friendship the king has for your husband that you were given such an honor."

"I am not involved with the king," Belle said calmly.

"We both know it is just a matter of time," Rolf replied patiently.

"Shall I invite Mavis to share my quarters?" Belle said.

"Mavis has a bed," Rolf said a trifle irritably. "Do not be a little fool, Isabelle. You know better."

*"I will not whore for any man!"* Belle hissed angrily.

*"I will not argue with you further on this matter,"* he retorted. "You damn well know that your first duty is to

Langston and Hugh. If that means personally serving the king, you must!"

"Hugh would hardly be pleased to find Henry Beauclerc lusting after me, Rolf, and well you know it. I will avoid the king's attentions as best I can, I assure you," she said firmly.

*"And when you can no longer avoid the king?"* he demanded.

"Pray that time does not come," Isabelle replied. Then curt-seying to her stepfather, she found her way from the hall to her own chamber.

"Were you much admired?" Agneatha asked eagerly as Isabelle entered the room. "Did you see the king? Was the queen there? Is she pretty?"

Belle laughed at her serving woman's enthusiasm. "Of course I saw the king," she said, "and the queen, too. She is certainly pretty, but she looks so tired. I imagine I looked the same way when I was carrying young Hugh. The meal, however, was horrendous. I will be so glad to get home. The venison in the stew was tough, and the meat, I suspect, had hung a bit too long."

Agneatha carefully helped Belle remove her beautiful tunic. The maidservant then examined the garment thoroughly. "Not a single spot," she announced triumphantly. She brushed the tunic with painstaking care, gave it a shake, and folding it neatly, packed it away in the storage trunk. She followed a simi-lar procedure with Isabelle's long skirts while her mistress removed her soft shoes, setting them aside. Agneatha filled a small basin with warm water, and Isabelle bathed her hands, neck, and face. Then she scrubbed her teeth with a small, rough cloth and a paste made up of finely ground chalk, propolis, and mint. Rinsing her mouth, Isabelle next undid her tresses from their caul, and sat down so Agneatha could brush the long red-gold hair.

"Lady Mavis's serving wench tells me they'll soon be hunting in the New Forest," Agneatha said. "There is a royal lodge where the king and his guests stay; and the other great lords have lodges there as well. Do you think we'll be invited, lady?"

"I expect so," Belle said. "Lind should be here soon with Couper, and Sir Rolf's falcon." She sighed. "I wish we were home, Agneatha. Oh, how I wish my lord husband were here and we were all home!"

"Ohhh, lady, I think it ever so exciting to be visiting here with the king and his court!" Agneatha enthused. "When we go home, I shall have traveled more than anyone of my station in memory at Langston. I like it here. Langston is boring, with its humdrum everyday life."

"Yet I prefer it," Isabelle replied.

The door to the chamber opened suddenly and the king entered, smiling, as Agneatha, open-mouthed, dropped the hairbrush. "You know who I am, wench?" he asked her in jovial tones.

Agneatha nodded, struck dumb, stumbling clumsily as she curtsied.

"You will wait outside your mistress's chamber with the guardsman, and not enter here or allow anyone else entry until I tell you it is permissible. Do you understand, girl?"

"Yes, my liege!" The maidservant's voice was strangled. Then she backed from the room, eyes wide.

Going to the door, the king bolted it behind her.

"How dare you intrude upon my privacy," Isabelle said in icy tones. She held herself straight, but her heart was hammering wildly.

He turned. "I thought you very beautiful this evening in your new gown," the king said, ignoring her obvious anger, "but I think you more beautiful now in just your smock, your lovely hair loose and shining." Reaching out, he fingered a silken lock. "It is like silk to my touch."

"My liege, you insult me," she rejoined angrily. "Worse, you betray a friendship my husband treasures."

"To be bedded by your king is counted an honor, Isabelle,"

he told her, and moved closer to her, snaking his arm out to capture her.

Belle moved even more swiftly, avoiding that proprietary grip. "I count it no honor to be forced into whoredom, *even for the king*," she said coldly. "You are a man, my liege. No less. No more. An accident of birth has set you higher upon the ladder of life than others, than my Hugh; but it should not give you the right to force yourself upon me!"

"If you were a man, I should set you to argue the law for my benefit, Isabelle," the king told her, amused. No woman had ever defied him as openly or as cleverly as she was now defying him. He had been intrigued from the first, but this new side she was showing him set him aflame. Isabelle of Langston was a magnificent creature. He wanted her now far more than when he had first entered her room. This would be a seduction such as he had never known. It would take every ounce of his skill as a lover, and skilled he was.

His shrewdest adviser, and good friend, Count Robert of Meulan, believed Henry's passions were driven only by political concerns, and said so; but Robert was wrong. Henry Beauclerc's passions were driven by his love of beautiful women. He could not, it seemed, get enough of them. No two were the same. Their variety was infinite. They were fascinating, charming, adorable creatures made for a man's pleasure. Women were treasures to be kissed and caressed, to be filled with a man's seed. His blue eyes glittered dangerously. Then quickly reaching out, he captured her.

*"Let me go!"* she said furiously, struggling, fists futilely drumming his chest.

Instead, with a single finger he traced the outline of her full lips. "Lips such as these, Isabelle, are surely better employed in kissing than in contentious speech," he told her. "I am fully prepared to woo you, sweetheart, but if rape is more to your fancy, I am equally skilled in that art as well."

"I am going to be sick," Isabelle said abruptly.

*"What?"* The king's grip loosened slightly and he looked nervously at her. Certainly he could not have heard her aright.

*"I am going to be sick!"* she repeated, swaying. *"Ohhh, God!"* She broke free of his grasp, and grabbing up the basin, spewed the contents of her stomach into it. The pungent stink of vomit quickly filled the room.

Henry Beauclerc was startled by this sudden turn of events. All thoughts of seduction fled him as he stood there gazing upon Isabelle of Langston, who was now pale and continuing to sway slightly.

"The venison stew was overripe," she moaned. "I knew it, yet I ate it, for I was hungry." She doubled over, groaning piteously.

"I will fetch your servant," the king said, swiftly backing away from her, unbolting the door and hurrying out of the chamber.

A moment later Agneatha entered, looking very anxious. "Lady, was it the stew?" she asked, concerned. Putting her arm about Belle, she helped her to her bed. "The king says he will visit you another time," the girl told her mistress.

"Is he gone?" Belle half whispered.

"Oh, yes, lady! No man can stand the sight of a woman disgorging her guts. Takes the bloom right off romance, it does," Agneatha declared.

Belle jumped from the bed, giggling. "Give me some wine to rinse my mouth out with, Agneatha," she said. The color was already flowing back into her cheeks.

Sudden comprehension dawned in the servant's bright eyes. "Ohh, lady, you made yourself sick!" she said low.

"I used to do it when I was little and my mother would not give me something I wanted," Isabelle said. "It's really quite easy for me to do." She grinned. "The stew *was* overripe, but it had been settling. Now, however, I shall be able to avoid the court for a day or two while I recover from my indisposition." She took the goblet Agneatha gave her, swishing the wine about in her mouth and spitting it into the offensive basin before swallowing the rest to settle her now roiling stomach.

Agneatha grabbed up the basin. "I'll get rid of this down the garderobe, lady. Open the windows to air out the stink, or we'll never get to sleep here tonight." She hurried from the room.

Isabelle unbolted the shutters over the window, flinging them wide. Outside, an almost full moon silvered the roofs of the houses below in the town. She leaned upon the sill, breathing in the cool night air. Was Hugh, wherever he was, seeing this moon tonight? If indeed he was, then the moon was a bond between them. She prayed that it was so, and that he would come back to her quickly. Her interlude with the king tonight had frightened her. How long would she be able to fend him off before he became offended? *"Hugh,"* she whispered, *"come back to me, my love!"*

For the next two days, Isabelle played the invalid, keeping to her chamber, having Agneatha bring her dainty little delicacies from the hall. Mavis came, and Isabelle told her of her encounter with the king. Mavis couldn't help but giggle.

"I should have loved to have seen the look on the king's face when you threw up your dinner, practically at his feet. I doubt any woman has dared to do such a thing before," she exclaimed. "Well, you did hold our lusty monarch off, at least temporarily."

"I do not know what I shall do when he approaches me again," Belle confided worriedly. "If only Hugh would come home!"

"I don't think you'll be able to escape the king's advances again," Mavis said matter-of-factly. "I've never heard of him to lose interest in a woman before he had satisfied his desires on her body. You would need to be very, very clever to escape his attentions, Isabelle, without offending him. I do not think it possible."

"Nor do I," Isabelle admitted softly. "Ohh, none of this

would have happened if I had not insisted upon coming to court!"

"Praise God that I'm a virgin!" Mavis said. "He never compromises virgins of good and noble families."

"You've never been married?" Isabelle was surprised. Mavis was surely at least her age. "How old are you?"

"Eighteen," Mavis responded cheerfully. "I've been betrothed three times now, and they've all died of boyhood complaints. I almost got the last one to the altar, but he got the pox a day before the wedding, and was dead two days afterward. My family is making another match for me now. This one is a widower about Hugh's age. Fortunately, he has no offspring, so my children will be his heirs. They're planning to have the wedding around Martinmas." She grinned at Isabelle. "Let's hope this groom survives to enjoy our wedding night."

Isabelle couldn't refrain from giggling. "You are really quite dreadful, Mavis," she said.

"Well," Mavis responded, "having three prospective husbands die on a girl doesn't make her look exactly like a good luck charm. If I don't get this one to the altar and into bed, I shall be gossiped about by the more kindly—and thought to be bad luck by the not-so-kindly, who unfortunately are in the majority. Besides, I am getting old, and I want children."

"Ahhh," Isabelle said, her face unguarded and soft for a moment. "I do miss my wee Hughie. Sometimes when I am most afraid, I close my eyes and think of him. I can just imagine him toddling on those fat little baby legs of his after my little brother, Christian. How I wish I could go home!"

"There is to be a hunt tomorrow," Mavis told her. "Nothing big, just outside the town in the fields. The king is growing restless and longs to hunt stag in the New Forest, but it's too early for it yet. Will you ride with me?"

"Am I expected to attend the hunt?" Belle wondered.

"Two days is all you can hope to gain from an unsettled belly," Mavis said in practical tones. "You're part of the court now, and if you do not show up, it will seem odd, particularly

if the king sends after you, which he's bold enough to do. I
expect you seek to keep a liaison with him a private matter."

Isabelle nodded. "I do," she admitted, and then asked,
"What will I wear? Certainly not one of my good new gowns."

"Nay, one of the gowns you brought from home will do
very well," Mavis said, "but of course you can wear a pretty
headpiece."

Agneatha bustled into the room, brimming with excitement.
"Lady, Lind has arrived from Langston with your merlin!"

"Then that settles it," Mavis told her friend. "Your hawk is
here. You *must* hunt tomorrow. I'll come by for you, and we'll
attend the mass together before we go off." She then departed.

The next morning, before the first light even began to stain
the horizon, Isabelle arose, washed, and dressed herself with
Agneatha's help. She chose a dark green skirt and a tunic top,
which she belted with a twisted rope of green silk and copper
metallic thread. Her soft leather boots felt cold to her feet as
she slipped them on. She braided her hair, looping the plaits up,
affixing them with tortoiseshell pins and covering them with a
copper embroidered veil over which she set a copper circlet
decorated with malachite.

"Give me the leather gauntlet," she instructed Agneatha, and
then tucked it into her belt, where it would remain until it came
time for her to take Couper upon her hand.

Mavis came, and together the two women squeezed themselves into the back of the royal chapel to hear the mass. Afterward Mavis pulled Belle along into the Great Hall, where they
snatched up bread, meat, and pears. They gobbled their meal,
washing it down with cider, then hurried to the stables to find
their horses. Mavis mounted a delicate white palfrey.

"I call her Daisy," she told Isabelle, who was in the act of
mounting her gray gelding. "Holy Mother, that is a big beast!"

"He's quite sweet-natured," Isabelle informed her.

"What do you call him?" Mavis was fascinated to learn her
friend rode such a large horse.

"Gris," Belle answered, settling herself atop her animal.

"Lady." Lind stood by her stirrup. "I have brought you Couper."

"Thank you, Lind," Isabelle said, drawing the gauntlet from her belt and sliding it onto her hand. Then reaching out, she took the merlin from the falconer. "Greetings, *ma petite*," she cooed at the bird, who ruffled her feathers at the sound of her mistress's voice.

"She traveled well," Lind remarked.

"Were you given shelter and food?" Isabelle asked him.

Lind bobbed his head. "Aye, lady. There's plenty like me here from other places. Your lady mother says to tell you that little lord Hugh thrives in her care, but she hopes to see you home soon." Then seeing the horses stir restlessly as the hunt began to move off, he said, "I'll be here to take Couper from you when you return, my lady."

The hunting party rode through the town and across the fields to the nearby river. The dogs were set loose in the marshes to flush out any waterbirds nesting there. It was a disappointing day, however, for few if any birds could be found, which was unusual, given the location and the season. Isabelle had no chance at all to allow Couper to fly. The king was in a bad humor, she could see. Henry didn't like being disappointed.

They returned to the castle, where all afternoon and evening Isabelle listened to talk of a bad year. The crops were not growing. The hay had been scant. There was little fruit on the trees in the orchard, and what was there was small. It all portended a bad harvest. And now no waterfowl to hunt! Others, however, said that the spring had merely been later than usual. As for the lack of waterfowl, it was easily explained. The nesting season was past, and the birds had probably gone upriver for the summer.

The queen had not gone hunting that day. Her advanced state of pregnancy forbade it. She sat at the high board that evening, pale and obviously very uncomfortable. Watching her, Belle suddenly had a clever idea. It was obvious that the queen was not hungry, or could she simply no longer tolerate the rich diet provided by the king's kitchens? When the queen departed the hall with her ladies, Belle arose and, pulling Mavis along with her, followed.

"Where are we going?" her companion demanded. "Don't you know that the king's been eyeing you all evening like a sugar comfit?"

"That's why we're going to hide ourselves in the queen's chambers," Belle said with a naughty little smile. "The lady looks very uncomfortable, and just possibly I can be of service to her instead of to her husband."

Mavis shook her head, but she was laughing.

"Well, would you want to be in my position?" Isabelle demanded.

"Nay," Mavis replied, "I would not, but you cannot hold off the king forever, Belle. He always gets his way in the end."

*"Not this time,"* came the firm declaration.

They entered the queen's rooms in the company of the other women. Not long after, the queen said, "If this child is not soon born, I shall die! I have never been more uncomfortable in all of my life. I am swollen like a grape and can hardly walk anymore." She paced her day chamber nervously.

"Perhaps I can help you, Your Majesty," Belle said, coming boldly forward and curtseying. "Your Majesty may not remember me, for I am newly come to court. I am Isabelle of Langston, the wife of Sir Hugh Fauconier. I had many of Your Majesty's symptoms when I carried my own son. May I share with you my mother's remedies that helped ease them?"

"Ohh, pray do, Isabelle of Langston!" the queen begged.

"Your Majesty is too much upon her feet," Isabelle said, taking the queen by the hand and leading her to a settle. "Mavis, bring some pillows for the queen's back and to prop her legs up with." She knelt before Queen Matilda and gently removed her shoes. The woman's feet, ankles, and legs were badly swollen. "I do not know why," Isabelle said as she stood up again, "but keeping your lower extremities raised seems to help the swelling, my mother said, and it did help mine." She tucked pillows beneath the queen's legs and behind her back.

"There could be something to that," the queen said slowly. "In the morning when I arise my legs are not swollen at all."

"Perhaps instead of walking about during the day," Belle suggested, "Your Majesty might be carried in a litter. After all, you are in a most delicate condition right now. You carry England's heir, and should be treated gently. The king, God bless him, is a most active man, as we all know, but it is not he who is having this child. It is Your Majesty who is bearing the burden of new life."

"The lassie speaks good sense," said Mary Malcolm, the queen's old nursemaid who had come with her to England. "Keep her by yer side, my lamb. She'll be of more use to ye than yon giggling group of fine ladies. The younger know naught of birthing, and the older hae forgotten."

"There is also the matter of the queen's diet, Mistress Malcolm," Belle said pluckily. "The foods offered her majesty are too rich, and too greasy. A lady in her condition has a squeamish belly. The foods offered her should be nourishing, and gentle."

"Aye, yer right," Mary Malcolm said, "and why hae none of us had the good sense to remember it?" She was very aggrieved, not just at herself, but at the others chosen to serve her precious darling.

The young queen laughed. "You have met with Mary Malcolm's obvious approval, Isabelle of Langston. Stay with me as one of my companions until my child is born. I can see I shall need your advice even more in the days to come. I hope you will not mind giving up your hunting. I have been given to understand that you have a fine merlin."

"My falconer can exercise the bird, Your Majesty," Belle said sweetly. "I am more than glad to remain with my queen as long as I can be of help to her. I am not used to idleness, being a countrywoman, you see. May I have a pallet here in Your Majesty's chambers?"

"Of course," the queen agreed, delighted to have this charming young woman, near her in age, and less fettered by the pomp and circumstance of the English court than the other women about her. "I, too, was once a countrywoman," she told Belle. "I lived in the convent my aunt founded after her husband's death. She was the abbess there, and I thought to be a nun, but then King Henry sought me for a wife, and my brother acquiesced, for it meant peace between our two countries." The queen turned to Mavis. "Go and tell Isabelle of Langston's serving woman where she is and where she will remain tonight, else the poor girl worry about her mistress's whereabouts."

Mavis arose from her place upon a stool by the queen and, curtseying, hurried from the room.

"You will be quite safe with me, Isabelle of Langston," the queen said perceptively, and in that moment Belle became aware that the queen knew of her husband's peccadilloes.

Taking the queen's hand, she kissed it. "I thank Your Majesty for her favor. I am an honorable woman, and will serve you with as much devotion as my Hugh has served the king."

"It is much better that way, I think," Queen Matilda said with a twinkle in her blue eyes.

In the morning, after the mass, the king saw that Belle was among the queen's women. "Have you taken a new lady into your service, my dear?" he asked his wife.

"Aye, my lord, indeed I have," Queen Matilda replied. "Isabelle of Langston has become invaluable to me." She smiled up at her husband, batting her eyes at him. "Now that I am so close to giving England its next king, I should not be denied anything that I crave, Henry. Surely you do not want to upset me by stealing Belle away to your old hunts? You have enough companions to join you, but I must stay here, practically alone, and surrounded by *old* faces. There is hardly a young woman my age amongst my ladies. Besides, Belle has already helped reduce the swelling in my legs and feet that troubled me so. She has recent experience in being enceinte. I simply cannot do without her!"

"Very well, my dear," the king said with apparent good nature, and then he turned to fix his gaze upon Isabelle. "And *you*, madame, are you content to serve your queen rather than sample *all* the delights the court has to offer? It is not often easy to please royalty."

"I am a simple countrywoman, my liege," Isabelle answered him with honesty. "The *delights* you speak of are far too heady for me. I am satisfied to serve the queen until my husband comes home." She curtsied most prettily, giving him a bright, public smile.

Henry Beauclerc grinned back at her, then bowed in return. A most clever wench, he decided once again. She had outwitted him for the present. She did not know it, although he expected that her servant would tell her soon enough, but he had been in her chamber awaiting her return from the hall the previous evening. He had sent the maidservant to the common sleeping area for women of her lowly rank, giving the girl orders not to return until the dawn. Then he had made himself comfortable upon Isabelle's bed, but she had not come.

At first he had been concerned by her absence, and then he began to wonder if perhaps that modest and sweet demeanor she affected were not a ploy. Was she with a lover? Then he had laughed at himself. Isabelle of Langston had not been at court long enough to take a lover. Her servant had obviously been expecting her. Finally, after an hour, he had left her chamber, finding his page, Henry Beauchamp, and sending him to seek out Isabelle of Langston. The boy returned to say she was with her friend, Mavis of Farnley, in the queen's chambers. The king had gone to his bed alone, irritated and amused by turns.

Now he watched Isabelle hurry off with his wife and her other ladies. Turning to Rolf de Briard, he said, "Does your stepdaughter not understand her duty to me, Rolf? Certainly you have told her."

"Belle is a headstrong woman, my lord," Rolf said quietly. Then he added, "Her serfs call her Belle from Hell, for she can be most perverse in her behavior. She will have her own way, I fear."

"Then we are, I think, at an impasse of sorts," the king replied, "for I will have *my* way in the matter sooner or later."

No woman had ever before refused Henry, and he was puzzled by it. Why could the fair Isabelle of Langston not comprehend the honor being tendered her? And he always recognized his bastards. Perhaps Rolf, who was a gentle fellow, had not related the situation to the girl clearly enough. That could be the only reasonable explanation for her behavior.

The king watched for a moment when he might take Isabelle aside privately and clarify everything for her, but she was very skillful at avoiding such a meeting, and a small niggling doubt began to creep into his mind that she really did understand, but did not wish to be his mistress. It was absolutely unpardonable. Nay! *It was treasonous!*

Then fate smiled upon him. He went to the falcon mews to exercise his gyrfalcon, and found Isabelle there with her merlin. Seeing the king, she curtsied prettily. Then handing the bird off to her falconer and claiming her duties called, Isabelle hurried away. With a wolfish smile, the king followed. The route she had chosen to get back to the queen's apartments would take her through a secluded, narrow hallway. He would trap her there, and they would resolve the matter on the spot.

Isabelle could hear someone behind her. Instinct told her who it was. She walked quickly, struggling not to give in to panic or break into a run that would clearly indicate her feelings to the king. As long as she simply avoided him, there could be no confrontation. Then she realized she was entering the little hallway that connected with the large public corridor leading to the queen's chambers. The queen's ladies used it because it was a shortcut, but it was quite deserted. Her heart sank, and then she felt a hand upon her arm.

"Wait, Isabelle of Langston," she heard the king say, and she was turned about so that she faced him.

"Ohh, my lord." She feigned surprise at seeing him. "Please let me pass, for I shall be late, and her majesty is expecting me. I was only allowed a short recess in which to exercise Couper, my merlin."

Skillfully he backed her against the wall, pressing himself against her body. "You are driving me to distraction, you little temptress," the king murmured, and he leaned forward to kiss her.

Isabelle turned her head, and to his surprise, she giggled. "Ohh, Your Majesty, you are so naughty," she simpered at him. "You must not approach me in such a wicked manner. I am an honorable woman."

"I have not forgotten that night I came to your chamber and you were in your smock with your lovely hair loose about your shoulders. I cursed the venison stew that made you ill, interrupting what promised to be a most delicious interlude," Henry Beauclerc said, and his fingers dug into her arms. "*I want you, Isabelle!* Surely you understand what I mean? I know damned well that you do! *I am your king.* A king may do whatever it is that amuses him. If he could not, there would be no point in being king." The back of his hand softly caressed her neck. Then capturing her chin between his thumb and his forefinger, he kissed her mouth hard. "I want to fuck you, Isabelle, and I mean to, my clever wench. You have been told there is no shame in being my mistress, and I always acknowledge my bastards. I will take care of you as long as we are together and Hugh is not here to know of it." His hands were fumbling with his clothing, fumbling with hers.

Isabelle knew that she had to act this instant to escape the fate the king had in store for her. He meant to rape her here in this dimly lit hallway, she realized. Mustering every ounce of guile in her soul, she burst into loud sobs of anguish. Surprised by this turn of events, the king loosened his grip on her, and in that instant she pushed past him, dashing with what appeared to be a noisy display of deep sorrow down the remaining distance that separated her from the door leading out into the main corridor. Behind her she could hear him cursing furiously. Stepping forth into the public hall, she was once more the picture of composure, and quickly made her way back to Queen Matilda's apartments.

Mavis, however, noticed her friend's flushed cheeks. "What happened?" she asked Belle, her voice soft.

"*He* caught me in the shortcut, and was about to do his worst, but I got away," Isabelle said. Then she chuckled. "He used some very colorful language, I might mention. I had never heard some of the words."

"You are playing with fire," Mavis said, shaking her pretty head. "Heaven only knows what he'll do if you drive him too far." Then she thought a moment. "Rolf is seeking you. He said he would seek you out in the Great Hall later."

Rolf had news, Isabelle learned that evening, that a young messenger had arrived from Normandy that same day. Her stepfather did not know what word of Hugh the messenger carried, however, for the king had not yet told him.

That did not stop Belle. With Mavis's help, she sought out the messenger, a young and inexperienced squire. Mavis flirted with the boy quite shamelessly. "This is my friend, Isabelle of Langston," she gigglingly told the messenger. "Did you bring the king any word of her husband, Sir Hugh Fauconier? He was at Duke Robert's court last autumn and winter."

"Was he the lord who brought my lord duke that fine gyr-falcon who hunts cranes? What a bird she is!" the squire said admiringly.

"My husband raised the bird, and trained her himself," Belle said with a friendly smile. "I am quite put out with my Hugh, however. He plays at the duke's court when we need him back upon the manor."

"Oh, he is not at my master's court any longer," the messenger told her. "He left before the feast of the Nativity to visit with the Sieur de Manneville. My master was quite surprised when his brother sent for word of Sir Hugh. He assumed him gone home this spring from Manneville," the young squire finished.

While Mavis remained to flirt further with the young Norman so he would not grow suspicious, Isabelle hurried off to find her stepfather.

"God's bones!" Rolf swore, hearing her news. "What if your brother has killed him in a misguided attempt to regain Langston?"

"Hugh is not dead!" Isabelle said quietly. "I would know if he were dead. Richard is a coward. He would not kill Hugh, for fear of being discovered, but he would imprison him. We must return to Langston! He may attempt to see that harm comes to my son. To murder a distant child is far easier than murdering a grown man. Children are so susceptible." Why on earth, she wondered, had Hugh gone to Manneville? Surely he understood how dangerous Richard could be when thwarted. Had she not told him?

"What if the king will not let you go, Belle?" Rolf asked. "Henry is slow to give you the news the messenger brought from his brother, if indeed he intends to give you that news at all. Hugh's disappearance is only to Henry Beauclerc's advantage, daughter."

"Then I must stay, Rolf, but you must go home. Mother is not strong enough, or brave enough, to fend off Richard's wickedness. Besides, you have the advantage over any assassin in that you will be expecting an attack. I'll keep Agneatha and Lind to serve me. Take half of our men and ride with all haste for Langston. Go this very day, Rolf. I sense that there is no time to waste. Tell Mother what has happened. Then watch carefully for any sign of treachery against Hugh Fauconier's son, and Langston."

Rolf de Briard did not need further urging. He agreed

completely with his stepdaughter's assessment. It wasn't until he was halfway back to Langston that he suddenly realized that Isabelle had said nothing at all about how Hugh might be retrieved from her brother's clutches. She certainly could not count on the king's aid unless she yielded herself to him. Of course! That was her solution, and she had sent him home so she would not be embarrassed before her family.

When he was safely home, Rolf discovered, to his great distress, that there was another answer. The king's royal messenger came to Langston, demanding that the lady of the manor return to court, which had now removed to the New Forest for the hunting season.

Astounded, Rolf told the king's messenger, "My stepdaughter is not here. I left her in Winchester myself several weeks back. She said nothing of returning home to Langston. Nor are her servants here. Tell the king I am at a complete loss as to where she might be, but if she returns home, I shall certainly tell her of his royal command and see she immediately rejoins the court."

The messenger departed. Two days later Agneatha and the men-at-arms returned.

"Where is your mistress?" Rolf de Briard demanded of the girl.

"Is not my lady here, my lord?" the maidservant replied.

Rolf shook his head. "No, Agneatha. She is not."

Agneatha began to weep. "I awoke one morning, my lord, and she was gone. Lind, too, their horses, and the merlin. I waited for some days, but she did not return. The queen was most distressed, my lord. The king was furious, and threatened to have me beaten if I did not tell him where she was, but I could not. I went to the lady Mavis, but even she claimed not to know what had become of my lady Isabelle. When the court decamped for the New Forest, the men and I began our journey home."

*"Richard!"* Alette's face was ashen.

Rolf shook his head. "Nay. He had no means of spiriting her from the court. Besides, if he had, why take Lind, their horses, and Couper? Nay, my sweet wife. Knowing her child safe with us, Isabelle has, I suspect, gone to Normandy to fetch Hugh herself. That can be the only answer, I fear. I hope she was wise enough to travel with someone else going her way, for to travel alone is surely to invite disaster. She'll probably go to Duke Robert and plead for his aid, since Richard is his liegeman. What a girl your daughter is, Alette. I want no headstrong offspring like that," he told his wife.

"Nor would I give you another like her," Alette said fervently. "I tried to be a good mother, Rolf. I did! But Belle was always too strong for me to handle."

"We must pray for our lady's safe return," said Father Bernard in soothing tones. "I know that God is with Isabelle of Langston, for her cause is a just one. Trust in God, and His Blessed Mother, my children. We know that the lady Isabelle will return safely to us in the Lord's time, and Hugh Fauconier with her."

The priest led them all to the chapel.

# ▓Chapter 12

*T*he king had not been forthcoming at all to Isabelle about the messenger from his brother. In fact he said nothing to her about Hugh, despite the fact she approached him when he was with the queen in the Great Hall and asked. Isabelle now knew what she must do. She sought out the household steward of Anselm, the Archbishop of Canterbury, who was about to embark upon a pilgrimage to Rome.

"Two of my servants, falconers, must travel to Normandy," she said. "May they travel with your train, Master Odo, that they be safe from robbers and other evildoers?"

"We leave on the morrow," the archbishop's steward said doubtfully.

"They can be ready," Isabelle replied. "They have a merlin for the duke's son, a gift from the king to his nephew."

"A merlin for an infant?" The steward raised his eyebrow.

Isabelle laughed. "I agree," she said pleasantly, "but the king would insist the bird be sent, and hand-delivered by my own falconers. What could I do?" She shrugged fatalistically.

"They may travel with us," the steward said. "They must provide their own food, however. I will see they are given drink."

"My thanks," Isabelle said, pressing a coin into the steward's fat hand. "They are good men, and I will rest easy knowing they travel in relative safety with the archbishop's train."

"They are fortunate to have so caring a mistress," the

242

steward said approvingly, his palm feeling the generous weight of the coin. "I will ask my master to pray for you and your family."

"I am honored," Isabelle said, curtseying and withdrawing.

"Lord Hugh is like to kill me," Lind said nervously when Isabelle sought him out and explained her plan to him.

"Lord Hugh can do nothing while he is imprisoned by my brother," she answered him.

"We will be discovered for certain, lady," Lind fretted.

"No one will penetrate our ruse, I promise you," Isabelle assured him. "We shall be brothers. You the elder, I the younger. I am called Lang. We are falconers, freedmen, traveling in our youth before settling down with a master. Though I have told the archbishop's steward we travel to the duke's court to deliver a bird, 'twas but a little lie. We shall not go there at all, and since the archbishop is not going there, his steward will not know whether we arrive at Duke Robert's court or not."

"Where are we going?" Lind ventured.

"To my ancestral home at Manneville," Isabelle told him. "My lord Hugh was last seen there, and I will wager he is still there, imprisoned in my brother's dungeon."

"And if he is," Lind spoke up more boldly now, "how can you and I rescue him, lady? If your brother is bold enough to jail my lord Hugh, will he listen to you? I think, lady, you will find yourself imprisoned as well."

"I do not intend to beard my brother in his own den," Isabelle said patiently. "All you and I are going to do is ascertain that my husband is at Manneville. Then we will go to Duke Robert's court and lay our evidence before him. The duke will see that Hugh is freed, *and* the men who traveled with him. We must not forget the six Langston men and Alain, your fellow falconer. They will have been incarcerated by my brother as well, else they would have come home."

"Unless they're dead," Lind said gloomily.

"I know my brother," Isabelle replied. "He will have forced

the Langston men, and possibly even Alain, to serve him; he does not like waste. He would not feed them unless they earned their bread. But he could not allow them to go free."

"And just how is anyone going to believe that you are a lad, lady?" Lind demanded. "You've not the look of a lad."

Isabelle gave him some coins from her small purse. "Go to the town market, Lind, and purchase us the food and whatever else we will need for our journey. Pack it in our saddlebags, but be discreet. The fewer people who see you, the less the likelihood of our true destination being discovered." She dismissed the falconer, then hurried off to find her friend, Mavis of Farnley.

"You're surely mad," Mavis said when Isabelle had told her of her plan. "I'm as big a fool for romance as you are, Isabelle. I'm not certain what you are doing is wise, but I'll help you with your wardrobe. The brother who used to chaperone me when I first came to court went home some months ago to wed, but he left some of his clothing. I can give you several pairs of chausses and two cotes. I think there is a mantle you can have as well. You'll have to find boots, Isabelle, that go halfway to your knee. You can't wear those pretty dainty shoes of yours. Ranulf left a rather worn pair of boots. You've got a large foot for a woman, and his was small for a man's. They just might do. And you'll need knitted hose as well. We'll need the privacy of your chamber to try these garments on. Can you get rid of your Agneatha?"

Isabelle nodded.

"Do so, and I'll bring my brother's clothing to you," Mavis said. "Agneatha doesn't know what you're planning, does she?"

"Nay," Isabelle said. "I cannot take her with me. Do not tell her that you know where I've gone, Mavis. It's better she remain ignorant else she be frightened into telling by the king. See that she and my Langston men go home as soon as possible."

"I will," Mavis pledged, and then she hurried off to fetch the promised garments.

Isabelle wended her way through the king's garden, where the two young women had been able to speak without fear of being overheard. Gaining her own chamber, she sent Agneatha off to Mistress Mary's stall in the market to find her a new head veil. It was unlikely Agneatha would run into Lind, and if she did, it would give Lind an opportunity to practice his deceptive skills upon the maidservant.

A soft knock came upon the chamber door, and it opened to admit Mavis, carrying a small selection of garments. All were well made, of good material, but not so rich that it would arouse suspicion. The colors were dark and simple. The warm, dark brown mantle had a clasp that was of greenish bronze in a Celtic design. Isabelle tried everything on, and it fit.

Mavis giggled. "You have too much bosom for a boy."

"Watch, and see," Isabelle told her. Turning her back, she bound her breasts with a length of cloth, then whirled about to face her friend again. "Is that better, Mavis?"

Mavis, more serious now, eyed her friend critically. "Aye," she nodded, "but what will you do about your lovely hair, Belle?"

"I shall cut it," Isabelle said softly. "And I shall dye it with dark stain else its bright color attract attention I do not want. I see no other choice, Mavis, do you?"

Large, fat tears began to run down Mavis's pretty face. "Your hair is so beautiful, Belle," she sobbed. "Oh, do not do this foolish thing, I beg you! Can you not remain with the queen? Surely she will protect you."

"I must find Hugh," Isabelle said. "There is no other way, Mavis, and you know it. I cannot hide behind our good queen's skirts forever. The king has still not told me of the messenger from his brother. I do not think he means to, either. Under those circumstances, how can I plead with him to send again to his brother, the duke, to go to my brother and search his dungeons? It is all hopeless! I have to go, Mavis. Who else is there to aid Hugh Fauconier but me?"

"You're right," Mavis sniffled. "I do not think I could be so brave as you are, Isabelle of Langston. God and His Blessed Mother travel with you, my friend!" Then Mavis of Farnley ran from the chamber.

Quickly Belle wrapped up the clothing she had brought, and hid the bundle away where Agneatha would be unlikely to find it in the few hours remaining before her departure. And when her maidservant returned from Mistress Mary's stall, triumphant, a beautiful veil of iridescent threads in her possession, Isabelle praised her mightily.

"It's beautiful, Agneatha. The loveliest veil I have ever seen. My silver circlet will be perfect with it!" She clapped her hands gaily. "Let us celebrate your cleverness, my lass. Pour us both a goblet of that fine red wine the king keeps me supplied with, and we shall drink to the prettiest veil in all of Winchester. Nay, England!"

Giggling at her mistress's good mood, Agneatha complied, pouring them both generous portions of the king's vintage. Isabelle, however, remembered how the rich brew had affected her servant the last time she had tasted of it, and sure enough, Agneatha soon fell asleep once again, tumbling into her trundle to snore the night away.

Isabelle slept herself for several hours, waking in the darkest part of the night. She lay for several minutes, and then slipped from her bed. Taking up her knife, she sliced through her thick braid, biting on her lip so hard she tasted blood as she felt her hair pull free of her head. The faint firelight illuminated the plait now in her hand. Stirring the coals in the tiny fireplace, she laid the hair upon them, and then went to open the window so the smell would not awaken Agneatha. Pouring water from the pitcher that had been set in the warm ashes, she mixed a dark stain with it and, bending, dunked her head until it was quite thoroughly soaked. The stain was walnut, and she knew it would take immediately. She toweled the excess from her head, adding the towel to the fire so it would not be discovered. Then carefully feeling her way, she evened out the line of her hairstyle, using the little pair of scissors that she possessed. She would take them with her.

Quickly she dressed, drawing on a pair of dark green chausses, gartering them tightly, and pulling the dark knitted hose on over them. Then she bound her breasts. Next came a linen jupe lined in soft light wool. The sea would be chilly. Over the jupe she wore two silk shirts, and finally a cote. Slowly she drew on the black leather boots Mavis had given her. She and Mavis had been delighted earlier to discover that the boots fit perfectly. The men's clothing felt strange to Isabelle. She picked up her mantle, put it around her shoulders and fastened it. Then reaching down, she picked up the bundle of additional clothing she was taking. Agneatha was still snoring loudly. Belle smiled softly, and opening the door to her chamber, slipped out into the corridor, where Bert stood dozing outside her door, as she knew he would be, leaning upon his pike, his blond head nodding. She tiptoed past him.

Down in the stableyard Lind waited with their horses. His eyes widened at the sight of his *brother*, Lang. Isabelle put a finger to her lips and silently mounted Gris, taking Couper on her gauntlet. Wordlessly, Lind mounted his own animal, and together they walked the horses to the castle gate. The guard nodded and let them pass.

"I told him we were traveling with the archbishop," Lind said when they were out of earshot. "I thought it better he didn't look too closely at you, my lady, but I must say you make a fine lad."

"I do not intend to speak a great deal," Isabelle told him. "It is difficult to keep my voice lowered and deep. I don't want to give us away before we've obtained our objective."

"Aye," Lind agreed, but frankly, he wasn't too certain this was going to work. Still, he was her servant, for all the lady Isabelle was a woman. It wasn't his place to question her decisions.

They reached the archbishop's courtyard, where his great train was assembled and just about ready to go. Isabelle pointed out the steward, Odo, to her companion, and Lind approached him, bowed, spoke a moment, and then returned to tell his mistress that they were to travel at the end of the train with several others who had attached themselves to the archbishop's party for safety's sake. They reached the coast late that day, embarking the next morning for Normandy.

Isabelle had never been in a boat on the sea, and she was frankly a little frightened. She, Lind, and their horses were loaded onto an open deck, and there they remained until they reached their destination two days later. They were fortunate, she learned from listening to the talk around her, to encounter no storms. In a sheltered corner of the deck, with Couper in the crook of her arm, Isabelle huddled with Lind, who was no less in awe of their situation than his mistress. Neither of them could eat anything but a little bit of bread, and they swallowed but a sip of wine now and then to keep from being thirsty. Watching the coast of England disappear had been the most terrifying thing Belle had ever known. Seeing the coast of Normandy coming nearer and nearer was the greatest relief. They left Archbishop Anselm's train, still pretending to be going to Duke Robert's court at Rouen. Instead they traveled in the direction of Brittany, for Manneville was located close to the border of that country.

As they traveled they could not help but notice the crops in the fields were not a great deal better than those in England. It was obvious that it was to be a bad year all around. The poverty, however, seemed even more deeply ingrained here. To their relief, there was little traffic upon the roads they took. Each night they would find shelter in the fields, for Isabelle dared not spare the few coins they carried on lodging, even in church-sponsored guest houses. Who knew when they might need the hard currency? Besides, masquerading as a boy, she would have been housed with other men, a situation she chose to avoid. They carried their scant food with them, supplementing it with small purchases in the few villages through which they passed. Finally, they reached the ancestral home that Isabelle had never known.

She saw Manneville for the first time from the crest of a hill. It was a small castle, not even as large as Langston Keep, built of grim, dark stones. There was nothing warm or welcoming about it. Belle could well understand now her mother's delight in leaving it for England. She stood silent for a long time, and then Lind spoke, breaking her reverie.

"Well, lady, what do we do now?"

"I must think on how we can best approach Manneville," Isabelle said slowly. "Can you see if there is a mews somewhere?"

"Every lord, high or low, keeps hunting birds," Lind said. He waited for her decision. She had really surprised him in the days that they had traveled together. On that first morning when the sun had finally risen and he had gotten a good look at her, he had been shocked. Gone was Isabelle of Langston. Next to him rode a gangly boy with short-cropped dark hair. He realized that she had cut her glorious red-gold hair and dyed it with walnut stain. Only then did he truly understand how deeply committed she was to finding her husband.

She rode by his side, Couper in her charge, and never once did she complain about the hours spent in the saddle, or the lack and poor quality of the food they ate. She was, he decided, a very brave lady. He had more confidence in her and their mission now than he had when they first started. He still wasn't certain, however, that they would get safely back to England, or even find Lord Hugh at all, but what an adventure she had led them on, he thought.

Finally Isabelle spoke. "Richard may have a few birds, but it is unlikely he keeps a falconer. Perhaps you could cajole him to take us on, Lind. My brother is very tight with a coin, but he must be convinced to let us stay so we can find out where he is keeping Hugh."

"Let us be off, then," Lind said, and together they rode down the hill to the gates of Manneville.

They were allowed into the little castle, and brought to the Great Hall where Richard de Manneville sat at his dinner. Isabelle struggled to keep her eyes to herself, but her quick glance about the hall showed it to be clean. She and Lind stood before her brother. This was the first true test of her disguise. Would Richard penetrate it? She scarcely breathed.

"Well, who are you?" Richard demanded.

"I am Lind, my lord. This is my brother, Lang. We are falconers, my lord. Freedmen."

"You are not Norman," Richard said, peering hard at them.

"Nay, my lord. We are English," Lind answered him pleasantly.

"What do you want, then?" Richard de Manneville demanded suspiciously.

"My brother and I have decided to go adventuring this summer. We have traveled from our home, near the New Forest. Whenever we find ourselves short of coin, we offer our services to the local lord. I saw your mews, my lord, as we entered the castle. If you do not keep a falconer, then perhaps there would be some work for us. And if you do keep a falconer, then we ask but a night's shelter, and we shall be on our way."

The man sitting to the Sieur de Manneville's left leaned over and murmured something to his lord. Sneaking a look at him, Belle recognized Luc de Sai. She held her breath, wondering what it was he had said to her brother. Surely he hadn't recognized her.

"I have no falconer," Richard finally said. "My birds are but rough-trained and could use some seasoning. If you do a good job, I may pay you in coin. Until then I will but provide food from my hall, and you can sleep in the stable loft."

"Thank you, my lord," Lind said, bowing, and poking at his *brother* to do the same. Together they backed away from the high board and found places at a trestle below the salt. Silently they ate wooden bowls of hot rabbit stew, and nothing, Belle thought to herself, had ever tasted so good. They hadn't eaten hot food since leaving England. Afterward, the castle's steward, a bent old man, showed them to the stables, where they would be housed along with their horses.

For the next week they worked diligently with the Sieur de Manneville's falcons, all of whom had been wild caught and only given the rudimentary lessons of training. Together they smoothed the birds' rough behavior until Lind was satisfied that the falcons could hunt with even Duke Robert's gyrfalcon. Richard was more than pleased. Isabelle could not ever remember seeing him so amiable. Then she learned her brother would be joining the duke's court in the autumn. Having such well-trained birds would but be a credit to him.

His young wife, however, would not be going. She had given her husband a son, lost a daughter, and was even now with child again. Isabelle had seen her sitting to her husband's right that first night. She was a quiet, pretty girl with soft blue eyes, and dark blond plaits that hung neatly on either side of her head. Isabelle could not help but wonder how her brother had attracted such a sweet girl, for it was obvious that all the servants adored her.

Richard was, nonetheless, oblivious to his good fortune in his choice of a mate. He never praised his wife for anything, but he was quick to criticize her loudly and publicly if everything was not to his liking. Seeing him behave so, Isabelle realized now how much like their father Richard was, and how the gentle Blanche de Manneville, for that was her sister-in-law's name, was much like her own mother. Dutiful. Silent. Uncomplaining. And obviously very unhappy except when in the company of her little son.

Isabelle and Lind had been at Manneville several weeks, and they knew their time here would soon be ending. They had seen none of the Langston men, nor any sign of Alain, the falconer. Manneville's dungeon was used for storing wine, they had learned. Isabelle was at her wits' end. "Where can he be?" she wailed to Lind as they sat in their hayloft one afternoon.

"I do not know, my lady," Lind replied, "but it is obvious that my lord Hugh is not here at Manneville."

"If Richard has harmed one hair on his head," Belle vowed, "I will personally kill him myself, Lind!"

Below them they heard a gasp of fright, and before she might say another word, Lind was over the side and down into the stable to catch their eavesdropper. Isabelle was close enough behind him to see the terrified face of Blanche de Manneville.

*"You are a girl!"* Blanche cried softly.

"I am your sister-in-law, Isabelle of Langston, and please keep your voice down, lady. We mean you no harm." But Belle did not suggest that Lind release his captive yet. Instead she came directly to the point. "My husband, Sir Hugh Fauconier, was last seen here at Manneville. He has not, however, returned to England. Do you know where he is?"

Blanche de Manneville's blue eyes were enormous in her fright, but it was not, Isabelle could see, they who were frightening her.

"Richard does not have to know who I am, or that you told me," Belle reassured her. "In fact I think it far better that he does not know," she finished with a small smile of encouragement.

"I am not afraid of my husband," Blanche finally said. "Not since the night he kidnapped me from my home and raped me so I would be forced to marry him. I was to be betrothed to another man, but Richard coveted my lands, which match with his. He wanted a wife, and he chose me for that reason. I may despise him, but I do not fear him. He is a coward at heart, but if you know him, you know that, Isabelle of Langston."

Belle nodded. "I do know that," she said. "If you do not fear Richard, then what is it that keeps you from speaking the truth?" she asked her sister-in-law. "Lind, let her go. She will not run."

"I fear the sorceress, and her brother," Blanche de Manneville replied. "Richard swore a fealty to her in secret before he went to England to try to steal your lands. She promised him that if he would be her man and be loyal to her, whatever he wanted would be his for the asking. She promised him she would cast the proper spells. You can imagine how angry he was when he returned home defeated at your hands." She smiled a small smile. "But the sorceress assured him he had but to be patient. She predicted that your husband would come to Normandy, and when he did, Richard would get what he wanted."

"Is Hugh dead?" Isabelle asked her with a sinking heart.

"Nay! The sorceress came to Manneville after Hugh arrived here with Richard last year. She immediately desired him, and somehow managed to rob him of his memory and his will, using her magic. She took him back with her to her own lands, and his men, too. Richard plans to send Luc de Sai to England when he is at court with the duke, thus providing himself with an alibi. Luc is to kill your son and force you into marriage. Your lands will then be Richard's, for Luc de Sai is his man, or so my husband believes," Blanche de Manneville concluded.

"Where is Hugh imprisoned, and who is this sorceress?" Isabelle persisted. "I will find him and get him safely back to England."

"It is hopeless," Blanche replied. "Her name is Vivienne d' Bretagne, and she is very powerful. Even the church turns a blind eye out of their fear of her. Your husband is lost to you, Isabelle. Go home, and be on your guard for Luc de Sai. Protect your child!"

"Where is this sorceress's lair, Blanche?" Isabelle demanded in a hard, fierce voice. *"Tell me!"*

"What of your child?" Blanche pleaded.

"He is well-guarded, and under the king's protection." Isabelle altered the truth only slightly to ease Blanche's worry, and to gain her own way. She had to know where Hugh was! *"Tell me!"*

"Vivienne d' Bretagne's castle is located on the coast, near Lamballe. Ohh, you must beware of her, Isabelle. She sees, they say, into a person's very heart, and mind, and soul. They say she is the devil's daughter."

"You have seen her," Isabelle said. "Tell me what she looks like, Blanche. Is she beautiful?"

Blanche nodded. "She is very, very fair. Her hair is like midnight, and she has eyes the color of violets. It is difficult to understand how one so beautiful could be so wicked, but she is."

"You will not tell Richard that I was here, will you?" Belle asked her sister-in-law.

Blanche de Manneville shook her head. "Nay," she said in her quiet voice. "I think that what my husband has done, and plans to do, is very wrong. I cannot fight him openly, you understand. I have neither the courage nor the means; but by telling you what you need to know, perhaps he can be foiled. I do not understand how you plan to gain the advantage of this sorceress, but I will pray to God and His Blessed Mother to watch over you and keep you safe, sister. If it were me, I should go home to England and to my child."

"Do you love my brother?" Belle asked her sister-in-law.

"Nay!" The answer was quick, and then Blanche flushed guiltily. "I am ashamed to say I do not, nor do I respect him, though he does not know it, or understand how I feel. My sole use to him is as a breeder."

"If I were married to Richard, I should feel the same way," Belle said to Blanche. "I would gladly leave *him* in the sorceress's hands; but I am not wed to Richard de Manneville. I am Hugh Fauconier's wife, and Hugh Fauconier is the kindest, most noble of men. I love him, and I will not rest until he is free!"

"Then if you are that determined," Blance said, "I will tell you the way to go, Isabelle of Langston."

* * *

Lind and Belle departed Manneville before dawn on the following morning. They had collected several coppers and a small piece of silver from the Sieur de Manneville, who was feeling unusually generous at the thought of how well his birds now performed and how they would certainly help bring him into the duke's favor. It was mid-September now, and while the sun remained warm above them in a luminescent sky, the morning air had an underlying chill to it. They guided their horses through the misty dawn. Their journey, Blanche had told them, would take two days.

"Be certain to get to the castle, which is called La Citadelle, before sunset. At sunset the drawbridge is raised, the gates barred, and a pack of wild dogs loosed upon the land. Any living thing found by these beasts is torn to bits," Blanche warned them.

Consequently, they rode hard the first day in order to be certain to reach La Citadelle on the following day before dark. Although they expected Vivienne d' Bretagne had her own falconers, they had decided to offer their services to her anyway, as a means of entering the castle grounds to seek for Hugh and the Langston men.

As they rode on the second day, they were struck by how desolate the countryside was about them. There were no villages or farmsteads. Just miles and miles of empty green and rocky landscape. The salt tang of the sea filled the air as they came closer to their destination.

In midafternoon they saw it: a great, grim, gray fortress, its four towers thrusting forth into the golden afternoon. La Citadelle was surrounded by a wide, deep moat on three sides. On the fourth side it clung to the cliffs, almost seeming to be one with them. Below it the seas roared endlessly, as they had for centuries before and would for centuries after. The two riders stopped for a moment to observe the fortress.

"If he's there, lady, we'll never get him out," Lind said, his fears returning tenfold. There was an air of wickedness about the place. The thought of crossing over that drawbridge was frightening.

"I cannot ask Duke Robert for his help if I am not certain whether Hugh is there or not," Belle said with logic. "As soon as we have proof, we shall leave, I promise you, Lind."

"We are no longer in Normandy, lady. This is Brittany," Lind replied, and his horse, sensing his nervousness, shifted restlessly.

"Duke Robert will speak to the Count of Brittany," Isabelle said firmly. "Come along now. The sun is beginning to get lower. We don't want to get caught outside when they loose the dogs."

Together they crossed the drawbridge. On the other side they were stopped by a burly guard. "State your business," he said.

"We are falconers," Lind replied, "come to offer our services to the lady, Vivienne d' Bretagne. We were at Manneville, and they said she might have use for us." Lind bobbed his head respectfully.

"You may pass," the guard said. "Stable your horses, and see the household steward in the Great Hall. He will know if you are needed. If not, you'll be safe the night here. We don't welcome strangers, but the laws of hospitality hold even here."

"We were warned not to arrive after sunset," Lind said, and the guard laughed.

"Aye," he said. "Our doggies would have made a nice meal of you two and the little bird." He laughed all the harder when Isabelle drew Couper closer to her, as if to protect the falcon.

The stables were clean, as was the bailey and the castle when they entered it. Yet there was something in the air that bade them be cautious. They found the steward, and to their surprise he was pleased to see them.

"My lady has only recently desired hunting birds, and intended to send to England for some falconers. You two are English, are you not?" the steward asked. He was a tall, spare man, but his face was not unkind.

"We are, sir," Lind replied. "I am Lind, and this is my younger brother, Lang. We are freedmen, and have been trained as falconers."

"What brought you here?" the steward inquired.

"We have been adventuring," Lind answered, "for we have not yet taken wives. We decided to see a bit of the world, and so we travel about, offering our services to those who can use them. We were at Manneville last, and were recommended here by the sieur's lady."

"The position here would be permanent," the steward said. "I want no vagabonds, you understand. The terms would be fair, and you would be housed, fed, and clothed. I would expect you to serve my lady for a year, at which time it would be decided if you suited us."

Lind pretended to think a moment, and then he said, "I agree for both Lang and myself, sir. This is a fine establishment, and traveling about the world is not really all that they say it is."

"Good," said the household steward, and then he asked, "You are competent at what you do, are you not? We already have one falconer, a gruff fellow, but an excellent man. He will not tolerate poor performance."

"We have been trained by a falconer who once belonged to the great house of Merlin-sone," Lind said. "We are more than competent."

"Good!" the steward answered. "I shall take you to Alain, and tomorrow he will test your skills. If they are all you say they are, then you will become part of this castle's company."

Their eyes had made instant contact at the mention of Alain's name, but now they bowed to the steward, who decided they had pretty manners and would do nicely, provided their skills were everything they claimed they were. They followed him from the Great Hall, back out into the bailey, across the courtyard to a fine stone mews.

"We're just beginning to collect birds," the steward explained. "Alain, are you there? Come forth!"

The door to the mews opened, and there was Alain. Isabelle

almost cried aloud with joy as he stepped out into the fading light.

"Here, Alain, I've brought you two young falconers come to the gates this day seeking a place. Take them out tomorrow, and if they are worthy of your own skill, we shall take them on. The taller is Lind, and the other, Lang."

"Why, Sir Steward," Lind said before Alain might speak, "this is the very man who taught both my brother Lang and me our skills. He was once a falconer in the house of Merlin-sone. Do you remember us, Alain of Worcester? Lind, and his brother Lang, of the New Forest."

Alain made an appearance of peering at the two, and then he smiled, saying to the steward, "I did indeed train these two lads myself, Master Jean." He turned back to Lind. "What brings you here, my friend?"

"We were looking for the right place, my brother and I," Lind said meaningfully. "I hope we have found it."

"You have indeed!" Alain said enthusiastically. "You will enjoy being in service to this house, my friends."

Master Jean beamed, pleased. "I shall leave these two with you, Alain. Bring them to the Great Hall for food, and find them a place to bed down. *She* will be most pleased by this turn of events, not that I don't believe she didn't cast one of her spells and arrange it herself. *He* has been restless of late, as we both know." With a nod to the trio, he then hurried off.

Alain shepherded them into the mews, where Couper was given her own perch. While Belle fed her bird they spoke in low, hushed voices.

"How did you find us?" Alain demanded.

Lind explained their adventures, and when he had finished, Isabelle said, "Are the Langston men safe, Alain?"

*"My lady?"* Alain was astounded. How could this dark-haired boy be Isabelle of Langston? And yet there was no mistaking her voice, or the merlin, Couper. Recovering his equilibrium, Alain said, "Aye, the men are safe, and in *her* service now."

"Can they be trusted, Alain? I do not think they would recognize me in my current state, but what if one did?"

"They want to go home, lady. We all do. If you can help us to get home to England, we will do whatever you desire of us," Alain said.

"Where is my lord Hugh?" Isabelle said.

Alain flushed. "*She* has bewitched him, my lady. I do not know what she did to him, but he does not remember his life before her. He is her lover, lady, and does whatever she bids him do."

"I must do what I can to help my husband regain his memory," Belle said quietly.

"Lady, perhaps it would be best if you returned home," Alain advised. "We are trapped here by our love for lord Hugh, and the fact that *she* will not let us go lest we tell my lord's family where he is; but you, my lady, you and Lind can yet escape La Citadelle on the morrow. I have but to tell Master Jean you are not as skillful as I had thought you to be."

"*No!*" Belle's voice was sharp. "Let me try to penetrate my husband's memory. If I cannot after a reasonable time, then I shall seek help from Duke Robert in this matter. Vivienne d' Bretagne cannot continue to hold Hugh captive, depriving his family, and his son."

"You may not want the man he has become," Alain said low. "He is not the Hugh Fauconier any of us know. He is a totally different man, my lady. He is hard, and sometimes cruel."

"He is my husband, and I love him," Belle rejoined quietly.

Alain shook his head. She didn't understand. Well, let her see for herself, and then they would decide. She was his mistress. He had to obey her. He sighed, and then said, "I will show you where you can sleep. Lind and I must, of necessity, bed with you, you understand."

Belle laughed softly. "I understand," she said. She wondered if Alain thought she feared for her virtue. She followed the falconer into a hay barn.

"We sleep up in the loft," he told her.

"Who else shares this place?" she asked him.

"They allow unimportant travelers to shelter here, but most of the time it has just been me," Alain said.

"Where do the Langston men bed?" Isabelle asked.

"In the barracks with the other men-at-arms," he answered.

"I think it best," she told him, "that no one know who I am, even the Langston men. When I see the lay of the land, then I will decide the matter. For now, only you and Lind will bear my secret."

"Agreed, my lady!" Alain said. "That way you'll be able to escape this place should it become necessary."

"The fewer who know, the fewer who can tell," Isabelle said wisely.

"We'd best go to the hall for the evening meal now," Alain told them. "There's no one at La Citadelle but *her*, her brother, and Lord Hugh. The rest is servants, or soldiers, and they're a rough lot. Keep clear of them. I generally sit with the huntsmen. There are two of them, and they're good men. I must warn you that you'll see things in *her* hall you won't see anywhere else. Show no fear, or you could regret it. Fear is counted as a great weakness here."

The hall was a large stone rectangle of a room. There were no windows in it, only two enormous fireplaces, one on either side. Lining the room, however, were arched alcoves where windows might have been. In two of these alcoves Isabelle saw naked men chained up.

"Why are they there?" she whispered to Alain. The men were both obviously exhausted, and their bodies were striped with lash marks.

"They're being punished for some infraction," Alain said. "It is permitted that any man may beat them while they hang there. Usually it's the soldiers. The drunker they get, the crueler they get. *She* will not allow them to be killed, though. She passes her sentence, a day, two, perhaps three. They are kept alive until they are released, and then they are expected to return to their duties immediately."

Alain led them to a small trestle that had been set to one side of the room. He introduced them to the two men seated there, the huntsmen, Paul and Simon. "Lang is yet a boy," he explained, "and mightily awed by all he has seen here so far. He speaks little."

"A lad who listens, learns," Simon, the elder huntsman said, "eh, boy?" He poked Isabelle with a friendly finger.

"Aye, master," she replied, bobbing her head.

"Good manners," Simon pronounced, and then ignored her.

The food was excellent, even here at their table below the salt. There was variety: fish, game, and fowl. The bread was warm and crusty. There was both sweet thick butter and a tangy Brie cheese. There was even a bowl of braised lettuces, and another of crisp apples. Their cups were kept filled with wine by a buxom serving wench who chucked Lang beneath his chin and then laughed heartily at the blush she coaxed onto his cheeks.

"If you've never swived a lassie, that Jeanne-Marie is a good one for a lad to practice his skills upon," Simon said with a rich chuckle. "There's not a man in the castle who hasn't enjoyed her favors."

"I've a lass in England I'm true to," Isabelle said in her Lang voice. "We swore an oath, we did."

"He's a fine lad," Simon said. "I wonder that this is a good place for him."

"When a man needs a position, he cannot be choosy," Lind said, and the others nodded, agreeing.

Isabelle let her eyes wander to the high board where Vivienne d' Bretagne, the mistress of La Citadelle, was even now taking her place. With her were two men. One was a very tall man who was obviously her brother, for he looked just like her. He was, Belle thought, the handsomest man she had ever seen. He sat on his sister's right. To her left, however, was another man. It was Hugh Fauconier, although Belle almost didn't recognize him for he had greatly changed.

His short, dark blond hair was now long, and drawn back into a horsetail. His once serious expression was now severe, and the look in his blue eyes was predatory. He did not smile. His whole look was hard. He was Hugh Fauconier, and yet he was not. What had happened to him? He was bewitched by the beautiful woman who sat by his side, they said. She was exquisite. Isabelle forced her eyes away from the high board lest they feel her interest. She must not draw attention to herself.

"You see now," Alain whispered to her.

Isabelle nodded, and then she said, "Love between a husband and a wife, Alain, is the strongest magic of all. I truly believe it." But she had lost her appetite suddenly.

Master Jean, the household steward, came to the trestle and said, "Lind and Lang, come with me. *She* wants to get a look at you. Alain, you come, too. I'll need your good word else she be difficult."

Belle brushed the crumbs from her forest-green cote and followed the steward with the others. They stood before the high board waiting for the mistress of La Citadelle to acknowledge them. Belle could feel eyes upon her. She did not look up. She was afraid of what she might see if she did. Instead she struggled valiantly to keep her eyes upon her feet. They stood, and they waited. She could hear Vivienne d' Bretagne's smoky laughter, and the deeper undertones of her companions.

Then suddenly the steward said, "I have taken these two young falconers into your service, most high lady. Alain assures me that they are worthy to serve you, do you not, Alain?"

"Though it is by chance they came here, most high lady," Alain replied, "I trained these two brothers in England. Their names are Lind and Lang. They will work well with me."

"Lind and Lang." Her voice purred their names slowly. "You may raise your eyes to mine, my young falconers." She turned to her companions. "Hugh, you are the expert with the birds. Will they suit?"

"If Alain says they will, then they will. He knows the penalty for disobedience, or lying, don't you, Alain?" Hugh Fauconier's voice was strangely harsh. He stood up and, descending the dais, walked across the room to one of the alcoves where a prisoner was hung. Picking up the whip that lay curled on the stone, he swiftly gave the hapless man several hard, cruel lashes, completely disregarding the pitiful cries of his victim. Instead he laughed, and, tossing the whip aside, came to face the falconers. "You will be well fed, and housed at La Citadelle," he told them, "but in return you will obey without question. If you do not obey, you will end like those two fools." He looked hard at them. "Do you understand, and agree?"

"Yes, my lord," they answered him, and he turned away from them, moving back up to the dais to sit with his mistress.

"They look like good lads," Vivienne d' Bretagne murmured, and then she said to the falconers, "You are dismissed," and turned back to Hugh.

They backed away. Isabelle was astounded. Hugh had stood right before her and shown not one iota of recognition. Of course she was dressed as a boy with short, dark hair, but could he, of all people, not see through her disguise? She was devastated, and suddenly felt sick. Was she being naive? Had she truly lost her husband to this beautiful enchantress?

"Come," Lind said, as if sensing her mood. "Let us get some rest, *little brother*. It has been a long day for us all."

She followed him from the Great Hall, but even as she did, once again she felt eyes upon her. Unable to contain her curiosity this time, she turned her head to see Vivienne d' Bretagne's other male companion staring at her. "Who is that looking at us?" she asked Alain.

He glanced back over his shoulder. "It is her brother, Guy d' Bretagne. Why?"

"He has been staring at us," Belle responded. "Why is La Citadelle not his? He appears slightly older than she does."

Alain shook his head. "I do not know. The castle belonged to their mother. It has always belonged to a woman. They are a race of sorceresses and sorcerers. Come, do not look back at him. He is very wicked, and has taken both boys and girls to his bed, or so I am told. You do not want him intrigued by you, lady."

"No," Isabelle agreed. "I do not."

Together they left the hall.

# Chapter 13

$A$lain was surprised at first, and then quite pleased by Isabelle's skill as a falconer. "You've taught her well, Lind," he praised his old friend. "I'm going to leave the merlins and the sparrow hawks to her. She's as competent as any I've known." He watched as the young woman brought her charges out to weather upon their stone block. The birds were all caught wild as nestlings, and not as easy to manage as Couper had been, but Isabelle acquitted herself admirably.

"She's got a touch with the birds the same way he always did," Lind said. "It's not me that taught her, 'tis Lord Hugh. What's happened to him, Alain? He ain't the same man we knew as our master."

"We came from Duke Robert's court to Manneville," Alain began. "At first all was well. Lord Hugh strove hard to overcome the sieur's bad temper, and his lady wife was most kind. The sieur, however, could not get it out of his head that Lord Hugh had stolen Langston from him. One night he drugged Lord Hugh's wine and had us all thrown into the dungeon. When Lord Hugh stirred before they imprisoned him, that Luc de Sai hit him a fierce blow on the head. I feared he'd killed him. There is a cage behind the barrels of wine. There we languished for several days without food, and precious little water. When Lord Hugh finally awoke, he began to rage over what he called his own stupidity in trusting Richard de Manneville. He shouted, and he cursed our jailor, until he could no longer speak. Luc de Sai came and struck him again to quiet him. After that he wasn't the same, and didn't know any of us.

"Then *she* came. We gaped like village idiots, Lind, for we had never seen anything so beautiful as her. The sieur said that if she wanted him, she could have him, but she had to take us all. She laughed and agreed. She came near our cage and smiled at Lord Hugh. Their eyes met, and it was as if he could not break the gaze. He followed her like a wee lamb to the slaughter, and we after him, glad to be free of Manneville. After we got here, the Langston men were told they had a choice. Swear their loyalty to her, or die. She had me stay by his side while she nursed Lord Hugh back to health again. I was there when she mixed her potions, and fed them to him. Eventually his voice returned, but it was now harsh and unlike his old voice. He seems to have forgotten absolutely everything about his past life but the birds, which is why I was set to catching them and raiding nests last spring. She wants him happy, Lind, for she has fallen in love with him."

"Does she continue to feed him her potions?" Belle asked, and they realized she had been listening all the time.

"I do not know, my lady," Alain said. "Once I was set to the task of the birds, another took my place serving my lord Hugh."

"We must find out!" Belle said. "If she needs this particular magic to keep him in her thrall, if we could prevent her from giving him the potions, then we might be able to restore his memory and free him."

"But how?" the two falconers asked in unison.

Isabelle shook her head. "I do not yet know," she said.

"Perhaps we should leave La Citadelle and take our evidence before Duke Robert," Lind suggested reasonably.

"It is too late! You have agreed to enter her service," Alain said. "There is no escape for you now. I warned you to flee that first day you came, but you would not heed me. It is not as if you were a pair of scullery boys running away. Scullery boys are easily replaced, and she would not care; but you are falconers. She needs you. You are now as trapped as we all are. May God have mercy on us!"

"No, I will not accept it," Isabelle said resolutely. "There must be a way to help Hugh, and I will find it, I promise you. Then we will go home to Langston!"

Their lives took on an almost strange monotony. They arose early each morning, breakfasted, and spent their day attending to the birds. Another meal was served at four o'clock in the afternoon, and then Isabelle would slip from the hall, which she found too rough for her taste, and retreat to her loft. She longed for a hot bath. Her ablutions were scant, and the water always cold. The scissors she carried with her kept her hair trimmed short. Her supply of walnut dye would keep her hair dark through the next few months, if they were forced to remain here.

She wondered about her son. Was he well? How he must be growing. In just a few months he would be two years old. He would have forgotten both his parents, of course, but she took comfort in the fact that her mother and Rolf would be loving and kind to Hugh the Younger. Isabelle sighed. What if she never saw her child again? The thought brought her to tears. She had yet to find a way around their dilemma. She could not spend the rest of her life pretending to be a boy! She hated this unnatural life she was living now, and she was condemned to it unless she could find a way to release her husband from Vivienne d' Bretagne's powerful spell.

Several days later they accompanied the mistress of La Citadelle, her lover, and her brother on a hunt. They had been directed to bring along several of the birds, although they would be hunting deer in the morning. Belle had brought Couper and a particularly clever sparrow hawk she had been training. Alain and Lind had a gyrfalcon and a peregrine. The huntsman and his assistant had stalked their quarry, a fine stag, earlier that morning with the dogs and their handlers.

"He's a grand big fellow, lady," Simon told his mistress. He spread his thumb and his forefinger. "His tracks are this big. The scratches where he rubbed his antlers on a tree were this high." He again used his hand to demonstrate, and then he held out his hunting horn. "Here's a sample of his fumes."

Vivienne d' Bretagne looked at the size of the droppings in the huntsman's horn. "You are right, Simon. He is a big one. I will have him before the day is out. Let us loose the dogs."

The huntsman bowed as his mistress raised her own ivory hunting horn to her lips, blowing a series of short notes. This was the signal for the greyhounds to be unleashed. Made familiar with the stag's spore, they dashed into the forest, baying wildly, the hunters coming behind them on their horses.

The falconers did not keep abreast of the hunters, for the pace was too quick for their birds. Instead they followed along at their own pace, always listening for the sound of the hunting horns and the baying of the dogs ahead of them. The chase would continue until they either killed the stag or it managed to elude them.

The falconers came upon the hunters again even as the dogs brought the stag to bay. It was a magnificent russet-colored creature with a full set of antlers. Simon, the head huntsman, offered up the lance to his mistress. Violet eyes glittering, Vivienne d' Bretagne slipped from her black mare and took the lance. She advanced upon the stag, moving through the pack of dogs fearlessly. With a swift thrust she killed the beast. Belle turned her head before the deed was done, unwilling to see such a brave and beautiful creature slaughtered.

"I am ravenous, my darling," she heard Vivienne d' Bretagne say gaily. "Let us picnic here in this glade while the deer is skinned and the meat divided up. Let the hounds share its skin, Simon. They have done well this day." She turned to her two companions. "Have you had your fill of hunting, my darlings, or shall we seek some ducks with the birds this afternoon? The marshes nearby are full of them."

"Whatever would please you, dear sister," Guy d' Bretagne

said. It was the first time Belle had been near enough to him to hear his voice. It was a deep, rich, almost musical one.

" 'Tis a good day to try the birds," Hugh agreed in his harsh voice. "Let us see if these new falconers are worth their keep, *mon amour*, or if they are to be hung in the hall and whipped."

Isabelle shivered beneath her cote. Hugh sounded as if he would enjoy whipping them. Oh, dear God, she silently prayed, help me to find a way to save my husband! Lind and Alain brought her some bread and cheese, but she could not eat. What if the birds did not perform to their best potential? Heaven forfend!

When the meal was done, the huntsmen and their dogs led the way to the nearby marshes, which were filled with waterfowl. The deer meat was carried back to La Citadelle by a train of servants. The dogs were let loose to flush the ducks from their hiding places within the reeds. Lind allowed the peregrine he had brought to circle about his head. When at last the dogs raised several ducks, the peregrine swooped down with quick success, then stood patiently by her kill. Belle then released Couper, who was equally facile in her duty.

"Well, *mon amour*," Vivienne d' Bretagne said to Hugh, "are these falconers worthy of my service?"

"Aye," he said. "They are."

She laughed. "How perfect this life is that we share," she said smugly. "Come, let us return to the castle. The sunlight is fading, and we shall have both venison and duck for supper!"

"The venison needs to be hung," Hugh told her.

"Just a taste," his mistress replied. "I like my meat freshkilled, *mon amour*, as you should well know by now."

While they had been speaking, Isabelle had dismounted Gris and gathered up the two birds. She lashed them together by the feet and flung them across the pommel of her saddle. Mounting her horse again, she called to Couper to come. The merlin landed upon her gloved fist. She swiftly hooded her, and gathering the jesses, drew them tight. Lind had hooded the peregrine, and in Alain's company they returned to La Citadelle.

Belle took the ducks to the kitchen, offering to pluck them in exchange for a bucket of hot water.

The head cook agreed. It was a small enough price to pay, as he was going to be hard-pressed to get those two damned ducks roasted in time for the evening meal. It never occurred to him to ask what the young falconer wanted with a bucket of hot water. He had other, far more important duties to attend to. He didn't intend providing an evening's entertainment on the whipping rings by displeasing the lady with a late, badly cooked meal.

Isabelle carried her precious bucket of hot water from the kitchens, across the courtyard, and into the hay barn. She moved slowly so as not to spill a single drop. "Find me some kind of tub to bathe in," she told Lind and Alain as she entered the barn. "And fetch me two more buckets of water from the well. I am going to have a bath, my lads!"

"Is it safe, my lady, for you to do such a thing?" Alain fretted, always cautious.

"Who comes to this barn but us?" she asked him. "Besides, if you are worried, then you and Lind watch the courtyard from the loft while I bathe. If you see anyone coming this way, I will have time to get out and hide. Do you know how long it has been since I had a proper bath? I cannot bear it another minute! The dirtier I get, the better the fleas like me."

"There's a small wooden washtub in the laundry," Lind said. "I've become friendly with one of the young laundresses. She'll loan it to me if I ask, and not wonder why if I give her a kiss or two."

"I'll fetch you another bucket of water," Alain said.

The two men hurried off. Belle could scarcely contain herself. She was to have a bath! Tentatively, she dipped her finger in the hot water, yanking it back almost immediately, for it was yet scalding. Oh, it was going to feel so good! How did the lower classes manage to live their whole lives without regular hot baths? She clambered up into the loft, and rummaging among her things, drew forth a tiny cake of soap. Then hearing the barn doors open, she scrambled back down eagerly. Turning from the ladder, however, she was startled to see Guy d' Bretagne.

"My lord!" Did her Lang voice squeak?

His deep violet-colored eyes gazed down at her for a long moment from his great height. He had to top Hugh by at least three inches. "Who are you?" he finally demanded.

*"My lord?"* What on earth did he mean? He couldn't know she was a woman, or could he?

"I have watched you ever since you arrived," Guy d' Bretagne said in his deep voice. "You play your role very well, my dear. There have even been times when I thought I might be imagining it; but today when you turned away at the kill, I knew I was right. You are a female. Now, tell me who you are, and why you have perpetrated this masquerade? Your sex will not protect you from my sister's wrath."

Isabelle was thunderstruck. For a moment she was even speechless with fear. What on earth was she to say to him? She certainly could not tell him the truth.

"She is my half sister, my lord," Lind said, coming into the barn with the tub in his arms. Placing it upon the ground, he continued boldly, "We have the same mother, you see, but her father was the lord of our manor. When he died, his legitimate son and daughter drove her from the place, though she had been gently raised with them. Our mother was dead. I was the only blood kin she had who would help her. I did my best by her. I taught her my craft, and we took to the road. What else could I do, my lord? She is helpless without me."

"If you are lying to me," Guy d' Bretagne said slowly, "it is a most clever lie; and yet I suppose it could be possible."

"He does not lie, my lord." Alain, having returned with his bucket of water and overhearing Lind, now backed him up. They had to protect their lady at all costs.

"Then you, too, knew of this charade?"

"Aye, my lord, I did. How could I send them away? The girl is defenseless without her brother, and she is as good at her craft as any man, as you yourself saw today. The merlin she carried is her own. She trained it alone."

"Did she, indeed?" Guy d' Bretagne was intrigued, and then he said, "What is the tub for?"

"A bath, my lord," Belle said softly, eyes lowered. "I wanted a warm bath. It has been months since I had one."

Reaching out, he tipped her face up so he might see it. "What is your name, wench?" he asked of her. His gaze locked onto hers, and she grew pale, for his look was a powerful one. It was as if he could see into her mind. The strength seemed to go out of her. She realized in that instant that he was silently bewitching her, and she was powerless to avoid his enchantment. She was like a moth, caught suddenly in a spider's web. She tried to break free of his potent gaze, but he would not let her.

"My name is Belle," she whispered, amazed she had any voice to speak at all.

"It suits you," he replied. Then, "So you want a warm bath, do you, Belle?" He laughed. "A falconer who desires to be clean. It is an amusing thought. *A bath!* Well, you shall have a bath, pretty Belle, but not in this tiny washtub with a bucket each of hot and cold water! How on earth did you manage to obtain hot water?"

"I plucked the ducks we hunted for the cook," she said. "He was glad for the help."

Guy d' Bretagne laughed again. "What a resourceful little wench you are, my dear!" He grasped her by the hand. "Come! You shall have your bath!"

"My lord! Where are you taking me?"

"My lord, do not, I beg you, hurt my sister! We meant no harm," Lind cried. "We will go away if it pleases you!"

"It does not please me, falconer. Cease your cries of distress. Your sister desires a bath. I am going to see that she gets one. Now remain here upon pain of punishment. You may only leave, and come to the hall, at the supper hour. Do you understand me? Both of you?"

Then he yanked Belle almost off of her feet and led her across the courtyard into the castle. He took a turn here, and another there, and she was forced to half run up a flight of stairs. She had absolutely no idea of where she was, having only seen the Great Hall of La Citadelle, and nothing more. They saw or passed no other living soul. Then it dawned upon Isabelle, as she finally began to gather her wits about her, that the castle had four towers and he was taking her up into one of them. She fell suddenly, bruising her knee.

"God's bones!" she swore softly.

Guy d' Bretagne laughed. "I thought you would have spirit," he said. "A weak wench could not have survived the life you have been living. Well, here we are!" He flung open an iron-bound oak door.

"Where are we?" she demanded as she entered the room.

"My apartments, of course," he said. "I have a bathing room, Belle, but you, of course, would not know of such things. Come! I shall show you. My grandfather was a Moor, and he introduced the amenity to La Citadelle." He flung open another door and drew her into the chamber.

Belle gasped. This was a room nothing like the utilitarian bathing chamber of Langston. The marble walls were smooth and white, veined with green. The floor was tiled with great blocks of white stone. In one corner of the room was a depression shaped like a scallop shell, with a gold drain in it. There was a long, rectangular tub of the same marble as the walls. Its interior was also carved to resemble a scallop shell. Near it stood a waist-high marble bench. There were alcoves set into the walls, filled with towels, all manner of decanters that held scented oils, and blocks of soap.

"Where is the water?" she asked him.

Reaching over the tub, he turned the tails of two golden fish protruding from the wall, and lo, there was water pouring forth from their mouths, which acted as spigots.

Belle gaped, which seemed to delight him. "How have you done this?" she asked him, genuinely amazed.

" 'Tis just some of my magic," he said quietly. "Now, let us get your clothes off, Belle."

She jumped back. "I am quite capable of undressing myself," she said nervously.

"But it will be more fun for me if I do it," he said, his dark violet eyes dancing wickedly. "Are you a virgin, then?"

She pondered the wisdom of lying to him, and decided against it. "Nay, my lord." She said no more, and he asked not.

"If you are not a virgin, then you know there is no reason for you to be shy of your nakedness, Belle," he told her in a gentle voice. "You must learn to render me complete obedience, my sweet. Come here to me now." He took her hand again, drawing her to him. Again his eyes met hers, and once more the weakness assailed Isabelle. "You are like a wild creature," his rich, musical voice murmured into her ear. "I won't hurt you, Belle. Nay, I only want to offer you pleasure, my pretty one." His fingers fumbled with her clothing, pinching a nipple sharply. She cried out softly, and he laughed low. "You are sensitive, eh? Then it has been a long time, I'll wager, since you had a good strong cock to fill you up. We'll remedy that soon enough, my beauty. Now," he said briskly, "raise your arms up so we can get your cote off, my pretty wench," and he pulled the garment over her head, dropping it on the floor. Then lifting her up onto the high marble bench, he removed first one worn leather boot and then the other, tsking at their sorry state. "How long has it been since you had a new pair of boots?" he asked her.

"I cannot remember," she answered him, avoiding his gaze. Not just the nipple he had pinched, but both nipples were absolutely throbbing.

"These don't even fit properly," he said, noting where her hose were worn. He rolled them down, relegating them to the growing pile of her clothing. Then he undid her garters, pulling her chausses off her shapely legs, which he silently admired, running his palms over her calves. He examined her feet, roughened by weeks of walking.

His big hands were warm. They slid up her legs to linger on her thighs a moment. Belle nervously slipped from the high bench to the floor. "The poor," she told him, "cannot be fussy about fit. The boots were hand-me-downs, and I was happy to have them. I have never had anything new," she added for effect. She had to keep her wits about her, and it was becoming more difficult with each passing moment. His magic was obviously robbing her of her puissance, and she was becoming ever more helpless to his will. Despite her bravado, Isabelle was now afraid. Had Hugh felt this way when Vivienne d' Bretagne began weaving her spell about him? Still, Guy must be convinced that she was a nobleman's by-blow, as Lind had so cleverly told him. "I wore my half sister's castoffs until Lind decided I should be safer being a boy."

Guy d' Bretagne did not answer, for he was far too intent on eliminating the remainder of her garments. He drew off the two smocks she wore, lastly unbinding her bosom from the length of cloth that had tightly suppressed its natural curves. Then he stepped back and looked. It was obvious that he was enchanted by what he saw. Finally he said to her, "Go and stand in the shell. I will be with you in a moment."

What do I feel? Isabelle wondered as she padded across the room on bare feet to do his bidding. Should not I at least be embarrassed by my situation? But she wasn't. Isabelle of Langston had divorced herself from Belle, the bastard girl. She had to if she was to survive. She had to if she was to save her husband from Vivienne d' Bretagne. If they should find out the truth of who she really was, Isabelle suspected her life would be quickly forfeit.

Through a twist of fate she had gained entry into the castle proper. She knew that she would not be leaving soon. Guy d' Bretagne was a big healthy man with an obvious appetite. He wasn't allowing her a real bath out of the kindness of his heart. He wasn't just amusing himself by bathing her personally. He meant to make love to her, and Belle realized that if she was to obtain her real objective, she was going to have to let him. She thought of her righteous outrage, and her noble indignation over the king's attempted assault on her wifely virtue. Yet she was now about to allow herself to be seduced by this mysterious man all in the name of aiding her husband. A year ago she could have never imagined such a thing.

God, and His Blessed Mother, forgive me, she thought, but I know of no other way. I could not have left La Citadelle until I knew for certain that Hugh was here, and when I did, I could not leave because they would have come after me, believing me a falconer. Life is very complicated away from home, but if I hadn't left, then there would have been no chance at all of regaining my husband. Is there even one now? What have I gotten myself into?

Guy d' Bretagne rummaged among the crystal decanters, and then finding what he sought, he uncorked it, sniffed appreciatively, and, walking over to the tub, poured a good dollop of the pale purple liquid into the water. Then he replaced the bottle, and leaning over, turned the spigots off. She watched curiously as he next poured wine into a carved amethyst goblet set in silver filigree, added a pinch of something, and swirled it about until the goblet appeared to be filled with a royal purple liquid laced with swirls of gold. He handed her the goblet.

"Drink it all down, it will calm you," he told her, then said, "The art of bathing is quite simple really. When one finally enters the tub, one should already be clean. To sit soaking in dirty water defeats the whole point of bathing. I will wash you first, Belle, and then you may relax in the perfumed water. When you are through, you will agree that you have never had a bath quite like this one, I promise you. Come now, drink all your wine down," and he gently forced the goblet to her lips, holding it there until the liquid was utterly consumed.

Next he filled a silver basin with water from the tub. Reaching into a nearby alcove, he drew forth a soft cloth. He selected a small alabaster jar and removed its gold lid. "The scent I have chosen for you is called freesia. It is a delicate flower that grows in the south." He dipped the cloth into the jar and held it out to her to sniff. "Do you like it, Belle?"

The aroma was sweet, yet heady and sensual. She did like it, and told him so. He smiled at her, pleased, and then began to wash her. Kneeling, he began at her feet, the cloth slipping between each toe, rubbing assiduously. He lifted each foot, washing its sole, shaking his head again over the condition of her feet. Carefully he washed each of her legs in turn, and when faced with her bush, said, "Is your hair naturally dark, Belle?"

"No, my lord," she answered him.

"Walnut stain?" he inquired calmly.

"Yes, my lord," she replied.

"I have something that will take it out right away," he told her. "And I have a special elixir that will help your hair to grow again. How long was it when you cut it?"

"To my buttocks, my lord," she said.

"And it is this wonderful red-gold color?" he asked, tweaking her flaming mont.

"Yes, my lord." What an odd conversation, Belle thought.

He laughed as if reading her mind, which made her decidedly nervous. "The hair on your head I shall appreciate, but no lady should have a bush, or legs overgrown with hair. Only peasants have such body hair. It hides a woman's natural glory, and I do not want that, Belle." He stood up, and reaching into another alcove, drew forth another alabaster jar, this one with a pink marble cover. Opening it, he dipped out a thick pink paste which he smeared over her mont, her legs, and beneath her arms. "We'll give it a few minutes to work while I finish washing you, and then we'll rinse it off." He returned to his task of bathing her. His hands moved over her belly, up her torso. The cloth swirled over her breasts, teasing at her nipples; up to her throat and over her shoulders. He turned her about and scrubbed down her back to her buttocks. The cloth rubbed between the halves of her bottom, and she stiffened. He laughed, and patted her reassuringly.

Turning the fishtail handle of a spigot in the wall, he filled a crystal pitcher with water several times over while rinsing her. As the water sluiced down her body it took with it the red-gold hair that had formerly covered her Venus mont, her armpits, and legs. Belle was amazed, and not just a tiny bit uncomfortable, with the plump pink flesh that was revealed. Her slit was so visible. *So voluptuous, and carnal.* Surely it shouldn't be.

He moved away from her, and returning, set a small wooden stool in the center of the shell. "Sit down, Belle. I want to wash your hair before I let you soak," he told her.

She sat, and almost at once he was wetting her dark locks, rubbing something fragrant into it, his fingers briskly kneading her scalp. She gasped as he dumped a basin of water over her hair, and then she felt him beginning the process all over again. When he had finished, he knelt before her again, gently cleaning her face with a fresh cloth. His touch was very light.

"You can open your eyes now," he said, and drawing her up, led her over to the tub. "Get in, Belle. You may soak for a few minutes."

She gratefully sank into the warm water. If the truth be known, she had never felt better in her entire life. This, then, was what bathing a person was really all about. She had learned a great deal from him this day, and she would remember it. She reached up and touched her wet hair. Was it really her own color again? She longed for a silver mirror in which to view herself. Perhaps he had one and would share it.

"Come now, it is time to get out," he told her, helping her from the water. He dried her quickly and efficiently, and then brought her back to the high marble bench. "I want you to lie upon it, facedown," he said, helping her up. Then he began to knead her flesh with the same oil that he had swirled into the bathwater.

It felt marvelous. Belle almost swooned with pleasure, but the pleasure was not a sexual one. She hadn't allowed herself to acknowledge how sore her muscles were until this very moment, but now his supple fingers soothed away all the aches, and she almost purred. If it was magic, then certainly it was very good magic, she decided. She had never felt more relaxed in her entire life. He rolled her over and continued his massage, and there was no lewdness in it.

Finally, when he was finished, he helped her up and brought her through a different door into another room, which she immediately recognized as a bedchamber. He had remained fully dressed the entire time he was bathing her, and standing next to him now, she felt more than just naked. She suddenly felt very vulnerable. Sensing her sudden change in mood, he poured a pale green liquid into a small, narrow silver goblet. "Drink this," he said, and she took it, but again was hesitant about drinking it.

"May I have my clothes back now, my lord?" she asked him.

"You would put those filthy rags on that magnificent, clean body?" he demanded.

"You could have my clean clothes sent up from the barn," she suggested.

"You will not wear boy's clothes again, Belle," he said. "Such a thing is a sacrilege against nature and the mother who created you."

"What shall I wear, then, my lord?" Belle inquired.

"I have not decided yet," he told her frankly. "Until I do, you will remain as naked as the day you were born. You have a beautiful body, you know. Though you be a big girl, you are delicately made. Now drink your drink. If you do, I shall fetch a silver mirror so you may see your lovely hair returned to its natural state."

"What is in it?" Belle demanded suspiciously, sniffing the goblet.

"It is a blend of wine and herbs I have formulated. It will not hurt you, you silly creature. I did not bathe you so tenderly to murder you," he said with a laugh.

Isabelle brought the goblet to her lips and began to drink, looking at him over the silver rim of the cup. He was surely the most handsome man she had ever seen in her entire life. He had to be the most handsome man in all the world. His fair skin

seemed even more so in contrast to his jet-black hair and violet
eyes. His features were absolutely perfect and symmetrical:
oval eyes beneath thick black brows; a high forehead, and
higher cheekbones; a long, perfect nose; narrow, perfectly
shaped lips; a square chin with a deep cleft in it. And he was
certainly taller than anyone she had ever known.

The last of the strangely spicy liquid slid down her throat.
He took the goblet from her and led her by the hand into an
alcove of the bedchamber that she had not previously noticed.
Within was a strange device, padded in a black leather; one end
shaped like an X, the other end like a cross. Before Isabelle
could ask, Guy d' Bretagne lifted her up and laid her upon the
device, quickly snapping manacles of gold lined in lamb's
wool over first her wrists, which were bound to the cross, and
then her ankles, which were spread wide by the X. Her torso
lay on the comfortable bench.

"What are you doing?" she asked him. Her head was spinning just slightly, but for some reason she wasn't afraid.

"I must join my sister and her lover, Hugh, in the Great Hall
for the evening meal. When I return, Belle, I will want to satisfy a different sort of appetite. As I sit with Vivienne eating
venison from the deer she killed this day; eating the ducks your
birds brought down; drinking my sister's excellent wine; I
shall think of you here, clean and fragrant; your beautiful, fair
body spread wide, eagerly awaiting me."

"I shall await you, my lord, for I can see I have no other
choice," Belle told him with a small attempt at humor, which
he greatly appreciated, "but I shall not be eager."

"But you will, Belle," he said softly. "I shall see to it that you
are." He moved to a small table nearby, and lifting the lid on a
long, carved box, drew forth an object such as she had never
seen. Holding it up, he asked her, "Do you know what this is,
Belle? Nay, of course you do not." He caressed it. "Look
closely, and tell me what it resembles, my beautiful wench."
He held it before her.

She looked upon it, her eyes widening. The object was made

of a soft, yet supple cream-colored leather. It was long and slender. Its shape was that of a manhood. "What is it?" she whispered, a tiny curl of fear knotting her belly.

At first he did not answer her. Instead he dipped his fingers into a vial of oily liquid. Then he tenderly spread the substance over her mont, spreading her netherlips wide to thoroughly massage it in. Belle, however, could not take her eyes from the thing he held in his other hand. The object was attached to an oval-shaped gold ring through which he now laced his fingers. "It is called a phallus," he said, noting her gaze. He dipped the phallus into the same liquid. Setting the vial down, he stood over Belle. Then, to her immense shock and surprise, he inserted the phallus smoothly within her, turning it just slightly once or twice, smiling at her gasp. "Now," he said softly to her, "when I return from the Great Hall, Belle, you will indeed be eager for me. The phallus with its special oils will act to prime your passion. You may cry out if you wish. This entire tower is inhabited by me alone. No one will hear you, but just imagining you here thusly, my own passion will burn brightly. We will give each other great pleasure this night, Belle. You are now securely within my power," he purred to her, and bending down, he kissed her mouth softly. Then he turned, leaving the chamber, and she was alone.

At first Isabelle lay stunned with shock by what had just happened. Oh God, she thought, her heart pounding. I am ensorcelled even as my poor Hugh, else I should never be brought to this condition. She was very aware of the phallus within her. It felt enormous, and it seemed to be throbbing. *That could not be!* It was nothing more than an inanimate object. She had never imagined being violated by such a thing. No woman could imagine it. She shifted her body just slightly, and gasped, for the merest movement was torture. The walls of her sheath seemed to cling to the phallus despite her desperate attempts to have as little contact with it as possible. She was beginning to tingle with her arousal. It was agony, and yet it was not.

* * *

Guy d' Bretagne entered the Great Hall of La Citadelle to find Vivienne and Hugh already at table.

"You are quite late," his sister said. Her beautiful mouth was greasy with the duck she was eagerly consuming.

"I have made a rather interesting discovery," Guy told them. "The young falconer, Lang, is in reality a girl! What think you of that?"

*"A girl?"* Vivienne was intrigued. Then she laughed. "I could trust you, dearest brother, to discover such a thing. You have a sharp eye for a pretty wench, but I did not notice anything odd about the young falconer Lang. How did you see it?"

He laughed. "It is difficult to explain, *chérie*. Just an instinct, I suppose. Then today when you killed the deer, Vivi, the young falconer turned away. No boy, not even a kindhearted one, would have done such a thing. A gentle boy would have watched lest he be mocked by his peers." Guy then went on to explain his visit to the hay barn where the three falconers slept; and what followed.

"Can you be certain that the other falconers did not lie?" Vivienne asked. "Is this some ploy to breach the defenses of our castle?"

She is beginning to grow jealous, Guy thought, amused. Vivi always grew jealous when he showed any interest in a female, although she did not expect him to be jealous of her lover. "The falconers told the truth," he said calmly. "The girl is obviously wellborn, for although she is a big girl, her bones are finely made. She is well-spoken from having been raised in her father's house. No, this is no ploy, just the desperate effort of a poor freedman to protect his sister. Now, however, I shall protect her."

"And will you share her?" Hugh Fauconier looked with hard eyes upon Guy d' Bretagne. "We've shared wenches before, my brother."

"No, I shall not share her with you yet, Hugh. As you have Vivi to yourself, I want this girl for myself for the present. I haven't even begun to explore her depths, and until I do, and tire of her, I will not share her with anyone, even you, brother."

"Where is she?" Hugh asked him. "Why did you not bring her to table, Guy?"

Guy d' Bretagne speared a piece of venison with his knife and took a bite. He chewed it vigorously, swallowed it down, and then took a healthy swig of wine from his goblet. Wiping his mouth with the back of his hand, he replied, "I have not brought her into the hall for several reasons. Since I have seen the condition of her boy's garments, I have ordered them burned. They were, I expect, vermin-ridden. I would not bring her into the hall naked, although that is the condition in which I intend to keep her in my chambers. For the time being I will keep her from everyone, even my servants. She will become dependent upon me for everything, even her food, which she will take from my fingers when it pleases me to feed her. I will become the whole reason for her existence, and her survival."

"Ohhh, brother," Vivienne said softly, "how deliciously diabolical! Do you think she is strong enough for such treatment?"

He nodded. "I will not break her spirit, Vivi, for that is not the purpose of the game."

Vivienne d' Bretagne was an extraordinarily beautiful woman. The violet-colored, almond-shaped eyes, set in her heart-shaped face with its little pointed chin, were avid with excitement. "Guy, do you think she is the one we have been awaiting?"

"I believe so, *petite soeur*. She is physically strong, and she has intellect. Her breeding is good, and this is better than spiriting off some swooning noblewoman whose family would be certain to come after her."

"Let us do it now!" Vivienne d' Bretagne said eagerly.

"No," he told her. "You have been enjoying your lover all these many months, Vivi. Now give me until next summer to enjoy mine. Besides, she must be willing to do my bidding no matter what it is I ask of her. I want no rape here. Do you understand me?"

She pouted at him, but Guy laughed.

"You know that my magic is stronger than yours, Vivi. Such a thing may not have been so in past generations of our family, but it is now, and you are well aware of it. I yield to you from custom only, but if you try my patience, I have the means to punish you." He patted her little hand with his long, delicate fingers. "Be a good girl, now, Vivi. If you promise me that you will trust my judgment in this matter, I will show you and Hugh my new toy."

"When?" Vivienne demanded.

"When you have finished your meal," he promised, a smile lighting his features at her enthusiasm.

Before the food was cleared away, Guy took a small silver plate and placed upon it some venison, a slice of bread, which he buttered, a pear, and a small bunch of grapes. He then sat back and listened while the castle minstrel sang a charming ancient lay about their ancestress, Vivienne, the wife of the great Merlin.

Finally, when the hall was almost emptied, Lind and Alain, the two falconers, begged leave to approach the high board.

"You may speak," their mistress told them.

"We merely wish to inquire," Alain began, his eyes on Guy, "about little Belle, my lord." Lind was silent.

"She is clean, and safe in my apartments," Guy assured him. He gestured toward the plate of food. "I am just about to bring her a small meal. You need not fear for Belle. She pleases me."

"Will she not be returning to her duties, my lord?" Alain said.

"Belle has been given other duties here in the castle, Master Falconer," Guy replied. "You will see her again eventually, but not for the time being. She will be too caught up in those new duties to spend any time in the falcon mews. See to her bird, will you? I know she puts great value upon the pretty creature."

"My lords, my lady." The two falconers bowed and

departed the hall. There was nothing more that they could do for now to help their lady, but they knew she was a resourceful woman. They would be waiting when she needed them, as would the Langston men as well.

Guy watched them go, a look of amusement upon his handsome face. "Are they not charming?" he said to his companions. "The concern was etched all over their faces. Now are you convinced, sister? It is no plot against us. Just the poor, doing the best that they can."

Vivienne jumped up. "Let us go and see your wench, brother!" she said excitedly.

"You may not come into the bedchamber," he told her. "I will take you and Hugh to the peephole so you may view her in all her glory."

"You have her on the black bench? All this time?" Vivienne was astounded. "Did she scream when you set her there?"

"No, she did not. She was surprised, I have not a doubt, but she made no cry of alarm," he told them.

The trio hurried to Guy's tower, entered his apartments, and continued to an interior hallway lit by torches. When Guy had unlatched several peepholes, he ushered the others forward to look.

"Ohhh, Guy, you are most wicked," Vivienne exclaimed. "You left her with the phallus to entertain her. Is it the one with the little pearl studs?" She did not fear being overheard, for the stone wall blocked the sound of her voice.

"Nay," he said. "She is not ready for such refinements yet."

"She is lovely. When her hair grows, it will be magnificent. What think you of her, Hugh?" his mistress asked.

"She's pretty enough, Vivi," he told her, "but no woman could hold a candle to you. Guy, go in to her, and rotate the phallus so we may see her pleasure peak." The naked girl in his view was exciting, and he wanted to rid himself of Guy so he might amuse himself with Vivienne. She would like that.

"Ohh, yes, brother!" Vivienne said excitedly. "Do it!"

He left them, and at once Hugh was behind Vivienne. He

pulled her tunic dress off. His fingers quickly unlaced her
smock and his hands gathered up her large, round breasts,
crushing them cruelly, which he knew she enjoyed, his lips and
tongue on her shoulders and neck. "If this corridor weren't so
damned narrow," he growled in her ear, "I'd fuck you till you
screamed your pleasure, Vivi!"

*"Look!"* she said, enjoying her lover's attentions, but
equally fascinated by what she could see through the peephole.

Guy d' Bretagne entered his bedchamber, and before the
startled eyes of his captive, removed all of his garments so that
he was as naked as she was. Coming over to the black leather
bench, he bent and kissed her mouth in greeting. "Has the
phallus kept you good company while I was away, Belle?" he
asked her, reaching down to grasp its gold ring. "Ahh," he said
softly, "I see you have bedewed it with your love juices. I will
teach you to be more restrained in the future."

*"Take it out!"* she whispered low.

"Not yet," he said. "I have yet to show you the pleasure it
can really bring you, *ma chérie.*" He began to rotate the phallus
with a delicate motion, smiling at her soft cry.

*"Please, no!"* she sobbed. She believed as she had lain there
all this time that she had finally managed to gain control over
her body, but now she could see it was not so. The enjoyment he was inflicting upon her was a sweet torment such as
she had never known. She writhed in an effort to escape him,
even while knowing that she could not. The phallus drove
deeper and deeper within her, until she was mindless with the
pleasure-pain he was giving her. She wailed her frustration at
being unable to defeat him, but her cries quickly turned to
those of a woman approaching the ultimate heaven. Then his
mouth closed over hers again, and she could remember little
else but for the wave after wave of pure pleasure sweeping
over her until finally it was no more.

She felt him withdraw the phallus as she lay gasping, her
body drenched in its own sweat. She hadn't believed that she
could survive his vigorous attentions, but she had. She found

she couldn't open her eyes; they were still too heavy with her satisfaction. Her body felt weak and totally limp. She felt him unlock the manacles that had bound her wrists and ankles. She lay exhausted, unable to even move. Then, to her shock, he began to bathe her sex with sweet warm water, working swiftly and efficiently. When he had finished, he lifted her up and laid her on his bed, drawing the coverlet over her. She heard the door to the chamber close, and slid away into sleep.

Guy found his sister and Hugh in the outer chamber. Neither was taken aback by his nudity. He smiled at them. "Did you enjoy my little spectacle? She is quite a marvelous young creature, isn't she?"

Vivienne nodded in agreement. "You could not see, for you were unable to resist kissing her, but at the moment she reached her peak, her body arched so high I thought it would fly off the bench, Guy! You brought her along quite beautifully, *mon frère*; neither too quickly, nor too slowly; but then, you have always been a master of very good, nay, exceptional timing," his sister praised him.

"And you, Hugh, did you enjoy watching the wench?"

"Aye!" Hugh said. "She has beautiful little breasts, and you know how I appreciate a woman's breasts, brother. I can see that she will prove a fine winter's amusement and companion." He paused, and thought a moment. "I think I once knew a girl with hair that color, but I cannot remember now."

"You do not have to remember, *chérie*," Vivienne said in a soft, purring voice. "All you need to remember, my Hugh, is how much you love me. You do love me, don't you?" Her look was for a brief moment vulnerable, much to her brother's surprise.

"I have never loved anyone before you, Vivi," Hugh said, "and I shall never love another even if I should live forever." He gave her a quick kiss. "Let us go to our bed now, *chérie*, and leave your brother to his new plaything. Certainly she will have regained her strength by now for the new bout of Eros he will treat her to," and Hugh Fauconier laughed wickedly as, putting his arm about his mistress's waist, he led Vivienne from her brother's apartments.

Guy watched them go, and thought it was unfortunate that Vivienne had fallen in love with her captive. Usually Vivi took a man for lust, but this one had lasted far longer than any of the others. It was obvious that she was in love with him. Still, Hugh was easy to live with. Guy shook his head. Love was a weakness people like he and his sister could ill afford, but Vivienne would not want to hear it. He smiled to himself. As long as Hugh Fauconier kept her amused, she would be happy, and Vivienne's happiness was really paramount. Picking up the plate he had brought from the Great Hall, he brought it into the bedchamber.

# *Chapter 14*

*B*elle lay sleeping, and for a moment Guy was tempted to leave her so, for he knew she must be exhausted after her long day. Then he decided against coddling her. The food would revive her, and he did not want to deny himself the pleasure of possessing her this night. There was a candle stand by the bed, and he set the plate upon it, all the while feasting his eyes upon her. She really was lovely, with her short, tousled red-gold hair and her white, white skin. Her fine breeding was more than evident. He sat beside her, running a finger down her bare arm, bending to kiss her soft shoulder. She stirred.

"I have brought you something to eat," he said. "Open your eyes now, Belle. You must eat."

She sighed, and reluctantly sat up. He propped pillows behind her back, drawing the coverlet down so he might see her charming little breasts as she ate. "I'm surprised that you remembered to bring me food," she said daringly. "Your other appetites seem greater." She reached for the plate, but he pulled it out of her reach.

"Unless I give you permission otherwise, Belle, the only food you will take will be from my own hand," he told her quietly, setting the plate back down and cutting a piece of venison off the small joint. He held it to her lips, smiling.

For a moment she debated telling him to go to the devil from whence he had obviously come, but then she decided against it. Who knew what this sorcerer might do to her? She had to have nourishment, and if this was the only way she could get it, then so be it. She opened her mouth and took the meat with her teeth, chewing it slowly. His eyes never left hers. At first she was uncomfortable in his gaze, but then she simply let it sweep over her, refusing to be the first to look away; defying him in the only way she knew how. She realized now that the gentle, musical voice and the tender touch were a sham. This could easily be a cruel and dangerous man. Yet if she pleased him, she would be allowed to remain within the castle. She would have the opportunity of reaching Hugh, and helping him break free of the sorceress's enchantment.

Guy fed the girl in his bed, wondering as he did just what she might be thinking. The meat and bread were finally all devoured. "Lick my fingers clean now, Belle," he ordered her, holding out his hands.

She took first one hand and then the other in her own two hands, bringing them to her mouth, slowly, and, to his pleasure, most thoroughly licking the venison juices and the butter from each finger, which she sucked individually. Her pink tongue lapped back and forth over his palms until they were completely free of any residue of her supper.

He smiled slowly. "That was well done," he complimented her. Then he quartered the ripe pear and fed it to her. The sweet juices dripped down onto her breasts. He bent his head to lick them off, his tongue sweeping across her flesh in search of an errant drop of pear juice. When the pear had been eaten, she again took his hands in hers, and bathed them with her tongue without his even asking. She was intelligent, and that pleased him. This girl, he believed, he might take further than any of the others before her. He suspected that she would not be arrogant, as so many of the little peasants had become once they believed that Guy d' Bretagne could not live without them. And when they became difficult, and too proud, he coldly gave them to his men-at-arms for a few nights of amusement. A proud wench's disdainful ways were invariably swiftly cured beneath the unwashed bodies of a dozen or more men, whose only objective was to release their baseborn seed as quickly as possible.

He saw Belle's eye go to the plate, which still contained the small bunch of grapes. "You may have two," he told her. "The rest are for me." He plucked the grapes and popped them into her mouth.

She ate them, saying, "I would have thought that in the length of time you were gone, you would have eaten your fill."

"I prefer my grapes a special way," he told her. "Do not be so greedy. I do not want you fat and bloated like some farmwife." He pressed her back into the pillows. "You took well to the phallus, Belle. You did not hold back your passion. Your former lover taught you well. How many lovers have you had, my pretty wench?"

"I had a husband, my lord. No lovers," she answered him.

"What happened to this husband?" he wondered.

"My brother killed him," she said, then amended, "not Lind. Richard, my lordly brother. I am not a woman of easy virtue, my lord."

"Women of easy virtue lack passion," he said. "You certainly do not. You yield to it most gracefully, and that pleases me." He leaned toward her. "Come, and kiss me of your own free will, Belle. I want to feel your luscious mouth moving with conviction beneath my own."

Isabelle looked into those deep violet eyes. She could feel her will being sapped once again, caught in that dark gaze. She could not, it seemed, fight him. Unbidden, her hand reached up to touch his cheek. His skin was so very fair, framed by his dark, dark hair. "I have never kissed a man I did not love," she told him softly.

"Ahhh, but you are going to love me, Belle," he answered her.

The words frightened her, for there was such a ring of certainty to them. Would she love him? How could she love him when she loved her dearest Hugh? But Hugh had forgotten her, did not know her. Guy's eyes bore into her green-gold ones, and she could feel the warmth of his desire in the look. She had to believe that her love for her husband could free him! But if she displeased Guy d' Bretagne, she would be cast out of La Citadelle, and there would be no hope left at all. She had to kiss him, and kiss him with honest ardor. This man was far too skilled in matters of the heart to believe a lie.

Her lips touched his tentatively. He scarcely breathed, for he feared to break the spell. It was all he could do not to sweep her into his hard embrace. Instead he let her lips find their own rhythm, and to his shock, his heart soared as it never had before. He was intrigued with the sensation, and relinquished himself to it.

His lips were petal soft, she realized, and yet they were also firm. Their mouths seemed to part as if in response to a silent signal. Her facile little tongue slid into his mouth, encircling his, teasing him until he could finally stand no more. With a growl, he forced her back against the pillows, his lips suddenly fierce and very, very demanding. He kissed her until she was near to fainting, for she could not breathe. Seeing it, he eased back, pulling himself onto the bed, where he might more easily have access to her.

She felt his lips, hot and wet, insistent and fierce, as they slowly, slowly, made their way down the column of her ivory throat. He lingered at the pulse that beat under his mouth, enjoying the sensation of the blood that throbbed beneath his lips, knowing it must be singing in her ears, even as it now sang in his. The lips slipped even more slowly across her chest, burning insistently against the swollen flesh of her nipples. She could not restrain the soft moan that slipped from between her lips.

He pressed close against her now, one hand taking a breast completely in his hand to fondle it, while his dark head moved to capture the nipple of her other breast within the warm wetness of his mouth. He tongued the nipple, encircling it again and again until it felt raw and aching. Then she felt his sharp teeth gently scoring the tender flesh, sending needles of fire throughout her body. Suddenly, he drew hard upon her, and she cried out softly, feeling a corresponding tug of desire in that hidden place between her thighs. Her body arched slightly.

He loosed the first breast, and his hand moved to insinuate itself between her legs, pushing past her moist, pouting nether-lips to find, with unerring aim, her tiny pleasure pearl. "Ahhh, Belle," he chided her tenderly. "Such impatience." He stroked her until she thought she must surely die of the sweetness he had loosed to pour through her veins. Abruptly, he stopped, and pushing a hard pillow beneath her buttocks, said, "Open your legs for me, Belle. Wider. Wider. Aye, that will do, my precious." For a moment his eyes gazed upon her vulnerability, and she blushed, the heat spreading from her chest up her face. "Nay," he said gently, touching a hot cheek. "You are very beautiful there, Belle." Then, to her shock, he began plucking the grapes and, with firm fingers, pushing them into her sheath one by one.

Isabelle's eyes widened. "You must . . . not . . . you can-not . . ." She faltered as his eyes met hers and he silently com-manded her to be quiet. What kind of man was this? she wondered, frightened. He was so tender, so gentle, and yet his actions were to her astounding. Confusion swept over her. He was not harming her, and yet . . .

Guy d' Bretagne pushed the last grape into Isabelle's sheath. "Now," he said softly, "you will remain very still, my precious one. I will shortly retrieve the fruit from the succulent bowl where I have but temporarily stored it. Keep your legs open, Belle," he commanded her sharply when her thighs trembled and threatened to close. He added a second pillow to the one already beneath her, elevating her body even higher. Then leaning forward, he delicately parted her plump netherlips and began to tongue her pleasure pearl.

"*Mon Dieu! Mon Dieu!*" she cried out, and her body writhed.

"*Stay still!*" he commanded her sharply, raising his dark head up so she could see his fierce look. "You must learn to control your instincts so you may enjoy your pleasures even more than you now do." Then he bent his head so he might taste of her once more.

I will not be able to bear it much longer, Isabelle thought, terrified. If she displeased him, what would he do? He would cast her from the castle. She had to bear it. *She had to!* He suckled hard on her, and her body spasmed, but she forced herself to remain still.

"Good!" he praised her. "I knew you could do it, my precious." Then she felt him push his head between her legs and begin to draw the grapes, one by one, from her sheath. She could feel him sucking deeply, and could feel the tiny fruit as they popped from her; feel the spurt of their juice as it mixed with her own. When the last grape had been brought forth, his tongue swept about her sex, seeking a last measure of the sweetness, and then he pulled himself level with her, yanking the bolsters from beneath her so she lay flat once more.

"That is how I like to eat grapes," he said, smiling into her eyes. "A difficult task to perform in the Great Hall, would you not say, Belle? You quite enjoyed it, my pet. Your honeyed juices were most copious, and quite overran the fruit's." He bent to kiss her deeply, plunging his tongue into her mouth, caressing hers. "That is what it tastes like," he said, breaking the embrace.

"I could have never imagined—" she began, but he cut her short.

"Of course you could not." He laughed. "Such things are quite forbidden by those who think of themselves as good, but here at La Citadelle, we are not good. We are a race of sorcerers, the damned, and so we may do that which others would not even consider."

"You are such a contradiction, my lord," Belle told him honestly. "One moment you are tender, the next fierce, and strange."

"I am all those things, and more," he said with a laugh, "but I am also just a man. I have been very patient tonight, but now,

my precious, I must slake my most basic thirst for you."
Swinging over her, he thrust deep.

Isabelle cried out in surprise, for she had not yet been
expecting his entry. A big man, his rod was both longer and
thicker than her husband's. Once well-lodged within her, he
ceased his movement to smile down into her face. As if in
answer to a silent command, she put her arms about his neck,
drawing him down to her. She could feel the dark hair upon his
chest tickle her sensitive skin. Her legs wrapped about him,
and she felt him slip even deeper into her soft body. He
throbbed within her, and she was at once reminded of the
leather phallus. Isabelle shuddered, and he whispered but one
word into her ear in answer to her unspoken question. *"Yes!"*

To her surprise, he had given her incredible pleasure over
and over again this evening. Now he set to work to gain his
own pleasure. His movements began slowly, augustly, his
manhood delving deep into her, withdrawing with a deliberately languid motion. But the movements became faster,
quicker, harder, until she was writhing beneath him, crying out
again with her joy. Her head was whirling for the hundredth
time in the last few hours. Then came the explosion of stars
behind her tightly shut eyes, and she heard him cry out in
delighted satisfaction as he reached his own apex. For a brief
moment he slumped atop her, and then he lifted his head and
looked deep into her eyes.

"There has never been a woman who pleased me as much as
you do, Belle. I do not think I shall ever let you go." Then
rolling off her, he fell into a restful sleep.

She had pleased him. Isabelle felt relief pour through her
body. He would not send her away, and she would soon be able
to free Hugh from Vivienne d' Bretagne's spell—and herself
from Guy's enchantment. She must learn just what it was that
was keeping her husband ensorcelled. And when you learn
that, a voice in her head asked, how will you know what to do?
For a moment she was overwhelmed with self-doubts, but then
she caught herself. Whatever happened, she would find the

way. She had not come so far to fail. She would rescue Hugh, save herself, and they would return home to Langston, to their child. *They would!*

To his astonishment, Guy d' Bretagne slept the entire night through, something he had never done in his memory. When he awoke, he took Belle back into the bathing chamber, and they bathed each other. When they returned to the bedchamber, he dressed himself and was about to take his leave of her when she said, "Where are my clothes, my lord?"

"I gave orders that they be burned, my precious. Besides, you will not need clothing for the interim, Belle," he said calmly.

"Why will I not need clothing?" she asked him.

"Because you will not be leaving these rooms for a while," he replied. "I want you all to myself. I want you when I want you. Now let me go and break my fast. I shall return with food for you afterward." Then he was gone, out the door, and she could not, of course, follow.

How was she to reach Hugh if she could not leave these rooms? Her heart sank. Then she calmed herself, remembering that Guy had said it was but for a short while. He did not intend to keep her penned up here forever. She was his new toy, and he merely wanted to keep the new toy to himself for the time being. He was a man, but like most men, he was a child. Isabelle returned to the tumbled bed, straightening it up, climbing in, and going to sleep once again. Guy d' Bretagne was both a tireless and an inventive lover. She would need all her strength to keep up with him.

Vivienne d' Bretagne was alone in the Great Hall of her castle when her brother joined her. "I had thought you would sleep till midday," she said mockingly. "Did you not spend the night playing?"

He joined her at the high board, pouring himself a cup of wine as he sat. "I had a most satisfactory night, *petite soeur*, and afterward I slept as I have never slept. The girl is fearless so far, and very passionate as well." He nodded to the servitor who spooned eggs poached in cream and dill onto his plate.

"Then you mean to keep her?" Vivienne asked.

Guy nodded. "She is the one we have been waiting for, Vivi. There is no doubt in my mind about it. Both she and Hugh are perfect for our purpose. We shall begin early next summer, but until then I mean to enjoy her to the fullest." He spooned the eggs into his mouth hungrily, washing them down with the rich red wine.

His sister tore a piece of bread from the long loaf upon the table, and, buttering it, handed it to him. "Tell me what you did with her, Guy. Did she fight you at all?"

He laughed at her eager desire to know all. "I began gently, Vivi. I do not want to frighten her." Then he went on to tell his sister in careful detail of his evening.

"And she did not struggle at the grapes? Wonderful!" Vivienne exclaimed. "I can see why you believe she has possibilities."

"By early next summer," he promised her, "I will have her completely trained to do whatever it is I require of her without ever questioning it. I am not allowing her to eat, except to take the food from my fingers. I thought she might object, but she did not. I could see her debating defiance, but in the end her common sense won out. I am very, very pleased with Belle, *ma petite soeur*."

"I am glad, Guy, for without her we should be lost, I fear. That the line of Vivienne, wife of Merlin, should come to such an end! Damn our ancestor Jean d' Bretagne for his rash and selfish act! He may well have doomed us all, Guy!"

Guy d' Bretagne nodded, but he took his sister's hand in his, patting it, attempting to offer her some small comfort. Their family descended from the wife of the great sorcerer Merlin, who was herself a sorceress and Merlin's equal. They were shunned by the local population from the beginning, and they far preferred it that way. Each generation that followed had produced a son and a daughter, who, at a time decided upon by their parents, mated and produced the next generation of a son and a daughter. The descendants of Vivienne, wife of Merlin, did not mean to mix their blood or share their secrets with anyone.

Then, almost two hundred years ago, the line had produced a son of unparalleled cruelty, Jean d' Bretagne. He had raped and murdered the only child of a nearby neighbor, a widowed noblewoman. Then he had raped his delicate victim's mother. The woman had survived to lay a powerful curse upon the d' Bretagne family. From that time on, no male d' Bretagne was able to reproduce. The curse did not affect their lustiness, but the family could no longer breed its children. And the women of the line were cursed as well, for they had produced Jean d' Bretagne. At some time in the future, the female line would also fail in its ability to reproduce. The d' Bretagnes would die as a family, even as the family of the murdered girl had died with her untimely death.

Jean d' Bretagne had laughed at the curse. His was a line of sorcerers. How could a mere mortal curse him? But as lusty as Jean continued to be, he produced no children with his sister. Finally, their aged parents, realizing that their spells and incantations were useless, had decided that their daughter must have a lover to give her a child. He would, of course, die after he had sired two children upon her. And so it had remained throughout the ensuing years. Each d' Bretagne daughter had taken a lover to continue her line, which is why the estates had fallen upon the female line, and not the male. The siblings had learned to work together to preserve their family.

But now in this generation, Vivienne had not been able to conceive. She had had a dozen lovers since she was fourteen, and she was now twenty-five. Not one of these men had been able to get a child upon her. Finally, she and Guy had faced the fact that the second part of the curse had fallen upon them. They were not, however, willing to allow their family to die out. They would have a child, even if it would not be of their own blood. They would make it theirs. This new life would break the curse laid upon their family so very long ago. When the next summer came, they would mate their two lovers, and the child of that union would become theirs. For now Vivienne loved Hugh Fauconier. She would love his offspring. As for the girl, Belle, her fate would be up to Guy d' Bretagne after she produced the desired children.

Finished with his meal, Guy arose from the high board and gathered up a small plate of food for Belle. "She should be ravenous," he said with a smile, and left Vivienne to her own thoughts.

"Get up, you lazy wench," he teasingly scolded Belle when he entered the chamber. "I've brought you a feast. Eggs, bread, and honey. Even cheese, and a crisp apple."

"No grapes," she teased him, and he laughed at her quick wit.

"No grapes," Guy said. "I have other games in mind, my pretty, but first you will eat." Setting the tray down, he helped to prop her up. Then taking a spoon, he began to feed her the egg dish.

"Ummmmm," Belle approved, her pointed little tongue whisking a dribble of the sauce from the side of her mouth. She quickly finished everything that he fed her. "I am thirsty," she told him, for he had offered her nothing to drink with her meal.

Guy arose, walked across the chamber, poured a goblet of red wine, and, returning with it, sat again by her side. "I will feed you the wine," he said. "You will take it from my own mouth, but you are not to swallow until I tell you you may." He took a sip of the wine, and, pulling her head to his, transferred the fragrant liquid from his mouth to hers. "Do not swallow," he warned her. "I think you can take another mouthful, Belle." He reached again for the cup.

Isabelle struggled to keep from swallowing the sweet liquid. She was terribly thirsty after her meal. His mouth met hers again, and he added more wine, again cautioning her not to swallow. He sat back, and, reaching out, began to play with her breasts. Belle felt some of the wine beginning to drizzle down her throat, but she did not swallow. His big hands crushed the flesh of her bosom. He dipped his finger into the wine cup and painted her nipples with the wine, slowly licking it off. Belle began to choke.

"You may swallow," he said softly. "You did surprisingly well for a first time. You don't want to obey me, yet you do. Why?"

"I was raised gently," she told him. "While I was grateful to my half brother, Lind, for his protection, do you really believe that I enjoyed such a rough life? Here in the castle with you, my lord, it is far more pleasant. I am bastard-born, raised between two worlds. Will you fault me for preferring a privileged life to a harsh one?"

"No," he said, intrigued by her honest reasoning.

"Am I to be your leman, my lord?" Belle further pressed him, amazed by her newfound ability to dissemble the truth.

The question surprised him, but he answered her question with a question. "Do you want to be, Belle?"

"I think so, my lord," she said. Better to not be certain than to be boldly assertive with this man.

His violet eyes grew warm as he said, "You were meant to belong to me, Belle. I have waited my entire life for a woman like you." He kissed her softly, and then said, "I will not always be kind, my precious. If you displease me, I will beat you. Have you ever been beaten?"

"No, my lord," she answered, her heart beginning to beat faster.

"I would not mark your lovely skin," he said soothingly. Then he stood up, reaching out for her. "Come! I will demonstrate. Do not be afraid. You are not like those poor wretches that get strung up in the hall every now and then for their disobedience." He pulled her from the bed and drew her back into the alcove where the bench was located. Placing her facedown upon it this time, he quickly affixed the manacles.

"Please, my lord, I am afraid," Belle told him.

"There is no need for it," he assured her, pushing a hard bolster beneath her belly so that her hips elevated themselves. "Even your church permits the occasional beating of a woman for disciplinary purposes. If I give you six strokes of my leather strap now, you will understand what is involved. It is unlikely, with a girl as intelligent as you, that I shall ever have to do it again. It is really better that we do this now instead of waiting until you disobey me, and anger me. If you angered me, I might give you twenty-four strokes of the strap."

As he spoke he was moving about the alcove, and she could not move her head to see him from her position. Finally he came and stood by her head. In his hands he held a leather strap, several inches in width. The ends of the strap were divided into several narrow strands, each one of which contained several knots. "If you truly angered me, I would use the leather on you, but as I only wish to demonstrate that I am capable of punishing you, I shall use the hazel switch. You are a brave girl, I know, and so I do not want you to cry out, for six strokes are nothing. If you displease me with any display of cowardice, I shall add one stroke for each cry you make," he warned her. "Tell me that you understand me, Belle."

"Yes, my lord," she whispered.

"Good!" he said, and then he moved away from her.

She felt his hand smoothing tenderly over her buttocks. "You have a bottom like a fine, ripe peach," he remarked. And then he brought the switch down across the pale flesh. Isabelle swallowed back her urge to protest. The second and third blows were more forceful, and by the fourth she realized her flesh was tingling.

"You're doing very well," he complimented her, and laid the fifth blow more gently across her helpless flesh. "And six!" The last came hardest, as if to imprint itself on her memory.

"There, my precious," he soothed her. "That was not really so bad, and you were very brave. Had this been a real punishment, I should have let you shriek your head off, but it was not." He undid her bonds, and bringing her back to the bed, laid her facedown upon it, again propping her hips high.

She lay silently, tears pearling her cheeks, and then, to her shock, felt his member seeking between her thighs. Before she might protest, he had lodged himself within her. His hands grasped her hips in a strong grip as he ground himself into her burning flesh.

"You are simply too tempting this way," he murmured into her ear, leaning forward over her prone form. "The heat from your pretty pink bottom is delicious, Belle. I may take to beating you on a regular basis just for the pure pleasure of it." He began to pump her with vigor. "You are as ripe and sweet as a summer's fruit, my precious!"

To her immense horror, Isabelle felt her traitorous body responding to his dark passion. *"No!"* she cried out in a desperate attempt to stop it. *"No!"* But he had taken her unawares, and there was no stopping the pleasure that began to swell within her. Together, this time, they attained the crest of their passion.

Afterward he smoothed an ointment across her sore flesh, soothing it. "You will never be disobedient, will you, Belle?" he said softly, cradling her against his chest. "No. You are far too intelligent, and you have learned from this little incident, have you not, my precious?"

"Yes, my lord, but I hate you for it!" she cried low.

He laughed, ruffling her cropped hair. "Nay, you do not." Then, the episode concluded for him, he said, "I must really give you something to help your hair grow quickly. But for those fine breasts of yours, you still have the look of a lad about you."

She was astounded by this change of subject, but then it was not his bottom that was still stinging from the blows he had administered to her. She would do whatever she had to do to avoid having to face that switch again. And then to have him mount her like a stallion put to a mare; aroused by the pain he had given her. Belle shuddered. His arms closed about her more tightly.

"There, my sweet Belle," he cajoled her. "It is over now."

Aye, Belle thought bitterly, it was over for him, but not for her. Again she silently berated herself for her folly in coming to La Citadelle. What had ever made her think she could rescue Hugh? But then, she had never anticipated that her disguise would be penetrated. For weeks she had managed to hoodwink everyone she and Lind had come into contact with that she was a lad; but none of them had been sorcerers. Isabelle hadn't expected a sorcerer's powers could extend to seeing into one's soul. Although Blanche de Manneville had told her the d' Bretagnes were a race of sorcerers and sorceresses, she had not thought someone as unimportant as a young falconer would attract their attention. That oversight was costing her dearly. Guy d' Bretagne had, so easily it seemed, found her out. Now she was his prisoner, caught in a tightly woven enchantment and playing a very dangerous game.

As the days wore on, there was no doubt in her mind that she was bewitched. Each day, her captor would mix deliciously flavored drinks, adding different bits of herbs, or colored powders, or even flower petals that had been dried, to his liquid potions. He would serve them to her in exquisite vessels of gold and silver, studded with carved jewels. At first he had to coax her to partake, but eventually, her willpower seeming sapped, she drank willingly. Unlike her poor Hugh, she retained her memory, however.

And the lotions he prepared were also part of his power over her. Smooth and fragrant, he would rub them onto her body in generous amounts after having bathed her. No part of her body was spared. Some were merely to soften her skin and keep it supple. Others, however, were concocted as a means to her arousal. Once he had her chained spread-eagled to the wall of his chamber. He massaged her with a pale coral-colored cream, paying careful attention to her intimate parts, and within moments she was writhing with desire. Facing her, he watched with amusement, laughing as she cursed him, her passion burning into her, and unable to satisfy it.

*"I hate you!"* she screamed at him until her throat was raw.

Guy d' Bretagne had finally released her, and commanded her to pleasure him. Belle desperately wanted to defy him, but his dark, violet gaze forced her compliance, and she obeyed, hating herself, but caught in the throes of his fierce and lustful enchantment, she could do naught but his bidding.

Because she was near hysterics afterward, he moved his hand before her eyes in mysterious fashion, and she fell into a deep sleep, awakening hours later, sore, and yet exhausted. Still, she had been happy to see him bringing her a plate of food, and equally happy to make love with him in the dark night hours that followed. Aye, she was enchanted even as her Hugh was, or else she would have surely killed Guy d' Bretagne by now.

Her master was, it seemed, very pleased with her behavior. One day he took her into the small private room where he liked to fashion his creams and other magical potions.

"I shall teach you how to mix love potions, and the special creams I enjoy using," he told her, and he smiled. "You are an intelligent wench, and if the time comes when you no longer amuse me, you will have another use to help pay for your keep, my beautiful Belle, but I cannot imagine such a time ever coming. Can you, my pet? *You are mine.*" He caught her chin between his thumb and forefinger. "Are you not, Belle?" His eyes bored into her very soul.

"I am yours," she agreed softly.

He smiled at her then, pleased, and said, "I shall teach you to make a potion guaranteed to inflame the bodily lusts. We will begin by boiling some water. Watch everything I do, and next time I shall allow you to do it." Ladling water from a bucket into a small black caldron, he affixed the kettle to a hook and swung it over the fire in the little fireplace in the corner of the private chamber.

No one was allowed in this room except a large orange male cat called Saffron, unless they were invited by Guy d' Bretagne. "Saffron is the king of the castle," Guy told her, laughing. "He has fathered more kittens than any cat I have ever known. I suspect him of lapping up the potions that sometimes fall to the floor."

He drew Belle over to a clean but worn wooden table, and handed her a small grater. "You will grate these almonds for me," he said, handing her a small bowl of them. Then he turned away to busy himself, and she watched him with wide eyes, fascinated. He took down from a shelf two jars. Opening one, he spooned out a thick, dark, gold substance into a narrow-mouthed pitcher. Capping the jar and returning it to its place upon the shelf, he opened the other vessel. She could not see what was in it, but he added two pinches of the contents to the pitcher. "Are the almonds grated yet?" he asked her.

"Aye," she answered, swearing softly as she nicked her knuckle.

"Give them to me." And he mixed the grated nuts into the pitcher with the other two ingredients quite thoroughly. When the water was boiling, he began ladling it into the pitcher until the small vessel was filled. Again he mixed the contents completely. Then taking two narrow crystal goblets from a cabinet, he poured the warm golden liquid into them, handing her one. "Drink it down quickly!" he ordered her, quaffing his own portion.

Belle drank, and it was sweet, yet there was a sharp underlying taste to the potion that she could not quite place, although it was familiar. The liquid coursed through her veins, and she was suddenly aware of a tingling sensation that seemed to concentrate itself in her nether regions. She shifted nervously, and then, to her amazement, he opened his gown to reveal his manhood, rampant with desire. Wordlessly, he lifted her up, impaling her on it as she wrapped her legs about him and clung to him as he backed her up to the very same table she had been grating the almonds upon. He began to piston her with long, slow strokes of his mighty weapon, quickly bringing them to mutual satisfaction.

Setting her down at last, he noted, " 'Tis not as strong as it should be." Then he murmured some words over the remaining liquid in the pitcher that she could not understand, his elegant hand making a graceful sweeping motion over the vessel. "There! That should do it. We shall give the remaining portion to Vivi and Hugh, and see what they think of it, eh, Belle?"

She nodded, and then asked him, "What is in the potion, my lord? Besides the almonds and the hot water, I mean."

"I will tell you next time," he promised her. "For now it is not necessary that you know. Not until I allow you to make it yourself. Did you enjoy its effects, my pet? I far more enjoy pleasing you than punishing you. Now, Vivi, she enjoys occasional pain. It seems to arouse her to extreme ardor. Hugh tells me he whips her with great regularity, and afterward she is wild with passion." Guy caressed Belle's hair, which, thanks to another of his potions, was growing longer and thicker with each passing day. "You did not take well to my hazel switch, did you, my beauty? You did not like it at all."

"Nay," Belle told him. "I did not, my lord."

In retrospect, Belle thought, it had been a good thing that he had beaten her that morning. The memory kept her strongly in mind of how dangerous this man was, and of how her very life was held in his hands. She could do nothing to help Hugh until she could gain Guy's full trust, and perhaps even his love, and get out of the confines of his apartments. She thought perhaps now that he was teaching her simple tasks in his magical chamber, she might be gaining his trust. Yet she remained fearful of Guy d' Bretagne, and helpless in the face of his spells and the pleasure-pain tortures which he continued to inflict upon her. As for love, was he even capable of it? Isabelle did not know.

One day before Guy left Isabelle, he fastened a narrow strip of gilded leather about her hips. A single matching strap hung from the front of the girdle. To it was attached a small phallus shaped like a thumb. The strap was drawn down between her netherlips and the phallus inserted in her sheath. It was made of leather, and studded with tiny freshwater pearls.

Then he pulled her into his lap and began to play quite suggestively with her breasts. Soon she could not help squirming against his knees. When she did, the phallus pressed against her, arousing her wickedly. Seeing the surprised look on her face, he laughed wickedly. "It is to remind you of your duty while you wait for me," he told her.

"I am bored just waiting," she told him daringly. "I can read." She sat very still now, lest she be tortured again.

"In what language?" he asked, fascinated by this new knowledge of her.

"English and French," she said.

"I will see you have manuscripts with which to amuse yourself," he promised, and then left her.

He kept his promise, and Isabelle read each day when she was alone. Still, it was boring lying about naked, waiting for Guy d' Bretagne to rejoin her.

Several weeks passed in this fashion. Then one day when Guy came back, he had with him a beautiful tunic dress and long skirts. He handed them to her. "You will join us in the Great Hall tonight," he said.

"There are no undergarments," she said.

"You do not need them. I have had the tunic dress lined in rabbit's fur for warmth," he explained with a small smile. "Are you not pleased that you are to join us?"

"Yes," she answered him, kissing his mouth sweetly. "While I do enjoy my own company, my lord, the company of others can also be equally stimulating."

The tunic was beautiful. Made of copper-colored silk, it was embroidered in copper metallic threads and sparkling golden gems she did not recognize. She had never seen so rich a garment, even at King Henry's court. The high neckline was round, and the long sleeves jeweled at the cuffs. The simple soft wool skirts were dark green in color and lined in a soft silk sarcenet. When he had bathed her and dressed her, he took up a brush and slowly groomed her beautiful hair, which had by now grown back nearly to her shoulders.

Brushing Belle's hair has become one of my most sensuous

pleasures, Guy thought as he drew the bristles through the thickening mass of red-gold. Then he sprinkled it with gold dust. "You are almost too beautiful to share," he said quietly when she was ready. "I hope I do not regret my decision to give you a small measure of freedom, Belle. Still, it is time for you to meet my sister."

"I have seen her in the hall. She is extremely beautiful, my lord. I wish," she sighed, "that I could see what I look like."

He laughed at her little vanity. "Come," he said, taking her hand and leading her over to a cabinet that stood against the wall. Opening it, he revealed an enormous oval-shaped mirror that was most wonderfully clear. "Voilà, Belle! Do you like what you see?"

"Is it me?" She was astounded by the woman staring back at her. "Is it really me? What is this mirror made of? It is not of silver. Is it magic, my lord?" She was fascinated by the image she saw, and turned this way and that. This woman who stared back at her was hardly the Isabelle of Langston she knew. That Isabelle was a pretty but practical girl. This creature was a beautiful, sensuous, and very voluptuous woman. Was this, too, magic?

"The mirror is a magic of sorts, Belle," he said to her, "but the thing it does best is it tells the truth. What you see in it is exactly what you are. Are you pleased by your image?" He stepped behind her now, and she saw his handsome face reflected back at her.

Isabelle nodded.

"Come then," he said, closing the cabinet and leading her from the room.

As they began to climb down the narrow stone staircase, Isabelle suddenly realized that she was afraid. There was a sort of comfort in the big warm hand clasping hers. It was good that she would see Hugh this night, for she was beginning to have feelings for Guy d' Bretagne that she knew she should not have, even if those feelings were engendered by his sorcery. She had to fight this enchantment. She was Guy's mistress for but one purpose: to free Hugh Fauconier, her husband, so they might return to England, to their child.

"Hold your head high, Belle," Guy commanded her as they entered the Great Hall, to traverse its length to the high board. The noisy hall was filled with servants and men-at-arms.

Isabelle focused straight ahead. There was Hugh! *Her Hugh!* Her eyes devoured the long, plain face and hawklike nose. They lingered upon his big mouth. She could almost feel the pressure of that mouth upon hers, and swallowed back a sigh. She liked the way he now wore his dark blond hair; long, and tied back with a length of leather. It gave him an almost primitive look she found strangely attractive. It was so different from the close-cropped hairstyle of the Normans. They mounted the steps to the high board, and Guy squeezed her hand.

"Sister," he said, "this is Belle."

Vivienne d' Bretagne looked straight at her, and Isabelle was struck at how much she looked like her brother. They could almost have been twins, each with thick-winged dark brows over almond-shaped violet eyes. Vivienne had heavy dark hair that tumbled to her shoulders, and a heart-shaped face with absolutely perfect features. From a distance she had been beautiful; up close she was spectacular. Belle wondered how she could win her husband back from such a woman. *Love.* She had to remember that the power of true love could overcome anything. *It had to!*

"You are very beautiful," Vivienne d' Bretagne said in a tone that was slightly disapproving. Never had she had to share the high board in her own castle with a woman who could match her beauty. Usually Guy's little mistresses were pretty, but no more.

"You are very beautiful, too," Isabelle responded, deciding that a bold approach was perhaps the better one in this instance.

For a moment Vivienne looked surprised, but then she laughed. "My brother said you were brave, and I can see he has not lied." She turned to her lover. "Hugh, *mon amour*, come and greet Guy's leman. Is she not lovely? One would never know that her mother was a peasant."

Isabelle's gaze swung to Hugh. His wonderful blue eyes surveyed her impersonally. Those eyes, which had once been warm and loving when they alighted upon her, were cold and assessing as they roamed over her now. He did not smile. "She's pretty enough, Vivi," he said, "but my taste runs to black-haired Breton wenches." He turned away from Belle, leaning over to kiss his mistress.

"Come, Belle, and sit," Guy said, helping her to her chair. Isabelle heard his voice speaking to her, and she obeyed him, but shock was coursing through her body. The man who called himself Hugh Fauconier looked like Hugh Fauconier. She could even hear an echo of Hugh's voice in the harsh tones of this man, but this Hugh was not her Hugh. Could she ever get him back? What had begun as an adventure was turning into a nightmare of horrendous proportions.

The menu was filled with foods known for their aphrodisiacal qualities: cold, raw oysters, taken from the sea below La Citadelle, and served in their half shells; roasted quail, and a rabbit stew with onions, leeks, and ginger; long stalks of pale green asparagus; and for a salad, braised *Brassica eruca*, a type of cabbage famed for its strong amatory powers. They ate from gold plates, and drank wine mixed with gentian root from carved pink quartz goblets. The addition of the gentian was to but increase their erotic tendencies. Everything placed before Isabelle was exquisite, but she had little appetite for the morsels Guy offered with his elegant fingers. Concerned, he murmured against her ear, "Are you all right, Belle?"

She was instantly on her guard. They must not know who she was and why she had come to La Citadelle. Turning her head, she managed a smile. "I think I am overawed by all of this," she told him. "I had gotten used to your chambers being my world. May I have a sip of wine to encourage my appetite? And perhaps a bit of quail, and some of those lovely grapes, my lord."

He held the cup to her lips, letting her drink her fill, and the wine seemed to restore her. He fed her the quail as she had requested, smiling as she licked his fingers clean with her facile little tongue. "A bit of bread and brie?" he tempted her, and she ate it. Then he fed her the grapes, one by one, and when she licked the juice from his hands, he reached out to take another small bunch, saying, "For later," and they laughed together. For a moment it was as if they were in their own little world, and she did not have to face the horror of what had happened to her husband.

She saw the falconers at their trestle with the two huntsmen. She nodded to them, and Alain's flick of an eye acknowledged her. She wondered if she might be allowed to visit the mews and see Couper. She knew that the mews had been stocked for Hugh. If she could only speak with Alain, she might learn when Hugh visited the birds. Perhaps she could break through Vivienne d' Bretagne's spell if she and Hugh were in familiar surroundings. It was all going to take time; more time than she had anticipated. And even if she could help Hugh, how was she going to break the spell Guy d' Bretagne had woven about *her*?

Guy now took her for walks outdoors, leading her down a narrow path in the cliffs below the castle. Usually it was gray and damp, but one early winter's day the sun shone, and across the sea she could just barely make out the darker line of land.

"What is that place?" she asked him.

"England," he said, and they continued their walk along the shelly beach, watching the gulls soar and dive. They could smell the salt tang of the sea, and the cold air was fresh and cutting. The deep blue water sparkled in the sunlight. "Do you miss England?" he asked her.

"There is nothing to miss," she lied. "I have found a far better life with you, my lord."

He stopped and looked down into her face. "Once I said that you would love me, Belle," he told her. "Now, I find that it is I who am falling in love with you. It is dangerous for a man such as me to love. Love is a weakness, and makes one vulnerable. Do you care for me at all?" His dark violet eyes bore into hers.

"I think so," she answered him. Reaching up, she caressed his handsome face. "You must never wear your heart upon your sleeve, my lord. It places you in grave danger."

He smiled down at her. "If you did not care, you would not warn me, Belle."

They walked on, and she felt some little guilt for the deception she was playing upon him; and yet had his sister not stolen her husband, and taken Hugh's memory from him, Isabelle of Langston would not have had to come to this place at all. And Guy d' Bretagne would have never fallen in love with her.

The Winter Solstice came and was celebrated at La Citadelle with much feasting. Great bonfires were lit upon the castle heights and the adjoining hills belonging to the d' Bretagne family. During the celebration it was easy for Belle to mingle among the retainers in the hall without suspicion. She easily found Alain and Lind. No one would question her about sitting with them for a moment or two. They looked relieved to see her.

"Are you bewitched, too, then?" Alain asked her.

"Aye," she said softly, "I fear that I am. Still, unlike my lord Hugh, I have managed to retain my wits."

"Our lord is lost to us," Alain said grimly. "Let us all flee La Citadelle before the winter snows set in and we cannot. If Lord Hugh cannot come, lady, then he must stay. Will you allow our master's son to be raised without either of his parents?"

"I am not ready to give up," Isabelle said calmly. "I do not yet know by what means of enchantment Vivienne d' Bretagne holds Hugh, nor have I discovered how Guy d' Bretagne holds me in thrall."

"What difference does it make?" the falconer demanded, his voice low with caution. "How can you thwart these sorcerers, lady?"

"I do not even know if I can, Alain," Isabelle answered him, "but would you want me to flee not knowing? How could I ever face my son if I did not do my best to free his father?" She arose from the trestle, smiling gaily for the benefit of any watching, and said, "I must go now, but first, Lind, tell me, how is Couper?"

"She pines for you, lady," he answered her.

"I will try to remedy the situation," she replied, and moved off back to the high board.

"You stayed overlong with the falconers," Vivienne d' Bretagne noted when Belle sat back down.

"They are concerned about my merlin, Couper," Belle answered her. "I have raised her from a nestling, and now we have been separated these many weeks. She pines, Alain and Lind tell me."

Vivienne d' Bretagne turned to her brother. "Why do you not let Belle have her merlin? The falconers tell her the bird is growing despondent for the loss of her mistress. It is not right that a fine creature be sacrificed, brother. Belle must have her bird."

"I do not want the creature in my apartments," Guy said. "Belle may visit the mews if she chooses. I have no objection to that." He turned to his mistress. "Will that suit you, my precious?"

"Of course, my lord. I shall go tomorrow. My thanks." She leaned over and placed a sweet kiss upon his cheek. "A token of my appreciation," she said with a little smile.

"I will expect far more than a token," he rejoined wickedly.

"And you shall have everything of me that you desire," Belle promised him, her dark lashes sweeping flirtatiously against her fair skin. "I am my lord's to command."

"You are becoming too artful," he complained, but he was not displeased with her at all. He had never known a woman like his Belle.

The following day he gave her a trunkful of exquisite garments to wear. She visited the falcon mews, taking Couper onto her hand, caressing the bird, feeding her, praising her lavishly.

The merlin brightened immediately at the sound of her mistress's voice, uttering small cries of welcome. Belle almost wept, for in her overwhelming desire to find a way to rescue Hugh, she had almost forgotten about her faithful Couper.

As she walked about the mews' yard, Couper upon her fist, she spoke with Lind, for Alain was angry that she would not leave Hugh and lead them home to England.

"How often does Lord Hugh come to the mews?" she asked.

"Almost every day," Lind said.

"Does he come at a particular time?"

"Usually in the early morning," Lind said.

Isabelle sighed deeply. It would be difficult if not impossible for her to get to the mews at that time of day. Guy usually awoke at first light, rested and filled with lust to pleasure himself before he began his day. There would be no chance of getting away from him then, except during the few days when her link with the moon was broken, which he respected. She had only recently finished her flow, and it would be several weeks until it came again. She had no choice but to wait. "Lind," she said, "does he not recognize you at all?"

Lind shook his head. "Nay, lady. He knew not Alain, either, but then Alain told him he was his servant. Lord Hugh remembers nothing but his love for the birds. We have been teaching him about them all over again. Sometimes one of us will mention his grandfather and the birds of the Merlin-sones. He thinks a little, and then he shakes his head and says it is not important; but we can see he is distressed he cannot remember. It seems to hurt his head when he tries." Lind frowned. "I am beginning to think that perhaps Alain is right, lady. Perhaps we should leave."

Belle shook her head. "Let us at least wait until spring, Lind. Perhaps by then I will have discovered the magic that binds my husband and me to the d' Bretagnes. Besides, we should never be able to cross the sea now. You have but to look at the water to see that. And where would we get a boat? If we attempted to go overland instead, they would easily find us and bring us back. No. When we go, there must be no chance that they will catch us, Lind. Tell Alain that, and beg him not to be angry with me any longer. We must remain united."

Lind nodded, agreeing with her.

Belle debated the wisdom of approaching Hugh too soon. In her heart she wanted to rush to him and tell him who she was, but she knew in his current state of mind it would be inadvisable. She forced herself to wait, for he obviously had eyes for no one but his mistress. He scarcely if ever even spoke to her, Belle knew, or acknowledged her presence.

Then one day in midwinter she was surprised to find him in the mews when she arrived for her mid-morning visit.

"Good morning, my lord," she said pleasantly.

He nodded curtly.

"I had been told that it was your custom to come earlier to the mews. If I disturb you, I will go," she told him.

"There is no need," his harsh voice grated.

Isabelle went immediately to Couper and took the merlin up upon her gauntlet. "Good morning, my darling," she said gaily. "You are looking particularly beautiful this fine gloomy day."

The merlin chittered back at the sound of her voice.

"She is very responsive to you," Hugh growled.

"I raised her from a nestling," Isabelle told him quietly. "She was a gift from my husband."

"He was a falconer?" Hugh asked.

"Aye," Isabelle said. "He was a fine falconer. Once he showed me how he trained a gyrfalcon to hunt for cranes."

"In the spring you will show us," Hugh replied. "There are cranes in the marshes hereabouts. I should like to hunt them." Then he turned abruptly and left the mews.

That night at table, however, he spoke indirectly to her, telling his mistress what she had told him about hunting cranes. "We will all hunt them together, will we not?" he said.

"Who was the gyrfalcon trained for?" Guy asked her.

"The king," Belle answered with a half-truth.

"Your late husband trained a gyrfalcon for King Henry?" Vivienne d' Bretagne was impressed. "He must have been a fine falconer."

"He was," Belle replied quietly.

Later in their chambers, Guy could not swallow back his jealousy. "You spoke of him as if you loved him," he accused her.

"Loved who?" Belle asked, not certain what he meant.

"Your falconer husband. Your rough-spoken Englander!" His eyes were almost black with invidiousness.

"Of course I loved him, else I should not have been so unhappy when my brother destroyed him," Isabelle said.

"Why did he kill him?" Guy demanded.

"Because my half brother lusted after me," she replied, quickly inventing the tale. "He tried to rape me, and my husband came upon us. He beat my brother for it. It is not wise to beat your overlord, is it? My brother hanged my husband for his crime, and he and my half sister drove me from our father's estate. Now you know the whole tale. Does it ease your jealousy any, my lord?"

"No," he said, but the anger was gone from his voice.

"What will ease it?" she asked him softly.

"To hear you tell me that you love me as you once loved your falconer. To hear you say it, and know that you mean it," Guy d' Bretagne burst out.

"Cannot your sorcery make me love you?" Belle said quietly. She was rather surprised by his intensity.

"True love cannot be forced! You mock me," he said angrily.

"I do not!" Belle cried, fearing the dangerous look in his eye.

"Aye," he said slowly, "you do, my pet, and you will be disciplined for it. Come! You will help me to fashion your own punishment." He dragged her from their bedchamber into his magic room. Saffron glared at them balefully, his nap disturbed, as Guy lit the lamps. Flouncing down from his perch upon the table, the cat departed. "Give me the silver cup!" Guy commanded her.

With shaking hands, Belle obeyed. Suddenly this room had become very frightening to her, the lamps and the firelight casting ghostly shadows upon the stone walls. And yet how many pleasant afternoons had she spent here? He had taught her to make several lovely creams and ointments that were used to improve pleasure and heighten the skin's sensitivity. She had, beneath his careful eye, mixed potions over which he had murmured strange incantations, but would not tell her what their use was. One had the most delicious ingredients: rose water, myrtle water, orange blossom water, distilled spirit of musk, and just a dash of a waxlike substance called ambergris. They had bottled it in crystal flacons encased in silver filigree.

Guy d' Bretagne took the cup from Isabelle. He had assembled several jars, containers, and bottles upon the table. Fearfully, she watched as he poured a dollop of clear springwater into the cup, adding a large pinch of something, stirring it vigorously, and then holding it out to her. *"Drink it!"* he said in a fierce tone.

Isabelle shrank back. "Do you mean to kill me, then?" she whispered. "Do not, I beg you! I will do your bidding, my lord!"

"I told you once that I did not mean to kill you, Belle, but you have greatly displeased me, and I will chastise you for it. *Now drink!*"

"What is it?" she quavered. Oh, God! His eyes were boring into her, and she could feel the all-too-familiar weakness sapping her will.

"It is called cantharides," he said softly. "It will arouse you as you have never been aroused before, and until it pleases me, you shall not be satisfied." He pushed the cup at her.

Despite herself, Belle accepted it, and drank the liquid down. It had an almost musty taste. He held out a piece of colewort to her. This herb, she knew, induced a love trance. The ancients, he had told her, had used it in their orgies. Unwilling, but afraid, she chewed the herb down, helpless to his will.

He led her back to the bedchamber, ordering her to remove her garments as he removed his. When they were both naked, he made her stand in the middle of the floor. He poured powdered purple cyclamen root in a circle around her, murmuring incantations all the while. Isabelle was terrified as she had never been before. What was worse, she was beginning to feel dizzy. Her blood felt boiling hot in her veins, and every single bit of sensation had drained from her entire body to center itself with a throbbing urgency in her sex.

Guy d' Bretagne smiled cruelly, seeing her distress. "Ahh, my pet, you are beginning to understand, aren't you? It will get worse before it gets better, I promise you. Do not move from this spot. I must fetch something I forgot in the magic chamber." He hurried out of the room, then returned. "This cream is called kyphi," she heard him say.

"The kyphi will make your skin exquisitely sensitive, my pet," he promised her, and in short order he had rubbed it into every bit of her flesh, even between her legs. Then, pouring a thin trickle of juniper oil atop the cyclamen powder, he lit it so that it caused a circle of flame to surround her. Again he muttered strange words she could not understand, all the while moving about the outside of the circle.

Then Guy d' Bretagne stepped over the flames into the circle of fire, putting a strong arm about his victim. His other hand began to caress her body. "How soft you are," he said low, kissing her earlobe, his tongue then exploring its pink whorl.

Isabelle moaned. His touch was gentle wherever his fingers and mouth met her skin, but the agony was almost excruciating because of the intense throbbing of her sex. *"Please,"* she sobbed. *"Please!"*

"You see, my darling," he told her, "I do not have to resort to the strap to punish you. How far more exquisitely painful this little chastisement is, eh?

"Open your legs for me," he commanded, and she quickly complied. "Now," he said in a deceptively gentle tone, "spread yourself for me with your fingers, and show me your dainty little pleasure pearl." Again she obeyed, and he continued, "If you close yourself to me without my permission, the torture you feel now will be nothing to the spell I shall cast upon you, Belle. Do you understand me, my pet?"

She nodded, wondering nervously what new torment he was about to inflict upon her helpless body. She watched nervously as he sat cross-legged directly before her and drew from nowhere a long feather with a sharply pointed tip. He applied the tip directly to her pleasure pearl. The sensation was the most pleasurable, yet painful feeling. Her eyes widened in shock. Relentlessly, he worked the feather back and forth across her exposed sex, sometimes giving her a moment's respite by sliding the tapered feather up and down her nether lips. "You are going to kill me," she managed to gasp.

He smiled cruelly. "You are bearing up quite well," he noted, and reaching out with his other hand, he lifted a goblet she had not seen before to his lips. These objects seem to come from the air, she thought.

"The drink I am drinking is called satyricon," he told her. "It will ensure that my weapon does not flag this night." Finishing his potion, he flung the cup from him, but she heard no sound of the vessel falling to the stone floor.

Finally, Guy d' Bretagne dropped the feather with which he had been teasing her. The ring of fire had burnt itself out. "You may close yourself for the moment," he said, and taking her hand, he led her from the enchanted circle to a goatskin rug before the room's fireplace. "Kneel down," he ordered. "I shall first take you as a stallion mounts a mare in a field." Moving behind her, he plunged his unusually swollen manhood into her burning sheath.

Isabelle cried out, half with relief, half with pain, for he was enormous tonight, and deeper within her than he had ever been before. It was only the beginning. For the next several hours,

he used her in a variety of positions; having her anoint his manhood with goat suet in between, which had a profound effect
upon a man's performance, and his was unflagging. She was
but half conscious when he finally decided she had suffered
enough. "You will never again mock me, Belle," he told her,
and then, making a motion with his hand, he willed her into
sleep.

When Isabelle finally awoke, she found herself in their bed,
but Guy was nowhere to be seen. She lay quietly, hoping that
she was alone in the room. Every muscle in her body ached,
and her love sheath felt raw and sore. Guy d' Bretagne had
shown a side of himself last night that she hoped never to see
again. *And why?* Because she had said she loved her husband,
and he had obviously felt threatened by it. *Cannot your sorcery
make me love you?* That had been the innocent question that
had caused him to erupt with violence and anger.

The question slipped unbidden into her head. *What true sorcery had she ever seen him perform, or Vivienne, either, for
that matter?* They made potions and lotions, it was true, but
never once had she seen them turn anything into something
else. Never once had she seen them call the wind, or make the
rain stop. Was that not what sorcerers did? Any old witch
woman in the forest could make love potions and ointments.
Sorcerers did really important things, or so she had always
believed. Other than Hugh's very odd condition, she had seen
no real magic of a serious kind. And what of that passionately
uttered cry he had made in his anger? *"True love cannot be
forced."* Was it possible there was no magic?

And if there was no magic, what kind of a woman did that
make her? Possibly a very gullible one; a very foolish one; a
very stupid one. Once, perhaps these decendants of the great
Merlin had been keepers of powerful magic, but somewhere in
the intervening centuries that magic may have lost its potency.
Were they using the memory of it to frighten their neighbors,
to keep others at bay? Why else had Guy d' Bretagne subjected
her to such a night of brutal passion? If he had any real power,

he would have simply cast a spell to make her love him and forget her husband. He would not have been angered by her love for a supposedly dead mate.

"What an incredible fool I have been," Isabelle of Langston said softly to herself; and then she was filled with a burning anger. What amusement she must have provided Guy and Vivienne with over these past few months.

Still they must not guess her suspicions. She must remain Guy d' Bretagne's obedient mistress for Hugh's sake, until she could find a way to free him. As long as she could make Guy believe she was acquiescent, she would be safe. Even without true magic, he was a dangerous, powerful man. Unless he believed she was really his, she faced the danger of being sent away, *or worse*.

"You are awake at last," he said, and she started at the sound of his rich, musical voice. Coming into her view, he seated himself upon the edge of the bed. "Have you learned your lesson, my Belle?"

She nodded, casting her eyes down in apparent abject obedience.

"And you will love me, putting from your mind any others for whom you might have ever held a tender passion," he commanded her.

"Have I not warned you, my lord Guy, that love is dangerous as well as sweet? I do not want you weakened by it. I enjoy your strength, for it is like none I have ever known in a man," she said daringly.

"After last night you must surely know I cannot be weakened," he replied. *"I must know that you love me!"*

You have lied to me, she thought to herself. I shall now lie to you, for it will, I am certain, help me learn the truth of you and gain my beloved Hugh's release. "After last night," she murmured softly, "how can you doubt my love for you, my lord Guy? Did you not behold my ecstasy? Could I have obtained such rapture with a man I did not truly love? Yet I have heard it said you discard those who care for you. I have but sought to retain your favor and remain within your sweet custody. I never meant to displease you, my dear lord."

*She loved him!* he thought. *And,* she had said his name for the very first time. In all the months he had kept her by his side, she had never once uttered his name, always addressing him formally, and most properly, as *my lord*. His heart soared with delight, and pulling her into his arms, he declared, "The knowledge that you love me has made me the happiest of men. Your love will not weaken me, Belle. It will but give me greater strength." Then he kissed her, and for a brief moment Belle let herself be swept away, melting into his embrace, that he not be made suspicious.

In the back of her mind, however, was a new knowledge. The power of the d' Bretagnes was most probably a false one. *There was no true magic!*

# ▓Chapter 15

*I*sabelle shared her revelation with Alain and Lind the following day when she visited the mews. Both were amazed.

"How can you be certain there is no real magic?" Alain said, suspicious as ever. His tone was disapproving, for he did not really understand or favor her association with Guy d' Bretagne.

Isabelle said wisely, "Think, both of you. Have you seen any sign of magic? Anything unusual, out of the ordinary? Nay, you have not. We have seen unspeakable cruelty, fear, and intimidation. We have been told the d' Bretagne history, and warned we must obey without question. But is any of this magic?"

They both shook their heads in the negative.

"And that," she said triumphantly, "is because there is no magic! They have traded on their family's reputation to keep everyone in awe and afraid of them. Hugh's memory has been kept from him by means of some kind of elixir, I am certain, not by enchantment. Did you not tell me, Alain, that Hugh's loss of memory originally came from a blow upon his head? Nothing that I know of could permanently erase someone's memory. Vivienne must continually dose him. If we know what to watch for, my lads, we shall be able to unravel the puzzle and free Hugh!"

"You are more likely to discover the potion than we are," Lind said. "You are with them more, lady."

"Perhaps," Isabelle agreed, "but I nonetheless want you to

323

keep a sharp eye out. Make friends with the serving wenches. Servants always see what they should not," she concluded with a chuckle, and they both grinned at her knowingly.

Now Isabelle deliberately set out to make friends with her lover's sister. She dared not be obvious, but she knew that if she could get close to Vivienne, she was more than likely to learn her secrets. Then one evening an opportunity came. Vivienne was complaining that the winter cold was dulling the sheen of her raven-black hair.

"Have you tried rinsing it with apple cider vinegar?" Belle asked the older woman. "I am told it is excellent for restoring a dark hair's shine, or so my mother, who was skilled in herbs and household remedies, always said. Lemon is good for lighter hair."

"Apple cider vinegar? I never heard of using it for that purpose, but it certainly cannot hurt to try," Vivienne said thoughtfully. "If you are wrong, though, I shall have you hung here in the hall to be whipped like any common miscreant. Do not think that because you are my brother's leman I cannot do it. *I am the mistress of La Citadelle.*"

"Lady, I would do you no intentional harm. If you would like it, I will wash your hair myself," Isabelle murmured sweetly.

Vivienne d' Bretagne thought for but a moment, and then she said, "Yes, I should like you to attend to my hair, Belle. If you are clever, and you please me, I shall give you a place serving me one day when you no longer amuse my brother."

"That day shall not come, sister," Guy said quietly. "From this day on I will take Belle as my wife. If she attends to your hair, Vivi, it will be for love of us both, not because she is your servant."

If Isabelle was astounded by his words, Vivienne d' Bretagne was even more so. "You would take her to wife, Guy? *Why?* Does she know that you cannot give her a child? Have you told her of the curse upon us? No d' Bretagne male has ever taken an outsider for a wife."

"Why should I not?" he rejoined. "Under the circumstances, what difference does it make, Vivi? I love this girl. I do not ever wish to be parted from her. If I cannot give her a child, at least I can honor her with our name, such as it is. She is too fine to remain merely my leman."

"My lord . . ." Belle touched his arm and looked up into his face. "I would cause no riff between you and the sister you have always loved. Whatever place you desire to assign me within your sphere, I am content to accept it."

"There can be no priest to say the words here, Belle, but I acknowledge you to be my wife from this time forward," Guy said quietly. "If my sister loves me as I have always loved her, she will accept this."

*"And what of our plan?"* Vivienne whispered desperately in a tongue the others in the hall could not comprehend.

Guy caressed her cheek, answering her in the same ancient Breton language, "It will be fulfilled as we desire it, *petite soeur*. What is more, you and I shall share in it. Trust me. I have never failed you yet, Vivi, but I want this girl to wife."

"So be it then," Vivienne d' Bretagne said, returning to the modern idiom. "If it will truly make you happy, Guy, how can I deny you?" She turned to Belle. "I welcome you as my brother's wife," she said softly. "You are now my sister, Belle."

"Sisters help one another," Belle replied. "I shall still wash your hair and help restore its shine for you."

How strangely fate had played into her hands, Isabelle thought gratefully. She sipped automatically from the cup Guy held to her lips.

"Where are you wandering?" he asked her playfully.

She focused her green-gold eyes upon him. She must not betray herself when she was closer than she had ever been to her goal. "I am marveling that with a few words you can make me your wife," she admitted honestly. "Why can you not give me a child?" She had frankly been amazed that in all the months she had been with him, she had not conceived.

"One of my ancestors managed to get us cursed by an angry parent," he said lightly. "For centuries the men of my line have been unable to reproduce, which is why the women rule at La Citadelle. Will you love me less for it, Belle?"

"Of course not," she told him, secretly relieved. When Hugh's memory was restored, he would surely forgive her her liaison with Guy d' Bretagne, but had she borne her lover a child, how could Hugh ever forget her infidelity whilst the evidence of it grew up in his house? It would have been absolutely impossible for them both, and for the poor, innocent child. It was so much better this way.

"I have a special way to celebrate our union," Guy said, nibbling suggestively upon her ear. "It is most delicious in a variety of ways."

"You know that I am yours to command, my lord," she murmured.

His violet eyes glittered. "You are surprisingly brave for a woman," he said.

"You are very naughty, my lord," Belle teased him dangerously. Her pointed little tongue ran across her lips.

"Tonight I shall teach you how to be very, *very* bad," he responded.

Her heart hammered. At the other end of the table sat her lawful husband, lost to himself, and perhaps even lost to her, but she had not yet really tried to free him. How easy, she realized with horror, it would be to give up, to remain here at La Citadelle as Guy's *wife*. But could she forget Langston? What of Hugh the Younger?

It was the one thing that kept her focused upon what she had to do. Their little son must not grow up without his father. And what of the other children they hoped to have? Children who would go unborn if she could not bring Hugh home. *If they could not escape La Citadelle.*

"Come!" Guy's voice was imperious. Taking her hand in his, he led her from the high board. "While you daydreamed, I gave certain orders," he said meaningfully. "I have spent many weeks teaching you the delights of your pleasure. Tonight I shall teach you how to pleasure me in a way such as you cannot imagine."

"Your creativity has always amazed me, my lord," Isabelle answered him, smiling. "I am intrigued as to what you have in store for us, but I have no doubt we shall both be pleasured by it."

In his apartments, Guy undressed her, and then she undressed him. They bathed together, returning naked to their bedchamber. He had a beautiful body that, while hirsute and unlike Hugh's, was graceful and finely made. Though very tall, his torso and limbs were in perfect proportion. She thought it sad that he would have no son of his own. Any children he sired would surely have been beautiful to behold.

In the alcove where he liked to play his special games, a silver bowl had been placed upon a table. Peering into it, she could see it was filled with an extraordinarily thick, creamy golden substance. Next to the bowl was a long brush with a silver handle. Guy lit the sweetly scented oil lamps he enjoyed on special occasions. The scent of aloe filled the room. He held out his hand to her.

"What is in the bowl?" she asked him.

"In time I will reveal its contents to you," he said, and then, "Have you ever taken a man's member between your lips, Belle?"

"No," she said, eyes wide. But then, why not? she thought. Did he not taste of her each time they made love? Why should she not taste of him as well? She slipped to her knees before him at the gentle pressure of his hands on her shoulders. His groin was smooth and white, devoid of the dark hair that covered his chest, arms, and legs. A curly growth but hid the glory of one's sex, he had told her when she had first remarked upon it.

Reaching down with his hand, he lifted the limp flesh and rubbed it across her lips. "Open your mouth, Belle, and take it in, my precious. Be careful not to score it with your teeth. Then you may suckle upon it and use your tongue to tease it," he instructed her.

Following his directions, she was enchanted to find the member growing within the confines of her mouth. It grew so swiftly that she could scarcely contain it, and choked just slightly. With his hand on her fiery head he encouraged her further. She was becoming very aroused by her actions, and dizzy with the pleasure she was obtaining.

Finally he said softly, "Cease, Belle," and when she opened her mouth, he withdrew his member, now enormous and fully engorged. He smiled down at her, pleased to see the rising desire in her green-gold eyes, knowing she had enjoyed the task. "Now," he continued, "place the bowl upon the floor near you, Belle, and using the brush, paint first my rod and then my jewels with the substance."

Fascinated, she obeyed him, lavishly spreading the thick, pale gold substance up and down his manhood. And then she painted his jewels as he had ordered her. Finished, she put the brush aside on the edge of the bowl and awaited his instructions.

"Now," he said, "using your mouth and tongue, wash it all off, my beauty. Every speck, for if I feel the least stickiness when you are done, you will receive six strokes of my strap, my pet."

Kneeling before him, she began to lick at his swollen member. *Honey!* There was honey in the mixture she had painted upon him. "Ummmmm," she murmured, "delicious, my lord!" She licked and suckled his manhood, her hot tongue moving quickly up and down its length, laving the flesh free of the syrupy matter until there was no more. She could feel a heavy wetness between her legs, and realized how fiercely aroused she was. Twisting her body, she bent very low, gently taking his jewels into her mouth to suck them free of the honey. The more her mouth worked him, the more excited she herself became. He said nothing while she attended to him, but his labored breathing was audible.

"Enough!" he finally groaned. "Enough, you vixen!" He forced her up, and lifting her into his arms, impaled her upon his raging member.

Belle wrapped her legs about her lover, sobbing with her own desire as he carried her across the room to their bed. Laying her back upon the coverlet, he stood above her, plunging himself in and out, in and out, until she was screaming with a pleasure she would not have believed existed. She felt as if she were going to die, and it mattered not a bit to her. Her breath was labored as she reached peak after peak after peak. The familiar starburst exploded behind her eyes, but this time in such a profusion of colors that she could not bear it. She felt his tribute thundering into her, and almost immediately afterward lost consciousness.

Her awareness returned with the feeling of his tongue on her torso, licking delicately. Belle forced her eyes open and watched as he painted her belly with the honey paste and then sensuously lapped it off her skin. "It is too delicious," she murmured. "Too delicious to bear, and if you stop, I shall die, my lord!"

"You like this little game," he said innocently.

"It is even better than the grapes," she assured him.

"Yes," he laughed low, "I noticed how much you enjoyed it, Belle. There was a moment or two there when I thought you meant to swallow me whole, my precious. You left me no excuse to beat you." He licked the last of the sweetness off her skin and laid his dark head upon her belly. "You have the body of an ancient goddess," he told her. "What a pity we cannot have a child together. Especially now."

"Why now?" she wondered aloud.

"When our ancestor was cursed," Guy told her, "the curse was not simply upon the males of the family. It was also upon the females. The story is that the noblewoman cursing the d' Bretagnes first laid her malediction upon my ancestor Jean and all those males who might follow him. Then, as an afterthought, she damned the female line, too, but that curse would

not come immediately. She wanted the family to suffer as they
had made her suffer. The women of the family would be forced
to take lovers to procreate their line, but one day a woman
would be born to the d' Bretagnes who would not be able to
reproduce our line, and it would end altogether. My sister,
Vivienne, seems to be that woman. She has taken lover after
lover since she was a nubile girl, but not once has she quick-
ened with a child."

"What has happened to her other lovers?" Belle asked.

"She has dismissed them, of course, when she realized they
could not give her what she most desired—a child," he said.

"And will she dismiss her Hugh?"

"Nay, she has fallen in love with him, even as I have fallen
in love with you. She will keep him by her side," Guy said.

"Who is he? Where did he come from?" Belle caressed her
lover's dark locks.

"I know little about him," Guy answered honestly. "He is
English, I believe. Vivienne has a liegeman, a great fool named
Richard de Manneville. This man was in de Manneville's
dungeon for some reason, and he wished to be rid of him. De
Manneville was too cowardly to kill him. Vivienne saw Hugh,
and despite his filthy state at the time, she decided she wanted
him. She took him, the falconer Alain, and six men-at-arms
who accompanied them, and brought them back to La
Citadelle."

"He must love your sister, else he certainly would have tried
to return to his own land," Belle noted.

"He has virtually no memory of his past life," Guy told her.
"The falconer told Vivi that his master received a blow on the
head. Then, too, my sister, I suspect, keeps his memory from
returning by means of some little potion she mixes up. If she is
happy, it matters not to me. Hugh is no more than a simple
knight, or else his family would have come seeking after him.
Besides, anyone doing business with Richard de Manneville
was surely unimportant." He pulled himself up and began
kissing her.

She forced herself to respond to his ardent embraces. There was so much more she wanted to know, but she dared not press him further.

In the morning, when Isabelle went to the mews, she asked Alain, "Why did you not tell Vivienne d' Bretagne that your master was Hugh Fauconier of Langston Keep, a companion to King Henry? Had you spoken up, we might all be home, and none of this would have happened."

"You were not there, lady," Alain said. "I was. The moment *she* laid eyes upon him, she was in love. Was I to tell a sorceress that she could not have the man she desired? That he was a married man with a child? She would have killed me, and then who would have taken care of him in those early days?"

"But could not you or one of the Langston men have fled this place, and returned home to tell me what had happened? We waited for months for word. Then I went up to court to ask the king's help, only to find myself a victim of his salacious seduction!" Isabelle paced nervously back and forth in the mews, which was their only place of privacy. "Well, it matters not now."

"What will you do, lady, if you cannot restore his memory?" Lind asked her. Lind might be a quiet fellow, but he always came directly to the point.

"I do not know," Isabelle told them, and turning abruptly, left the mews. *What would she do?* She loved Hugh, and she wanted their simple old life at Langston restored to them. Yet would she ever be happy again with her good Hugh, having known Guy? Guy who, despite his deception, was dark and complicated, and showered her with a passion such as she had never known. But deep in her heart she knew what had to be done.

Vivienne's serving woman came to Isabelle and said that her mistress wished to see her. "Go and fetch me an egg and a small pitcher of apple cider vinegar," she told the servant. "I

can find my way to your mistress's quarters. It is the south
tower, is it not?"

"Yes, lady," the woman said.

She found the mistress of La Citadelle lying in her lover's
arms, clad only in her long skirts. Hugh absently played with
Vivienne's breasts, his eyes flicking to acknowledge Belle's
entry, but he said nothing. "I have sent your woman for what I
shall need," Belle said.

"I hope this works," Vivienne d' Bretagne said petulantly.
Then, "What is this magic spell you have cast over my
brother?"

Isabelle laughed mockingly. "There is no spell, unless you
believe that love is magical, lady. If my lord Guy is content
with me, would you seek to deny his happiness?"

"I sense you are a threat to me," Vivienne said honestly.

Isabelle almost shivered, but she did not. "I am no danger to
those I love, lady," she replied evenly. Then she smiled. "Can
we not be friends, lady?"

"I have no friends," Vivienne d' Bretagne said.

"Ahh," Belle answered, "here is your woman with the
vinegar."

Water was brought, and a fine gold basin. Using a soap fragrant with lilies, Isabelle washed Vivienne d' Bretagne's hair.
It was very dirty, and Isabelle was not in the least surprised that
the hair had lost its sheen.

"What!" Vivienne cried. "You are washing it again?"

"The first time was for the dirt, lady. The second is to restore
its shine," Isabelle said, cracking the egg the serving woman
had brought her. She mixed it with a bit of the soap and
scrubbed it into the woman's head vigorously.

"I smell egg!" Vivienne said, and her serving woman
giggled.

"Indeed you do, lady. It's in your hair right now, but if you
will be patient," Belle replied sweetly, "I will soon have it
washed out. Egg is very good for the hair."

"Your old mother's remedy, I have not a doubt," Vivienne

replied sarcastically. "I do not care if my brother declares you his wife, if this does not work, I will see that you suffer!"

"Pour the vinegar into the large pitcher of warm water," Belle said calmly to the serving woman. "Mix it with your hand. That's good." She rinsed Vivienne's hair first with clear water, then the vinegar, and then with clear water again. "I am done," she told the servant. "Towel your mistress's hair dry with vigor to stimulate it, and then brush it out till all the water is gone. Then rub it with a length of silk. The shine should be restored." Then, without another word, Isabelle departed Vivienne d' Bretagne's chambers, a small smile upon her lips.

"I did not say she could go!" Vivienne said waspishly.

"Nonetheless, *chérie*, she has," Hugh murmured. "She is a most independent creature, isn't she? I can see why your brother enjoys her. She reminds me of someone, but of course, I cannot remember." He laughed. "It doesn't matter though, Vivi, does it?"

"I sense she is a danger to us," Vivienne persisted.

"Are you fearful she is a sorceress like yourself, and perhaps with stronger magic than you possess?" he teased her.

"She speaks of love, and her face lights up," Vivienne d' Bretagne said. "There is no such thing as love, Hugh. There is lust, and passion, and hate, but love? It does not exist!"

"Of course it exists, Vivi," Hugh said. "Love is the sun to hate's moon, *chérie*. You feel it for me, else I should not still be in your good graces, and would have gone the way of all of your previous lovers." He bent to kiss her damp shoulder. "I think the problem is that you are jealous Guy has found a small measure of happiness that is not connected with you. I know how deeply you care for your brother."

"If she should harm him . . ." Vivienne warned.

Hugh laughed. "Vivienne, when will you realize that Guy is far stronger than you have ever been, or will ever be? Because this family of yours is a matriarchy, you naturally assume you are the stronger, but my pet, you are not." He kissed her pouting mouth. "Now cease your fretting over the girl, Belle."

* * *

The winter progressed slowly. The sea rumbled noisily beneath the castle, sending fingers of icy green water into the caves below. They had days that were cold, cloudless, and blazingly sunny, but more often than not the days were gray, dank, and mist-filled. On the good days, Isabelle would go with her falconers into the fields above the sea and exercise the birds, who chafed from too many days of confinement in their mews. Isabelle loved watching Couper soar on the whorls of the wind.

"If we had wings, we could fly home to Langston," she said to her falconers one bright day. In her enthusiasm she had forgotten that Hugh was with them. Alain and Lind looked nervously at her.

"Where is Langston?" Hugh asked her.

"It is a place in England we once knew, Lind, Alain, and I," she said, knowing he would ask no more, for he really wasn't interested. "My lord Guy says that you lost the memory of your past before you came to La Citadelle. Is it true that you remember nothing? Not a wife, or family? Naught?"

For a moment he looked at her curiously, and Isabelle's heart leapt in her chest, but then he said, "Sometimes I see images in my head, but they come and go so quickly that I cannot retain anything. You must not tell Vivi that, however. It will frighten her."

"What kind of images?" Belle gently pressed him.

"Mostly it is of the falcons, which is why Vivienne keeps them for me," he said slowly, "but sometimes I see a stone tower, and a river. At other times I see the phantoms of people, but I cannot see their faces." He smiled gently, for the first time looking like the Hugh of old. *Her Hugh.* "I cannot, Belle, have been a man of any importance, else someone would have come after me. Ahhh, look at your merlin! How she soars, the pretty little devil!"

Afterward, Isabelle said to her falconers, "Do not tell me that he cannot be coaxed into regaining his memory, for I believe he can! We must help him, and I must learn what it is *she* feeds him to prevent his recovery."

"I've made friends with one of the young serving women in her chamber, a maid named Jeanne," Lind said. "Jeanne says that each morning before lord Hugh is allowed from his bed, he is brought a small silver cup with what Jeanne says is a strengthening potion so that Lord Hugh will not lose his virility, for Lady Vivienne is insatiable in her appetite for passion," the falconer finished with a deep blush.

"That must be it!" Isabelle cried. "Lind, Jeanne must find out what is in that cup. Tell her you want it so you will be potent with her. There is no other way I can learn what we must know."

"Even if you discover what is in the cup," the practical Alain reminded her, "how can you prevent her from feeding it to him?"

"I do not know," Belle said, "but I will find a way! Have we not come a great way already, my lads? We cannot fail now!"

"I will see what I can do," Lind said, "but remember, lady, I must move slowly with the maid lest I arouse her suspicions. I will have to begin to court her in earnest so she will tell me her mistress's secrets." He sighed. "You will not tell Agneatha when we get home, lady, will you? She will not like it at all."

*Lind and Agneatha?* She hadn't realized it, but of course! "No, I will not tell Agneatha, and neither of you will tell of my little adventures, either, will you?" She smiled at them.

"We've all done what we had to do," Alain said bluntly.

There were small signs of spring; a bit of greening here, a violet by a sunny wall there. One afternoon three swans flew over the castle as Belle walked upon its heights. The soft whirring of wings made her look up suddenly, and there they were. She shared her sighting with the others at the evening meal.

"Swans in the marshes, a certain sign of spring," Hugh said.

"How would you know a thing like that?" Vivienne asked him.

He shook his head, confused for a moment. "I do not know," he finally replied in his harsh voice, "I just do."

Belle laughed. "I think I mentioned something like that to Hugh yesterday, and now here today the swans are back." She worried that if Vivienne believed Hugh's memory were returning, she might grow desperate and give him some new and stronger potion.

"How do you know so much about swans?" Vivienne demanded.

"Remember, I grew up in the country," Belle said. "You live in the country. Certainly you know about swans, too."

"Swans do not interest me except as food," Vivienne replied.

Guy chortled. "Vivi, you are being quite cruel, and silly," he told her. "Swans are beautiful creatures."

"Who make excellent eating," his sister rejoined stubbornly.

"I once had two swans for pets," Belle said. "Everyone was amazed for they are dreadfully mean birds, but they were quite gentle with me."

"You do have magic about you!" Vivienne cried. "I knew it! Guy, you must send her away! Surely you see that now!"

Her brother took Vivienne's hand in his. It was such a petite hand that it was almost lost in his big paw. Yet in features they were alike enough to be twins.

"Vivi," Guy said softly, "if my precious Belle does indeed have magic about her, how much better than if she were just a simple girl. You are beginning to become tiresome in your jealousy, *petite soeur*, and I am losing my patience with you." His violet eyes darkened as he looked into her face.

For a brief moment Isabelle felt sorry for Vivienne d' Bretagne. Somehow, Guy's displeasure was much greater with his sister than with anyone else, and it was obvious she felt that displeasure.

"You are right, Guy," she said low. "I forget our goal."

The meal continued with small talk, and Belle was relieved that the conversation had been turned from Hugh's memory. Once she caught him looking at her questioningly, but when she met his gaze, he turned away from her, leaning over to murmur something into his fair mistress's little ear. When Vivienne laughed, Belle felt a stab of jealousy, but her face remained smooth and did not betray her.

Spring came on full now, the fruit trees and flowering bushes bursting into glorious bloom. The fields about the castle grew green and lush, tended by La Citadelle's serfs. On the hillsides, fat cattle grazed, while in other, greener meadows, white sheep dotted the landscape.

Midsummer's Eve was upon them. The serfs were freed from their labor for the day, as was the custom at Langston, and that night fires blazed from the walls of the castle and the hillsides in the long, lingering twilight. The air was soft with summer, and above La Citadelle the stars echoed the bright firelight.

Guy had ordered that their apartments be newly decorated for the occasion. Their huge bed was hung with cloth-of-gold hangings upon which had been embroidered silver crescent moons and glittering, deep blue stars. The always fresh lavender-scented snowy sheets had been exchanged for sheets made from midnight-blue silk. Although it was warm enough to forgo a fire, the hearth was filled with lighted, scented candles in all sizes and shapes. There were also candles on every flat surface in the room. On the table next to the bed had been placed a silver tray, and on it were pale gold quartz goblets set in silver filigree, several crystal decanters, and half a dozen different-colored marble jars. The shutters were back on all the windows, allowing the bright moonlight to join the candlelight, and a gentle breeze wafted the intoxicating scent of flowers into the chamber.

Guy and Belle had finished bathing. Gently, he dried her pale skin, smoothing foliatum, an erotic ointment made from spikenard, over her. The ointment was pale pink in color and had an exotic scent that was quite heady. It would be absorbed through her skin, making it highly sensitive to any sort of touch for hours to come. She had grown quite used to his ministrations, and had actually learned to enjoy them. How could she not, even now when she knew there was no real enchantment? Such delicious treatment was simply impossible to resist, and Isabelle refused to feel sinful about it. After all, he would hardly be pleased with a weeping, guilt-ridden woman. He would have replaced her in an instant with a more willing partner, and then how could she have helped Hugh?

Guy now held a cup to her lips. "Drink it," he commanded her.

She sipped the bitter liquid, curious, for she had never before tasted this particular mixture. "What is it?" she asked him as she drained the cup off.

"A special little elixir I have mixed especially for you on this occasion," he told her. "It is red wine combined with wormwood, which you will find a strong aphrodisiac."

"I need no aphrodisiac to be aroused by you, my lord Guy," she told him, knowing it would please him.

"I know that," he replied, smiling, "but tonight Hugh is to join us in our love revels. I would have you eager to receive his lusty attentions, my adorable Belle. You cannot be shy, my pet."

*"Hugh is joining us?"* Certainly she had not heard him aright. Was the wine already muddling her wits?

"Aye, he is," Guy answered her, drawing her into his embrace and fondling her breasts lovingly. "How I love these little fruits," he murmured, bending swiftly to kiss each berry nipple.

*"Why is Hugh joining us?"* Isabelle pulled away from her lover. Had Guy d' Bretagne grown tired of her at last, and willing to share her with other men? Was the next step to be her banishment from his side to the guardroom, where she would

serve as the new whore? Her lovely face betrayed her concern to him almost immediately.

He drew her back firmly into his embrace. "Do not be fearful, my fair Belle. Do you not know by now that I truly love you and would do nothing to harm you? Tonight, however, is a magical night, and we need that magic badly. You have noted the new bed hangings, I know, but do you not see the flowering branches, the branches heavy with fruit, and the sheaves of wheat that have been set about our chamber?"

Belle looked about her. Indeed there were branches of flowers, and fruit set in great containers about the room, and sheaves of wheat stacked near them, *and beneath the bed itself!* She looked questioningly to him, and he smiled, the smile lighting up his handsome face, extending from his mouth to his magnificent violet eyes.

"Tonight, my perfect love, you will conceive a child for the d' Bretagnes; a daughter who will be La Citadelle's next mistress. To ensure your fruitfulness," he continued, "these symbols of fertility have been placed within our chamber." He caressed her shining hair gently.

"But you have told me that you cannot produce a child, my lord Guy," she said nervously. What had Hugh to do with this?

"I have told you the truth. Neither Vivienne nor I are capable of having children, but certainly you and Hugh are. My sister and I have decided that you and Hugh, now being a part of the d' Bretagne family, will together conceive the next generation for us."

"Ohh, my lord, do not ask such a thing of me," Isabelle protested. The thought of a child of hers and Hugh's belonging to the d' Bretagnes was absolutely horrific.

He misinterpreted her disquiet. "Do not fear, my precious one," he reassured her. "I shall not leave you alone with my sister's rude lover. I will be with you the entire time. You will lie safe in my arms, and taste my kisses upon your sweet lips each time he mounts you and fills you with his seed. Then he shall cradle you as I enjoy you to the fullest. If you did not know the secret of the d' Bretagnes, you would believe me if I told you the child was of my issue; and indeed, my passion will ensure that you conceive this night, Belle."

"Am I some prized mare to be put to the stud of your choice?" Isabelle demanded furiously. True, she thought, any child conceived would be lawfully born, since Hugh was her true husband, but neither Guy d' Bretagne nor his sister was aware of that. What if they had chosen some other man to perform this *service*? The thought was too terrible, and she shuddered with distaste.

Again he misunderstood, and, believing her disinclination stemmed from her love for him, said in his beautiful voice, "My darling, I know it is an idea that will take a moment or two for you to digest and comprehend; but surely you can understand. You know our history, Belle. We cannot allow our family to die out. We will not allow it. Now, the moon is almost in the perfect position for us to begin. Let me call Hugh to join us."

"What of Vivienne?" Belle demanded, desperately attempting to forestall what she realized was inevitable. "Does she know that you plan to use her lover for such a purpose? She is very jealous of him, and has punished several maidservants for even looking at him in what she believed was an admiring manner."

"Vivienne knows, of course, and wanted to join us," Guy answered her, "but I felt it best she did not. You are absolutely correct about her jealousy. I do not believe she could have borne seeing Hugh using another woman. Besides, I need her to do the incantations that go along with our efforts and are necessary for our success. My sister understood. After all, she will be the child's mother as the matriarch of our family." He stroked her hair again. "Are you all right now, my precious?"

Isabelle nodded. What choice did she really have? However, she now knew what she must do, for she would not give her child over to Vivienne d' Bretagne. If she became pregnant and still could not find a way for Hugh to regain his memory, she would be forced to leave him and flee back to Langston. Perhaps if King Henry had overcome his lust for her, and certainly he must have at this point, mayhap he would help her get her husband home to England now that she knew where he was. She would die, and the child with her, before she would allow Vivienne d' Bretagne to have her babe.

She looked up at Guy. "You realize, of course, that his attentions may arouse me, my lord. And if they do, I will enjoy them. Will you punish me for it if I do?"

"You came to me with an ability to enjoy passion," Guy said calmly. "I do not expect you to deny your feelings, Belle, even if it is Hugh who pleasures you. You do not love him. You love me." He led her to the door of their bedchamber, and opening it, called out, "Hugh, come in and join us now."

Hugh entered the room solemnly. He was freshly washed and shaved. His dark blond hair was tied back with a delicate gold chain. Seeing his dear, familiar body once again, Isabelle felt herself melt inside. She watched as the two men prepared for what was to come. They drank down the wine she had previously drunk, which was now having a very erotic effect upon her. Seeing these two, well-made male creatures before her, she was becoming aroused. Guy, she had to admit, was certainly the more handsome of the two. Still, Hugh's plain, honest face was the more attractive to her.

Guy picked up the largest of the marble jars. It was black, with white and gold veins running through it. Taking the carved, golden lid off, he scooped a fingerful out and ate it. He then passed the jar to Hugh, who did the same and then passed it to Belle, who followed their example and made to hand the jar back to Guy, but he shook his dark head. "Nay, my love. Ingesting the pyrethrum will aid our arousal, but you must also rub it into our manhoods. It will work to make them quite rampant."

Isabelle said nothing, but obeyed. Carefully and quite thoroughly she anointed the two well-made sets of genitalia displayed before her. Within moments of her ministrations each became fiercely upstanding. Wordlessly, she replaced the lid on the jar, licking the excess from her slender fingers, and looked to Guy for further instructions.

Together the two men guided her to the open window. They stood on either side of her, and the moonlight streamed in, touching their naked bodies as it reflected off the sea below. She felt them grope for her hands, and finding them, each held one of hers within his own.

"Great Mother, and Maker of all creation," Guy said in his strong voice, "make fruitful this woman, whose garden will tonight be sown with the seeds of life. Let her ripen as the fruit in the orchards and the wheat of the fields ripen. This I ask of you in the name of our great and powerful ancestress, your daughter, Vivienne."

"Make it so, Great Mother of all the Earth," Hugh's rough voice echoed. "Let my seed take root in this woman's fertile body. This I ask in the name of the great and powerful sorceress, Vivienne, your daughter and devotee."

"When the moon again waxes in all its silver glory," Guy concluded, "let this woman's womb be ripe with new and growing life."

When his words had died, there was no sound for a few moments but the gentle slap of the waves upon the rocks of La Citadelle below them. Without another word the three of them moved across the room to the large bed. Guy climbed in first, drawing Belle with him. Moving her limbs so that he could display her, he said to Hugh, "Look how fair her skin is against the dark sheets." Hugh stared hard at Belle, and then he entered the bed on the other side, so that she was nestled between the two men.

They drank from the gold quartz cups in the silver filigree holders. Guy added a touch of erithraicon to the mixture. This, Belle knew from her afternoons in Guy's magic room, was another member of the satyricon family, and helped to induce unbridled lust. Her lover was taking absolutely no chances that Hugh would fail in his mission this night. Guy massaged her

breasts and belly with more foliatum. Then he playfully rubbed
pyrethrum into her netherlips and over her already throbbing
pleasure pearl. The pyrethrum, which was made from a plant
called pyrethrum parthenium, which had been pounded down
and mixed with ginger and essence of lilac, set her afire with
lust, and she moaned hungrily, her hips beginning to imitate
the rhythm of love. The two men grinned wickedly at each
other, their passion rods stiff, unyielding, and ready to pleasure her.

Guy cupped one of Belle's breasts in his palm, displaying it
for Hugh. "I know Vivi has fine big breasts, my friend," he said
in pleasant tones, "but observe these perfect little apples my
adorable Belle possesses. Her nipples are very sensitive
always. Taste one and see," he encouraged the other man.
Then taking her face in his grip, Guy turned her face to his and
began to kiss her.

His lips were warm and tender; his tongue gently sought
her tongue, found it, and teased it playfully. She responded to
his kisses as she always did, with pleasure; and then, to her
shock, she felt a mouth on her breast. She stiffened, her mind
confused.

"It's all right, my precious," Guy assured her. "Hugh is but
pleasuring himself, and you as well. To be loved by two men is
a rare and special treat for a woman. I want you to enjoy it,
Belle."

*Enjoy it?* It was madness, Belle thought, and yet, though she
struggled with herself to keep the notion unborn, it bloomed,
and she was forced to admit that it was also very thrilling. Neither of these men was behaving in an unkind or cruel fashion.
Indeed, they drew her this way and that, hands caressing, lips
kissing her tenderly. The arousal was constant, and her own
desire rose with each passing moment despite her reservations.

Guy sat up, a wall of pillows behind his long back. He drew
Belle between his open legs, murmuring low, "Spread yourself
for him, my precious. That's a good girl." Each of his big
hands held one of her breasts, his fingers crushing the soft

flesh. His breath was hot in her ear. "You are wonderful, my darling," he purred encouragingly.

Hugh knelt between Isabelle's milky white thighs, gently caressing her plump mont. She was really very lovely, he thought. Leaning forward, he spread her netherlips with his thumbs and gazed on her little pleasure pearl. It was larger than Vivi's, but most perfectly formed. Bending lower, he began to tongue it with at first delicate and then harder strokes that demanded a response.

It was as if fire had touched her. Belle's body writhed, and she moaned from deep in her throat. *"Mon Dieu! Mon Dieu!"*

Without a single word, Hugh mounted her, thrusting deep. Sobbing with desire, Belle moved back to wrap her arms about Guy's neck. Leaning forward, Hugh kissed and licked at her breasts as her body arched against him with unbridled passion. Within moments he was pumping her full of his love juices, and she cried his name. Hugh then rolled off her, his face hidden from her.

Guy was quickly atop Isabelle, driving deep inside her with a ferocity she had never experienced, even with him. He could see the pulse in the base of her throat throbbing madly, and he was filled with a jealousy he forced himself to swallow. She had, after all, warned him that Hugh might arouse her passions.

Hugh lay dazed as Guy used Isabelle. Just a brief moment ago when she had cried out his name in her passion, his memory had returned in a blinding, searing, white-hot flash. *He remembered absolutely everything that had happened before he had arrived at La Citadelle and since then.* What he did not know was how his wife had gotten here, and how he was going to keep himself from killing Guy d' Bretagne. But he realized immediately that he could not reveal himself to the d' Bretagnes lest he endanger Isabelle. Brother and sister were ruthless in pursuit of their own desires. He must continue to pretend he was the same Hugh that Vivienne d' Bretagne had brought from Manneville. It would not be easy, given the fact that the woman he loved, the mother of his son, was even now yielding herself with cries of undisguised pleasure to her lover.

Guy d' Bretagne rolled off his mistress, gasping with his efforts. His manhood was still stiff, as was Hugh's now, too. "Mount her again, brother," he said to his companion. "She is a tireless little witch, and nowhere near her peak."

Masking his emotions, Hugh pulled Isabelle atop him, saying roughly to her, "Come, my pretty little bitch, and let us see how well you can ride me to a finish." He lifted her up and impaled her firmly upon his passion rod.

Her own lust high, Belle pressed her breasts against his hard chest, and their lips met for the first time. Sucking her tongue into his mouth, he moaned as she rode him with slow, teasing motions. Suddenly, she felt Guy's hands upon her hips, his manhood pushing against her in a place she never thought to entertain a man.

"Arch your back more," he growled into her ear, and pushed with fierce determination until the muscles protecting her yielded.

She gasped, shocked, but Hugh held her tightly, not allowing her to rise. She could not help but continue her subtle motions while behind her Guy ravished her. The two men were maddened by the juxtaposition of their throbbing members within her lush body. They both delved deep within her sweetness, thrusting and groaning as they sought to find the zenith of their passion. Caught between them, Isabelle's head swam with a combination of the wine, the lotions, and her own natural ardor. Her little cries filled the air, exciting the two men even further. Finally the trio collapsed, limbs entwined, and barely sated, but the hour was yet young, and there would be many to follow.

The rest of the night followed a pattern. The men made love to Isabelle in turns, then they would bathe and drink restorative liquids that Guy had brewed up for them. Guy would feed her small tidbits from time to time.

"To help keep up your strength, my pet," he murmured.

In the end exhaustion overcame her and she fell asleep.

"You did well, my friend," Guy d' Bretagne said to Hugh. "She has surely conceived this night, but if not, we shall try again in another few weeks."

"I did it for Vivienne," Hugh said. "A child will make her happy, she says, though I do not believe it."

Guy barely heard him. His attention was turned to Belle. She was pale, but she slept a normal sleep. He did not hear Hugh leave the chamber, but, finally noticing he was gone, Guy put his own head down and slept.

"Was it necessary to remain with them for the entire night?" Vivienne asked her lover peevishly as he entered their bedchamber.

"Your brother wanted to make certain that I impregnated her," Hugh answered. He, too, was exhausted, and wanted nothing more than to sleep. He did not want to have to answer her jealous questions.

"How many times did you use her?" Vivienne demanded.

"Three, four, I cannot remember. Guy kept feeding us all some damned aphrodisiac he had brewed up to enhance our desire. Vivi, I want to sleep and not speak on this. Leave me be now. I have done your bidding because it will make you happy, but I am tired."

Aye, he was tired. He realized, too, that he had the problem of deciding what he was going to do about the situation that he and Belle were caught in. First, however, he needed sleep. Making decisions from a position of weakness was not a very wise thing.

"Very well, my Hugh," Vivienne said, "sleep. I suppose you have earned it this night." Then she grew silent.

When Hugh awoke, it was midday, and Vivienne was gone from their bed. He lay quietly, considering his options in light of his newly returned memory. Was he to tell the d' Bretagnes he knew everything? And what of his wife, Isabelle, who so easily played the whore to Guy d' Bretagne? How had she come here, and why? His two falconers would, of course, have some of the answers. He slung his legs over the bed, his feet making contact with the floor, and stood up.

He did not bother calling for a servant, dressing himself instead. Entering Vivienne's day room, he startled the women serving there. One of them jumped to her feet, and hurrying to a table, poured a small cup of pale amber liquid into it. Seeing her, he waved her away. "I need nothing to strengthen me, Marie," he told her. The damned stuff has probably helped keep my memory at bay, Hugh thought. Vivi knew all kinds of little potions and nostrums for everything. She was always mixing up something. She was probably even now in the little interior stone room where she brewed her elixirs. "Where is your mistress?" he asked the serving woman.

"In her special chamber, lord," came the answer.

"I will see her before I go to the mews," he told the woman. That should keep her from hurrying to tell her mistress he had refused his daily libation. Instead he went directly to the falcon mews. "Lind, Alain, to me," he called upon entering the stone tower.

At once the two falconers were by his side, chorusing in unison, "My lord!"

"I remember," was all he said.

"Praise be to God and His Blessed Mother!" Alain answered.

"No one else knows, and I have not yet decided whether I shall tell them. Only we three know," Hugh explained.

"What of the lady Isabelle?" Lind asked.

"How did she come here?" Hugh Fauconier asked the young man.

"She and Sir Rolf went up to King Henry's court to seek word of you, my lord, when you did not return. My lady was frantic with worry. The king promised to help them, but then he took a fancy to my lady and forced her to remain at court. She avoided him quite skillfully, my Agneatha said, hiding herself among the queen's ladies. One day she told me we should go to Normandy for she had learned that you were last seen in the company of her dastardly brother, Richard de Manneville. Sir Rolf did not know, and I begged my lady to reconsider her decision, but she would not. She gained boy's clothing, I know not how, and she cut her hair, dying it dark with walnut stain. We traveled to Normandy in the train of Archbishop Anselm, for my lady had convinced his high steward that her two falconers would be delivering a merlin to the duke's infant son, a gift from the king to his nephew.

"When we left the archbishop's party, we went directly to Manneville, where we stayed for several weeks training a bird for my lady's brother. Sieur Richard's lady wife befriended us, and my lady revealed herself to the lady Blanche. It was she who told us where you had been taken. Again I counseled caution, but my lady Isabelle said she must be certain that you were really here before she appealed to Duke Robert for aid. Once we had agreed to serve the d' Bretagnes, however, we were unable to leave La Citadelle without drawing pursuit. Then lord Guy discovered that my lady was no lad, and you know the rest."

"Nay, the rest my wife must tell me," Hugh said in a dangerously dark voice.

"My lord," the practical Alain interjected. "We all did what we must do to gain your release. Now we must take the first opportunity to flee this place and return home to Langston. You have a son waiting there. My lady's one fear was that the child would grow up without his father. She is a good and brave woman who has risked much to free you."

"What time of day does she usually come here?" Hugh asked them.

"In mid-morning, my lord," Lind replied.

"I will try to come then on the morrow," Hugh said. "If I

cannot, do not tell her that my memory has been restored. That must come from me and no one else."

The two falconers nodded, in complete agreement with their lord.

# Part IV

# LA CITADELLE AND LANGSTON

*Late Summer 1104–Autumn 1106*

# ▓Chapter 16

"Marie tells me that you did not take your strength-ening elixir today," Vivienne said to her lover as they lay abed that night. She ran her beautiful slender fingers across his smooth chest.

"I do not need any further medication, Vivi," Hugh Fau-conier told his mistress. "Surely your brother told you of my fine performance with his precious Belle last night. I need no potions, Vivi, unless, of course, you are dosing me in an attempt to keep my natural memory from returning. Why should that frighten you?" He caught her hand in his and, bringing it to his lips, began to nibble upon the fingers.

"It does not, Hugh," she lied, but her heart thudded nervously.

"Good!" he said, "then it is settled," and rolling her beneath him, he pushed into her, her cry of pleasure ringing in his ears. This was all she wanted of him, he realized; his ability to give her pleasure and to dance obedient attendance upon her. His lack of resistance to her authority, his meek acquiescence these past months, had led her to believe she loved him. For now he would continue to please her. *Until he decided what he was going to do.*

Isabelle was what confused him. He had every right to go, and leave her behind to the fate she had chosen for herself. Why could she not have remained at Langston like a proper wife? And yet, he smiled to himself, was what she had done—disguising herself as a boy, and coming after him—totally out

353

of character for Isabelle of Langston? She had always been a hellion. Responsibilities and motherhood had not changed her, he realized. And if she had not come seeking him, would his memory have returned as it had last night when she cried his name in her ecstasy? Perhaps without her he would have remained under the d' Bretagnes' enchantment forever. It was possible he owed her a greater debt than he could ever repay.

But could he forget that for these past months she had been Guy d' Bretagne's most complaisant mistress? *And what of your beauteous mistress, now lying by your side?* the voice in his head prodded him. *That was different.* A man might have a mistress, but a woman should remain faithful and true to her lord. Yet how could Isabelle of Langston have remained true under the circumstances in which they both now found themselves? Would he really have preferred her to fling herself from the battlements of La Citadelle in remorse? He had to speak with her. And he had to begin thinking of a way that they could all leave La Citadelle. If he had indeed impregnated his wife, the d' Bretagnes must not obtain possession of his child.

He slipped from the bedchamber in the morning, leaving Vivi sleeping soundly after an active night. Making his way to the mews, he found Isabelle already there, fussing with Couper.

"Good morning, Isabelle of Langston," he said quietly.

Her startled green-gold eyes met his blue ones. *"You remember?"* she whispered softly. "Ohh, Hugh! Tell me that you do remember!"

"I remember, ma Belle," he murmured, and then she was in his arms, weeping, clinging to him.

*"How? When?"* she asked him.

"When you cried out my name in your passion," he said.

She looked up at him, blushing, her dark lashes wet and spiky. "No one would help me, Hugh. The king even tried to seduce me. He wanted me to remain at court for his pleasure. Rolf did not know what to do. I knew that you were not dead. I just did not know where you were, but I had to try to find you, Hugh! Are you terribly angry with me?" The words tumbled out one after the other as she tried to explain it all to him. Would he understand? Or would he hate her for what had happened?

"Why did you not remain at Langston, Isabelle?" he asked her.

"*And if I had?* The Langston men who were captured with you were so fearful of the d' Bretagnes' magic, they did not even try to help you, or escape so help might be obtained for you. If I had not sought you out, Hugh Fauconier, who would have? Your playmate, Henry Beauclerc, was more interested in seducing your wife than he was in finding you. When you think that you went to Normandy at his behest, it is disgraceful! And Duke Robert was little better. If Lind and I had not come seeking you, you would have been attempting to get a child upon some other female two nights ago!" Her temper was engaged now as it had not been in many months.

Hugh could not help but laugh. She was the most outrageous woman in the entire world, a perfect hellion who would brave anything, obviously, to get back her own. He pulled her into his arms and kissed her firmly. For a moment her mouth softened beneath his, and then she pulled away, hitting him a blow that staggered him. "Belle!" he protested.

"What kind of a great trusting fool would go off to Manneville knowing what a wretch my brother Richard is? Could you not have made the peace he tricked you into believing he was offering you at Duke Robert's court? Did you have to go to Manneville with him?"

"It seemed impolite to refuse his invitation, especially since he was being so publicly contrite and pleasant before the duke," Hugh said, rubbing his arm. The hellion had bruised him, he was certain.

"This is all your fault, Hugh Fauconier!" Isabelle hissed at him. *"Every single bit of it is your fault!"*

"My lord, lady," Alain came into the mews. "The castle

courtyard is astir. It is no longer safe for you to speak at length here."

"He is right," Belle said. "We should not be seen together too frequently else we arouse suspicions. We will communicate through our falconers, Hugh."

He agreed, but before he left her, he asked, "Are you with child, ma Belle?"

"It is much too soon to know that," she replied, "but one cannot say you did not do your best to give Hugh the Younger a brother or a sister, my lord." She offered him a small smile.

"Do you love *him*?" Hugh demanded.

Isabelle looked at him cryptically, and then without another word left the mews, Couper on her glove. He watched as she set her merlin out on the stones to get the air and fed the bird bits of its favorite raw chicken. Why had she not answered him? It had been a simple enough question. Did she love Guy d' Bretagne? And if she did, what of them? Of Langston? Of their son? He was about to take his peregrine and join her outside, but when he looked again, Isabelle was gone. He needed to speak to her again, but he knew it must not be for several days. This Isabelle was not the Isabelle he remembered. This was a much stronger woman. One might almost say formidable. To have such a woman for a wife was a sobering thought.

The summer ripened along with the grain in the fields. The d' Bretagnes watched Belle when they believed she was not aware of it; but she always knew. She understood what it was they sought: some confirmation that she was with child. Guy's fascination with her belly had become paramount. His big hand would smooth over it in gentle, circular motions. He was constantly feeding her tidbits he thought she might enjoy. She felt like a goose being stuffed for slaughter.

"Do you think you might be with child?" he finally demanded after several weeks had passed. She knew how anxious he was.

"I cannot be entirely certain," she admitted honestly, for she knew he was aware of her moon cycle. "Perhaps, but I must wait a bit longer to be sure, my lord Guy."

"I think it so," he told her, catching her hand in his and kissing it. "We will let Vivienne pretend she is a mother," he said softly to her, "but you shall be the child's mother. It is at your breast the babe will nurse and be nourished."

"And loved," Belle responded quietly. "But for my sake, wait awhile longer and say nothing. I really am not quite certain, my lord."

The same day a rider came to La Citadelle, the first visitor Isabelle had seen since she and Lind had arrived those many months ago. Vivienne allowed the man time to eat and otherwise refresh himself, and then she called for him to present himself before her and state the nature of his business at La Citadelle.

The young man bowed politely. "My master, the Count of Brittany, demands your fealty, lady," he said. "You are to present yourself at court by Michaelmas, with your brother, to do Count Alan homage. At that time he will offer you a choice of gentlemen from which you will choose a husband, who will hold La Citadelle in the count's name, keeping it safe for Brittany." The messenger bowed again.

Vivienne d' Bretagne looked astounded. *"Fealty?"* she said. *"Homage? A husband?* Is your master mad, then, that he would beard me? *Does he not know who I am?* My brother and I are the direct descendants of the great enchantress Vivienne, wife of Merlin. We give our fealty and homage to no one, least of all to a puny Count of Brittany. As for this count of yours choosing a husband for me . . ." Her laughter echoed throughout the hall, and even her servants and retainers laughed with her. "Tell your master I want no husband except one of my own choosing. I have already taken a mate for myself. The d' Bretagnes have always held La Citadelle on their own. Tell your count if he thinks us helpless to do so now, that I welcome him to try to take it from us!" She laughed again. "I shall enjoy turning your master's army into a horde of toads!" The hall again erupted into dark chortles. "We will give you shelter this night, but be gone by morning back to your lord, and tell him what I have said. His interference is not welcomed here."

When all had gone from the hall but the d' Bretagnes and their two lovers, Guy said to his sister, "Are you wise, *petite soeur*, to be so forthright with the count's messenger?"

Vivienne's violet eyes darkened with her outrage. "Do you think I do not know what it is Count Alan seeks to do? He wishes to annex La Citadelle for himself, and this is but the first step. I will not allow it! I can but hope our reputation for magic will now keep him away since my rebuff has been so strong."

"It might be wise," Hugh said in his harsh voice, "to gather in the harvest as early as possible, *chérie*. La Citadelle is defendable, but you do not want to lose your crops. If the count takes your challenge up, Vivi, the first thing he will do is fire your fields. In a good year you barely get enough to survive on, and must buy food stocks to supplement what you grow from your neighbors. If your neighbors learn that you are at odds with their liege lord, they will not sell to you, so you must protect all you have now."

"How do you know things like this?" she asked him suspiciously. He had become more independent of late. Was he beginning to remember his past life, whatever it was? She did not know, of course, for Richard de Manneville had never enlightened her. Frankly, she had not cared at the time. His plain face had attracted her as no other man's face had, and she had wanted him. That had been enough. Now she was not certain she should not have learned his history.

"What I have told you is simply common sense," Hugh answered his beautiful mistress. "I know you can understand it. You are simply angry at having been approached in such a cursory manner by Count Alan. I would not mind if you took a husband, *chérie*. What fun we would have cuckolding him on a regular basis." He laughed darkly.

Guy nodded. "Hugh is correct about making a defense, *petite soeur*. Think a moment, and you will see. We must begin to plan as if we were already at war."

"Perhaps you are both right," Vivienne d' Bretagne said slowly. "It was indeed thoughtless of the count not to come himself to speak with me. It says he thinks little of our family, and only wants our lands. I can but imagine the prospective bridegrooms he has chosen. Big, honest, clumping knights devoted to him and him alone. Aye, we had best prepare to defend ourselves against him."

"He will not wait until Michaelmas, I suspect," Hugh said.

*"How do you know such a thing?"* she again demanded of him.

"He has offered. You have refused, Vivi. You have dared him to take by coercion what he sought to gain by cajolery. Alan of Brittany is a battle-hardened knight. He must now attempt to take La Citadelle by force, or else be embarrassed before his peers."

*"Your memory has returned!"* Vivienne d' Bretagne cried out.

Isabelle held her breath, wondering what her husband would answer his mistress. Would he admit to her charge?

"Vivi, though I cannot remember in detail my past life, we both know that I was a soldier. I speak to you as a soldier now. My feelings are instinctive. There is nothing more. I am still with you. Can you not be content with that? Why is it so important to you that I remember nothing of my life before you?" Hugh's gaze was direct and honest. He took Vivienne's two little hands in his big ones. *"Chérie?"*

"I do not want you to leave me," she said low.

"Do not be foolish," he responded. "Besides, where else should I find such an easy life, and such a beautiful woman to love, if not here at La Citadelle? You have said yourself that as no one came after me, I must have been unimportant. Unimportant men do not live as I live here with you."

Isabelle was amazed at Hugh Fauconier. Never would she

have suspected that her husband was so adept at dissembling. This was a Hugh she had never seen before. Had he ever masked his own feelings for her? It was something to think about.

"I think," Guy said, "that we should leave the defense of La Citadelle to Hugh." His sister agreed.

The following morning Hugh Fauconier saw the count's messenger off. "How came you?" he asked the man.

"By the coastal track," the messenger answered.

"Take the track across the moor when you return to Count Alan," Hugh advised him. "The way is a bit longer, but there is a storm coming, and the coast road will become impassable."

"My thanks," the messenger said.

As Hugh watched from the castle ramparts, the count's messenger turned onto the coast road. Hugh smiled. He had told the man the absolute truth, but of course, having had a poor reception from Vivienne d' Bretagne, the messenger assumed he was attempting to trick him; perhaps even murder him. Hugh looked out to sea. The cloud bank was already thick, and rushing toward the shore. The hapless messenger would have to take shelter somewhere along the route for the next few days. It would take him far longer to reach his destination than if he had taken the advice. That was good, since they needed the time.

He descended to the mews, finding Isabelle there. It was the first chance he had had to speak with her since their initial meeting a few days ago.

"Have you no control over *that* woman?" his wife demanded angrily. "She is about to start a war with the Count of Brittany. How will we escape if she does that? We shall all be killed!"

"You are with child," he said calmly. He recalled Isabelle having grown extremely irritable when she was newly enceinte before.

"Of course I am with child!" she snapped.

"You did not answer my question the other day," he said to her.

"What question?" she said, but she knew.

"Do you love him?" Hugh asked her.

"Of course I do not love him, though he believes I do for I have told him so that I not be sent from the castle. If they had sent me away, how could I have been of help to you? How can you even ask me such a stupid question, Hugh Fauconier?" Isabelle demanded. "My love for you has always been true."

"You are certain?" His tone was very grave.

"We have our children," she answered him, and then, "Do you not care even a little for Vivienne d' Bretagne, Hugh? I have seen how protective you have been with her, even after your memory returned to you."

He sighed. "Aye," he told her. "She is so helpless, despite all her cruelty. Vivi is in a strange way yet a child. She clings to a way of life that is long past, and by doing so, she has condemned both herself and Guy to great unhappiness, though she recognizes it not."

"We shall never forget, either of us," Isabelle remarked, "but we must forgive, Hugh."

"First," he said, "we must escape La Citadelle and return to Langston. It will not be simple, ma Belle."

"Perhaps you should go and leave me here," Isabelle suggested. "You could come back for me, for I am your lawful wife, and the child I carry is our child whatever the d' Bretagnes may imagine. It would be far easier for you and the Langston men to escape now before we are besieged than later and burdened with a woman, my lord."

"Nay," he said. "I will not leave you. Not this time. I will find a way, I promise you."

"I must tell them I am with child," Isabelle said. "Guy already suspects, and I dare not lie to them."

"Do not," Hugh said. "Your condition is to our advantage. Remember, a woman in your condition is always demanding and must be catered to, Isabelle. Remember, they want this child badly."

She reached up and gently stroked his cheek for a moment. "But for your poor voice, you are yourself again, Hugh. I am relieved to find the kind man I married restored to me. I did not like Vivienne d' Bretagne's rough, cruel lover. I wonder why your loss of memory made you so? Still, you must continue to play that part else they suspect." Then, kissing his cheek, Isabelle hurried off.

*"I knew it!"* Guy crowed that evening when Belle announced her condition to both brother and sister.

Vivienne said nothing. For the family's sake, she wanted the child, but she herself was not particularly excited over the birth that would come. Her main worry now was that their way of life was being threatened by Count Alan. Though she might menace the count with magic, she knew well the kind of magic she truly needed to keep her enemies at bay was no longer available to her family. Somehow, somewhere, they had lost that great and wonderful power. They had ruled La Citadelle and its lands these last few generations by fear and intimidation. The Church had never had any power on d' Bretagne lands. Their serfs were an ignorant, superstitious lot, and La Citadelle was sufficiently isolated on its headland that no one bothered with it. Why was the Count of Brittany suddenly concerned with them? Would her severe threat to his messenger be enough to warn him off? Vivienne d' Bretagne hoped so. She simply wanted to be left alone in peace.

Hugh, however, began preparing the castle as if they were going to war. The peasants were driven into the fields and forced to work day and night getting in the harvest, which would be stored within La Citadelle's walls. Hay was stuffed into the barns until they were overflowing. Fruit was picked from trees and vines. Only those serfs with skills would be allowed to shelter with their families within the bailey. The others would be left to fend for themselves. Of peasants, there seemed to be an unending supply.

The gates were locked early, the drawbridge pulled up and not lowered again until morning. On the ramparts of the castle a twenty-four-hour guard paced. But it was not quite as vigilant as it might be, for one morning the guards awoke to find Count Alan's army camped outside the walls. Before the gates were piled the bodies of the fierce dogs who roamed the castle demesne each night.

Hugh smiled grimly when he was told. "The count has accepted your kind invitation to come calling, my dear Vivienne," he said dryly. "You have the choice now of defending La Citadelle until it either falls or we are starved out of existence, or you have a last opportunity to make your peace with him." He peered down at the gathered knights and soldiery. "I would suggest you make your peace."

"Are you mad?" she shrieked at him. "Accept a husband, and pledge my fealty to that fool? *Never!*"

"Guy, can you not reason with your sister?" Hugh asked him.

Guy d' Bretagne took the angry woman's hands in his. "We Bretons are known for our fierce tempers, Vivi, but you know we are in no position to seriously oppose the Count of Brittany. We did not believe he would really take up our challenge, but he has. Accept the count's offer of a husband. Can we not overcome this man, and then continue on as we wish? The count will be happy believing our lands secure; and we will be happy because he has taken his army and gone away. Bridle your temper, *petite soeur*, and let us make peace before it is too late for us to do so. If you persist in your foolishness and La Citadelle falls, what think you will be our fate? The stake, I've not a doubt. Our family will be gone, but the count will have our castle, which is what he really wants."

She said nothing, but, finally sighing, Vivienne nodded her head slightly.

"Hugh," Guy said, "ride out with the white flag and make

the arrangements for us, as you seem to understand this sort of thing."

"Can you say nothing?" Vivienne demanded of her lover.

"What would you have me say?" his hard voice grated. "You will take a husband, and we will cuckold him. I do not intend to give you up, Vivienne. Perhaps you would like it if both of us had you as your brother and I had Belle?" His laughter was dark, but he knew his answer pleased her childish vanity.

*"You do love me!"* Vivienne exulted happily. "Ohh, Hugh, I will do whatever you want me to do as long as we are together." Her violet eyes shone like jewels.

Hugh Fauconier, mounted upon a great black warhorse, gave the order that the drawbridge be lowered, and then slowly walked his mount forward, a white silk banner of truce in his hand. He was met by his equal on the other side and brought to the count's tent. He debated the wisdom of telling Count Alan the truth of his presence at La Citadelle, but he knew the count had little use for either of William the Conqueror's sons, even though he was married to their sister. And how could he explain Isabelle's outrageous behavior in all of this? No. It would be better if he simply followed the plan Guy had outlined. He did not want to become embroiled any further in their dispute with the count. Let them be distracted by this bridegroom while he planned an escape.

Hugh Fauconier bowed low before the Count of Brittany, and, given permission to speak, said, "My lord, the lady of La Citadelle has, in the manner of all women, changed her mind. She will accept a husband at your hand, and pledge her faith to you in all things."

"You are not Breton," the count said.

"No, my lord, I am not. I am English. My name is Hugh. I remember no other, nor have I any memory of my being before the d' Bretagnes found me, injured, and brought me here to heal me. I remained to serve them, having nowhere else to go. I owe them my life, and now I would try to help them."

"You appear wellborn, and you are well-spoken," the count remarked slowly.

"They believe me a knight, for I seem to have knightly skills," Hugh replied, not wanting the count to think he was being insulted, treating with a mere freedman.

"What sort of a husband would you suggest I choose for the lady of La Citadelle, Sir Hugh?" the count candidly asked him. "I have never met her, although her family's reputation for sorcery still lingers, and might frighten some. Still, we Bretons are Celts, but whatever magic was once in this land I believe long gone, else my army should be croaking at this very minute, eh?" He chuckled knowingly.

Hugh allowed himself a small smile. "The lady is skilled in medicinal potions, my lord, a talent needed by every good chatelaine responsible for her people," he said. "As for a husband, I should choose a very strong man to husband the lady, for she is strong herself, and has a most fearsome temper. It will take a robust and tenacious knight with a lusty nature to manage the lady Vivienne, I think."

"I have just such a man," the count said with a smile. "I appreciate your candor, Sir Hugh. While loyal to the d' Bretagnes, you understand the duties of a liegeman as well. If you desire it, there could be a place for you at my court."

"I am grateful, my lord count," Hugh said, "but a man such as myself, with no memory of his past, is better here. Besides, my lady's brother and I are the only knights this castle has."

"Leave the drawbridge down," the Count of Brittany said. "I will come with a small party of my retainers, and the bridegroom, at the noon hour. Ask your mistress to await us in the Great Hall."

Hugh bowed low and backed from the count's tent, returning to the castle to tell them what had happened. The drawbridge remained down on his orders, for he realized such an action was to be an act of good faith between the d' Bretagnes and the count.

"Well?" Vivienne demanded as he rejoined them.

"Count Alan will enter the castle at high noon and join us in the Great Hall. He will come with a small party of his retainers, and your bridegroom."

"I was to have a choice!" Vivienne cried out.

"You forfeited that right when you first refused him," Hugh said bluntly. "He has made his own choice, and you have none but to accept it. Now go and prepare yourself to meet this man while I remove my possessions from your apartments. When you want me, Vivi, you will have to come to me from now on, for we can hardly carry on our liaison in your nuptial chambers."

Guy watched them, amused. It was a most difficult situation for his proud sister. For the first time in her life she would have to behave like other women. At least temporarily; he chuckled to himself softly.

"I know what you are thinking," she snarled darkly at him.

"Then you know why I laugh," he said.

"I hate you all!" Vivienne cried passionately.

Now Guy laughed aloud. "Come, Vivi," he said, "you must only behave yourself for a short while. Count Alan will come and stay the day. Your bridegroom will be some stolid, dull, and absolutely loyal knight who will take one look at you, only to be lost in his admiration for you and his lust to get between your legs. You will wrap the poor devil about your dainty finger. The count will depart, content that his man will hold La Citadelle for him, and life will return as we know it. Nothing will be changed except Sir Whoever will be with us." He put a protective arm about Isabelle. "When the child is born, we will poison this husband, inform the count you have an heir, and alas, have been widowed, but that we will continue to hold this castle for him. It is unlikely he will send a replacement husband for you as long as he is content we are no danger to him."

"We are no danger to him now," Vivienne protested, "yet here he is outside our gates demanding I marry some stranger."

"We are probably the only family of note in all of Brittany who has not sworn fealty to him, Vivi," her brother said.

"Remember, the count is bordered by Normandy, and there is Poitou and Aquitaine to his south. He must be certain of his own lands. He believes that if we are not with him, then surely we are against him."

"Men are ridiculous!" Vivienne d' Bretagne said, and stormed from the Great Hall.

"She will do what she must no matter her ire," Guy said. "She is not so sweetly obedient as you, Belle. Open your mouth now, *chérie*, and eat this bit of cheese. We want a strong child." He popped the morsel into her open mouth and then kissed it. Then he lifted her into his lap where he stroked her breasts absently. "I am sorry, Hugh, that you are to lose my sister's company for a time. I would not like to lose Belle for any reason."

"If my lust overcomes me," Hugh said dryly, "there are a number of willing servant girls to keep me amused." Then, rising, he left the hall. It was impossible to remain there, watching as Guy d' Bretagne fondled his wife so possessively. Seeing Isabelle lay her head back against Guy's shoulder in that sweetly adoring manner galled him. Still, Hugh knew that, like him, she but played a part. He knew that she trusted him to find a way for them to escape La Citadelle. *But how?* For the first time in his life he was at a loss for a plan of action. He did not know what to do, and Belle, his falconers, and the rest of the Langston men were all counting upon him to come up with a way to get them home.

In the hall, Belle snuggled into her lover's lap, murmuring with pleasure as he caressed her. Her condition had freed her from the torture of the little phallus. For some reason, Guy's hands relaxed her now when before they had only irritated or aroused her. "Let us walk by the sea, my lord," she said. "I have a fancy for it even though the path be steep and rough. I am not big yet, and still very limber, as you can attest."

"If you want to go to the sea you may," he said indulgently. "We do not have to climb down the cliff. We can reach the beach from within the castle itself, my precious." His big hand smoothed her hair.

Isabelle looked up into his face, surprised. "We can?"

"Aye," he told her. "There is a staircase that goes from the cellars directly down through the cliff to the beach. Our ancestors built it. We cannot go today because of Count Alan, but when he has gone, I shall show you, and you may walk the beach whenever you so desire, provided you let someone know when you go."

Isabelle could scarcely contain her excitement. They had, at last, a means of escape! She could barely wait to tell Hugh. She kissed Guy's mouth sweetly. "Thank you, my lord," she said gaily. "I do so love the beach!"

"You must watch the tides, my precious," he warned her. "When the moon is full they can rise quickly, and fill the caves beneath the castle. You do not want to get caught on the beach then."

At the noon hour Duke Alan and a small party of men crossed over the drawbridge into the bailey of the castle. Entering the Great Hall, they found Vivienne d' Bretagne awaiting them. She was arrayed in her favorite hues of purple, her skirts dark, her tunic lavender brocatelle embroidered with silver and gold threads, small pearls, and crystals. Her dark hair floated like a cloud about her shoulders, contained by a silver and gold circlet studded with amethysts and moonstones. She was very beautiful, and very regal, the color high in her pale cheeks.

Next to her stood her brother, whom the duke could identify because Guy d' Bretagne looked so much like his sister. On the other side of the lady of La Citadelle stood Sir Hugh, and next to Guy was an equally lovely woman garbed in a dark green skirt and a tunic of spring-green, embroidered in sparkling golden crystals. Her red-gold hair was neatly braided in two long plaits and contained by a polished copper circlet with an oval malachite center.

Count Alan bowed to Vivienne d' Bretagne, holding out his

hand to her. "Come, lady," he said, "and meet the man I have chosen to be your husband and your protector."

Vivienne stepped daintily from the high board and came forward, nodding in acknowledgment of the count's greeting. "My lord," was all she said, her eyes surreptitiously sweeping over the count's companions. There were six, one a priest. Then, before she could hazard any kind of a guess, the count was speaking to her, and she turned her beautiful violet eyes upon him, listening.

"Your beauty, lady, is legendary, and having now seen you for myself, I can but go forth to tell the world the legend does not do you enough justice," he began gallantly. "However, a lady of your obvious delicacy needs a husband to protect and cherish her. La Citadelle is a great responsibility for so gentle a creature as yourself."

"My lord count," Vivienne said boldly, "while I am happy to pledge you my loyalty, although such a formal pledge has never been required of the d' Bretagne family for we have never either betrayed the counts of Brittany or, for that matter, involved ourselves with them, I am not pleased that you would take it upon yourself to choose me a husband. The women of this family are unorthodox in the matter of selecting mates, it is true, but we have survived nicely over the centuries."

"Times have changed, lady," the count said. "The power your family once wielded has waned. It is necessary for me to secure La Citadelle for Brittany. I'm certain that your brother understands. Sir Hugh assured me that he did when he came to offer your friendship this morning. I regret I can give you no choice but to do my bidding."

"Then let my brother Guy hold La Citadelle for you," Vivienne suggested to the count.

"This family has always descended through the female line," the count said smoothly. "I do not wish to change that, lady. You know how superstitious our people are. Such a radical change would distress them. Nay. You will marry the man of my choice before the hour has ended, and he will hold La

Citadelle for me. It is my wish." He beckoned to his companions, saying, "Simon de Beaumont, come forth."

From among the five knights a large man stepped forward. He was as tall as Hugh, but much stockier. His hair was as black as Vivienne's, his eyes dark. He had a short, well-barbered beard that darkened his jaw and encircled his fleshy mouth. "My lord," he said.

"This then, lady, is the knight I have chosen for you to wed. Father Paul will perform the sacrament now."

"My lord!" Vivienne was outraged. "Am I not to be allowed to get to know this stranger you have decided is to be my husband?"

Isabelle's eyes met Hugh's for a brief second in a moment of déjà vu. She actually felt sorry for Vivienne d' Bretagne. Simon de Beaumont did not look like either a patient or a kind man. His eyes were even now boldly assessing the woman who would shortly be his wife; they lingered on Vivienne's full bosom, and he licked his lips.

"There is no better way to know a man than to become his wife," the count said. "There is nothing unusual in a bride and groom meeting for the first time on their wedding day. Come, Father Paul, let us proceed. I have already wasted enough time here at La Citadelle."

"And if I once again change my mind, and refuse you, my lord?" Vivienne demanded in a final attempt to retain control of her destiny.

"I will kill you and your brother where you stand, lady. Given your reputations, I could hardly be faulted," Count Alan said, and, taking Vivienne's tiny hand, he placed it in that of Simon de Beaumont.

Vivienne made to snatch her hand away, but her intended clasped it tightly, growling, "Come, lady, do not be foolish."

The priest performed the ceremony as quickly as he dared. He was not comfortable in this Great Hall of the d' Bretagnes. It was surely a cursed place. He doubted the word of God had ever been heard here, nor would be again. When he had finished, he hastily made a sign of the cross over the newly married couple and nodded to the count.

"Now," said the Count of Brittany jovially, as if this were a happy occasion, "have your servants bring wine, lady, and we shall drink a toast to you and your new husband, and afterward you and your brother will both swear your fealty to me."

When they all had goblets in their hands, the count, raising his, said, "Long life, and many children!"

Simon de Beaumont grinned, showing surprisingly white teeth against his tanned skin. "We'll do our best to give your lordship a generation of loyal sons and daughters for Brittany." His arm was clasped possessively about Vivienne's tiny waist, but he was finally forced to release his firm hold on his new bride that she and her brother might pledge their loyalty to the count.

"Before I go," Count Alan said, "will you tell me who this other lady is who has been with us?"

"The lady is my wife," Guy d' Bretagne said.

"She is lovely," the count remarked. Then, turning back to Simon, he said, "You have your instructions, de Beaumont. Keep La Citadelle secure for me." The count and his small party departed the castle.

"I will watch from the ramparts," Hugh said, "and bring you my report, lady." He bowed, and was quickly gone from the hall.

"Your people must learn that I am now lord here," Simon de Beaumont said sternly.

"You are my sister's husband, de Beaumont," Guy told him, "but La Citadelle belongs to Vivi. You may plan its defenses for your master, but your wife is mistress here. Without her goodwill, no one will heed your orders. Count Alan is gone now."

"You would defy Brittany's ruler?" de Beaumont blustered.

"There is no challenge here," Guy said. "You do not understand. Allow me to enlighten you, but come let us be comfortable while I speak." He returned to the high board, seating himself and taking Belle into his lap, where he began feeding her morsels of bread and cheese. "Here at La Citadelle we live beneath the benign rule of a matriarchy. This castle has been inherited by its eldest daughter for so long that no one can quite remember when or where the tradition came from, de Beaumont. These women sometimes take husbands, and other times not; but no matter, they remain first and foremost mistress of La Citadelle. Their husbands and lovers are nothing more than pleasant conveniences. Oh, by the way, do you know that my sister has been taking lovers since she was fourteen? I hope you are a good cocksman, Brother Simon. Vivienne has a voracious appetite for passion. You do understand now, don't you? We will not prevent you in any way from doing your duty to Count Alan, but you must not interfere in the way of life that we enjoy here at La Citadelle."

Simon de Beaumont was outraged, but, looking around him at the band of ruffians inhabiting the hall, he knew he had little chance of survival should he object. They probably wanted him to object so they could kill him. What kind of a den of evil had his master sent him into? His new male relation smiled at him wolfishly, and he was angry. He would not allow this man or his sister to intimidate him.

"Why do you feed your lady?" he asked Guy, changing the subject.

"Belle is allowed to eat and drink only at my pleasure," Guy d' Bretagne said. "She is a very obedient little wife." He caressed her breasts beneath her elegant tunic. "I bathe her, too, do I not, my precious? She is very delicious, are you not, Belle?"

"If you say so, my lord," Isabelle replied, her tone amused.

Guy laughed. "You see, Brother Simon. She is a treasure!"

Hugh reentered the hall. "The count's army has gone over the hill," he said. "I have sent riders after them to make certain they are really gone, and this is not some ruse." He sat down on the other side of Vivienne, reaching out to take up the wine pitcher. Pouring himself a healthy dollop, Hugh drank the potent liquid down.

The meal was brought in, and they ate in relative silence. Afterward Guy said wickedly, "I think, sister, that it is time you took your bridegroom to your bed. He looks as if he may prove a sturdy mount." He turned to Simon. "You will be careful not to crush her beneath your great weight, will you not? You will be delighted at how delicately made she is, and none has fairer skin."

"You speak as if you know," Simon de Beaumont said.

Guy laughed uproariously. "Of course I know. Who do you think was my sister's first lover? *I was!*"

The count's knight grew pale with shock. "Such a thing is forbidden," he said.

*"Forbidden?"* Guy laughed again. "Nothing is forbidden to the d' Bretagnes, brother Simon. *Absolutely nothing at all!*"

"Ohh, Guy," Vivienne chided her brother. "Must you tell all our secrets?" Then she giggled. "Well, perhaps not *all!*"

"Lady," Simon de Beaumont said sternly, "you will behave like a good Christian wife from now on, or I shall be forced to instruct you in the ways of propriety."

Vivienne laughed. "Do you want me to be more like Belle, Simon, my lord husband? Belle is very docile. At my brother's request she lay with both him and Sir Hugh for their pleasure. Shall we allow Sir Hugh to lie with us one night after we have gotten to know one another better?" she purred into his ear. Then her little tongue flicked about her lips.

Simon de Beaumont was shocked, and not certain he believed her at all, but her tone was very exciting. She was utterly exciting. He could feel his desire for her rising, and, standing, he pulled her up. "Take me to your chamber, Vivienne," he said. "I am of a mind to be better acquainted with you. Be warned, lady. I am a tireless lover."

"So am I." Vivienne laughed again, and led him away.

Guy stood up. "Let us follow their lead," he said, drawing Belle from the hall after him.

Hugh sat alone. In a sense, he was relieved to be quit of them all. Tonight he would sleep alone for the first time in months. Standing, he left the hall and joined his falconers in their hay barn.

"Have you been able to approach the Langston men?" he asked them. "What did they say to you?"

"They will not leave unless the lady Isabelle goes, too," Alain said. "Damn fools! As if we would leave the lady behind."

"She suggested it," Hugh told them, "but I have told her that when we go, we all go together, my lads."

"But how, my lord? And when?" Lind asked him.

Hugh shook his head. "I feel like a dunce," he admitted to them. "I do not yet know. I have wracked my brain, and yet I cannot think of a way. I debated telling Count Alan our tale, but I feared he would do nothing. I will come in the morning when ma Belle comes to visit Couper. We will talk then, and perhaps she will have some suggestion of sorts." He left them and returned to his new apartment in the castle to sleep.

When the dawn came, Hugh went to the mews and found Belle there.

"I know a way from the castle without going through the barbican and across the drawbridge," she told him excitedly. "I learned of it yesterday, but then I could find no moment in which to tell you, with all the ado about Vivienne's wedding."

"What is the way?" he asked her excitedly.

"Guy is to show me today. There are stairs from the deepest cellars down through the rock to the beach below. We must learn the tides for they sometimes flood the caves, and if we were caught, we could all drown," Isabelle told him. "Hugh! Hugh! At last we have a chance!"

"Aye," he agreed with her, and then said, "We will also have to learn how far the beaches extend up the coast toward Normandy, and if they are passable. We must find a way to get our horses away, and Couper."

"Perhaps the Langston men could leave through the gates, taking the horses with them for exercise. I can bring Couper on my gauntlet. No! Let Lind and Alain bring her. They will take the birds into the fields to exercise them. No one will question them about it. That is what we will do!" Then she thought, and said, "But where shall we go, my lord? To Duke Robert's court at Rouen? Certainly he would help us return to England. I know of no other way, do you?"

Hugh shook his head. "We can but pray he is on good terms with King Henry, ma Belle. If the brothers are at war, we shall be caught in the middle once again. For two people whose only desire is for a quiet life . . ." He chuckled, and she laughed with him.

# ※Chapter 17

$T$he impossible had happened. In the space of a single night Vivienne d' Bretagne had fallen out of love with Hugh Fauconier and madly in love with Simon de Beaumont, her husband. She could scarcely believe it herself as she gushingly told her brother.

"*He* is wonderful, Guy! He is everything I always wanted in a man. A tireless lover! And unafraid of us, brother. *He beat me*," she finished in a whisper.

"*He what?*" Guy d' Bretagne was outraged. Surely he had not heard aright. While he enjoyed gently chastising a woman, it was always done with love, never brutality. Vivienne's fair skin bore bruises, he now noted. Guy d' Bretagne had never marked a woman's skin like that. *Never!*

"I was very naughty." Vivienne giggled inanely.

"Have you lost all your wits?" her brother said furiously. "You are Vivienne d' Bretagne, not some silly female of lesser blood. This man is not even your equal, or he would have his own lands. How dare he lay hands on you in violence?"

"*I liked it,*" Vivienne said softly. "Do you not comprehend, brother? This man is stronger than I. All my life I have been the great Vivienne d' Bretagne, of a race of sorcerers, and dangerous to behold. Every lover I took feared me. Perhaps not Hugh, for without a memory Hugh knew not what fear was, but I will tell you something I have never dared to utter aloud, although I knew it in my heart. Hugh has loved before. Whoever she is, even without the memory of her, he yet loves her. He never ever gave himself to me fully, although he has certainly never been disloyal. I loved him, but I dared not to give myself to him completely for fear that his memory would suddenly come upon him and he would then despise me.

"It is not that way with Simon. He does not love me yet, but he will, brother. I love him as I have never loved any man. He will have me completely! My body, my mind, yea, even my very soul; or he will kill me. He has said it. I am his gladly!"

Guy d' Bretagne was horrified. "Vivi," he said in his gentlest voice. "You are behaving like a silly child. People like us do not dare to love as you describe it. It weakens us." He took her hand in his. "*Petite soeur*, enjoy your lusty stallion, but do not love him with such deep and undying passion. It will be the death of you."

"And you, brother," she replied in equally soft tones. "Do you not love your pretty Belle that way? Do not lie to me. I have seen the way you look at her."

"Yes," he admitted, "I do love her, Vivi, but I should never allow her to have the upper hand over me as you are allowing your new husband to have over you. I am always in control of our passion."

"I am weary of being in control. I am tired of being feared," Vivienne said. "I want to be like other women, Guy."

"You will never be like other women," he told her angrily, "and when you wish otherwise, you shame our heritage! We are d' Bretagne! We descend from a great race. You, my sister, are like the finest mare ever bred, but you have taken for your mate a common rutting boar of the forest. I hope you do not live to regret it!"

"You must send Hugh away," Vivienne said, ignoring her sibling's anger.

"Nay," Guy responded, "I will not do it. You will tell him of your feelings for your husband. Then, sister, you will offer him the choice of remaining as a knight for the castle, or leaving. I pray he will stay, Vivi, for I believe we will need him in the days to come else your *husband* fill La Citadelle with his kind."

"Will you at least remain with me when I tell Hugh?" Vivienne asked her brother. "If he grows angry, I know you can stem his ire."

"I will stay. Where is Simon now?"

"He sleeps," she said, blushing. "I will return to him shortly."

Guy snorted with disbelief. For one thing, he had never in his entire life seen Vivi blush like a maiden. It was all very disconcerting, and not just a little distasteful.

Hugh came in from the mews in the company of Belle, but both of the d' Bretagnes were too distracted to make note of it.

"Come and break your fast, Hugh," Guy invited him. "Vivi has news of a somewhat startling nature." He filled the goblets set at their places with newly pressed cider, and tore a large chunk off the fresh loaf which he pushed down the board to the other man. "Sit in my lap, Belle, and I will feed you while my sister speaks."

Isabelle dutifully settled herself in his comfortable embrace, opening her mouth like a baby bird for the bread and brie he offered. She had become quite used to eating this way.

"Hugh," Vivienne said low, "you must not tell Simon that you have been my lover. You must not even allude to it. Do you understand what I am telling you?"

"If you wish it, lady, I am yours to command," Hugh answered, wondering what this was all about. Usually Vivi was bold about her lovers. Now, suddenly, she was stammering like a maiden. Fascinating.

In her quiet, dramatic voice, Vivienne d' Bretagne gave the reason behind her request. She concluded her remarkable explanation by saying, "You may remain at La Citadelle as a knight of the castle, or you are free to go with your men, but never again will there be anything between us, Hugh. You do comprehend me, don't you?"

He was dumbfounded. A day ago she had been professing

her absolute, undying love for him; outraged and ranting over Count Alan's decision to supply her with an unknown husband. Now, suddenly, all she had shared with him was quite unimportant to her in light of her new grand passion. Hugh was relieved more than anything else, but he was also slightly offended. For the briefest moment his eyes met Belle's. Then he swallowed hard. With the merriment he saw dancing in those green-gold eyes, it was all he could do to maintain his own composure.

"Can you say nothing to me?" Vivienne demanded. She had expected protest; a declaration of love, not silence.

"Lady, I am astounded by your words," he began.

"You will not tell Simon?" There was desperation in her voice.

Hugh shook his head. "You nursed me back to good health, and I am grateful. I have no desire to fight over you with that great beast you have wed, Vivi. In time when this new passion of yours wanes, and it will, you will want me back in your bed, *chérie*."

"Will you stay, or will you go?" she asked testily.

How much easier for her if I were out of sight, Hugh thought, but he could not leave La Citadelle until he could find a way to take his wife with him. *The wife they did not even know he had.* He laughed harshly. "You would like me to go now, I know, but I will remain in your service for now. I have no other place where I might go."

"Aye!" Guy said enthusiastically. "That pleases me well enough!"

Vivienne looked decidedly uncomfortable at this, so Hugh decided to give her something else to concentrate upon.

"I did not want to tell you, for I know how you feared such a thing," Hugh said contritely, "but several days ago I regained my memory. I have confirmed my identity with my men-at-arms, who dared not aid me in my quest to regain my past for fear of you, lady."

*"I knew it!"* Vivienne said triumphantly, sounding surprisingly relieved.

"I am Hugh Fauconier, a simple knight from Worcester. I am a younger son, and was traveling about with my men seeking a place. The Sieur de Manneville promised me one, but when we could not agree upon terms, he threw me into his dungeons, where you found me."

"You have no wife?" she asked.

"Nay, lady, but a sweetheart back in England who by now may have married another," Hugh said ingenuously. "Perhaps one day I shall go home and find another girl, but for now I have nothing to offer one."

Vivienne felt the relief pouring through her. The return of his memory was greatly to her advantage. He would not now betray her. So she said, "I am grateful to have you in my service, Sir Hugh Fauconier." She smiled at them all, and gathering up some food, said, "Now I must return to my husband. He will be waking, and want to break his fast." She hurried off.

"She has lost her wits completely," Guy said angrily as his sister departed the Great Hall. "She is like a maid with her first man. I am relieved you are staying, Hugh. I may need your help to protect what belongs to the d' Bretagnes from this bully the count has inflicted upon us. It is as if my sister were bewitched." Suddenly his eyes glittered. "That has to be it. The sorceress has been ensorcelled!"

"Nay," Belle said softly, "but she does believe she is really in love, my lord. Do not deny her her happiness."

"I never before did," Guy said, "but Simon de Beaumont is like a dangerous boar in the underbrush. I do not like him, nor do I trust him. He is the count's man first, and my sister's husband second."

"A man's sworn fealty must be to his liege lord first," Hugh said reasonably, "and then to his wife. Let us see how this man behaves with Vivi."

Guy nodded glumly. There was nothing he could really do for the moment. If Simon de Beaumont was the man he believed, then he would betray himself eventually, and they could act.

Isabelle sought to distract Guy d' Bretagne from his mood. Leaning over, she nibbled delicately upon his ear. "I can but imagine what your sister and her bridegroom are now doing, my lord Guy. Can you?" She blew softly into his ear. "Shall we occupy our time in the same manner? Hugh can see to the more mundane details of La Citadelle, can he not? Ahhh, how these garments chafe me!"

Guy d' Bretagne stood up, cradling his mistress in his arms. Then, without another word, he walked from the hall, leaving his companion behind.

Hugh watched them go, understanding the tact Isabelle had taken with Guy, but jealous nonetheless. There was no escaping the fact she was Guy's mistress, and Hugh hated it. When he had himself possessed Vivienne, it had not seemed so bad. Now, however, everything was different, and he was the odd man out. Had he been foolish not to leave La Citadelle when Vivienne gave him the chance? But how could he have taken Isabelle with him? Had she disappeared, they would have quickly realized where she had gone. There had to be a way to spirit her from the castle so they might return home to England.

Perhaps he could persuade Simon de Beaumont to take Vivienne to Count Alan's court. Then Hugh shook his head. He had not a doubt Simon de Beaumont would enjoy showing off his beautiful wife, and the mastery he held over her, but they were not the problem. Guy was the problem. They would not want to take him with them, and Guy would not want to leave Isabelle. His obsessive passion for her was obvious. Hugh silently struggled to find the answer.

Simon de Beaumont had brought with him news of the world around them when he came to La Citadelle. He sat at the high board in the evening, playing the lord of the manor while Guy d' Bretagne silently seethed with anger. Guy had named him well: *the Boar*. He was fully as tall as Hugh, but very stocky, and strongly built. His dark eyes were small and porcine. They glittered like jets, darting here and there, rarely still as he took in everything about him. Little got past him, although subtlety escaped him entirely.

"The Conqueror's aging whelps are at odds again," he told them, his meaty fist wrapped about his goblet. "Count Alan is wise. He sits back and watches, but does not involve himself."

"How can he?" Hugh said. "He is married to their sister, and cannot favor one over the other unless it is to his absolute advantage."

"Aye!" Simon said, banging his goblet down upon the high board, "and it is not to his advantage to become involved, although both of them have importuned him to join them." He swallowed a large draught of wine.

"What has happened, my lord Simon, to cause the brothers to quarrel once again?" Belle asked quietly. They needed all the information they could obtain, as they would have to cross Normandy to reach England.

" 'Tis those wretched Montgomeries again," Simon said. "Duke Robert has welcomed Robert de Belleme with open arms into his court. And this after King Henry sent him from England for his rebellions. The English king was mightily offended by his brother's actions."

"Aye," Belle said. "I can certainly understand why he would be."

"Did Henry act merely because his brother has become reconciled to Robert de Belleme? Certainly there must be more," Hugh said.

"Aye," Simon answered knowledgeably. "De Belleme has been plundering the Norman lands of those men loyal to the English king. The duke either could not, or would not, contain him. Then Duke Robert accepted de Belleme's presence with much cordiality into his court. Naturally Henry Beauclerc was offended." Simon reached for a joint of venison, and, biting into it, began chewing vigorously. He grinned, pleased, as

Vivienne personally refilled his silver cup with dark red wine, giving her an approving wink.

"Did the English send an army?" Hugh wondered.

"A small one," Simon answered. "Those Normans! Such a people! You cannot trust them at all, but then you native English know that. The duke's most important nobles took the English knights in and fully cooperated with them. Not that it made any difference. Then some other high Norman noble, one William of Mortain, left England, and conspired against the king with the duke. The king has seized Mortain's lands in retaliation. Pfaugh! Normans! At least in Brittany a man knows plain and simple who his enemies are." He took another swallow of his wine. "In Brittany a man's enemies never change. If you make an enemy, you are enemies until one of you is dead. It's much easier that way."

Hugh couldn't help but grin. "Aye," he agreed. Then he said, "I suppose Normandy is yet a dangerous road to travel. 'Tis good we're far from it all here at La Citadelle, eh?"

Simon de Beaumont nodded his agreement. "I've had enough of battles to last me a lifetime," he said. "I was with Count Alan in the Holy Land. I'm ready to be settled and have a family."

He was rough-spoken, Hugh thought to himself, but basically not a bad fellow, despite Guy d' Bretagne's dislike of him. Simon de Beaumont was a blunt, forthright man, loyal to his liege lord. How many like him did he know? Hugh wondered. He would make the most of the opportunity given him, and hold La Citadelle for his master. As I would hold Langston for Henry if I could but get home, Hugh thought to himself.

The situation as described by Simon de Beaumont was a bad one. Hugh knew he dare not take Isabelle and attempt to cross Normandy. It was much too dangerous, especially for a woman in her condition. He doubted if even he and his men could get through without casualties. And they could certainly not seek refuge at Duke Robert's court now. Hugh was King Henry's man without a doubt. He would not betray his old friend and childhood companion. Both he and Isabelle would be in danger in Rouen, particularly if Richard de Manneville were there and in Duke Robert's favor.

Isabelle knew from Hugh's face what he was thinking. They were trapped, and would be unable to escape La Citadelle at any time in the near future.

"Take the men and go yourself," she pleaded with him when they next met in the mews. "I know I should be a burden to you, but surely you could get through. I am secure here. You can come back for me, Hugh."

"Are you anxious then, lady, to be rid of me so you may continue to cavort with your lover without guilt?" He hated himself even as he said the words.

Quick tears sprang to her eyes, but she said nothing to rebuke him, turning instead to leave the mews.

"She carries another man's child," Alain said. " 'Twould be best if you did leave her, my lord."

Hugh swore beneath his breath. "She carries my child, you busybody, none other," he said angrily. Then, because he had no choice if Isabelle's good name was to be cleared of future suspicion, he told Alain and Lind the truth.

The two falconers were astounded by his tale.

"Those d' Bretagnes are surely the devil's own," Alain finally managed to say. The elder of the two falconers was pale with shock.

Lind said nothing, but Hugh could but imagine what he was thinking, for he adored Isabelle. She was *his* lady.

Isabelle's condition was now beginning to become evident in the gentle rounding of her belly beneath her skirts and tunic. The autumn came with its lovely, clear warm days and its cool, lengthening nights. The dark erotic passion that had always inhabited Guy d' Bretagne's soul was mellowing as he watched Belle ripen with the child he had now come to consider his own. The manner of this child's actual conception was of no consequence to him, for had he not shared Belle's

sweetness with Hugh Fauconier on that night? Hugh's partici-
pation in the creation of the infant to be born in the spring was
no longer of any account. Guy considered the baby his child,
and anyone who dared to suggest otherwise would suffer the
consequences. Simon de Beaumont did not know the truth.
Vivienne would not share it with him, for then she should have
to admit her own complicity in the matter.

Guy hated his brother-in-law. He was such an ordinary man.
He had taken the beautiful, exotic Vivienne, and before her
horrified brother's eyes, was turning her into an ordinary
woman. She now wore her wonderful dark hair in plaits, her
head covered modestly by a white veil. She looked more like a
damned nun than she did an exciting flesh-and-blood woman.
When he had remarked upon it one night, his brother-in-law
had spoken up rather than allowing Vivi to explain.

"The old-time Saxons used to make their brides shave their
hair all off as a gesture of submission," he chortled. "A woman
should be modest in her appearance. Vivienne was too flam-
boyant, but then she did not know it, having been isolated here
all her life. As her husband, it is my duty to correct her. Am I
not right, my angel?"

"Oh, yes, my dear lord," Vivienne said dutifully, taking up
his big hairy hand and kissing it. "I am yours to do with as you
will."

Guy felt physically ill at the display. What had happened to
his proud and independent sister? Unable to bear it, he arose
from the table and left the hall. I must kill that bastard who has
so changed my wonderful Vivi, he thought, and if I do not do
it soon, she will be so changed I will never be able to get her
back again.

Belle had been shown the stairs down to the beach, and having
learned the tides, now climbed down and up daily in order to
walk along the sands. She went alone most days, which she far
preferred. The winds and the mists seemed to soothe her,

giving her a peace she knew nowhere else. The tension between Guy and Simon became worse each day.

Simon de Beaumont at first had tried to soothe Guy d' Bretagne's feelings over Vivienne, but when it became obvious he would not succeed, Simon ceased his efforts, enraging Guy even further by firmly telling him that he, Simon de Beaumont, was master at La Citadelle. If Guy did not like it, he could seek a home elsewhere. Vivienne had stood by his side, a smug smile upon her beautiful face as Simon spoke.

"Vivienne knows I cannot leave," Guy said softly. His voice had a dangerous edge to it, and hearing it, his sister paled.

"Be silent, brother!" she cried. "You know you are welcome here as long as you choose to stay and respect my husband's authority." She turned to her husband. "Oh, my lord, you must try to get on better with my brother."

"Why must he remain?" Simon demanded, his patience worn thin.

"Because it is my child, the child my Belle now carries, who will inherit the d' Bretagne holdings," Guy responded.

"This house's line descends through the females," Simon said.

"Aye, but you claim you will only father boys on my sister, yet I have seen no evidence that she is with child," Guy answered, *any child*. Consequently my daughter—for I am certain Belle will bear me a daughter—will inherit this castle. I would hardly raise my daughter away from her home, my lord." He smiled. "It is our way."

"Times change," Simon growled. "I do not intend seeing my boys robbed of their heritage by a girl!"

Again Guy smiled. He had the upper hand. "When your wife gives you a son, my lord, we will discuss this further. Until then it is foolish to talk." His dark violet eyes met those of Vivienne's, challenging her to deny him, *deny his daughter*.

# *Chapter 18*

Guy d' Bretagne continually sought for a way to dislodge his brother-in-law, Simon de Beaumont, from Vivienne's heart. The antipathy between them was obvious to all. One day the woman who had nursed both the d' Bretagnes as children came privily to Guy and said, "You wish to be rid of *that man*, lord, do you not? I will help you, for I like not the way he treats my sweet mistress." She nodded toothlessly at Guy, her one good eye glittering.

"What do you know, my dear Marie?" he asked her eagerly.

"He will break my mistress's heart, he will," the old woman said. "She alone does not satisfy him, my lord Guy." Again she nodded knowledgeably, her finger to her nose, her head bobbing up and down.

"Tell me," he said softly. "Tell me, and I will give you a potion to take the ache from your old bones, Marie." His elegant hand stroked her gnarled fingers tenderly.

"Two kitchen maids, a milkmaid, and the blacksmith's middle daughter service that lusty stallion. All are already with child. His bastards will be legion, my lord, and my poor lady's spirit will be crushed when she learns of it. We all know how she dotes upon him, and the poor wenches fear her wrath when she learns of his perfidy, for she will surely turn her vengeance upon them, and not her husband. She will hear nothing said against him, so great is her infatuation."

Guy d' Bretagne could scarcely contain his delight. "You are wise to tell me this, Marie," he said to the old nursemaid.

"If Simon de Beaumont is betraying her, Vivi should know it. Do not fear, old Marie. I shall protect my sister, and we will soon be rid of Simon de Beaumont."

The old lady nodded once more. "I knew if I told you, my lord Guy, that you would make it aright. Do not let that great boar harm my pretty girlie." She patted his arm. "You are a good brother."

So de Beaumont was helping himself most generously to the charms of the female serfs. Guy chuckled to himself. How predictable it all was; he should have thought of it himself. But now, thanks to dear old Marie, he had the weapon he needed to dispose of his brother-in-law. He hurried to his magic chamber without telling anyone, particularly his sweet Belle, who would be horrified by his plan of action and attempt to talk him out of it. Nay. Tonight would see an end to Simon de Beaumont, and then everything would be as it had been before Count Alan came to La Citadelle and forced Vivienne to wed.

That evening they sat at the high board, Vivienne in the elegant garments she had worn on her wedding day. The mistress of La Citadelle was encouraging her husband to partake of a fine red wine she had caused to be brought up from the cellars for his delectation, for Simon de Beaumont did like his wine. Her simpering was enough, Guy thought, to make one ill.

Isabelle thought that Guy seemed unusually edgy this night, and wondered why.

"Let us have a toast to my brother-in-law," Guy said suddenly, standing up and raising his goblet on high. "I give you Simon de Beaumont, knight, whose prowess with his cock surely cannot be any greater than that with a sword!"

De Beaumont looked decidedly uncomfortable, and Vivienne puzzled. "What kind of a toast is that, brother?" she demanded of Guy.

"Why, sister, did you not know? I cannot believe it, for you always know everything that happens at La Citadelle. Your husband is quite the bull. He will have at least four bastards by summer. Are you not yet with child, dearest Vivi? Certainly half the female serfs are, courtesy of Simon de Beaumont." He smiled cruelly at her.

Vivienne grew pale with shock. Her large violet eyes turned to Simon questioningly. "My lord?" she said low. "Is this true?"

Simon de Beaumont gulped down more of his wine. "Aye! And what if it is true?" he demanded belligerently. "What is the use in seeding a barren field, lady, for certainly you are infertile, else you would be filled with my child. Do you think these are the first bastards I have fathered? I want sons, lady. You cannot give them to me. I shall recognize the most able of my bastard sons when they are grown. When my lads no longer need to nurse at their mother's breasts, they will be brought into the castle to be brought up. You, lady, can teach them gentle ways. At least you are good for that. I shall not evict you from your home. I am not a cruel man." Draining his cup, he set it back down again, belching noisily.

The beauteous Vivienne was devastated by his harsh words. She could not speak for the moment.

Guy smiled cruelly. "Do you hear him, *petite soeur*? He plans a fine future for his bastards. Does it please you to know that you will have a part in the future of those lads? A foster mother to teach them gentle ways?" Guy laughed knowingly, and then his dark violet eyes grew black with anger. He fixed a hard gaze upon his brother-in-law. "I will not allow you to shame my sister like that, de Beaumont. Even now the poison I administered to you, you great rutting boar, is beginning to burn through your guts. Can you feel it?" He laughed once more, and the sound sent a chill through Isabelle. Her eyes briefly met those of Hugh Fauconier questioningly.

*"Guy! What have you done?"* Vivienne cried out, as Simon de Beaumont's broad face grew ashen and he doubled over with the terrible pain assaulting him. The dying man's face was beaded with perspiration and he gasped for air.

"Did you really think you could take my sister and embarrass her publicly, de Beaumont? Did you truly believe that your Count Alan's might could overcome the power of the d' Bretagnes? When your master bothers to inquire to your health, we shall tell him of the illness that struck you down, and of how we mourned your passing." Guy smiled cruelly at his victim, watching as death entered his eyes.

The big knight writhed in horrendous agony as his death throes came quickly upon him. "Y-you . . . d-d-devil," he groaned. His body jerked for several seconds in awful spasms, and then he lay still, his breathing ceased.

Isabelle was frozen with horror. She could not quite believe what had just happened. Granted Simon de Beaumont was not a particularly lovable fellow, but he had just died a terrible death at Guy d' Bretagne's hand.

Vivienne began to wail in her grief, tearing at her beautiful dark hair in her great and deep sorrow.

"For pity's sake, Vivi," her brother said scathingly. "The man was an absolute brute. He beat you. He betrayed you. He shamed you before others, and you mourn his death? I should have killed him the morning after you wed him. Now at least we may get back to normal. We'll throw his body over the ramparts into the sea below for the fish to feed upon. What a fine meal he'll make, eh?"

Vivienne's beautiful face was bleak as she looked up at her brother. "You do not understand, Guy. *I loved him.* No matter what he did to me, I loved him!" Gazing at him through wet eyelashes, she asked, "How did you do this awful thing, Guy? *How?* We all drank of the wine tonight. Why are we not all poisoned?"

"Vivi, Vivi," he lamented, shaking his dark head. "Have you so easily forgotten that one does not have to murder the entire hall to kill a single enemy? I did not poison the wine. Had I done so, I should have endangered us all. I simply poisoned the cup from which your husband drank. The moment you filled it, the poison was released to flow into his greedy mouth. I should never harm you, or Hugh, or my beloved Belle, *petite soeur.*"

Isabelle arose to console Vivienne. She put her arm about

her to comfort the other woman, but Vivienne shook her off angrily, saying, "My Simon is dead! I shall never be happy again, but you, brother, you have your beautiful Belle. It is not fair!"

"Hugh is here to comfort you, Vivi," Guy said.

*"I do not want Hugh!"* Vivienne screamed at them. *"I want my husband!"* She turned on Isabelle. "How I wish my brother had never found you! *I hate you!"*

"Nay, Vivi," Guy chided his sister, "do not hate Belle, for next to you, I love her best in all this world."

"Do you brother? *Do you indeed?"* Vivienne's violet eyes glittered dangerously. "You want it to be as it always was between us, Guy, or so you say. Very well then, I shall make it so!" She raised her arm, and in her hand was her silver knife. Vivienne plunged it down toward Isabelle's defenseless chest.

With a cry of alarm Guy d' Bretagne threw himself between the two women. Vivienne's knife drove deep into his breast, to the carved dragon hilt. Astounded, Guy stared at the weapon protruding from his body.

*"Guy!"* Vivienne shrieked in horror as her hand fell away from the knife. Her eyes grew wide with the realization of what she had done. "Guy! Oh, brother, forgive me!" Then snatching up Simon's cup, Vivienne d' Bretagne drank down the remaining wine. "I cannot live without both the men I love," she declared, slumping back into her chair. "We will meet death together, my beloved Guy."

Guy d' Bretagne slipped to his knees as the blood spurted forth to color his black velvet tunic. *"Belle!"* he gasped as he collapsed, dying at her feet.

Isabelle's hand flew to her mouth to stifle her cry. Her green-gold eyes moved from Guy to Vivienne, who was barely alive. It was obvious that she was now in terrible pain, but she would not cry out. Her body writhed with her death agony, but her beautiful eyes still mocked the woman she had always considered her enemy.

"N-Now," she said slowly, but distinctly, "you w-will not

have h-h-him, either. Guy w-will always belong t-t-to me."
Her head fell onto her chest, and in a last burst of strength she
gasped, "La Citadelle will . . . always . . . be . . . m-m-mine!"
Vivienne's body shuddered, and then she, too, was dead.

The hall was deathly silent for a long moment, and then a
faceless voice cried out, *"La Citadelle is curst! Flee! Flee!"*
And the Great Hall emptied of servants and men-at-arms, who
ran out to spread the word that the d' Bretagnes were no longer
alive. Only the six Langston men, the two falconers, Hugh, and
Isabelle remained.

"Isabelle. *Isabelle!*" Hugh's voice pierced her consciousness.

She focused her eyes on him with some difficulty, for the
enormity of the tragedy had caused her to cry, and she could
not seem to stop the tears now pouring down her face.

"Are you all right?" he asked her gently, wrapping his arms
about her comfortingly. "We are free now, hellion. We can all
go home."

"We must bury them," she answered him. "We cannot leave
them here like this, Hugh. *We cannot!*" She was managing to
regain control of herself, and wiped the tears away with the
back of her hand.

"Aye," he agreed. "They must be buried before any dese-
cration can be done to their poor mortal bodies. Lind, find
a secret place before the light is completely gone. Then
come back, and we will do what needs doing. We will have to
remain here tonight, but tomorrow we leave La Citadelle for
England."

"Yes, my lord, at once!" Lind replied, grinning at Alain
and the other Langston men. It was good to have Hugh Fauconier back again, he thought, and he knew the others agreed
with him.

The castle had emptied of all human life, but for them. In the
stables, however, the falconers found the chief huntsman and
several others.

"Take whatever you want," Alain said, "for certainly you
deserve it, but leave our horses that we may escape this place,

too. They came with us, and they will go with us. And leave the lady's horse as well. It is hers, and not d' Bretagne property. She will come with us."

The chief huntsman nodded. " 'Tis fair," he agreed. "You were forced to serve your time with *them*, too. It is only right you depart with your horses, but why do you take the lady? Being with child, will she not slow you down?"

"She is English, and she is Lind's half sister," Alain reminded them. "He would not leave her, and he is one of us."

That made sense to the Bretons, and taking all the livestock from the stables except that belonging to the English, they departed.

Lind found a secluded spot near the outer walls of La Citadelle. It was near a corner, and close to it a grove of trees had sprung up. With the help of his companions he quickly dug three deep graves. Returning to the Great Hall, the Langston men carried out the bodies of Simon de Beaumont, his wife Vivienne, and, lastly, Guy d' Bretagne. Isabelle, her lips moving in barely remembered prayers, and Hugh escorted them. Vivienne was laid to rest between her brother and her husband. The Langston men waited as their lord and their lady prayed silently over the bodies of the trio.

Hugh barely glanced at the two men. He had eyes only for the beautiful woman who had taken him from his brother-in-law's dungeon, and then for a time given him her love. She had saved his life, and for that he owed her much. She had been cruel, selfish, and wicked. Had he been himself, he should have never loved her. Aye, he thought secretly, I did love her for a time, may God help me.

Belle's green-gold eyes flicked from Simon de Beaumont past Vivienne to Guy d' Bretagne. She had never before seen the face of death. It was frightening in its finality. While she regretted the deaths of Simon and Vivienne, she could not believe that Guy was really dead. He had been so full of life. She had never known such a man before, and suspected that she would never know such a one again. His passion for lust was the most wildly erotic thing she had ever experienced. While she would never discuss it with Hugh, her now restored husband, she knew that Guy had truly loved her, and while she had never admitted it to herself before, Isabelle knew she had cared for him in a strange way as well. It was over. She would not forget, but she would not dwell upon it ever again. *Farewell, my lord Guy,* she said silently.

"Cover the bodies, and finish the burial," Hugh ordered his men. "Try to disguise the graves so they will not be discovered. Let the superstitious believe the devil came for his own, and leave the legend of the d' Bretagnes intact." He chuckled. "They would like that."

When they had all gathered back in the Great Hall of the now eerily quiet castle, Hugh and Belle put their heads together to decide the route by which they would make their way back to England. The Langston men and the two falconers sat quietly as their lord and lady argued back and forth.

"Boulogne to Dover is the shortest crossing," Isabelle said. "I would be just as happy to spend as little time on the sea as possible."

"It's too far for us to travel overland, with the king and his brother still feuding. Do you not remember what Simon de Beaumont told us? We may not even be safe in some parts of Normandy, with Robert de Belleme on the loose. And do not forget William of Mortain. His lands are very near. Both these men know me, and would count it a coup to have me in their dungeons. Although I am neither rich nor important, I am still the king's good friend. The roads in Normandy are far too dangerous to travel for very long, *chérie.*"

"Then what are we to do?" Belle demanded of him. "Certainly you are not suggesting that we remain here at La Citadelle? Though Vivienne and Guy are dead and buried, even now I can feel their presence about me. The castle is already haunted, and the sooner we leave, the happier I will be, my lord!"

"I agree," Hugh replied in irritatingly mild tones. "In the

weeks since Vivienne's marriage, I have had far greater freedom than I had in the months prior. The d' Bretagnes possess a small fishing village several miles up the coast to the north. We will go there at first light and commandeer the boats and men we need to sail across the Channel to England."

*"At its widest part?"* Isabelle shrieked, causing the Langston men to cease their own talk and look to their master and mistress.

"There are several islands, ma Belle," Hugh soothed her. "We will sail from one to the other in gentle stages, and from the last of those islands, Alderney, straight across to Weymouth Bay. The final part of the journey will take us no more than a full day, with good winds. We have just enough time to make the crossing before the northerlies set in and make the Channel difficult, if not impossible, to cross for the next few months. Even if we could reach Boulogne in safety, which I doubt, the winter winds would have begun," Hugh explained.

"What about the horses?" she challenged him. "We cannot afford to leave ten horses behind. Your liege lord, Henry Beauclerc, will certainly not reimburse us our loss," she said scathingly, "and what of the birds? I will not leave Couper!"

"We are not going in just one boat," he replied. "The horses will be given passage as well as the birds."

"I had best pray for fair winds, then," Isabelle said dryly, "for I see you are determined to put to sea."

"We will be in England all the sooner," he promised her with a small smile. "It is really better my way, *chérie.*"

"We will see," Isabelle of Langston said ominously.

She returned to the apartments she had shared with Guy to gather up a few of her possessions. The place reeked of memories. She could almost feel him within these very walls, his sensuous mouth curling with amusement as he watched her, all the while planning some wicked passion for them to share. She took a few pieces of plain, sturdy, serviceable clothing, and the other small things she would need for her journey. Pulling a small stone from the wall, she drew out a soft chamois bag, putting it among her other possessions. It was Guy's private cache and contained silver pieces. She would keep it for the new baby. One piece, however, she took out, clipping it carefully into smaller pieces for the journey, sewing them into the hem of her skirts.

A rumble of thunder caught her ear, and, going to the window, she flung back the shutters. There was a storm out over the sea. She watched as the lightning forked down into the roiling waves. Lovely, Isabelle thought irritably. Pray God it has cleared by tomorrow. Behind her she thought she heard laughter. *Guy's laughter.* She whirled about but there was no one there. She was alone. *Or was she?* Quickly gathering up her bundle, Isabelle fled the apartments without another backward glance. She had been right. La Citadelle was haunted. Guy and Vivienne would never leave it. They would be in possession for eternity.

They all slept on pallets in the hall near the fire, waking even before dawn. Lind and Alain foraged in the kitchens, competent to boil up oat stirabout, finding day-old bread and half a wheel of cheese. A small basket of apples was discovered, and Isabelle ordered that they be taken, along with whatever else could be found that was edible. They ate quickly. As they left the Great Hall of La Citadelle, Isabelle thought how strangely silent it was now. Only yesterday at this time it had been so alive and vibrant.

Outside in the bailey she waited for the horses to be brought. Lind and Alain had gone to the mews to release the birds. They would only take Couper and the young peregrine Lind had personally trained. He was so fond of the bird that he could not bear to leave the beautiful creature behind. The other birds they set loose. Left in the mews, they would have soon starved and died. Isabelle watched as the creatures, freed of their hoods and jesses, were at first confused. But then the gyrfalcon, boldest of all, took wing, soaring into the bright morning skies above, screeching his delight. The others quickly followed suit. Hugh had wanted to keep the gyrfalcon, but it was too great a responsibility, considering the journey ahead of them.

The horses were ready, but they would not ride them yet. Hugh had decided they were less apt to attract attention if they departed the d' Bretagne holding by means of the interior staircase to the beach rather than riding out across the countryside. The tide was now almost out, and they would have plenty of opportunity to reach the little seaside village of Bretagne-sur-Mer, which was well isolated from the rest of the holding. The villagers might not yet have heard of the murder-suicide of their master and mistress, and believing the English came on orders of the d' Bretagnes, they would cooperate.

Leading their animals into the castle, the men followed Isabelle and Hugh through a wide hallway that led directly to the staircase. The steps were broad and the gradient downward not steep. Slowly, carefully, they led the animals down the slope. For a time all was silent save for the clopping of the horses' hooves, but then they began to hear the sea, its roar growing louder as they moved forward. At last they came out into a large, high cave, and, mounting their animals, rode forth into a sunny morning. To their left the sea was spread out in bright blue splendor.

"Pray the weather holds," Isabelle said as she took Couper on her wrist, then, kicking Gris gently, moved ahead.

It took very little time to reach the village. The sun was just coming up, and the fishermen had not yet put to sea. Isabelle could see the wariness in their faces as the mounted party approached, but no one fled, for the villagers knew that only someone from La Citadelle would have approached them from that direction. The party came to a stop before the fishermen and their boats.

"Who is in charge here?" Hugh demanded in harsh tones.

For a long silent moment no one spoke, and then a tall, bearded man stepped forward. "I am headman, my lord. Did they not tell you at the castle to ask for Jean-Paul?"

"I was simply told that the headman would arrange passage

for us back to England," Hugh answered. "I am Sir Hugh Fauconier, lately in service to the d' Bretagnes. I am now returning home with my wife and my men-at-arms. I will need passage for us all and for our animals. There will be a silver piece, half to be paid now, half when we reach England, for each boat that will take us. What think you, Master Jean-Paul? Will the weather hold for the next two or three days?"

The headman nodded slowly. A silver piece for each boat? It was a fortune, and none from the castle had ever been as generous with them. Ten passengers. Ten horses. The two hunting birds were no problem. Most of the village boats were small, but there were three that were large enough to make the voyage; his and two others. "The weather will hold for the next week, my lord," he answered Hugh. "We can take you. Guilliame! Luc! Make ready your boats." The headman turned back to Hugh. "The silver, my lord?"

Hugh took three coins from his pouch. He clipped each piece in half and gave them to the headman while the other fishermen looked on enviously. Without another word the three vessels were pushed into the surf. Five horses and three men each were loaded onto the boats belonging to the men called Guilliame and Luc. Isabelle, Hugh, and the two falconers boarded the headman's ship, but not before Belle had carefully divided the foodstuffs among the others. Barrels of water were brought aboard to ensure that they not go thirsty.

The winds were fresh, blowing evenly yet not too hard as they departed Bretagne-sur-Mer. The seas rolled gently, and there was no sign of rain or fog. Gradually the coastline disappeared, and finally Isabelle could see nothing either ahead of them or behind them but the sea. She shivered, drawing her cloak about her tightly. She did not like the sea, and God willing she would never have to face it again once she was safely home to Langston. *England,* she thought to herself. *Langston.* There had been times she had thought that perhaps she would not see it again. Now she could barely wait to step within her own hall, to see her mother and her little son again.

How wonderful it would be to live a quiet, normal life once more. When Hugh's arm slipped about her shoulders, she smiled up at him, and within her the child moved as if it were giving them its full approval. She put her hand upon her belly in a maternal gesture.

"The baby is as eager as we are to get home," she told her husband. "Have you thought of what we shall call it, my lord?"

He laid his hand atop hers. "We will have to call him Henry if it is another lad, ma Belle; but I should like Matilda if it is a little girl, after our own good queen," he teased.

"I shall never name a son of mine *Henry*!" Isabelle said indignantly. "Had it not been for the king, none of this would have happened! We have almost been robbed of our lives, and certainly we have been robbed of the chance to watch our son grow. And why? Because of Henry Beauclerc! *No Henrys!*"

"Had it not been for the king," Hugh reminded his irate mate, "we should have not been wed, hellion. Besides, it was your idea to come after me, certainly not the king's. I cannot help but name a second son Henry, especially if I am to retain his favor."

"If I had not come after you," Isabelle reminded him for possibly the hundredth time, "you would not have regained your memory. Besides, what choice had I? Had I remained at court, I would have eventually been forced into the king's bed. Would you have found that preferable?"

"By not remaining at court," he said softly, "you were forced into Guy d' Bretagne's bed. As to which was preferable, I do not know."

"At least all England will not know of my shame," she countered, "and at least the child I carry is true-born because of Guy's inability to father a child. The king is known for his potency. Would you have enjoyed raising a royal bastard, my lord?" she concluded icily.

"Touché, hellion," he responded. She had done it once again; taken a logical argument and turned it to her advantage. "You are an impossible woman," he said.

Isabelle turned from her view of the sea to gaze up at her husband. "Aye," she agreed placidly, "but would you have me like my sweet-tempered mother? Alette could have never survived what I have, my lord. She is much too gentle and kind."

At that moment the subject of their thoughts was hurling oaths from the new tower at Langston down upon the head of her stepson and his unpleasant henchman, Luc de Sai. "Villain! Cowardly devil's spawn!" Alette de Briard shouted. Then she hurled the contents of the night jar down upon their heads.

Richard de Manneville leapt aside none too soon, avoiding the noxious dousing, but his companion was not so fortunate and was splashed. De Manneville snickered, but then he shouted back at his stepmother, "Lady, you are being foolish. I will eventually gain entry to your refuge, and you will regret having denied me access. Langston is mine now. I hold it for England's rightful king, Robert of Normandy."

"King Henry is England's rightful king, you stinking oaf," Alette returned. "When my husband, Hugh Fauconier, and your sister return, you will wish that you had never been born, Richard de Manneville!"

"Hugh Fauconier will not return," Richard said with certainty, "and as for my sister, should she come back to Langston, she will find me in charge not only of this keep, but of her person as well."

"My grandson is master of this keep should his father not return," Alette said smugly. "King Henry will uphold little Hugh's claim, and kick your skinny rump straight across the Channel back to that damp pile of stones called Manneville." She then disappeared within her tower, slamming the shutters closed behind her.

"Give the little bitch to me," Luc de Sai said darkly. "I'll teach her better manners." He shook his wet sleeve, but he knew the stink would remain until the garment was washed.

"When I secure the place," Richard said, "you can do what you want with my dear stepmother, but if Isabelle returns, you must wed her in order to secure my claim to Langston. Hugh Fauconier will never escape the d' Bretagnes alive. If he isn't already dead, he might as well be." He laughed nastily. "Alette for a mistress, and Isabelle for a wife. You will be most comfortable, Luc. If Duke Robert cannot take England from his brother, then I will swear my fealty to Henry Beauclerc for these lands, and you will continue to hold them for me. I cannot lose, my dear Luc. I cannot lose."

In her tower Alette fumed aloud. "I cannot believe that Richard was able to simply walk into Langston and take possession of it. Ohhh, if only my Rolf had been here, he would not have dared!"

"That is most true, lady," Father Bernard agreed. Rolf de Briard had gone to answer the king's call to arms and was in Normandy with all Langston's experienced, well-trained men-at-arms, leaving only a group of unseasoned, callow youngsters to guard Langston Keep. They did not know Richard de Manneville, nor did it seem likely to the inexperienced defenders that two knights accompanied by four men-at-arms were a danger to Langston. Even Rolf would not have expected such boldness. "Sieur de Manneville must have watched for Lord Rolf to leave," the priest said, "knowing that the king would call him, leaving Langston defenseless to him."

"Praise God and His Blessed Mother," Alette said, "that I was able to escape to my tower with the children. If Richard knew which of the boys was little Hugh, he would kill him without so much as a thought. Then if Hugh did not return, there would be no male heir to Langston." She shuddered. "I thank God we have our own well within this tower, and that the servants are able to smuggle food in to us, but good father, how long can I hold out? I am not fearful for myself, you understand, but for the children. Richard is as cruel as his father was. The children must be protected at all costs."

"Your tower is secure, good lady," the priest assured her. "The sieur is not clever enough to learn how we obtain our stores. He will not be here for long, I promise you. I know the king, and I know Duke Robert. Henry Beauclerc will prevail. He will retain England, and he will have Normandy before another year has passed, I promise you. The king would *never* give Langston to Richard de Manneville. We will be able to hold out until Lord Rolf returns, I am certain."

In the hall, Richard de Manneville sat at the high board with Luc de Sai. For all his bravado, he was uncomfortable, and just a little afraid, for he was in truth a coward. The servants were extremely polite, and gave him no cause for complaint, obeying his every order. He and Luc had even been supplied with pleasant and enthusiastic bed partners from among a group of pretty serf girls. Yet Richard de Manneville knew he was trespassing in his sister's house. His stepmother was barricaded in her tower with her children, and with the true heir to Langston. The priest came and went, although Richard had not yet been able to discover how.

The priest now warned him that his soul was in mortal danger. "Duke Robert will not prevail, *mon seigneur*. Go home to Manneville, and give up this foolish quest to have Langston as well."

"Langston was my father's keep, and as his surviving son, it should be mine by right," Richard replied.

"I know that your father, may God assoil his soul, made over Langston to your sister, the lady Isabelle," the priest answered him. "Both King William Rufus and King Henry recognize her rights over yours. Now she is wife to the Saxon heir of these lands. You have no claim. You have done no damage, *mon seigneur*, although the lady Alette fears for the children. Return to Normandy now while you have the opportunity."

*"Never!"* Richard de Manneville blustered.

Father Bernard sighed. "Then may God have mercy on you, *mon seigneur*, for neither Rolf de Briard nor Hugh Fauconier will when they find you in residence at Langston."

"Hugh Fauconier will not return to Langston," Richard said with certainty. "My nephew is yet a babe, and children are always subject to sudden complaints, many of which prove fatal. I am the only logical lord for Langston. If Duke Robert does not take England, then I will plead my case to King Henry. The de Mannevilles have always been loyal followers and liegemen of his family."

Father Bernard reported this conversation back to Alette de Briard.

"Why is he so certain that Hugh will not return?" she wondered. "And where is that daughter of mine? Gone over a year, and not a word! I shall certainly have something to say to Isabelle when she comes home. The very idea of her running off like that, and leaving Hughie; but then, was she not always willful?"

"So you have said, lady," the priest responded dryly. While Alette de Briard was indeed a model wife and mother, he sometimes found her a bit annoying. He had to admit he had missed the lady Isabelle. Father Bernard had prayed for her every day she had been away. He had prayed for Hugh, too, and looked forward to their return to Langston. They would both come home. He somehow knew it. In the meantime he must keep the lady Alette and the children safe, and pray harder for their deliverance from Richard de Manneville.

# ⵎ*Chapter 19*

*D*eliverance was at hand. Hugh Fauconier, his wife, and their party landed safely in England after three days at sea. They disembarked on a rocky beach bordering upon Weymouth Bay. The Breton fishermen were paid the remaining silver that had been agreed upon, and immediately set back to sea for Bretagne-sur-Mer. Before they departed, Hugh told them of the d' Bretagnes' demise.

"You are free, my friends," he said to the astounded men. "You need fear the d' Bretagnes no more. Their magic has died with them."

Jean-Paul shook his head. "Perhaps, Sir Knight," he said.

Isabelle didn't know who was more relieved to be back on dry land, herself or the horses. She actually had no cause for complaint, the voyage having gone swiftly and without incident. Still, the crunch of sand beneath the stones upon the beach was music to her ears. They found water for the horses and set off for Winchester, where Hugh hoped to have news of the king. Isabelle was not pleased that they might see the king again, but Hugh reassured her.

"His attempted seduction of you was a quiet effort. You did not publicly embarrass him when you left court, but he is aware of the set-down you gave him. He will not try to breach your defenses again, especially as I am now with you, ma Belle."

"He should not have attempted to breach them in the first place," Isabelle said tartly.

"He is the king," Hugh answered her with a shrug.

"That is no excuse for his bad behavior," Belle replied firmly.

Hugh did not bother to answer his wife, for how could Isabelle understand a man as complex as Henry Beauclerc? While he was certainly none too pleased to have his wife accosted by the king, kings were in fact different than the rest of the populace. It would never have happened, he knew, had he been with Isabelle. If she had listened to Rolf and remained at Langston, the incident would not have occurred. Of course, had he said that aloud, Isabelle would have reminded him once again that had she not come to court, and then gone to Brittany, he would still be without his memory, and possibly yet the captive of the d' Bretagnes. Hugh Fauconier smiled to himself. It was better in this instance to remain silent, and not receive a stern lecture from his wife regarding the deplorable state of King Henry's morals.

At Winchester they found the king in official residence, but gone hunting for a fortnight. Hugh Fauconier sought the king's personal chaplain and left word with him that he had returned to England and was now going home to Langston. As he departed the chaplain's quarters, he saw Rolf de Briard in the hallway and called out to him.

Hearing his friend's voice, Rolf turned, a look of delighted surprise and relief upon his handsome face. The two men embraced, and then Rolf said, "Where the hell have you been, Hugh? And is the lady Isabelle with you? We can't go home to Alette without Isabelle."

"Aye, Belle is with me," Hugh replied. "Thanks to my dear brother-in-law, both Belle and I ended up imprisoned by friends of Richard de Manneville's. We have been in Brittany, which is why we couldn't be found, although Belle managed to track me. With the help of the Langston men, and our falconers, we were able to escape only recently and get back to England. I will say that ma Belle and I whiled away the hours of our captivity most pleasantly. We will have another child in the spring."

This was the tale he and Isabelle had concocted to explain their absence. The falconers and the Langston men had agreed that it was a good explanation and sworn they would support it. They knew little of what had actually gone on in the castle, but what little they had seen frightened them. Like the fishermen of Bretagne-sur-Mer, they were not entirely certain that the sorcery of the d' Bretagnes was ended. The less said about their sojourn in Brittany, the better.

Isabelle was delighted to learn the king was off hunting, and doubly delighted to see her stepfather. "Do not scold me now, Father Rolf," she told him. "Hugh would not have gotten home without my help."

"He probably would have gotten home sooner without the burden of a wife to worry about," Rolf answered her, still irritated that she had tricked him so neatly in making her journey to Brittany.

"Nay," Hugh defended his wife, adding just a trifle more to their tale. "I had suffered a blow to the head, and until Belle aided me in regaining my memory, I could not recall who I was. Belle was the key to my recovery."

They began their journey home the following day. The city of London seemed even noisier and dirtier than Isabelle had remembered it. She was glad to be quickly quit of it and on the well-traveled highway to Colchester. *Home!* They were so close now. Even the air was beginning to have a familiar smell to it, she thought, wrinkling her nose with delight.

They reached the river Blyth on a rainy, misty afternoon. As they waited for the ferry to come and carry them across to the other side, Isabelle noted that Langston Keep now had two stone towers. Finally their transport arrived, and the ferryman gaped at Hugh and Isabelle with surprise and relief.

"My lord! My lady! We thought you was dead," he exclaimed.

"Who told you such a thing?" Isabelle demanded, a touch of her old imperiousness in her voice.

"Ancient Albert said we should ne'er see you again. He sorrowed over it mightily before he finally died," the ferryman said, and then he looked to Hugh. "I cannot take you across now, my lord. I am to tell all visitors that entry is barred to Langston Keep, which is held in Duke Robert's name currently." The ferryman shuffled his feet nervously and dug his pole deeper into the mud of the riverbank to steady his vessel.

"Who holds Langston?" Hugh asked quietly.

"The lord Richard de Manneville, son of him who once held it for King William, my lord Hugh," the ferryman answered him.

"What of the lady Alette?" Rolf asked.

"She has locked herself with the children in New Tower, my lord. They say she hurls curses daily upon the head of him who's taken the keep when he comes to demand her surrender," the ferryman explained.

"How many men has Lord Richard got with him?" Hugh asked.

"There is another knight, and four men-at-arms."

"How the hell did he take the keep with only four men-at-arms and a single knight?" Hugh exploded. "Surely the lady did not let him in?"

" 'Tis my fault, I believe," Rolf said. "I took the more experienced men with me when the king called. We were sent to Normandy to reconnoiter for the king's eventual invasion, and to make contact with those lords loyal to King Henry. You cannot travel in Normandy these days without a heavily armed escort. I believed at this point the Sieur de Manneville had lost interest in Langston. I left only inexperienced men to guard the keep. De Manneville probably walked right in, for those green lads would not think two knights and four men-at-arms a threat to the keep."

The ferryman nodded. "Aye, lord, 'tis just what happened."

"Go back, and if you are asked, say it was just a party of

travelers seeking shelter. Then, when it is dark, return to ferry us all over that we may retake Langston. See that word is brought up to the keep to see to Richard de Manneville's special pleasure tonight, that we may capture him unawares. There is another knight, you said?"

"Aye, my lord. One Luc de Sai, and a mighty unpleasant fellow he is, too," the ferryman replied. Then he pushed off, poling back across the Blyth to the other side.

Isabelle sneezed. "The rain is getting heavier," she said. "How long must we wait? Is there any shelter nearby?"

"We must move back into the trees so we cannot be seen from the keep's walls," Hugh said. "Our party is large enough to alarm your brother should he see us, and I don't want the gates barred to us."

"It doesn't matter," Rolf said. "When New Tower was constructed, we built a tunnel that exits just outside the keep's walls for emergency purposes. When it is dark, we will ferry across, and using the night for cover, we will be able to enter the keep. There is no interior passage connecting New Tower and the original tower yet. We had intended to build it later on. When we built the tower, we opened a section of wall to fit it in, but it is accessible only by means of a door on the main level, or this secret tunnel."

"Excellent!" Hugh smiled wolfishly. "Richard de Manneville is very superstitious, for Vivienne d' Bretagne told me so. I have the perfect plan to remove him from Langston, and it will not cost us a single life."

"You would be better to kill him, and his henchman," Belle said grimly. "He will not give up the idea that he should have Langston easily. Unless he is dead, we will spend the rest of our lives wondering when he will next turn up. He will pass his erroneous idea onto his sons, and we will never be rid of the de Mannevilles. Kill him now while we have the opportunity, my lord." She sneezed again.

"There is a cowshed nearby where the lady may shelter," one of the Langston men said, interrupting them.

They quickly found it. Wood, not yet soaked, was gathered, and a small fire was made with it and some scraps of dried hay from within the shed. The birds were set down in a wooden enclosure that was used to contain straw for bedding the cows. The shed was crowded and soon warm with the press of bodies. They were all hungry and tired, and eager for dry clothing.

"What do you intend to do with de Manneville?" Rolf asked when they were finally settled down to wait.

Hugh smiled slowly. "The people who imprisoned Belle and me were believed by the local populace to be sorcerers. They traded on their family's reputation to keep their serfs in check and their neighbors at bay. Richard swore fealty to them, and they promised that he should have Langston. The first time he came, after Isabelle sent him packing, he returned to these alleged sorcerers most angry. They reassured him if he would be patient, he would get his way in the matter. How they laughed at him behind his back, for they were, of course, frauds," Hugh told Rolf, making light of the whole matter. "I, however, shall convince Richard de Manneville and his toady that I have been given some magic powers, and will punish him with my magic if he does not return home to Normandy and remain there."

"He will never believe it!" Rolf said skeptically.

"Oh, yes he will." Belle giggled. "When I was a little girl I always remember that Richard was fearful of certain things. If a black cat crossed his path—and we had an old tabby who kept producing black kittens—he would cross himself, turn about three times, and spit. If it thundered in winter, which it sometimes does, he would claim that it was the devil making noise. He is afraid of anything to which he cannot give a logical explanation. I am sure that with a suitable ruse, Hugh will be able to convince him that he now possesses magic powers. Nonetheless, I still think we should kill him," Isabelle concluded. "My brother cannot be trusted."

"Let us try to conclude this matter peacefully," Hugh said.

They waited until it was almost dark, then rode down to the river, where the ferryman was awaiting them. The rain had finally stopped, but a fine mist was rising from the water. The Langston men were ferried across first so that in the event of a surprise attack their lord and lady would not be undefended. Rolf went in the first boatload. The last crossing was made by Hugh and Isabelle and their two falconers. The boat slid up onto the beach, and Isabelle prodded Gris off, followed by her companions. Slowly, they rode through Langston village. In the dimly lighted doorways the villagers stood in silence, but they were smiling, every last one of them.

The wind rose, and once again it began to rain as they made their way up the hill to the keep. As they had suspected, the gates were barred. Rolf led them around the walls to where the second tower now rose. Pulling away carefully arranged undergrowth, he revealed a door. Taking a key from his tunic, he fit it in the door's lock. The door swung quietly open on well-oiled hinges. Dismounting, the others tied their horses within the shelter of the trees where they could not be seen and followed Rolf de Briard into the tunnel. He waited until they were all inside, motioning them with his hand to move forward in the passageway, and then locked the door behind him.

Taking torches from a stone container, he lit them one by one from the single stone lamp burning in the dim corridor, passing them along so that they would be able to light their way. Then, coming to the head of the line, he said, "Follow me!"

They hurried down the stone tunnel. The air was still, cold, and slightly fetid. They walked for a few short minutes, and then before them they could make out the outline of another door. Without warning it swung open and light poured into the passage. A faceless figure loomed in the opening for a short space, and both Hugh and Rolf reached for their swords.

"I thought you would come this way, my lord," Father Bernard's voice called out. "Welcome home! Is that my lady Isabelle I see with you?" The priest ushered them from the tunnel into a square hallway which quickly filled up with the Langston men.

"Where are we?" Hugh asked the cleric.

"This is the entrance to New Tower from the bailey, my lord," he answered. Then he let a tapestry that had covered the tunnel entry fall back against the door and pushed an oaken table in front of it. "Your mother is awaiting you upstairs, lady," he told Isabelle. "I have prayed long and hard for the safe return of you both."

"Your prayers did not go unanswered, good father," Isabelle responded graciously. There was no need to say that she wished God had worked faster. The priest, for all his upbringing in the Norman court, was an innocent. He could not possibly ever imagine what she and Hugh had been through. Instead she ran up the stairs to find her mother awaiting her at the top.

Alette took one look at her daughter and burst into tears. "Praise be to God and His Blessed Mother Mary!" she sobbed.

Isabelle embraced her, scolding her as she did so. "Madame, must you always weep and wail? I have returned safe and sound to you, and you will soon have a second grandchild to spoil. Where is my son? I would see him this very instant!"

"The children are sleeping, Isabelle. You cannot wake Hughie. He is still just a babe, and you will frighten him. Then I shall not be able to get him back to sleep. You must wait until morning."

"But I have not seen my son in over a year!" Belle protested.

"That is not my fault," Alette said, "nor is it Hughie's fault that his mother ran off and deserted him when he was barely past his first year. You will wait until the morning. I will not have the nursery roused at this hour. Besides, I want to know how soon your husband will rid us of Richard de Manneville."

"Hugh will have to tell you that, Mama," Belle said. She was disappointed at being denied access to her child, but knew in this particular instance her mother was absolutely correct. She looked at Alette, and a smile lit Isabelle's face. "You are with child, too!" She laughed. "How many will this make, madame?"

"Three," Alette said smugly. "I hope it is a daughter this time, for I should like to have a daughter to comfort me in my old age."

"Meaning," Belle said, just a trifle offended, "that you do not believe you can rely upon me, eh, madame?"

"You are too independent a female, Isabelle," her mother replied. "I would need you, and you would be off on some adventure or other. I want a meek, gentle daughter who will grow into a woman like me," Alette said, "not some hellion who would be careening all over the countryside." She folded her hands over her burgeoning belly. "Now, where have you been all these months?"

Isabelle carefully offered her mother the gentle version of the truth that she and Hugh had decided upon. When she had finished, Alette nodded, and, to her surprise, agreed that her daughter had been absolutely correct in following her instincts and going after her husband.

"I would not have thought you would believe me right in this matter," Belle said, "for, as you have pointed out, I will go my own way."

"Hugh could not have found himself again had it not been for you, Isabelle," Alette said. "It is quite clear you did the right thing."

Hugh and Rolf now entered the little Family Hall in New Tower. Alette ran to her husband, holding her face up for a kiss which he gladly gave, wrapping his arms about her protectively.

"You have been most brave, as well as clever, my love," Rolf said to her proudly.

"I am not brave," Alette said. "I have never been afraid of Richard, my lord. He is a coward in his heart. How will you kill him?" she demanded. "And when?"

"It may not be necessary to kill him," Hugh interjected.

"If you do not kill him, he will never leave you in peace,"

Alette warned her son-in-law. "That is the way the de Manneville men are. Welcome home, Hugh," Alette said as an afterthought. "Isabelle has told me of your adventures."

"Where are the Langston men?" Isabelle asked her husband, suddenly noting their absence.

"They have slipped out of New Tower to the barracks," Hugh explained. "They must seize your brother's four men and secure them so that there is no alarm given. Then one of our men will slip into the Great Hall to ascertain the state your brother and his henchman are in at the moment. If they are not drunk yet, they will be helped along by our people. When they have finally been rendered unconscious, we will move them across the river to that cow byre to sleep off their excess of wine."

"Where is Agneatha?" Isabelle wondered aloud, looking to her mother. "Is she safe?"

Alette nodded. "She is hidden in the village, for she is far too pretty to be around your brother, or Luc de Sai. We will send for her, my daughter, and glad she will be to see you."

A Langston man arrived shortly thereafter to tell Hugh Fauconier that the Norman men-at-arms had been taken and were even now locked away. The servants had been told that their true lord and lady were safe within the keep. Richard de Manneville and Luc de Sai were being fed the best of the keep's wines, laced with an herb that would make them sleep a deep sleep for the next ten hours.

"It will be a while before they can be moved," Hugh said. "I think you should get some rest, ma Belle. If I could, I would help you out of those wet clothes." His eyes twinkled at her.

"I want a hot bath," she replied.

"Not until we clear your brother and his companion from the hall, *chérie*. As I recall, the last time you desired a hot bath you got into difficulties." His voice was very low, so that only she could hear his words. "This time you must possess your soul of patience."

"Only this one time," she said with a small smile.

"Will you rest?" Alette asked her daughter.

"Nay, not yet," Isabelle replied. "Though my cape is wet, I am fairly dry beneath. I would like some wine, though, and something to eat, madame. Come, Rolf de Briard, and tell me of Langston's prosperity during our absence." She removed her cloak and settled herself before a large fireplace that burned hot with large logs. Alette pressed a goblet of warm, mulled wine into Isabelle's hand, and then busied herself slicing bread and cheese.

"The summer you left, as you will recall," Rolf began, "was very bad. The crops did poorly, both grain and fruit. We had much animal disease, and consequently death among the cattle, although the sheep survived. On St. Lawrence Day morning there came a horrific wind such as none you have ever before seen. It did tremendous damage, and there wasn't a roof left in any of the villages. This year has been better, although the king's taxes to pay for his war with Normandy do not help us recover. No one is spared. He will wring the coin from all of us, and we in turn must wring it from our serfs. I exempt them where I can, and I have made certain that they understand that we all must sacrifice for England. Most understand, and even last winter I saw that no one starved. We do not have rebellion at Langston as on some estates."

"You have done very well, my lord," Isabelle said, "and I thank you for it. Without you, Langston would have fallen prey to who knows what. Hugh and I will not leave it again."

"Hugh owes the king service, Isabelle," Rolf said. "If he calls us, we will go. It would be treason to do otherwise."

Isabelle sipped her wine thoughtfully, but said nothing. There was nothing to say. She could only pray Henry Beauclerc would forget about Hugh Fauconier and Rolf de Briard when the time came to take Normandy back from his brother, Robert. More tired than she realized, she fell asleep by the fire, her goblet tilting from her hand, to spill the remainder of its contents upon the floor.

Hugh took the cup from her fingers and then sat down to eat.

"Let her be until we have removed the intruders from the keep," he said quietly. "Then I will waken her, and we will seek our own bed after all these months."

"The story she told me was simple, yet I sense there is more to your adventures," Alette said with a perception he had not anticipated. "Is there more to your tale than my daughter would tell?"

"If there is," Hugh said grimly, "it is better you not ask ma Belle. We have told you only what you need to know. There is no more for either of us to say, Alette. Do not, I beg you, allow your curiosity to gain the better of your good sense." Hugh Fauconier could only imagine his mother-in-law with her delicate sensibilities learning of the perversions practiced by Guy d' Bretagne and his sister. The knowledge of those depravities would have shocked Alette terribly. He would not even discuss them with Rolf de Briard, his best friend. He and Isabelle, however, would have to speak on them eventually.

Near midnight one of the men-at-arms came to tell the two knights that both Richard de Manneville and Luc de Sai were sleeping heavily in the hall. Hugh and Rolf went immediately to oversee the removal of the two intruders. They grinned at each other upon entering the hall and hearing the noisy snores coming from the two Normans. The drugged and sleeping men were carried outside and their bodies laid in strong slings which were suspended between a pair of horses. The animals and their burdens were led from the bailey of the keep, down the hill, and through the now-slumbering village onto the keep's ferry, which made its way across the darkened river to the other side. There the horses were led off the little vessel and to the cowshed where Hugh and his party had earlier sheltered. Richard de Manneville and Luc de Sai were then removed from their transport and placed, still soundly sleeping, in the straw.

"How I should like to be here on the morrow when our two *friends* awaken." Rolf chuckled. "I wonder what they will think happened to them."

"They'll be confused at first, I've not a doubt," Hugh replied, "but then they will decide that they somehow got across the river themselves in their drunken state. The first doubts will begin to set in when they recross the Blyth and reenter the keep to find us in possession of it. It is then that the game will truly begin."

They returned back across the river with their men and horses. There was a new lightness of mood that was almost palpable as Hugh Fauconier, lord of Langston, rode into the bailey. The gates of the keep were barred once more, and Hugh went to find his wife, to return her to their own hall. Kneeling by her chair, he kissed her cheek.

Belle opened her eyes slowly. "Is it done?" she asked.

"Aye, 'tis done, ma Belle. Richard de Manneville has been dispossessed along with his henchman," he told her, drawing her up. "Come, and let me take you to our own chamber." He picked her up and walked from New Tower back into the original tower of the keep. Isabelle's head lay quietly against his shoulder. She was very, very tired.

Agneatha appeared out of the shadows, a smile upon her face. "Welcome home, my lord. Welcome home, my lady." Her gaze flew to Lind, and the look he returned her told Agneatha all she needed to know. He yet loved her. She struggled to regain her composure, her own moist look silently saying what he wanted to know; that she loved him, too. "While you was taking *that* intruder off," Agneatha said, "I roused the maids and we cleared the solar of *his* things and put fresh linens upon the bed, my lord. You'll both sleep well in your own bed this night. Shall I stay and help my lady with her garments?"

"I think she's too tired to disrobe, lass," Hugh said in kindly tones. "Go to your own bed, and in the morning your mistress will greet you happily, I have not a doubt. I'll just take her boots, and tuck her in beneath the coverlet. As you can see, she's already asleep."

Isabelle could hear their voices. Familiar voices. Instinctively she knew she was safe, and with a murmur slid into a comfortable sleep.

Awakening with the first light, Isabelle wondered for a moment where she was, and then the wonderful reality came to her. *She was home!* Home at Langston in her own bed!

"You are awake." Hugh's voice sounded next to her.

"We are home," she said happily.

"Aye, but before we may take our ease and slip back into our old lives, we have several matters to settle, ma Belle, the first of which is your brother. Will you help me in our little deception?"

"Of course, my lord," she replied, "but I think you a fool not to kill him. It may be the end of the matter for you, but it will not be for Richard. He will trouble us as long as he lives over Langston."

"Nonetheless, *chérie*, I am lord here, and it is my will that is law. This is the way I wish to settle the matter," Hugh told her.

His tone irritated her. He was being a pompous fool, Isabelle decided. Richard de Manneville was dangerous, and you did not end such a danger by turning your back upon it. There was certain to come another time when Hugh Fauconier would regret that he sent Richard de Manneville packing upon his horse instead of in a wooden box. "I seem to recall hearing Agneatha's voice last night before I was totally lost to sleep," Belle said to her husband, turning the subject neatly.

"You did," he replied, "and I will wager she is even now nearby."

He was correct. Agneatha came bustling from the bathing room.

"I've a bath all ready for you, my lady," she said as if Isabelle had never even been away. "Ohh, what a fright you gave me when I awoke that morning at Winchester and you was gone. You were very naughty. I fretted for weeks afterward, wondering what had happened to you."

Isabelle bathed beneath the eye of her servant, and the two

spoke of the version of Belle's adventures she was telling everyone. Once her beautiful red-gold hair was washed, dried, and neatly braided into a single plait, Belle dressed in her favorite green, then hurried with Agneatha to see Hughie.

"You ain't going to believe how he's grown, lady. Ada, his nursemaid, took real good care of him. He walks, and he can even talk, and him not yet three! Everyone loves him. Old Ancient Albert would sit outside his cottage in his last days and wait for wee Lord Hughie to come by. He'd carve little wooden animals with his old gnarled fingers for the small laddie."

They hurried through the Great Hall and across the bailey to New Tower. Upstairs in the nursery Isabelle's eyes widened. *It could not be!* Yet she knew it was. The small boy brought by the faithful Ada was his father's mirror image. Isabelle held out her hand.

"Hugh, my son, come and greet your mother."

The boy hid shyly behind Ada's skirts.

Isabelle smiled softly. "Hughie, *mon petit*," she said, "in the springtime, perhaps on your very birthday, I shall give you a little brother or sister for a present. Would you like that?"

Hugh the Younger thought a moment, and then he nodded solemnly. "Can I play with it?" he asked her.

"In time, my son," she said, enfolding the boy into her warm embrace. "Ahhh, *bébé*, I have missed you!"

Hugh Fauconier came then, equally amazed to find a small boy when he distinctly remembered a chubby-cheeked infant. "I am your father, young Hugh," he told the child, who looked up awestruck at the tall man. Hugh bent down and lifted his son up into his arms. "Men," he said, "should always speak face-to-face." Then, kissing his child, he set him back down again and looked to Belle. "Let us go into the hall to await our guests, lady," he suggested.

In the hall the servants' faces were all wreathed in smiles as they greeted their lord and their lady. Fresh sweet cider was served along with eggs in cream and dill, oat stirabout with raisins, fresh bread, newly churned butter, and a large honey-comb. Isabelle's appetite was the best it had been in many months, although the experience of feeding herself again was still a bit strange. Hugh also enjoyed his meal. He had posted a lookout, he told his wife, and they would have plenty of warning when Richard came back across the river.

When they had finished their meal, Hugh called for all his servants to come into the hall. He then explained to them that he had been held captive along with his wife for these many months in Brittany. He told them just what they needed to know about the relationship between Richard de Manneville and the d' Bretagnes. "Now," he said, "when my brother-in-law returns to the keep this day, I will convince him that I removed him by means of sorcery and that my powers are strong enough to punish him should he ever attempt to gain control of Langston again. Since I do not want my own people to fear me, I tell you that there is no magic, but Richard de Manneville must not know that. He is superstitious and will be afraid. He will go and not trouble us again." Hugh looked out over the upturned faces. "Now trust me, and go about your daily chores," he told them.

Toward the noon hour word was brought that Richard de Manneville was seen in the company of Luc de Sai on the other side of the river, calling for the ferryman to come and get them. The watch on the battlements monitored the two men's progress as they returned to the keep.

Upon entering the hall, de Manneville shouted for wine, and then he stopped, the color draining from his face as he saw Hugh Fauconier and his sister Isabelle standing behind the high board.

"Well, brother," Isabelle said in distinctly unfriendly tones, "I see you returned despite my warning to you last time you visited. Are you so stupid that you do not learn? You are not welcome at Langston, and yet I return from Brittany to learn you have penned up my mother and my son in New Tower and are threatening them. It will not do, Richard. It simply will not do."

*"You were in Brittany?"* Richard de Manneville was ashen. "What were you doing in Brittany, you little bitch?"

"Seeking my husband, whom you lured to Manneville and then gave into the hands of Vivienne and Guy d' Bretagne," Isabelle said. "You have much to answer for to us, *brother*, but my lord will now attend to you and your companion, Luc de Sai."

"Did you sleep well, Richard?" Hugh asked innocently. "Was your cow byre comfortable?" He laughed insinuatingly.

"How did you know where we slept?" the Sieur de Manneville asked nervously. "I don't even know how we got to such a place."

"I put you there," Hugh said softly. " 'Tis a little trick my friend, Guy d' Bretagne, taught me, my lord."

*"Taught you?"* Richard was now openly frightened.

"A small bit of magic," Hugh told him. " 'Twas nothing, really. Was your friend nearby? Sometimes when one does this little trick, it does not always happen properly. Were you also in the shed, Luc de Sai, or were you outside it?" Hugh cocked an eyebrow questioningly.

"We were on opposite sides of the shed," Luc de Sai answered slowly. His dark eyes were filled with fear.

"Good!" Hugh replied. "When Guy d' Bretagne first taught me that trick, I transported a servant from Guy's magic room to the peak of La Citadelle's highest tower instead of into the Great Hall. Poor fellow was so frightened he fell to his death, but then he was only a serf. We all have plenty of serfs to spare, eh, Richard?" The rough voice had the ring of truth to it.

The Sieur de Manneville shuddered. "I do not believe you," he quavered.

Hugh smiled a slow, devilish smile. "Do you not?" he rasped. "Shall I transport you both back to Manneville, then, Richard? Of course I am not really as good at long distances as

Guy d' Bretagne was. You could easily end up in mid-Channel. Do you swim well, de Sai?"

"My lord!" Luc de Sai began to babble, terrified. "I will leave Langston this very moment, but do not, I beg you, place a spell upon me! You will never see my face again, I swear it!"

Hugh seemed taller than normal to all those in the hall. He looked down coldly at Luc de Sai and told him, "Get you gone!" Then, gazing at his brother-in-law, he suddenly snapped his fingers, and at once there was a small flash of blue flame that seemed to spurt from his fingertips. *"Well, Brother Richard?"* he asked.

Richard de Manneville's eyes widened at the burst of fire from Hugh Fauconier's hand. His heart began to pound violently. He opened his mouth to speak, but no sound came out. Then he collapsed upon the floor.

"Is he dead?" Isabelle demanded of the servant who knelt by her brother's side, seeking a pulse.

"Aye, lady, he is," came the startled reply.

*"Good!"* Belle said triumphantly.

Luc de Sai took to his heels, running from the hall as fast as his legs would carry him. They would not see him again.

"Do not bury Richard's body on English soil," Isabelle said firmly to her husband. "Let his men take him home to Manneville. It is late autumn, and the body will not rot before it gets there. My sister-in-law will not long mourn his passing."

The servants hurried to do her bidding, and the body was removed from the Great Hall of the keep, to be placed in a box and returned to Normandy by Richard's four men-at-arms. Isabelle wondered if her brother would reach Manneville or if the men-at-arms would abandon his body along the road and seek service elsewhere. At least Langston would not be bothered by Richard again.

"How did you make the fire come from your fingers?" Belle asked Hugh curiously.

He smiled at her. "Some things are best kept secret, ma Belle," Hugh told her. "I did not mean for so simple a trick to frighten your brother to death, but his own fear of magic did him in, I suspect."

"He was a fool," Isabelle said. "I know you think me hard, my lord, but I am glad he is dead. He will trouble us no more, and now we may take up our lives anew without fear."

"There are other things we must settle before that can happen, ma Belle," Hugh told her seriously.

"Not today," she said. "Let me enjoy being home for at least today, and then we will talk, my lord." Then she left him, hurrying through the hall and out into a bright, late autumn day.

Hugh sighed. He could understand her reluctance to clear the air, but until they did, there would be no real peace between them. He wanted a true peace with Isabelle, not just a charade for the sake of their family.

That night when they were ensconced within the solar he forced the issue. Pouring them goblets of sweet wine, he told her, "We must settle this now, ma Belle."

Isabelle sighed. Men were so difficult. Could not Hugh be content that they were safely home, and that she loved him? "I do not know what there is to say, my lord," she told him.

"You told me once that you did not love Guy d' Bretagne," he began.

"I did not," she agreed. "I told him that I did because I knew it pleased him, and it allowed him to trust me. I needed that trust if I was to help you, Hugh Fauconier. Why do you refuse to understand?"

"Yet, I believe, you enjoyed his passion," Hugh replied grimly.

Isabelle thought a long moment, and then she said, "Sometimes, aye, I did," she admitted, "even when the pleasure was forced from me. I seemed to have no control over my body, but that is not love, my lord. And you, did you not enjoy yourself with Vivienne d' Bretagne? And until you came to yourself again, thanks to my efforts, did you not have a small tendresse for the bitch? What is the difference between us, Hugh? Tell me that, and I will beg your forgiveness."

*"I am a man, madame,"* he declared loftily. "A man, good or bad, may do as he pleases within the tenets of the law. A good woman must remain chaste no matter the circumstances."

Isabelle threw her goblet of wine at her husband. "You great donkey!" she cried. "What in the name of heaven has your maleness to do with anything? I will speak with you no further since you cannot be reasonable. I am going to bed." She climbed into their bed, turning her back on him.

Hugh was astounded, and his first instinct was to grab her and beat her soundly. To his credit, he did not. Instead he slammed from the solar without another word.

The next morning it was obvious to both Alette and Rolf that something was very wrong between the lord and lady of Langston. When they had left the hall, Alette looked unhappily to her husband.

"I fear, Rolf, that our peaceful days are over. There is, it would seem, a breach between my daughter and her husband. Can it be healed, I wonder?"

"If it can," Rolf told her, "they must do the healing, *ma petite*. They are neither of them easy people. Isabelle is headstrong, and Hugh proud. My duty is to steward Langston, and yours, I believe, is to see that the children, ours and young Hugh, are not unduly troubled by the war that will be fought between Hugh Fauconier and Belle from Hell."

*"Do not call her that!"* Alette snapped at her husband, who laughed at her ire. "I shall never forgive Ancient Albert, may God assoil his soul, for calling Isabelle by that awful sobriquet!"

Hugh did not return to the hall that night. Alette was careful in her conversation with her daughter, but she need not have worried. Isabelle was distracted; her main interest seemed to be her son, and she spent her day playing with him, tucking him into his bed that evening herself. She would not remove Hughie from the nursery in New Tower, for he was happy there with his two little uncles. In the solar she slept alone once more.

In the morning Belle entered the hall to find Hugh at the high board, pale and sipping something from a silver goblet. "Have you found yourself a rustic mistress then, my lord?" she asked him tartly, signaling a servant to bring her some food.

"I spent the night alone," he told her.

"It would appear that you also spent the night imbibing a great deal of bad wine, my lord. You are as white as fleece," she replied.

"Is that concern I hear in your voice, ma Belle?" he murmured. "Did you miss me in the night? I might have stayed, but your sharp tongue and your temper do little to encourage me."

"Nor does your arrogance please me," she snapped. "Sleep where you please, my lord. It matters not to me at all." Her hand reached for her goblet.

Reaching out, he quickly grasped her wrist. "Do not, lady. I am weary of your bad disposition."

"And I of your disdain, my lord," she told him. "Let me go, Hugh. I merely mean to drink the cider, not hurl it at you. I shall be bruised by your brutality, I fear." She shook him off.

"Is my brutality then not as refined as Guy d' Bretagne's?" he demanded of her.

"You are despicable, my lord," Isabelle said wearily, and then suddenly her voice was calm and measured. "Guy is dead, Hugh. I would not be alive had he not taken the blow Vivienne meant for me. Would you have preferred it that way? That I died, and the babe with me? We both owe him a debt of gratitude, strange as it may seem."

"Whatever I may have owed him, lady," Hugh said coldly, "you, *ma Belle*, repaid the debt a thousand times over."

"Ahhhhh, that is the crux of the matter, isn't it, Hugh? Guy d' Bretagne was my lover, and you cannot let that go, can you? I can forgive you Vivienne. Why can you not forgive me Guy? I did not love him. *I love you!*" She glared angrily at him. He was being so pigheaded, damn him! Did he think her memories of him with Vivienne were any less painful than his memories of her with Guy? They both had to put it behind them, or they would never be happy again.

"I would have preferred that you remained at Langston like a good wife, and that you had not come seeking me," he said, his voice rising.

"How many times must we go over this, my lord?" she demanded of him. "Had I not sought you out, we should not be home today. You should be grateful to me instead of angry! When you came to Langston, did I inquire of you how many women you had swived?"

"I was not married to you then, damnit! How do you think I feel knowing that Guy d' Bretagne made love to you, held you in his arms, kissed you, made you cry out with pleasure? I love you, too, Isabelle, but I do not know if I can ever forgive you!" His plain face was anguished.

"Then you are a fool, Hugh," she said quietly. "You are allowing your pride to stand between us. I should not have believed such a thing of you, my lord. I thought you wiser than that."

"Then what are we to do?" he said, and his voice was sad.

"Unless you can put the past in the past, my lord, I do not know what we can do," Isabelle responded softly. "I am ready to pick up the threads of my life again as the lady of Langston Keep. You must fight your own demons, Hugh." She arose from the high board, and without another word to him left the hall.

Hugh Fauconier watched his wife go, her head held high. For a moment he could almost believe it was as it had been when they were first married; but then his big shoulders slumped and his head fell into his hands. Isabelle had lain with another man. He could never forget it, and if he could not forget, how could he forgive her? It was a terrible conundrum he was unable to solve.

\* \* \*

During the weeks that followed, Langston appeared to have returned to normal. The servants behaved as if Isabelle had merely been away for a short time and had now returned to assume her duties as their chatelaine. Even Alette deferred to her daughter without difficulty. Young Hugh was making up for lost time with his pretty mother, following her about as she tended to her duties, snuggling into her lap to gaze up at her adoringly when she sat in the hall by the fire.

Only Hugh Fauconier seemed unable to shake the images of his wife that tormented him: Isabelle, her red-gold head against Guy d' Bretagne's shoulder. Guy, his dark glance possessive; his elegant, long fingers offering her a tidbit, a sip from his cup; thrusting the phallus into her writhing body while she cried with pleasure. Guy had owned Isabelle as Hugh had never believed it possible for any man to own a woman. Had she really resisted him? That doubt troubled him greatly, and he knew he should not have any doubts about his wife. She appeared to have been absolutely forthright with him, yet his suspicion lingered, for he could still see Isabelle nestled in Guy d' Bretagne's lap, complaisant, and more beautiful than he had ever before known her to be.

Now she moved again through her familiar world with a dignity and a serenity he would not have believed her capable of, her belly growing rounder each day. She was more assured of herself than she had ever been, and he had had absolutely nothing to do with it. Had Guy? Why was it that the d' Bretagnes yet had a hold on their lives? They were dead and buried, both of them, still their sorcery lingered.

Finally Alette tried to intercede with her daughter. "You and Hugh cannot go on like this," she gently scolded Isabelle.

"What do you want me to do, madame?" Isabelle asked patiently. She could not confide the truth to Alette. How could her sweet, sheltered mother possibly understand?

"Well, there must be *something* that you can do," Alette replied.

Isabelle laughed. "Can you turn back time, lady? If you can, then do it, I beg you. I like not this rift between myself and my husband any more than you do."

Rolf, too, tried broaching the subject as he and Hugh rode across the estate one winter's afternoon. "Alette and I are disturbed that you and Isabelle cannot manage to overcome your differences, whatever they may be," he began. "What can we do to help you both to a reunion? We cannot bear to see you so unhappy."

Hugh realized then that he had absolutely no choice. The burden he was carrying was simply too great for him to bear alone. "You must never tell Alette what I am about to tell you," he said, and then he revealed to his friend in detail the truth of his and Isabelle's time at La Citadelle. He concluded by saying, "If you can help me erase the memories I have of my wife with another man, then do so, my friend. I live in agony with those memories, for I love Isabelle above all women, yet I cannot forget."

Rolf was stunned by the revelations Hugh had just made. Still, he was a sensible man. "Hugh, you are being foolish," he said. "Your wife is not responsible for what befell her at La Citadelle. She knows that or else she could not live with her shame. How could a girl as basically innocent as your wife have known that a woman's body will respond to *any* skillful lover, Hugh? You were her only lover. Can you imagine her shock at finding out that another man—a man she did not even love—could coax a response from her? Yet she kept her wits about her, brave woman that she is. My sweet Alette would have crumbled and gone mad. Not Isabelle. She accepted what she could not change, and everything she did, Hugh, she did in order to free you from the enchantment you believed imprisoned you. She sacrificed herself totally for her beloved husband. No woman could love a man more than that! She is formidable, and you should be proud of her."

*"I see them together!"* Hugh groaned unhappily.

"What you see," Rolf said sagely, "is clouded by your damned overweening pride, my friend. Isabelle is to shortly bear you another child. Though the circumstances of that child's conception are odd, to say the least, it was conceived by you both. Replace the old memories that taunt you with the new memories that you will make together now that you are home again. Only then will you be able to exorcise that which distresses you so greatly. You know in your heart that Isabelle loves you, and always has; and I know that you love her."

Suddenly there came a shouting from behind them. The two men turned about to see a serf running toward them, waving his arms and shouting. Turning their horses, they hurried toward him.

"The lady Alette," the man gasped, almost out of breath when they reached him. "Her says the babe is a-coming, my lords!"

Hugh and Rolf galloped the few miles' distance back to the keep, but as they entered the hall, Isabelle came toward them, smiling, a swaddled bundle in her arms.

"I have a little sister," she said gaily, and placed the infant in her father's arms. "My mother says she is to be called Edith, for that was the queen's name before she came to England."

Rolf gazed down, awed by the dainty pink and white creature in his arms. She had a tuft of golden hair, and her blue eyes regarded him most carefully. "She looks just like my Alette," he said, teary-eyed.

"I saw," Isabelle said with a small chuckle. "Let us hope she is indeed the daughter our mother so desperately desires, and not a whit like me." Then she laughed aloud at her stepfather's look of concern, teasing him, "One never really knows with children, Rolf."

In the days that followed Edith's birth, Hugh Fauconier thought of his friend's words. He had never known Rolf de Briard to speak with such wisdom. Rolf had always been so carefree. Suddenly his friend seemed much older, and filled with sagacity. Hugh pondered to himself everything Rolf had said. Was it possible that he was right? Could a reconciliation with Isabelle be the key to obliterating his memories of what had happened? Was it really that simple? God only knew he wanted a rapprochement with his wife. *A new beginning.* But what if Rolf were wrong? What would happen to them then?

Hugh knew that he had to think on it further before he decided what he would do. Would Isabelle even welcome his overtures now, or would she angrily rebuff him? Still, he had seen her glancing at him when she thought he was not looking. Her gaze was always one of deep sadness, yet if his eyes met hers, she was always proud and defiant.

*Something had changed.* Isabelle sensed it. Hugh was suddenly not quite so combative whenever he approached her. Yet he had said nothing that would lead her to believe he had overcome his aversion dilemma. What had happened? Had anything happened, or was she just imagining it? Neither her mother nor her stepfather had said anything out of the ordinary. Isabelle knew if there was the slightest change in Hugh's attitude, her mother would have come to her joyfully with the tidings.

Belle's labor began early in the morning of the last day of March. Suddenly Hugh was with her, as he had been when she birthed Hugh the Younger. His was a calming presence, and in the early stages of her labor, while Alette directed her, he saw that the baby's cradle and swaddling clothes were nearby, and that Ida, the sister of little Hugh's nursemaid, Ada, was ready to take charge of this new child.

Isabelle made herself as comfortable as a woman in her condition could upon the birthing table. She half sat, her smock pulled over her hips, legs wide apart, waiting. The child would come when it would come, and not a moment before. Little Hugh's birth had been easy, she seemed to recall. He had come very quickly, and her mother had complained how easy a time she had had of it. Isabelle winced. This birth, she sensed, would not be as easy.

All through the day her pains came, easy at first, harder as the hours passed; but the child remained unborn. Alette was almost smugly satisfied that at least this time Isabelle was behaving as a birthing mother should, totally forgetting how quickly her own new daughter had come. Hugh would not leave his wife's side. The servants brought him food and wine, but he ate sparingly, his main concern for his Belle.

Finally, in the hour before midnight, it became obvious to everyone that the child was close to being born. Belle pushed and strained, and slowly the baby slid from her body.

"It is a girl!" Alette crowed.

"She is not crying," Isabelle said, aware, and frightened.

To both women's surprise Hugh, with some inborn instinct, took his daughter and, placing her on Belle's body, parted the infant's lips, inserting a finger into the baby's throat to gently lift a clot of mucus from it. Then, bending down, he blew softly into his daughter's mouth several times. She coughed, her eyes flew open, and taking a great gulp of air, the baby began to wail at the top of her lungs.

Belle wept wildly with relief. Then, clasping her child to her breasts, she soothed it. "You saved her, my lord! *You saved her!* How on earth did you know what to do, Hugh?"

He was amazed himself, and shook his head. "I do not know, ma Belle," he answered her honestly, "but I could not let our daughter die after all we went through to have her."

The baby was taken up by her nursemaid, cleaned, and set in her cradle while her mother finished the birthing process. Afterward Hugh sat by his wife's bedside, her hand in his. For a while they continued in silence, and then he spoke.

"She will be called Matilda, after the queen."

"She will be called Rosamund, my lord. Matilda indeed! It is a name I dislike, although I like the queen," Isabelle responded. "No Henrys and no Matildas, thank you."

He laughed. "You may have your way, madame. I do not really like the name Matilda, either."

"And you would have saddled our daughter with it? For shame, my lord!" Isabelle scolded him.

"I remember how good the king's mother, the first Matilda,

was to me as a boy. It was more to honor her, I think," Hugh said. For a moment they were as of old, but then the wall between them sprang up once again.

Several weeks later the king's messenger arrived at Langston requesting that Sir Hugh, Baron Langston, and Sir Rolf de Briard, along with the other two knights belonging to Langston Keep—Sir Fulk and Sir Giles, formerly squires, who had been knighted in the absence of their lord and lady by Rolf—attend the king, who was planning his campaign for Normandy. The service was owed, and must be paid.

"You cannot mean to go!" Isabelle said to her husband.

"I can hardly refuse the king," Hugh said testily.

"We are barely home six months," she shouted, her temper boiling over at long last. "I cannot believe that Henry Beauclerc is so lacking in knights that he must have you. Was your earlier service in Normandy not enough? It almost cost us each other! Rolf, Fulk, and Giles are going. Are three knights not enough service from Langston? I would have my husband safe at home for a change, and I should like to tell the king that, damnit!"

"Madame," Hugh roared back at her, "the king will hear *nothing* from you! You will shut your mouth and let me do my duty as I have always done it! What kind of an example would I set for young Hugh if I shirked my service to my overlord?"

"Go, then!" Isabelle said angrily. "But if you do not come back safely, I shall never forgive you, Hugh Fauconier! *Never!*"

Hugh Fauconier's sense of humor suddenly welled up at the ridiculousness of her words. He burst out laughing. "Ahh, ma Belle," he said, "if I did not come back to you, I should never know whether you forgave me or not for being such a fool, *chérie.*" Stepping forward, he gathered her resisting form into his arms. "Isabelle, Isabelle, what are we to do? I love you so, and I cannot be angry with you any longer. You have injured me to the core of my very being, but I yet love you with my poor, sore-wounded heart. I cannot live without you." He stroked her soft hair, delighting in its lavender fragrance.

"Ohhhhh, Hugh," she sniffled, burying her face against his shoulder, "I love you, too. I only wanted us to be together again." *He will never really understand my part in our adventures in Brittany,* Isabelle thought silently to herself, but what did it really matter? She had wanted her husband back, and now she really had him. She snuggled harder against his shoulder, sighing happily.

He laughed once more, but softly this time. "You chose an odd way of accomplishing your end, lady," he said.

"Are we then reconciled?" she asked him ingenuously. "I cannot let you go off to war if we are not reconciled."

In answer he picked her up, and, walking through the hall, found his way to the solar. She made no protest, instead cuddling in his arms and murmuring to him. There were no servants about; they had all disappeared, as had everyone else. Hugh laid his wife upon the bed and fell upon her. Her face was dwarfed by his two hands as, holding it, he rained kisses down upon her. Happiness overcame her. She kissed him back avidly, her hands caressing, stroking, touching him; and all the while the thought sliding through her head, *It has been so long.*

He wasn't quite certain how it happened so quickly, but they were suddenly naked, limbs intertwined, still kissing and caressing. *It was as if we had never been parted,* he thought, surprised. She was, as she had always been, warm and loving and giving of herself. His mouth found her left nipple. He tongued it, then suckled upon her, his teeth gently grazing the tender flesh. Her sigh swept warmly over him as her fingers tangled themselves in his dark blond hair. Now his kisses covered her entire body, moving down her torso, turning her over to press his mouth against her supple spine, making her shiver with delight until he finally turned her about again, to lie beneath him.

"I have missed you so, my dear lord," Isabelle said softly to him. Her full breasts pressed against the smoothness of his bare chest as she wrapped her arms about him.

"It has been hell without you, ma Belle," Hugh said, equally low. His knee pressed between her thighs, levering them open.

"Say that you forgive me my transgressions as I have forgiven you yours," she demanded. She could feel the hot head of his manhood seeking her channel. She wrapped her legs about him.

"You are forgiven, you impossible, but utterly irresistible hellion," he said with a lusty sigh as he sheathed himself deeply within her. "Totally . . . completely . . . unequivocally . . . forgiven. Ahhh, ma Belle!" he groaned, and then he began to move with vigor upon her.

The pleasure he gave her was unlike any she had ever experienced, and Isabelle knew why. It was because they loved each other absolutely. This was not blazing lust. *It was love!* She gave herself up to it with a happy cry, soaring among the stars until she spiraled down into a dark and warm contentment, weeping with the emotions that overcame her.

"Ahhh, ma Belle," he comforted her, "do not cry. Do not cry!" But Hugh Fauconier was crying, too, the tears sliding down his plain face. They had almost lost each other for good and all, and over what, really?

"I am so happy," Isabelle sobbed as they cradled each other.

In the Great Hall the servants moved softly, all knowing of the reunion taking place at this very minute, for things like that could hardly be kept secret. Alette looked to Rolf hopefully. She had heard no shrieks of outrage, or breaking crockery from the solar. Dared they hope that Hugh and Isabelle had resolved their differences at last?

They had, and Langston was all the better for it. Isabelle was still not happy about her husband going off to war, but she knew his honor would not allow him to do otherwise. She was grateful to have settled their dispute before he went, not because she believed he was in any danger, but because she loved him, and wanted his mind free to concentrate upon the business of survival.

How different it is now, she thought on the morning of their departure. Just a few years ago Langston had been a keep with one tower, and now it had two. There had been two knights, and now there were four. There had been a small complement of crossbowmen, and now there were fifty. Kissing her husband, and bidding them all Godspeed, Isabelle of Langston felt great pride.

King Henry gathered a great troop of men and knights about him, leaving for Normandy in late August. There, he was met by the bulk of the powerful Norman families who had pledged their fealty to him the previous year. They had remained loyal to Henry Beauclerc, having decided that of the Conqueror's remaining sons, he was best suited to lead them and reign over them. Conspicuous in their absence were those two great lords, Robert de Belleme and William of Mortain. De Belleme had come to England the previous winter, attempting to make his peace with Henry, but the king had ignored him, not trusting him, but choosing not to imprison him.

Finally, on September 28, in the Year of Our Lord eleven hundred and six, exactly forty years to the day William the Conqueror, Duke of Normandy, had landed his armies in England, his youngest son, English-born Henry, fought a mighty battle at Tinchebrai Castle for control of Normandy. At day's end he had won it. Duke Robert was defeated and sent to England, where he spent the rest of his days in comfortable but spartan confinement. With him, and suffering the same fate, went William of Mortain. Robert de Belleme fled the country, but was later captured and imprisoned. To everyone's amazement, not a single knight was killed in this battle for Normandy, but Hugh had been wounded, losing an eye.

"It was," Hugh Fauconier said to his wife when he had returned home, "as if God Almighty simply wanted the matter settled once and for all."

"And you will no longer go to war, my lord?" Isabelle asked him.

"I will if my king calls," Hugh said mischievously, "but Henry Beauclerc says he has no need for a one-eyed knight; even one with a strong sword arm." He put that arm about her, drawing her tightly to him. "So, ma Belle, you are sentenced to my company for all of your days, I fear."

Isabelle Langston, turning her head to look up into the plain but honest face of her husband, answered him with a smile. "It is a sentence I deserve, and right glad am I to accept it!"

*"Amen!"* said Father Bernard wholeheartedly, and the hall erupted into happy laughter.

"Amen indeed," rejoined Isabelle of Langston, who always had the last word.

# ☙*Afterward*

Henry Beauclerc, better known as Henry I, reigned in England and Normandy until his death in 1135. A warrior, he fought intermittently with the King of France, the Count of Anjou, and the Count of Flanders. It was his policy never to fight a war until he had obtained the diplomatic advantage first. In 1119 he defeated Louis VI of France. Anjou had been secured with the marriage of Henry's only son, William, to the daughter of the Count of Anjou. Unfortunately, Prince William died shortly afterward, in November 1120, in the wreck of the White Ship while crossing the Channel, and in sight of England. The king's only surviving legitimate heir was his daughter, Matilda. His Scots queen had died in 1118.

Two and a half months after his son's death, Henry I married Adelaide of Louvain, but no children were born of the marriage. Although the king had acknowledged more than twenty bastards, none could inherit his throne. When his daughter's husband, Emperor Henry V of Germany, died in 1125, the king recalled his daughter, made his barons swear to accept her as their ruler should he die without male issue, and saw Matilda married off again, very much against her will, to the sixteen-year-old Geoffrey of Anjou; but the Norman lords were not enthusiastic about being ruled by an Angevin.

Henry's death at age sixty-seven from eating too many lamprey eels set his kingdom afire with civil war. Stephen, a young son of the Count of Blois and Champagne, and his wife, Adela, Henry's elder sister, was at the center of the disputed throne.

For the next nineteen years, Stephen and his cousin Matilda fought over England. Each had powerful allies. Stephen was married to the heiress of Boulogne, giving him domination of the Channel. The Anglo-Norman lords also preferred not to have their loyalties divided again, and supported him.

Henry's daughter, however, had her supporters as well, among them her uncle, the King of Scotland; her half brother, Robert of Gloucester; and her husband, Geoffrey of Anjou. Both England and Normandy suffered in the squabble. When all the battles were over and done with, and all the diplomatic ploys sorted out, it was agreed that Stephen would be allowed to reign for life, and be followed by his cousin Matilda's son, Henry, Lord of Normandy and Anjou *and*, thanks to his wife Eleanor, Master of Aquitaine as well.

With Stephen's death, the Norman dynasty of eighty-eight years ended.

# ▮*A Note from the Author*

I hope you have enjoyed *HELLION* and will look for my next title, *DARLING JASMINE*, coming soon from Ballantine Books. As always, I invite you to write to me about my books at P.O. Box 765, Southold, NY 11971-0765. I'm slow, but the mail is eventually answered. So, until we meet again, I remain your most faithful author, Bertrice Small.

# SKYE O'MALLEY

## by Bertrice Small

There has never been a woman like Skye O'Malley. With ebony hair, deep blue eyes, and silken gardenia skin, she is beautiful, hot-tempered, and made for love. The seafaring captain of her own fleet and the shrewd overseer of vast wealth, Skye is spirited enough to win a battle of wits with none other than Queen Elizabeth herself. From the glittering green hills of Ireland to a lush Algerian hideaway, join Skye on a timeless journey filled with tender romance and the promise of eternal love.

Published by Ballantine Books.
Available in bookstores everywhere.

The O'Malley Saga continues…

# ALL THE SWEET TOMORROWS

## by Bertrice Small

A pawn in the bitter war between England's Queen, Elizabeth Tudor, and Mary Queen of Scots, Skye is forced to marry the Duc de Beaumont de Jaspre, whose Mediterranean principality is vital to England. Just as Skye begins to transform her bitter new life through the sheer force of her passionate nature, she learns her beloved former husband might be alive in Algiers. A daring flight into eroticism and danger leads Skye to her heart's true destiny—a destiny as bold and sensual as Skye herself.

Published by Ballantine Books.
Available in bookstores everywhere.

Another chapter in
the Skye O'Malley saga…

# WILD JASMINE

## by Bertrice Small

India, 1605. Princess Jasmine, favorite
daughter of the royal Mughal, flees to
England after her beloved husband is
killed by his lustful half-brother.
The beautiful Jasmine turns to the
grandmother she has never met,
the legendary Skye O'Malley, in her hour
of need. The indomitable Skye
introduces her granddaughter to the
court of St. James and a legacy of passion
and everlasting love. Igniting a whirlwind
of grand and erotic passions,
the tempestuous Jasmine will risk her
very soul in the name of love.

Published by Ballantine Books.
Available in bookstores everywhere.